Praise for *Kill Cinderella*:

"Imagine looking into a missing person case when the face of one of the people with whom you're meeting is shattered by a bullet. Chaos ensues. This is how J. Lee Taylor opens her newest Cindy Nesbit book. From the opening to the ending, Taylor keeps you on a suspenseful ride. Well done. This is the best Cindy Nesbit book yet!"

- E. R. Westphal

Praise for *Cinderella and the Vampire*:

"J. Lee Taylor has elevated sly humor to an art form in this vampire tale. This story is a delight, so if you're looking for a dark, depressing, real bloodsucker, this may not be the book for you. But if you enjoy dry wit and a brief trip into the weird, with an intriguing setting, great characters, and a clever "voice," then polish your fangs and chomp down."

- Ramona Butler

Books by J. Lee Taylor

Cindy Nesbit Mysteries
Cinderella and the Vampire
Cinderella and the Wolf (Cinderella - Dog Gone)
Cinderella - Slay Bells for Santa
Kill Cinderella

Jax Hollister Mysteries
Murder by Haggis

MURDER
By Haggis

A JAX HOLLISTER MYSTERY

J. Lee Taylor

 Lucky Bat Books

A Lucky Bat Book
with JLT Publishers

Murder By Haggis
Copyright 2014 by J. Lee Taylor
All rights reserved
Cover by Katrina Kirkpatrick
Cover Design: Katrina Kirkpatrick

ISBN 978-1-939051-75-2

LuckyBatBooks.com
10 9 8 7 6 5 4 3 2 1

For the real-life Hooligan, who isn't deaf, although he treats commands with selective hearing loss when it suits him.

Acknowledgements

To Ellen Westphal, Ramona Butler, Barbara Smith, and Lyla Dusing for your editorial input and continual encouragement. You are so good at what you do.

To Don and Dale Schafer, Judith Simpson, and Helen Nolte-Goddard, for reading the manuscript. Your suggestions and support mean so much.

To Donald Long, DMV of the Animal Medical Center in Reno, Nevada for his expertise. All my dogs have benefited from his knowledge and care.

To Molly Kirkley, a long-time friend, who discovered the article on the pearls of Scotland.

To the Scottish people, who twice extended their warm hospitality to a traveling stranger.

The town of Heather Hill overlooking Loch Linnhe exists only in my imagination. In Fort William, the location of the Italian restaurant, nursing facility, and jail are completely fictional. I take full responsibility for any mistakes, misconceptions, misrepresentations, or errors.

Scottish Folk-Tales and Legends, retold by Barbara Ker Wilson, Oxford University Press. Oxford, England, 1954. Ian's tale of the *kelpie* was adapted from this marvelous book.

If a man with dark hair, coal in one pocket and salt in the other is the first to cross the threshold after the stroke of midnight of the New Year, good fortune will fall on all present. But if a woman with red hair is first across, bad luck and disaster will follow. [Scottish prophesy.]

CHAPTER ONE

PHILIP LEBECK spent the last birthday of his life doing what he loved best; hiking to the top of his favorite mountain, alone. He savored the view of Fort William perched at the head of Loch Linnhe and the snow-covered switchbacks that snaked down the flank of the rocky peak. Darkening clouds lurked on the horizon. All too soon he'd have to leave the quiet solitude of Ben Nevis and return to his busy law practice.

He looked over his shoulder at the unexpected crunch of footsteps. Few people used the back trail at this time of year. "What are *you* doing here?"

"Have you changed your mind?" the other hiker asked.

"No, and I won't. I've given you time to tell her. Since you haven't, I must follow Michael's wishes."

"Were there written instructions?"

"I-I—"

"I knew it! He made a new codicil, didn't he?"

"It was what Michael wanted."

"If you tell, it will ruin everything."

LeBeck glanced from side to side, searching for an escape from the escalating argument. He slid a foot backward, felt his heel slip off the edge, and struggled to regain his balance.

A sudden shove sent him into thin air. "Stubborn old fool."

Loosened pebbles followed Philip LeBeck down the mountain. A howling wind out of the north swallowed the sound of the final thud. Snowflakes, pushed from the Highlands, blew sideways against the boulders. Moments stretched into minutes before the other hiker was satisfied no movement came from the body.

Only the mountain heard his epitaph.

"Happy Birthday, Philip."

CHAPTER TWO

Heather Hill, Scotland
New Year's Eve

'D EXPECTED MY godfather, Philip LeBeck, to pick me up outside Customs at the Edinburgh airport. He wasn't waiting at the exit. I paged him and called his cell. When Uncle Philip didn't answer, I began to worry. He's not a forgetful man.

I desperately needed to see his friendly face. My flight "across the pond" had been a disaster from beginning to end, including a mechanical delay which resulted in several missed connections. The trip from Hell ended when the last bus from Fort William dumped me at Heather Hill's only hotel. More bad luck—my reservation had gone missing. The clerk apologized for the mix-up, explaining how the storm and Hogmanay, the Scottish New Year, left them with no vacancies. She made a few calls and found someone at the local pub who had a studio apartment I might rent.

I'd settle for a broom closet, any place to rest my jet-lagged, weary head.

To the peal of church bells tolling midnight, I left the hotel and stepped into a winter gale sweeping over Loch Linnhe. A single street-light reflected off the wet cobblestones. Gusts of wind-filled sleet knocked my pull-along suitcase to one side. I righted it, tugged my ski cap over my ears, and plodded toward the pub sign. Within feet of my destination, a short figure lurched around the corner, ricocheted off my body and landed in a heap against the bar door.

A whisky-laden belch filled the air.

Wonderful. I'd knocked over the town drunk.

I wormed my way between the entrance and the inert body, grabbed him under the arms, and bumped the door open with my hip. In the process, my boot caught on the threshold, and I fell, keester first, into the crowded room.

Heavy silence greeted my undignified entrance. Half the village must be inside. Everyone stared at me with expressions of astonishment and horror.

"Could I have some help here?"

"Welcome and Happy Hogmanay, lass." A rumbling voice with the burr of the Highlands came from behind me. "Dr. Ian MacKenzie. How may I help?"

"It's this drunk who needs the help." I pointed to the small fellow wedged between my knees. I hip-walked backwards a few inches and used both hands to push off the floor.

I suppressed the urge to rub my sore tush and held out my hand instead. "Jax Hollister."

A rough-looking man at the bar stared daggers at me. "Another bloody foreigner. Be she here for the Coulter bidding?"

I was. My company had sent me to Scotland, but this was not the warm Scottish welcome Uncle Philip had promised. Perhaps I should wait for him to complete the introduction. I reached for my phone, until I remembered the battery was dead. Where was Uncle Philip?

"Ian, be that Dickie Campbell you're dragging head first into the room?" The female voice came from beyond the fireplace.

Dr. MacKenzie settled Dickie the Drunk in a chair. "Aye, and I'd say he got himself a head start on first footing this year."

"*Blootered* already," someone said.

I dropped onto a nearby bench, peeled off my ski cap, and finger-combed my flattened hair. The pub patrons moaned. I heard the word "red" whispered from person to person.

The doctor turned toward the bar. "Maggie, will you pour some coffee for Dickie and a shot of brandy for our visitor?"

He'd directed his request toward a petite bartender with auburn hair the color I would die for. My carrot-colored mop sitting atop six feet of clumsiness had always been the bane of my existence.

"Thank you," I said, "but I'm looking for a room. There was a mix-up at the hotel."

Discussions at the bar spilled over to include a table nearby. "She dinna come through the doorway *foot* first."

"Dickie wasn't first across, either." A round dumpling of a woman rapped the table with her beer mug for emphasis. "The lass couldn't have known he's been our first footer for twenty-five years."

The expressions of dismay lingered on some faces.

"Why are they all staring at me?" I asked the doctor.

"Do you know the beginning part of our first footing tradition? About a dark-haired man with coal in one pocket and salt in the other will bring good luck."

I nodded. "My Scottish grandfather told me."

He handed me a glass of amber-colored liquid. " 'Tis the second half you might not know. If a *woman* with *red* hair crosses the threshold *first*," he paused for effect, "it spells disaster for the coming year."

Wasn't that just dandy. Once again, I'd jinxed everything. Old year, New Year, foot first or otherwise. It didn't matter. Minutes into the New Year and I'd hexed an entire town for the next twelve months. In the past, my jinx had extended to my sorry excuse of a marriage, my brother's tennis matches, my whole damn life. Was it wishful thinking that it wouldn't affect my chances to acquire the Coulter property?

The door opened and the wind blew in another customer. A man pulled my suitcase behind him. "Someone left their bloody travel bag outside so I could trip over it."

My first impression? He was unusually tall. (Anyone taller than my six feet seemed unusually tall.) I guessed he was in his mid-thirties, with dark hair and a frown as deep as the Grand Canyon.

Before I could claim my suitcase, Ian asked, "Blake, did you find Philip?"

"I just came from the police station. Hikers saw something on Ben Nevis yesterday." He looked at his watch. "It took until five to get the body off the mountain. I confirmed the identification an hour ago. It was Philip."

A body? I dropped my glass. "Philip? Philip LeBeck? He's dead?"

The man named Blake gave me a look that riveted me to the bench. "Who are you?" he asked.

"Jax Hollister. Philip LeBeck is my godfather."

"Blake Ramsey, one of Philip's law partners." He glared at me. "You must be the American he was expecting. The one representing Fairway Golf here to bid on the Coulter estate?"

"That's right. And you're the friend he wanted me to meet." My voice broke in a repressed sob. I bowed my head to hide the beginning of tears. The realization that I would never again hear my godfather's Scottish accent and laughter booming off the rafters of my parents' Lake Tahoe home struck my heart with the impact of a sledge hammer. Hiking the Tahoe Rim Trail with him last summer had pulled me out of a depression no grief counseling could have. He gave me self-confidence in my physical ability I'd never had. A chasm of grief opened before me.

"How did it happen?" Ian asked.

"The police think it was a hiking accident."

Maggie, the bartender, came over with a dustpan to sweep up the shards of my broken glass. "Maybe he slipped and fell," she said.

I swiped away a tear and leaned over to help. "An accident? No, that can't be right. Uncle Philip climbed the seven highest peaks in the world."

"He was a much younger man when he accomplished that feat," Ian said.

"Age doesn't—didn't matter, not to Uncle Philip. He was strong and sure-footed when we hiked together. He was going to take me up Ben Nevis when my job here was over. He climbed in all conditions, including ice and snow. No, he couldn't have slipped."

"If not an accidental fall," Dr. MacKenzie said, "then there can be only one other explanation."

"He was pushed? Not possible." Blake was emphatic. "Philip had no enemies." The pub patrons nodded in agreement.

Perhaps not, but my first-hand knowledge of his abilities, combined with logic and intuition, convinced me my godfather had not been alone on that mountain. "If the police are calling it an accident, then they aren't looking at any other options." I turned to Blake. "You must get them to expand their investigation."

"Based on what evidence? You and Ian are speculating he was pushed because you don't think he could have fallen."

"What else could it be?" I waited for an alternative explanation. Blake didn't have one. "Perhaps there was a witness. Did Philip climb with a friend?"

"Not on his birthday." Blake's expression mirrored my sadness. "It was his tradition to hike alone, his way of greeting his new year and saying goodbye to the past one. He couldn't have been pushed."

"It wasn't an accident." Determination rode side by side with my sorrow. "I won't believe it until I see where it happened."

I **FOUND OUT** it was Blake who had the studio for rent. We left the pub and battled the windy sleet until we reached the two-story building he owned. The ground floor contained a mini-mart and laundromat.

The second floor contained two apartments, Blake's and the studio I would rent.

"Annie will bring you some milk and such," he said. "The market is closed for the day." He opened my apartment door, put my suitcase inside, and handed me the key.

I slipped out of my wet boots and looked at my accommodations. "I don't see a phone. I have to make a call, but my cell battery needs charging."

"It's the middle of the night." Exasperation tinged his voice. "Who's so bloody important you need to call at this hour?"

"It's not that late in Nevada. My father needs to know. He and Philip were at Oxford together and were best friends."

In the face of my explanation, his frown evaporated. "You'll have to use the one in my flat." He led the way down the hall and showed me to a phone next to a data port. He turned to give me some privacy, but I put a hand on his arm.

"Blake, wait. When Uncle Philip spoke of you, it was obvious he thought you were the son he never had." I felt a tremor run through his body.

He straightened as if to shake off his feelings of loss. "Philip looked forward to his visits with your family." He gave me a polite smile. "Lake Tahoe was a favorite place of his. He admired your father."

"I've known Uncle Philip all my life." I waited for him to say something. He didn't.

Was my unhappiness clouding my ability to read people or was something besides sorrow affecting Blake's attitude toward me? "I can't believe he's gone. When do you think we can go up Ben Nevis?"

"After the storm is over."

"If we wait, the snow will cover any clues that might be there."

"The storm has already wiped away any evidence. Besides, Philip wouldn't want us to climb in bad weather. It's not a good idea. Give it up." He left the room so I could make my call.

I didn't know how to tell my father his friend was gone except to come right out with it. "Dad, I have some bad news." I fought to keep my voice steady. "Uncle Philip is dead."

"Oh, my God. No. There must be some mistake."

"Dad, it's no mistake." I gave him the few facts I had.

"I can't believe it. Give me a minute."

Through the phone I heard him blow his nose, then a long silence. I visualized what he looked like when his mental wheels were churning. He'd get a take-charge expression on his face.

"Okay. I'll be on the next flight," he said. "When is the funeral?"

"I don't know, yet. Dad, you can't come. Your doctor is operating day after tomorrow for your blood clot. He won't let you fly."

"Damn, you're right. Your brother is in a tennis tournament and can't leave until it's over. You'll have to represent the family." He sniffed and cleared his throat. "I don't understand how this could have happened. I called Philip three days ago to wish him happy birthday. He mentioned he'd be making his yearly trek up Ben Nevis."

My father was barely holding on to his emotions. I made the decision not to tell him my suspicions surrounding Philip's death until I had more facts.

"Come to think on it," Dad added, "Philip sounded worried. Said there were things he had to tell you. There might be some problems with the sale of that Coulter place."

"Did he mention what kind of problems?"

"He thought they'd be taken care of by the time you got there."

Or not? I hoped they hadn't been the kind to get him killed.

"I don't like any of this, Jax. You going back to work so soon and all. I know you think you're ready, but you suffered a big loss, honey. The miscarriage and that damn divorce. Now Philip's death. I counted on him to ease your way. Give you some support. Now he's gone. Forget the job and come home."

"It's time to go back to work, Dad. I need to do this." At thirty-one, I couldn't continue recuperating at home. "My boss has confidence in me. I can't let him down."

And I had to make sure the police found Uncle Philip's killer.

SLEEP DIDN'T come easily. My sadness would not allow me peace until I prayed that Uncle Philip's heaven would have perfect weather and unlimited access to all his favorite mountains. Despite the lousy sofa-bed mattress, my emotional exhaustion and jet lag finally kicked in. Hours later, the barest sliver of gray light leaked through the drapes. With one eye barely open, I couldn't tell if it was early morning, late afternoon, or a cloudy day, but the tapping on the door kept me from slipping back to sleep.

"Be right there." I struggled into my parka that doubled as a robe when I traveled. I banged my knee against the end table and hobbled to the door. Must be the klutz phase of the moon. Again. I cracked the door and peered out.

"Miss Hollister, 'tis Annie Duncan from the pub last night."

Vague recognition registered. "Yes?"

"Blake sent us to bring things for your refrigerator. There be nothing open 'til tomorrow."

"Come in, please."

"This is my grandson." She pointed him to the efficiency kitchen. "Put the sacks on the counter, Bobby." She bent over. "Oh, my, here's a note someone slipped under your door." She picked it off the floor. "And I have a message for you from the hotel." She handed the two pieces of paper to me before bustling into the one-room apartment.

I opened the first folded page. Someone had pasted letters from a magazine on cheap paper.

YANKEE GO HOME.

Trite and childish. I glanced toward Annie's grandson; he was texting on his smart phone. I dismissed the note as a prank and stuffed it in my pocket. The second message was on hotel stationery. It was from my ex-husband, Raul Montoya.

He was in Scotland? He was supposed to be on his family's horse ranch in Argentina. The note said:

> *Mi Corazon, good fortune has brought us together in this village. Imagine my pleasure to find we are once again bidding on the same property. We must talk. Have dinner with me. I am at the hotel, Room 12. I have missed you. Raul.*

My dismay changed to disgust. His egotism had never been clearer. He couldn't imagine my not wanting to see him. It was still all about him. After the miscarriage, he'd never shown concern for *my* feelings. We'd lost a child. All I heard from him was how I'd lost *his heir*. It seemed to be more important for him to assign blame than console me. His mother, the Argentine Dragon Lady, felt the same and had made my life miserable.

I stuffed the note into my other pocket and concentrated on what Annie was saying.

"I run the market, postal station and the wash and dry on the floor below. I brought you some sandwich makings, instant coffee and milk, soup and Black Bun, a traditional cake. You can gather what else you need tomorrow."

Annie stopped unloading the sack and turned in a half circle. "Why, it's freezing in here. Isn't the heat on?"

"I didn't notice. I've been sleeping."

"The control is set right." She felt the floor register. "That's odd. There's no heat coming from the vents. I'll tell Blake to have the furnace serviced immediately. At least you have electricity. You can run the fireplace." She opened the door to a linen closet. "Here's an electric blanket."

"Thanks for the groceries. The soup smells delicious. I'll settle the bill with you tomorrow."

Without a word of farewell, she ushered her grandson out the door and closed it behind her. She'd been nice enough to bring me food, but hadn't smiled once. The stereotypical dour Scot?

I stood over the sleeper sofa and debated going back to bed. The ache around my heart returned, and with it the realization that this was the first day of my life without Uncle Philip. It was tempting to crawl back under the covers and sleep my sorrow away. It had been Uncle Philip who pointed out that focusing on my sorrow wouldn't change it. Move forward, he said. Exercise and work. Do something you love. Wise words.

I dressed, folded the sleeper sofa away, and shuffled into the kitchen. The soup was warming. Back on the sofa bed-now-couch, the electric blanket and fireplace held the cold at bay. I unplugged my phone from its charger. I checked for messages, hoping against hope for one more call from Uncle Philip. There were none listed, but there were several from my office. I contacted my immediate supervisor and mentor, Mike Lemon.

"Where are you? We tried calling you at the hotel. They told us you were staying with Blake Ramsey?"

"In his apartment *building*. My reservations at the hotel got lost."

"Be careful, Jax. You know how Mr. Atkins feels about fraternizing with the competition."

Ramsey was a competitor? He said he was a law partner with Uncle Philip. Had it been an oversight or had he deliberately failed to mention we were both bidders for the estate?

"Who does he represent?"

"SLFS, Scottish Lands For Scots. He's probably the toughest bidder against you. Didn't you get the files we emailed?"

"I don't have WiFi here. I have to locate a dial-up connection. Give me the short version on Ramsey."

"He's the counsel and representative for the conservancy branch of SLFS. They buy up property so developers can't. Watch your back. We hear Ramsey has taken a personal interest in the Coulter estate."

The stress knot between my shoulders tightened. My ex, Raul, and my landlord, Blake. Two potential problems.

"What is Raul Montoya doing here?" I asked. "He wasn't one of the original representatives."

"We didn't know Montoya would be there until you were in the air. He's the last minute replacement for the South American consortium rep who got the flu."

I heard a voice in the background. Mike said, "Mr. Atkins wants a word."

He transferred me to my employer. I repeated my travel woes and mentioned the death of Philip LeBeck.

"I know he was executor for Michael Coulter and the estate," Mr. Atkins said. "I want an update when they get someone else to handle the bids."

His attitude seemed harsh until I realized he didn't know Philip was my godfather. And in business, the job goes on. No one is expendable.

Why didn't Philip tell me he was the executor for the Coulter estate? Did he think our friendship would be viewed as a conflict of interest? If so, he was in a law practice with Ramsey, another competitor. Another conflict of interest? Were these the problems he mentioned to my father?

"Have you seen Montoya?" Mr. Atkins asked.

"I received a note from him."

"Is it going to be a problem with him in the picture?"

"No, I can handle him."

"It's not wise for you to stay with Blake Ramsey. No need to remind you of your past mistake?"

"No, sir. Ramsey owns the building with the only available room in town. I'm staying down the hall. He won't be a problem."

"Don't be overconfident, Jax. You asked for a second chance. Don't make me regret granting your request. Stick to the bidding cap, but I want that property."

"Yes sir." I couldn't afford to fail. Financially, my six-month sick leave had left dust bunnies the size of polar bears in my checking account. Professionally, I needed to reestablish my reputation as a top negotiator. "I won't disappoint you, Mr. Atkins."

"I sent Rosalind to lend a hand," my boss said. "She'll be there tomorrow."

Damn. Double damn. "I wish you hadn't, Mr. Atkins. I don't need her help."

I *had* counted on Philip for support. He was supposed to introduce me to the local folks. That wasn't going to happen. I mentally stiffened my spine. I could do this. I'd be fine . . . except I was saddled with Rosalind.

"I expect you to work with her. Make it happen."

The dial tone signaled the end of our conversation.

A short pity party was in order. My boss believed I needed help. Worse, he'd sent Rosalind. Her last name was Sweet.

She wasn't.

Advancing years had ended Rosalind's successful career as a lingerie model. She'd tried real estate and had done well. She had sales figures to match the size of her mountainous bra. (Meow) An executive head-hunter had introduced her to the chief of personnel at Fairway Golf. I'd heard rumors how and whom she scored on the interview process. (Double meow) Fairway Golf's Acquisitions Department had acquired her. I'd managed to avoid working with Rosalind until now.

The idea of her imminent arrival in Heather Hill sent me rushing for the aspirin bottle. A few minutes later, I felt ready to do the last item on my business agenda for the afternoon. Bookkeeping wanted an accounting. I must discuss my rent with my landlord and competitor.

CHAPTER THREE

WALKED DOWN the hall and knocked on Blake's door. A bird chirped from inside, accompanying the strains of Vivaldi's *"Four Seasons."* The door sprang open. Blake crossed his arms over his chest.

I didn't need a book on body language to know I wasn't welcome. "Sorry to bother you, but we have some business to discuss. Is this a good time?"

"No." He slammed the door.

How rude.

I knocked again. I could hear him stomping across the floor.

He flung the door open so hard it knocked against the wall. "What do you want? I'm working."

"So am I." I took a cleansing breath. "I need to notify my accounting department what you're going to charge for rent."

He glowered. "We'll discuss it later." He tried to slam the door again.

Being compassionate about his loss, one I shared by the way, only went so far to excuse bad behavior.

I stopped the door with my foot. "I'm trying to be professional, while you're being impossibly impolite. Besides interrupting your day, have I done something else to make you angry?"

"Ah, there's that famous Yankee brashness. Getting right to the point, aren't we?"

God, he sounded like one of those stuffy British BBC announcers. I did a fast count to ten.

"No, *we* aren't. *I'm* getting to the point. What's with the attitude?"

"I don't like how you planned to use your godfather, Philip, to win the bid."

"I did not! That's a cruel thing to say." I fought to keep a rein on my temper and other emotions. "Philip is dead. How can you be so unkind?"

"He was my friend, too, and you were going to use *your* relationship with him to further your chances."

"I repeat, we had not discussed it. I think we have a case of the pot and the kettle. Conflict? You were Philip's law partner."

"We had solved that problem, *Miss* Hollister. Returning to business, I don't like who you work for."

"Fairway Golf?"

"And its CEO."

"Mr. Atkins has a stellar reputation."

"Atkins's resorts are not eco-friendly. Tourists bring trash and trouble. You foreigners build it, take the money, and leave. Your only concern is the bottom line."

"B-but—"

He held up his hand to keep me quiet. "A warning, Miss Hollister. Many of us in Heather Hill don't believe a mega-golfing resort is the best use for the estate. Philip tried to remain neutral, but he knew the construction could damage Loch Linnhe and cause irreparable harm to the aquatic life in it. Scottish Lands For Scots and I are prepared to preserve the area, whatever it costs."

I tried using reason. "Have you ever met Mr. Atkins?"

Blake remained silent.

"I didn't think so. If you had, you'd realize he is the most responsible developer you would ever meet. He respects the land. Philip knew

Fairway had done the required environmental studies. Since when doesn't the birthplace of golf have room for another golf course? No, don't bother to answer. I will outbid you, *Mister* Ramsey, whatever it takes."

We glared at each other until I said, "When do you want me to move?" I'd considered that option, but I liked the idea of keeping an eye on the competition. And staying away from Raul made sense.

Surprise sent both of his caterpillar eyebrows climbing his forehead. "I didn't say you should move."

"You aren't going to kick me out?"

"Much as I regret it, it wouldn't be right to go back on my word."

"I can stay until I acquire the property?"

"You may stay until I outbid you."

There had to be a catch somewhere. "How much are you going to charge me for eight days?"

He looked me over from head to toe. Slowly. His scrutiny was unnerving.

I refused to squirm. "You gonna charge me by the inch or the foot?"

"Under the circumstances, it wouldn't be fair to charge more than what the hotel charges."

"No, it wouldn't. Will you provide maid service? Breakfast?"

"Certainly not."

"The hotel includes both." I calculated what I might negotiate at the current rate of exchange. "You should take at least twenty percent off the daily rate."

That amount should reduce the total bill and stretch my cash and credit card balance until my next expense check. Blake Ramsey didn't need to know I never ate breakfast.

"That's high. All right, twenty percent it is. Anything else?"

"The heat doesn't work. I won't pay until it's fixed. I'll expect to see at least two days deducted from my final bill." I pulled the note from my pocket and threw it at him. "Tell your childish friends this Yankee won't go home until I win." I stomped down the hall. Blake slammed his door behind me.

Oh, that went well. I was mad at myself for losing my temper and angry at him for being such an anti-American, tree-hugging, judgmental ass. I knew his narrow-minded, ecology-loving type—it was his way or the highway. Nothing in-between.

Back inside the apartment, I curled up in the blanket and replayed our argument. It had temporarily taken my mind off my loss. That was a good thing. Arguing with my landlord and competitor? Not so smart. Possibly I hadn't been diplomatic enough. He must be grieving, same as me. I could have shown more compassion. I'd apologize first thing tomorrow and get an update on the police investigation into Philip's death. Making sure the local constabulary searched for the killer was one thing Blake Ramsey and I could agree on.

Inspiration struck. During his rant, Ramsey had given away his strategy. He claimed Fairway Golf would ruin the ecology. To me, that meant SLFS planned to preserve the estate by keeping it the same. They'd do practically nothing to the land and the buildings. I could spin that to Fairway Golf's advantage. I'd stress improving the local economy with jobs and careful and thoughtful adaptive reuse of the manor house. That should sway the locals and the town council. It sounded better to me than Blake Ramsey's do-nothing approach.

CHAPTER FOUR

I WOKE THE NEXT morning to find a message from Rosalind on my cell. She reported she'd been able to book a room at the hotel after one of the holiday tourists departed.

My two least favorite people were in the same hotel. I was *so* glad I'd decided not to move.

Rosalind went on to say that she was suffering from jet lag. She'd see me tonight to develop a strategy.

Hah. I already had a plan—I'd tour the property for last-minute ideas, make the bid and inform headquarters when I won. What I needed Rosalind to do was stay out of my way.

On second thought, knowing the man-hunting Rosalind as I did, she might be a distraction for the male bidders. If she turned her sexy ways on Blake Ramsey, so much the better.

I wished Uncle Philip were here. Were there other problems I should know? Other than his contentious law partner being one of the bidders?

I went downstairs on a mission of discovery. The mini-mart on the street level had everything I needed. Cookies—I don't know why they are called biscuits in the UK—instant coffee and soup would meet my meager meal requirements. A friendlier Annie Duncan showed me the executive center located in one corner of the store. It was complete with a second-hand copier, fax machine, printer and, best of all, internet access.

With my tablet from upstairs, I logged on and dashed off an email to Fairway Golf. I explained how Blake Ramsey's local and emotional involvement could increase the price beyond what the acquisitions department had given me. I needed some leeway in the bidding cap. I clicked Send and noted the time difference. I'd have to wait for a reply until business opened in New York.

In the meantime, I downloaded the files on my competition. I'd dealt with and outbid the German and English agents in the past. The last time Raul and I had been bidding for the same property, he'd won by seducing me. True, we married soon after, but it didn't last long. When I finally saw the egotistical philanderer for who he was, I divorced him. Currently, Raul was representing a Peruvian group of investors. I didn't think their usual plans for time-share resorts would find favor with Scottish Lands For Scots or the locals who might be against foreign development of the estate.

The file on SLFS and Blake Ramsey highlighted past successes to keep out foreign investors. It sounded like they had unlimited funds. Good thing the sales process wasn't a public auction where Blake could out-bid us all. Michael Coulter's will stated the bidding would be sealed. I had to find a way to play the other foreign investors against SLFS. I needed them to pay attention to each other, not to Fairway Golf.

To get a feel for local sentiment, I read the area's on-line newspaper. The lead story reported the death of Heather Hill's prominent lawyer, Philip LeBeck. According to the article, the continuing storm prevented the police from finding the exact spot from which the deceased had fallen. The case was considered an accident, but the investigation remained open.

Idiots! The police had no suspects, so they called it an accident. He had *not* fallen. Nothing could change my mind. Someone had pushed Uncle Philip off that mountain.

I emailed a friend who writes crime novels, gave her the details that were in the paper, and asked what she knew about accidental falls—could they hide a homicide? I'd caught Ellen online and she replied:

Homicide? Difficult to prove unless there are footprints or other forensic evidence. Send more information when it's available, girlfriend. I may get a book out of this. You take care. Where there is one murder, another could follow, especially if I were writing the book.

Another murder? Why would the killer stay around? Unless he was local and thought he could hide in plain sight?

But Uncle Philip was well-liked. He had no enemies. Ellen said the killer in a murder mystery needed motive, method, and opportunity. The method and opportunity had happened on that mountain. I could discover the motive if I kept my ears open and paid attention to Heather Hill's population.

Any new developments in the case in the last twelve hours? Those would be in the police case file. Computer access was restricted. I needed Cindy, my hacker friend in Reno, to work her magic and left a message for her.

In the meantime, there might be another way to get an update. Blake Ramsey was a lawyer, or attorney, or solicitor, whatever they were called over here. He would have access to the police and could find out what I couldn't.

If he ever spoke to me again.

Before dinner, I'd make nice with the enemy if I had to. Uncle Philip had been there for me. I felt I owed it to his memory.

The rest of the day, I spent catching up on emails. Afterwards, I went upstairs, locked my door, steamed the wrinkles out of my clothes, and took a nap. My stomach grumbled at the same time someone knocked on the door. Annie Duncan appeared in a much better mood than when she'd delivered my groceries. She invited me to dinner at the pub.

"Maggie is serving Sean's famous game pie tonight at the *Heelster Gowdie*."

"Where?"

"The Head Over Heels pub, where you landed the other night. The *Heelster Gowdie*." Her eyes crinkled at the corners with merriment.

"Landed is right. Are you sure I'll be welcome?"

"Well, you did create a wee controversy, to be sure."

She pronounced it con-*trawf*-a-see. It took me a second to translate it into American.

"Half the town thinks it was you who first footed," she said. "For them, this New Year might be less than prosperous. The other half remembers that neither you nor Dickie's *feet* came over the threshold first." She held out my coat. "Life goes on, as it will. Please accept, Jax. I feel badly for being so abrupt the other day. Philip's death 'twas such a shock. Join us and meet my friends. Tonight, after dinner, 'tis the pub's regular darts night."

"I don't play darts."

"Oh, no, dear, only the men play. We ladies have a wee bit of gossip and a card game of Hearts while the men play with their pointy missiles."

Although part of me longed to avoid the pub, the scene of my last embarrassing debacle, it would be discourteous to turn down her invitation. "Thank you, Annie, I'd like to meet your friends." It was also a good way to gauge the amount of anti-foreign sentiment in the village. And I'd keep my ears open for some news about Philip's death.

Jet lag and my worry for Uncle Philip had blurred my first impression of the *Heelster Gowdie* on New Year's Eve. Tonight, I felt immediately comfortable in furnishings similar to most pubs I'd been in when traveling to the British Isles. Benches lined two of the walls with maroon faux leather cushions to soften the hardwood seats. A cheery fire crackled in the stone fireplace, adding to my sense of well-being. The one jarring concession to the modern age was a flat-screen TV behind the bar.

Mouth-watering aromas drifted from the kitchen. The individual game pies lived up to their reputation. Flaky crusts covered tender bites of rabbit and venison cloaked in a wine-tinged gravy. Maggie gave credit to her brother who did the cooking for the pub.

After dinner, another woman joined us. She was as tall, thin and severe as Annie was short, plump and merry.

"Maude Hampton owns Pins 'n Needles down the street," Annie said. "Maudie, you've heard of Blake's tenant? She's from New York City."

We shook hands, one businesswoman to another. She wore a sensible pantsuit, white blouse, no ruffles, no jewelry. Maude gave me a wary smile and a thorough inspection. She sat next to Annie and across the table from me. "I'm curious, Miss Hollister. How did you come by the name Jax? It's an unusual one."

Annie shot an elbow into her side. "No need to be rude, Maudie. Not everyone knows your direct ways."

"That's all right," I said. "It's a question I'm used to. It's usually mispronounced Jack. That caused lots of misunderstandings in school. Long story short, my mother wanted to name me after one of her brothers. Because Jason, Alistair or Xavier didn't fit a girl, she took the first letters of their names. Please call me Jax."

Annie accepted my explanation with a chuckle, Maude's lips twitched in a suppressed smile. The two women pulled cards from their purses, riffled the decks and set them on opposite corners of the table. Hearts was the card game my family played at reunions—no explanation of the rules was necessary.

Annie indicated the television. "On the telly, we see how New York City looks so dangerous. Why do you live in that big city? All those murders and such."

I'd heard it before and countered with, "I'm cautious. I've taken self-defense classes, and I lock my doors. Other than that, I refuse to live in fear. I'm sure your Edinburgh has its share of crime."

"In a small town such as this," Annie said, "we have no reason to be locking our doors."

Maude took a pad and pencil from her purse. "After Philip's death, we may have to start." She aligned them precisely with the edge of the table.

Annie sent her a sharp look. "You don't think it was an accident?"

"For heaven's sake, he hiked the Alps. Ben Nevis is an anthill by comparison."

"Perhaps a heart attack or stroke had something to do with the fall," Annie argued.

"No, the coroner won't find anything like that. Ian gave him a physical last month. Philip was healthier than most men his age. His death is very peculiar."

That was a conversation stopper, but it felt good to know someone else thought like I did.

"Oh, look at Jax's face, Maudie. You've put your foot in it now. Philip was Jax's godfather."

"I'm sorry, I'd forgotten the connection."

I knew my smile was a sad one. "I agree his death couldn't have been an accident. He was as sure-footed as a mountain goat."

Annie's expression changed to one of concern. "Maybe I will be locking my door tonight." She fiddled with the deck of cards.

Maude looked toward the pub's door. "Where is Bea?"

Annie explained. "We're waiting for Bea Kestle of Kestle's Corgis. She's been to another dog show."

"Her last. The newspaper confirmed she's retiring. Now she has time to start her dog rescue."

"Dogs are her life," Annie said. "Bea has a real soft spot, especially for those wee ones with disabilities."

The door swung open and a tiny woman entered, trailed by two dogs. To my surprise, she was the spitting image of the Scottish grandmother I knew from black and white photographs. The resemblance was so uncanny that I planned to research our family tree.

Maude smiled for the first time that night. "Here she is with her new champion, Winona, and of course, Hooligan."

Bea Kestle made a quick show-ring trot through the pub with the two tailless animals. I suppressed a laugh at the red-and-white, medium-sized dogs with stubby legs as they pranced around the room.

After Annie introduced us, Bea pointed to the floor. "Sit, Winnie." One dog obeyed. The other sniffed our shoes and jumped up on the bench by my side. I swear he gazed into my soul.

Bea sat on my other side. "Well, I'll be! Hooligan is deaf and usually stays clear of strangers."

I returned the corgi's stare and melted. I'd never had a dog when I was a child because my younger brother had allergies. Currently, my job required weeks of traveling. Not a sensible arrangement for keeping a pet.

"If you don't want him sheddin' all over your clothes, point down. He'll obey."

Before I could follow her instructions, Hooligan settled the matter. He curled up at my side and plopped his head in my lap.

It felt as if everyone in the room was looking at me. "What have I done this time?"

" 'Tis Hooligan. Everyone knows I've tried to find a good home for the lad. Because of his special needs, I made up my mind he should pick his owner. In the past, he's investigated potential buyers and always walked away. I'd given up hope he'd find a match." Bea gave me a penetrating stare and nodded her head. "I'll gladly gift him to you, Jax, if you will have him."

I longed to accept her offer and take the little guy home with me, but that was the problem. I didn't have a home, not since I sub-let my condo in New York. For the time being, I was homeless. Without going into lengthy details, I said, "That is so kind of you. Unfortunately, my apartment has a no-pets policy, though he's won my heart."

The women at the table murmured their understanding. Bea gave my hand a quick squeeze. "I wish you'd reconsider, dear. I trust my dog's instincts. You are a special person to capture his attention. I think you two belong together."

Maude leaned toward Bea after her pronouncement. "You should be more cautious, Bea. You don't know Jax. Besides, she's here on business and will leave soon. She can't take Hooligan."

"I disagree." Bea turned to Annie and Maude. "Jax Hollister is here on more than business. Some deeper purpose, a deeper need. Whether she knows it or not, she will be having an influence on Heather Hill."

"Another of your famous premonitions?" Maude quipped. "Jax, you should know Bea has so many we can't keep track of those that come true and those that don't. I wouldn't cancel your plane reservations based on her prediction."

"You two are embarrassing our guest." Annie pointed at me. "Look how she's blushing."

I fanned a hand in an effort to cool my heated cheeks. "The curse of redheads."

"I dinna mean to put you on the spot," Bea said. "Someone please change the subject."

"I can." Maude pulled a clipping from her purse. "You made it official. You're retiring. No more spotlight?"

"I'm tired of the travel, and I have the savings for my rescue operation. If I hunger after the competition, I'll try the local herding trials with Hooligan's cousins. They've been holding their own against Hamish McTavish's dogs, those long-legged McNabbs. And my little devils are as foolishly fearless as Tommy's border collies."

Hooligan raised his head and snorted. Maude and Annie laughed at his timing. It was hard to believe he hadn't heard and understood every word Bea uttered.

At the other end of the pub, men were moving tables and picking teams. One or two cast curious looks my way. Some appeared downright hostile. Angry enough to warn me out of town?

I scooted closer to Annie and surreptitiously pointed toward the group of young men seated near the fireplace. "I realize your tradition says I spoiled the New Year for some, but is there something else going on I should be aware of?"

"The oyster lads? Those are Sean's friends."

"Sean and some locals have started an oyster farm in the loch," Maude said. "It's a salt water lake. Ian is a partner, and Blake does some legal work for them, too. They're worried run-off from construction will spoil the oyster farm."

The men looked more like mobsters than oyster lads. "Are they against all building or is it just Fairway Golf?"

"The rumor going round," Annie explained, "is that your company builds huge resorts. The more construction, the more silt in the run-off. Don't give them a thought." She dismissed them with a flick of her hand. "It's true not everyone wants the Coulter land developed. The lads wouldna harm a soul."

Despite Annie's reassurance, I saw one of the so-called lads glaring at me. He pushed to his feet. The man nearest him placed a restraining hand on his arm and murmured something I couldn't hear. He returned to his seat.

My writer friend's warning of danger clanged in my memory. Maybe I'd been hasty to dismiss the Yankee-go-home note as a prank. "Who is the big man looking my way?"

Bea looked over at the table. "Niles Gordon? He's not such a bad sort. Full of bluster, he is. He had a rough time of it after his father died. I know his mother."

Blake and Ian were next to blow into the pub. Blake waved hello to Annie, Bea, and Maude on his way to join the dart players. He ignored me. If the enemy chose to make his animosity public, I could ignore him, too. So much for finding out any news in Philip's case.

Ian bypassed the darts game and sat at our table. "Ladies, if I'm called out, you may leave my winnings with Maggie."

Annie poked his shoulder. "Ye be that sure of yourself, Doctor?"

"The faeries must have whispered in your ear the secret of beating us," Bea said.

The good-natured banter seemed ritualistic, a part of their weekly card game and not something an outsider felt comfortable joining. I was content to listen and observe my fellow card players' habits. Maude sorted her cards into order then snapped them shut, crisp and business-like. When Bea led out a suit, she took command of the table. Annie dithered. Ian held his cards as if they were surgical instruments.

In the normal course of conversation, the subject of the Coulter sale came up again.

"Jax, don't allow Maude to win the game just because she's on the village council." Ian sorted his cards. "She can't be influenced. When do you have a look at the manor house?"

"Tomorrow noon. Have the others had their tour?"

"The German fellow took his this morning," Annie said, "and the English lady went this afternoon. That South American fellow will go tomorrow morning. Maude, what was his name?"

Maude jumped as if stuck by a pin and dropped a card on the floor. "Montoya?" She bent over to pick it up. "Yes, I believe that's his name. Do you know him, Jax?"

I forced a smile. "We've met." I wasn't sure how I'd handle my emotions when Raul and I inevitably ran into each other. I hoped to put it off until . . . never.

Wouldn't you know it? He was the next person in the door.

I concentrated on the cards until my peripheral vision picked up Raul's perfect, white smile advancing on our table.

"Raul asks himself where are all the beautiful women of this village?" He stood between Maude and me. "Here you are. How grand!"

The accent I once considered charming sounded phony and forced.

"And Jax. I'm pleased we will be competing again. We have much to discuss."

He placed a hand on my shoulder. I shrugged it off. A familiar scent clung to his clothes. Rosalind Sweet's distinctive perfume.

OMG, even for Raul, that was fast work. Or did Rosalind initiate the, um, contact?

My inner therapist asked how did I feel about Raul and Rosalind?

I felt a twinge, not of jealousy, but sadness. Raul, the womanizer, would never change.

The threat of possible collusion between bidders sent up a red flag. My boss would have a fit if he knew Rosalind had been with Raul. All the more reason to keep my distance, but I couldn't control Rosalind. What was she up to besides sex? I'd heard rumors she was after my job.

Raul moved closer to me, crowding Hooligan. The corgi stiffened and growled. Raul jumped back.

"Good boy, Hooligan." I forgot the dog was deaf.

Bea, Ian and Annie squirmed in their chairs and kept their eyes on their cards. No one invited Raul to sit down. The room quieted and the dart game stopped. The sound of the wind whistling around the eaves accented the snap and pop from the fireplace. Blake stared in our direction.

I had the uncomfortable feeling that my past with Raul would soon become public. Or was it already common knowledge? Rosalind-not-so-sweet?

"You are interrupting a private game, Raul." My mother would be proud how polite I sounded. I glanced to see his reaction.

Used to charming a woman to get his way, he frowned at my dismissal. His face had thinned in the past six months with new lines creasing his forehead and around his dark eyes, eyes that communicated a desire to get me alone.

"We will talk another time, Jax. Soon." He turned his smile on the rest of the card players. "Pardon. I see the beautiful Maggie has reserved a place for me at the bar. I will take myself there." He bowed.

Annie nudged me. "Well done, Jax. The man 'tis much too smooth."

I managed a weak smile. After an awkward pause, the conversation returned to the topic of the sale.

Bea asked Ian, "Will there be a delay in the bidding because of Philip's death?"

"I don't think so. Elizabeth appointed the third partner, Sam Bascombe, to act as executor and take over the sale," Ian said. "She thinks the transition will go smoothly."

Bea led out a three of spades. Maude followed suit with a nine of spades. "A real estate friend of mine confirmed the sale process is unusual, giving the town council the final say. It is legal. We're fortunate Michael Coulter wanted Heather Hill involved in the eventual outcome and that Elizabeth agreed."

"She will be glad when all the papers are signed, I'm sure," Bea said. "That house 'tis such a burden. First the death duties, taxes to you, Jax, then the roof repairs and plumbing. She'll be right glad for the money."

"And a great deal of money it should be." Annie slid a knowing smile at me, along with the black queen.

My king of spades was a singleton. I stifled a groan. There was no way to duck the queen. I'd be buying the next round.

I returned lead with a club. Annie asked, "Isn't there a minimum bid for the property? A high one?" She turned the question toward me.

It was time to set some business ground rules with my new friends. "Only Elizabeth, her attorney and the five bidders know what the minimum figure is. I can't divulge that detail or how much Fairway Golf is willing to pay. You'll have to wait until January ninth, when I plan to negotiate the winning bid."

Ian played a small heart on the trick. "Our Blake will have a say in that."

"No matter who wins the bidding," Maude said, "I hope Elizabeth finds a financial advisor to help her manage the funds. Someone not too close."

The three women exchanged meaningful looks.

Ian gave an exasperated sigh. "Don't keep Jax in the dark. Explain your skeptical expressions. She can tell you're bursting to say more."

Annie winked at me. "We've been caught out. Elizabeth's fiancé, Richard Hyde, has experience with money matters. He, no doubt, will have some input."

"Input?" Maude slapped down a card. "He'll tell her to put the money into his next fly-by-night idea, one of his archeological digs. More chasing of myths and legends. I don't care if he is English the same as her, she shouldn't trust him with her money."

"Maude, be kind," Bea chided. "Richard idolizes her. Flowers in the middle of winter, delivered once a week, like clockwork."

Annie dealt the next hand. "Elizabeth does dote on him. I'm thinking she's lucky. Her inheritance means nothing to him."

"How can you be so sure?" Maude asked. "After the sale, Elizabeth will be a rich woman. Richard could be putting on an act. You'll be meeting him, Jax. He seldom leaves Elizabeth's side."

Ian sipped his tea and remained silent. A smart man not to get involved in the women's gossip.

At the other end of the room, Blake rapped his tankard of beer on a table. "A toast to Philip LeBeck."

The crowd stood as one and raised their glasses.

Blake hoisted his drink. "A good friend. A better man. He will be missed."

"Hear, hear," everyone said.

Maude asked, "When's the funeral, Blake?"

"As he wished, there will be no funeral or memorial. I'll spread his ashes on Ben Nevis when the storm clears."

A cold draft worked around the room when another customer opened the door. The town's single pub appeared to be a central meeting place.

If Raul's arrival had soured my mood, Rosalind curdled it. She headed in my direction. One look at her and I knew how she'd cured her jet lag. That recently-bedded gleam in her eyes was a dead giveaway and confirmed how Raul got her perfume on his clothes. Her coat gapped open to reveal a tight pencil skirt and an animal print sweater cut low enough to expose considerable cleavage. As if on a high-fashion runway, Rosalind glided across the room on four-inch high "slut" heels. She exuded sex appeal. Every male in the pub turned his antennae in her direction.

"Jax, there you are. You must turn on your cell phone. I've been trying to call."

Yeah, right. In between boffing sessions with Raul.

To avoid appearing impolite, I introduced her as an associate from New York. "As you can see, Rosalind, I'm in the middle of a game. I'll meet with you tomorrow after I tour the manor."

"But Mr. Atkins sent me to help. Shouldn't I go with you?"

"That won't be necessary. Stay here, study the photos and add any details for my approval. We'll discuss them later."

She tried to hide her feelings, but the slight tightening around her mouth told me she didn't like taking my orders. She slithered past the dart game and gave a playful skip that could have bounced her bountiful bosom into a wardrobe malfunction. She ducked Blake's toss and it went wide. She apologized and batted her eyelashes. I heard her offer to buy him an I'm-so-sorry-drink. He declined.

The oyster lads made room for Rosalind by the fire where she attracted a swarm of admirers. She and Raul ignored each other. They didn't fool me. Raul concentrated his attention on Maggie, but I caught him glancing first at me, then Rosalind, via the mirror behind the bar.

I focused on the game. The teasing and laughter resumed. The one time I allowed myself to glance at the dart game, my landlord glowered at me. He didn't linger after Maggie made the last call. Neither did Rosalind. Blake opened the door for her and they left together. If she had him in her sights, look out, Blake.

Bea pulled on her coat. "I wonder what has Blake's kilt in a twist tonight."

"Philip's death, I would imagine. They were close," Annie said.

Bea gathered the two dogs. "The kennel is on your way to the manor, Jax. Why not stop in tomorrow for a cuppa? My dogs will be helping Mitch Connelly gather in his sheep. Come watch."

"Thanks, I'll do that."

Annie walked me back to Blake's building. In the window of the closed downstairs market, I noticed a bicycle rental sign and arranged to rent one for the rest of my stay. It had been years since I'd ridden a bike, but after three years of remedial spinning classes, I thought I could handle it. Hiking with Uncle Philip had been a real confidence builder.

I wanted to survey some of the countryside.

"Why not rent a car?" Annie said.

"Oh, I'm too sensible to drive in a country where people use the wrong side of the road," I joked, "and further confuse things with those silly roundabouts."

Annie waved off my thanks for including me in her evening outing and turned up the hill. I envied how she, Bea and Maude had remained friends after finishing school. In my move to New York, I'd lost touch with most everyone in Reno and Tahoe except my family and Cindy Nesbit, my study partner from Stanford.

I inserted the key to my apartment and felt a tap on my shoulder.

I yelped and reacted. Elbow thrust to a stomach, a stomp on an instep. I whirled to face my attacker, arms in front of my body like I'd been taught in self-defense class.

Relief washed over me. "Oh, it's you."

Blake struggled for air. He turned on his heel and limped toward his apartment.

"It was an automatic reflex, Blake." I followed him down the hall. "Are you hurt?"

He gave me a death glare over his shoulder.

Uh, oh. I knew I'd screwed up whatever chance we had to be friendly competitors. Both hands up in surrender, I backed away. "I'm sorry. I didn't know who it was." I stopped.

"Wait a damn minute. *You* should be apologizing to *me*. For all I knew, you were a mugger or Philip's killer. Don't ever sneak up on me again." I slammed my door.

CHAPTER FIVE

That Same Evening - Coulter Manor

ELIZABETH COULTER snuggled deep into the cushions of a leather wing chair. She wrapped her feet in the afghan and sipped her port. The book-lined walls of the study kept out most of the drafts, but no fire could warm the floors of the oldest room in the manor. The cornerstone dated to the fifteenth century. Add-ons and renovations to the rest of the building created a hodgepodge of styles, winding stairways and narrow hallways that occasionally ended in closets. She had passed many blissful hours exploring the house on her summer holidays. This room was where she and her father, Michael Coulter, had spent their happiest moments.

The study had been her father's favorite room and, over time it became hers. At the beginning of each summer, she and Michael would each pick a different book, race to see who finished first, then find another. They spent evenings in front of this ancient fireplace discussing their readings. So many good memories.

She sobered at the idea of leaving. In the two years since his death, the ancient plumbing system and other necessary repairs had drained her trust fund until she had no option but to sell. Momentary anger at her father's financial ineptitude threatened to spoil Elizabeth's mood, but with the money from the sale of the manor and surrounding lands, she would build a new home up the coast. She'd leave this antiquated village with its women pitying her because she was thirty-five and unmarried. That would change and soon. A new house, a new husband, a worry-free, new beginning. Thank the good Lord, her Richard loved Scotland as much as she did. She'd never have to return to London.

Her father's last wife, outwardly grief-stricken during the reading of the will, inherited the London house. That woman loved the city, swearing the property in Scotland held too many memories.

Remembrances were the very reason Elizabeth treasured the gift of the land and manor house. She planned to spend the rest of her life here, until Philip LeBeck had gone over the accounts with her. That was when the reality of death duties and the repair bills impinged upon her fantasy future. She looked around the last room in the house she would pack away. Here were all the books, documents, and her father's correspondence. What to save? What to donate to the library in Fort William?

"You'll give the American a tour of the house tomorrow afternoon?" the man in a matching wing chair asked.

Elizabeth gazed fondly at her fiancé. How fortuitous that he had attended her father's funeral. She hadn't seen dear Papa's business acquaintance in years. When he held her hand and offered his condolences, there had been an immediate attraction. He proposed on New Year's Eve. They planned a spring wedding, after the sale.

"I hope she is nicer than the German," Elizabeth said.

"Jack Hollister is a she?"

"Yes, dear. Didn't you hear? It's Jax with an 'x'."

"What a strange name. What are the gossips saying?"

"The cook said Jax Hollister has managed to stir up the anti-foreign investment fanatics and the save-the-world ecology supporters, Blake included. Ian and the other investors in the oyster farm are siding with the ecologists." Elizabeth chuckled. "Then there is the rumor that Jax and Blake may be more than competitors. Cook heard they tried to ignore each other at the pub tonight."

"How can that be important? Blake is determined to win. He must be toying with her. When he learns what her bid will be, he'll drop her. That could work to our advantage. You know, drive up the price." He puffed on his Meerschaum. "Does it bother you that Blake is interested in another Yank?"

"I doubt she'll be able to compete with Maggie. I couldn't. I was never part of the lovers' triangle. Ian, Blake and Maggie, the Three Musketeers. If Cook is correct and Blake and the American are interested in each other, I doubt it's anything more than a passing fancy on Blake's part. His previous engagement to an American didn't end well. Besides, he wouldn't allow anyone to influence his plan."

"Do you want his bid to be the highest?"

"Not at all. I've given it a great deal of thinking. Whoever buys the place will have to follow the terms of Papa's will. This room with the cornerstone and the chapel ruins must remain intact. As long as Papa's wishes are met, I don't care who has the winning bid."

Richard stood and added another log to the dwindling flames. "Won't it be difficult for you to leave the manor? You've told me your best memories are within these walls."

He understood her so well. "Yes, but I can take them with me when we move. We'll create new memories in our new house."

A comfortable silence stretched between them. Elizabeth hesitated to break the quiet, but a potentially contentious subject needed broaching. Reluctant to look at him, she examined her engagement ring.

"How is your research coming?" She hoped she'd kept any judgmental tone out of her question.

"I've come up against it once more. There is no mention anywhere of William Wallace's dirk. Not after Reginald Coulter's death. That means the knife has to be here."

"Hmmm." She feigned interest over a topic her father had belabored. "I'm not surprised it hasn't surfaced. Great-grandpapa had five brothers and a sister. I'm sure one of them, shall we say, appropriated it and hid it away from the others."

Richard relit his pipe. "And never mentioned they had something that important? A Scottish hero's dagger? I suppose it's possible, but the popularity of that movie, *Braveheart*, should have motivated someone in your family to put it up for auction. It would bring a fortune. That never happened."

"Dear Papa looked for it every summer. He paid one of the gardeners to walk the grounds at night with a lantern to perpetuate the legend that Wallace's ghost guarded the dirk. It helped keep the treasure hunters away."

Elizabeth looked up to find Richard gazing at her. She knew what he would say next.

"No slight intended against your father, my dear. He wasn't a trained archeologist. If the dirk is on the property, I will find it."

CHAPTER SIX

DEEP INTO MY unresolved problems, I pedaled my bike to my meeting with Bea Kestle. I hadn't slept well. The companionship and fun I'd enjoyed with Maude, Bea and Annie had been stimulating and taken my mind off Uncle Philip's death. The motivation behind Blake's actions in the hallway kept me tossing and turning. He'd ignored me in the pub, and then sneaked up on me in the hallway. What could he have been thinking? Blake Ramsey didn't strike me as a prankster. He was too proper and humorless. Had I misread his intentions? My therapist had told me it was normal to have trust issues after what I went through. Maybe I had overreacted. Could he have wanted to apologize for being so rude?

He wasn't the only person I worried about all night.

What had Rosalind been doing with Raul? Besides the obvious, what kind of plot was she hatching?

One more distraction I didn't need.

The brisk air cleansed my brain of business intrigues and of my unfathomable landlord. I gazed into the northerly distance, where clouds continued to shroud Ben Nevis. The more reality sank in, the more I knew there was no point in finding where Uncle Philip had fallen off the mountain. Any evidence, footprints, and such, would be covered with piles of snow. The current newspaper reported nothing new in the case.

I paid attention to the area surrounding Coulter Manor. It perched at the top of a rolling hill. The paved road would need widening to accommodate construction vehicles. Would Fairway Golf need to obtain easements? Bea's farm was on the downhill side of the estate. I wondered who owned the land on the other side.

At the wooden sign of a corgi, I pulled into a dirt and gravel drive that separated a small house with a neat yard from a medium-sized converted barn. I bypassed an animal transport trailer backed against a loading chute, surrounded by a corral. The sound of barking dogs came from inside the barn.

Bea emerged from her backdoor and motioned me to park my bike by the steps. She handed me a mug of coffee. "Will black do?"

"Perfect."

"We can walk and talk. Let's see how Mitch is gettin' on with my dogs."

Bea set a brisk pace toward an area bordered by a wooded hill to the north and a fast-moving river to the east. The ground was soft, but not muddy. The smell of sheep reached us before the bleating did.

A flock of about twenty sheep milled about. One red-and-white dog dashed to the left and another spurted to the right.

"That's Tilly and Regan," Bea said. "They follow Mitch's whistles. Hooligan hangs back and looks for any woolie that decides to break for it. See how Mitch aims them toward the corral."

A crooked man, bent over and limping, blew on a whistle. He waved a staff and the dogs edged the sheep to the right.

Bea hooked her arm through mine. "Hooligan can't hear the whistle and doesn't need the hand motion. It's like he reads Mitch's mind. Sheep are such silly animals. One never knows which way they'll jump, but Hooligan seems to read their minds, too."

We stood in the sunshine and savored the warmth of a winter sun. Bea's eyes gleamed with pride. She watched her animals do what their breed had done for centuries. Hooligan dashed one way and then the other. When the sheep went into the corral, Bea called Tilly and Regan to her side. Hooligan's job was to move them into the chute. One bark did the trick. The loading complete, Hooligan joined us. He recognized me and tried to climb my legs for a petting.

"Oh, dear. He got your slacks muddy. Put your hand in front of his nose. That means to stay down."

I did as instructed, and Hooligan dropped to the ground. The muscles in his rear end didn't know he lacked a tail, and his entire butt wagged from side to side. He wiggled and grinned up at me. I couldn't help laughing at his obvious joy.

The old gentleman approached and favored Bea with a courtly bow. "Thank you, Bea, for the help. They did right good, they did. Your Hooligan is the best heeler I've seen in some time. Not since Old Bob."

Bea introduced us and explained that Old Bob had been Mitch Connelly's border collie.

"Been gone six years now," Mitch said. "Never be anuther like 'em. Well, best get me sheep to market so's I can pay that piddlin' amount Bea calls a grazin' fee."

After he drove away, Bea said, "Come inside." She closed the dogs in a side porch. "We'll get that mud off and have another cuppa."

A stiff brush did away with the dirt on my slacks, and a corgi-shaped boot scraper handled the last of the mud. Inside, Bea settled me at the kitchen table and bustled to refill my cup. The combination cooking and eating area was as neat as Bea and her dogs. A glimpse of the living room showed a display of trophies and ribbons on a sideboard.

"How long have you been showing corgis?"

"My husband and I began breedin' the year before he died. At the urgin' of my friends, I did my first show a year after his funeral. Kept me busy." She gave a rueful chuckle. "Truth be told, it kept me sane. They're a lot of trouble, but they fill a hole in my heart." She sent me a shy smile. "I'm thinkin' you have a similar vacancy?"

I stammered a weak denial.

"I don't mean to pry, Jax, but I sense you have a sadness inside."

"I will miss Philip." Tears brimmed my eyes when Bea patted my hand. She handed me a tissue.

"Thank you. I hope you won't think me presumptuous, but you remind me of my grandmother when she was your age. And she had premonitions, too." I checked my watch. "You've been so kind. Thanks for the coffee and the opportunity to watch your dogs. I can see why you love them. I don't mean to rush, but I don't want to be late for my tour."

Hooligan sat by the door and watched me leave. He raised a paw to the glass, as if waving goodbye.

Foolish sentimental thinking.

I pedaled away without a backward look and refused to cry. Between Bea's perceptive observation and Hooligan's plaintive expression, I was an emotional wreck.

A black sedan crested the hill and approached me on the wrong side of the road. I swerved out of the way.

Dammit! I was on the wrong side of the road.

The driver stopped and got out.

Raul.

Head down, I rode on. Raul caught the seat of the bike and forced me to a halt.

"Jax. We must talk." His dark eyes tried to plead his case.

I reined in my temper. "I have nothing to say to you."

"It has been a long time. We must discuss—"

"We have nothing to discuss. What good would it do? We're finished." For emphasis, I poked him in the chest and paid little attention when another car drove by.

"I have apologized, beautiful one. The affair meant nothing. Is it not possible for us to settle our differences? Have dinner with me tonight. I know we can settle things if we could be alone." He stroked my arm.

He'd used that ploy once too often. "Don't touch me, Raul. Go play with Rosalind and leave me alone. You do your job, I'll do mine."

Red-faced, Raul grabbed my wrist. I jerked out of his grasp to the sound of my coat tearing. I slapped his face, six months-worth of anger and hurt behind it.

I mounted the bike. My pent-up rage propelled me up the hill until I came to the paved driveway mentioned in Annie's instructions. My breathing was much too rapid and shallow. I pulled off the road before the anxiety attack could take hold. The counselor had taught me to take deep breaths and concentrate on something other than the cause of my anxiety. It usually helped, but my physical reaction to seeing Raul again told me the time was fast approaching when I would need to confront my deepest emotions.

Down the hill, Raul's car was gone. The empty road stretched beyond Bea Kestle's property. Her land hadn't been included in the prospectus for future expansion. If she was retiring, would she be willing to sell any or all of it? I'd ask the next time we met.

I rested my arms on the handlebars and inhaled the scent of pine trees and damp earth. The aroma reminded me of my parent's home at Lake Tahoe. My memory of the ever-changing blue of the lake chased away the last images of Raul. Serenity wrapped around me like the mist enveloping the Scottish mountains. They were mere hills compared to the rugged Sierras I'd hiked with Uncle Philip.

The pine trees whispered from a gentle breeze, making me homesick once more. I made a promise. After I found who was responsible for Philip's death, I'd fly to Tahoe for a short visit. I looked forward to Mom's vegan cooking and viewing Dad's latest crazy invention. Then it would be time to pack up the rest of my belongings and move back to New York. It was past time to get on with my life.

I found a dirt path circling the estate. Beyond the obligatory putting green nestled a gazebo in a grove of trees. On closer inspection, I noticed chipped and peeling white paint. I leaned the bike against the rickety railing, climbed the wooden stairs, and took a seat inside. From this angle, gazing back at the manor house, I saw what I'd missed on the way in. The shrubs and trees needed trimming. No one had edged the mown lawns. Small things, but to my practiced eye, a sign of benign neglect or limited funds for upkeep.

Overgrown shrubs surrounded the ruins of a chapel on the north edge of the property. How many families had it served? How many baptisms, weddings, and funerals had it seen? I strolled over to see if the grounds included a cemetery. There were no visible headstones. I took out my notepad and sketched the crumbling stones of the kirk, glad that the historical ruins had to remain undisturbed. I wrote a memo to myself to seek the aid of a preservationist. There had to be a way to slow the natural erosion caused by the damp and lichens. A discreet fence around the area would protect it from curious golfers. Our architects planned to demolish the non-historic outbuildings and replace them with individual cottages for groups and families. There should be room for a tennis court, swing sets, and picnic tables.

My gaze returned to the main house. Mr. Atkins wanted my opinion. Should Fairway Golf remodel it or demolish and build around the cornerstone? I knew my boss trusted my eye for detail, not Rosalind's.

A brief gust of air carried the sound of rushing water. According to the land map, the Muckle River ran behind the property adjoining the Coulter's land and dropped down through Bea Kestle's farm. I'd read the Scottish equivalent of an EPA study that mentioned the river passed under the village before feeding into Loch Linnhe. Our chief golf course planner knew the river would make a worthy water hazard. I wandered down a short trail to investigate. The Muckle wasn't wide by Mississippi standards, fifty feet across, I guessed. A wooden footbridge provided access to the other side. I stood in the middle of the span and looked down at the strong current. I couldn't see the bottom. An errant shot would cost the golfer a stroke.

On the opposite side, pines and a few leafless trees needed thinning to make way for the back nine. The gorse and shrubs along the steep banks rustled. The air was quiet. A rabbit or deer? I strained to see through the brush.

A boy or small man scurried deeper into the woods and disappeared. I started to call out, common sense choked back the words. Why had he run? He must have seen me.

I returned to the gazebo. A sense of fleeting time pushed away the thought of the near encounter. I hurried to finish a sketch of the rear of the manor house. The mixture of architectural styles with the added-on wings was a charming bonus. There'd been no mention in the report that the manor was structurally unsound. Few modern resorts could offer their guests a fifteenth-century house made into a hotel. If the inside was equally quaint, I'd recommend saving it. The marketing department could advertise the house to history buffs who liked to golf.

Out of nowhere came a bullet of red and white fur. The corgi looked like Hooligan. I called his name before remembering he was deaf. He flew up the steps, stopped at my feet and went into a frenzy of barking. He dashed down the stairs, then returned to me, barking all the time. On his last back-and-forth trip, he jumped, put his front paws on my knees and stared at me, beseeching me to do something.

He ran down the stairs again and headed across the lawn toward the Kestle farm. I mounted my bike and followed, feeling like Timmy pedaling after Lassie. Hooligan cut across the path and into the woods. The trees separating the properties made it difficult to keep up with him. He doubled back to make certain I followed.

We burst through the woods and hit a steep slope down to Bea's house. I careened into the dirt yard to the sound of barking dogs and the smell of smoke.

Smoke!

I took my attention off the ground to look for the source. The front tire hit a rock and pitched me over the handlebars. My hands broke the fall, saving my face from a bad scraping, but my palms stung and my right knee ached. The sound of crackling wood penetrated my pain.

There, near the barn, a shed was on fire.

Hooligan ran at the door, barking and whining before the flames forced him back. I pushed the hair out of my face to make sure I wasn't imagining the unmoving hand and arm that lay across the shed's threshold. Hooligan leaped in front of me, licked my face, barked and ran to the shed. I pushed to my knees to follow and heard the sound of tires crunching on the gravel driveway behind me.

"Bloody Hell!" Blake knelt at my side. "What happened? Are you hurt?"

I pointed at the spreading blaze. "Someone's inside."

Blake raised his arm, shielding his face from the heat. He fought his way inside and dragged Bea Kestle out of the burning shed.

Hooligan sniffed Bea's face, then limped to huddle against my side. He turned his head toward the sky and howled.

CHAPTER SEVEN

BLAKE CALLED the emergency crews and moved me out of their way to a bench on the other side of the yard. His face was pale under his normal tan.

"Did you burn yourself?" I asked.

He shook his head. "It's hard to comprehend. I've known Bea a long time.

"I had coffee with her maybe two hours ago."

Blake didn't comment. His abrupt attitude suggested there was something else going on. Hooligan distracted me from asking more. The dog yelped when he jumped into my lap. He was hurt, but I didn't know where. I held him in a loose embrace. Soon the place was swarming with vehicles. The fire crew attacked the shed, but it was a total loss. The police kept the growing crowd outside the fence.

Blake stood off to one side while I told the policeman in charge, Constable Trask, how I happened to be in Bea Kestle's yard.

The cop raised a disbelieving eyebrow and pointed to Hooligan. "That the deaf one I've heard of? He came and found you at the manor?"

I looked to Blake for help. "Hooligan is whimpering. I think he's been hurt."

"I'll find Bea's veterinarian," Blake said. "He's examining the other dogs in the kennels and making arrangements for them."

The constable studied me, his skepticism easy to read. "Stay a moment, Blake. I've a few more questions for you and Ms. Hollister. You both arrived at the same time?"

"Close enough," Blake said.

Trask pulled his notepad from his trench coat pocket and took a step into my personal space. His lanky frame hunched over me.

"Tell me again. The deaf dog came onto the Coulter property and got you to follow him back here?"

"Yes." I hid Hooligan's eyes from the constable's stern stare.

"The shed was already on fire?"

"Yes."

"And you saw no one in the yard?"

"No one. I stopped in earlier and watched the dogs herd sheep for Mr. Connelly. After that, Raul Montoya and one other car came from the direction of the Coulter property. Oh, I did catch a glimpse of someone beyond the footbridge, behind the gazebo."

Trask flipped to a new page. "Did you recognize him?"

"No, he ran off."

"Which direction?"

"East."

"Big man?"

"I had the impression it was a small man or boy."

"What was he wearing?"

I shut out the memory of Bea's arm in the shed door and closed my eyes to concentrate on the mental snapshot of the brief encounter across the river. "There was nothing remarkable about his clothing. He blended in with the brush and trees. A brown, all-weather jacket, and matching pants. Rubber boots or Wellies. And one of those newsboy caps. Brown heather tweed."

I opened my eyes to find the constable staring at me. "You're positive what he was wearing?"

"I have a photographic memory."

"Did you see his face?"

"His hat was pulled low on his brow. The rest was shadowed by the pines."

"Humph. Any idea what time this was?"

"Seven minutes 'til twelve."

"How can you be so sure of the exact time?"

I didn't have to be a detective to hear Constable Trask's accusatory tone and disbelief. "I had a noon appointment with Elizabeth Coulter to tour the manor. After I saw that person, I returned to the gazebo and looked at my watch. It was five minutes before the hour by then. That's when Hooligan showed up."

"How did the dog know you were at the Coulter place?"

His interrogative tone made me feel like a suspect. I didn't like it. "I don't know, Constable. Why don't you ask him?" I turned to Blake. "I want the vet to check Hooligan. Now. No more questions."

"Walk with me, Constable, I have to find MacDonald," Blake said.

Blake and another man returned a few minutes later. Blake introduced Kent MacDonald, Bea's veterinarian. Hooligan continued to shiver. His eyes were glazed and vacant.

MacDonald used gentle hands to examine the dog.

"He yelped when he jumped up into my lap," I said.

The vet prodded Hooligan's left hindquarter. The corgi stiffened.

MacDonald stood back and studied him. "There's a swelling on his hip. Nothing feels broken. He's in shock. I'll take him back to my surgery and keep an eye on him tonight."

"No!" I surprised myself with my sudden outburst. I ran a hand over Hooligan's head. We both were trembling. "Is there any reason he couldn't stay with me?"

"I suppose not, but if he's limping tomorrow, bring him in for an X-ray. You're staying at Blake's building?"

"Yes."

"He can tell you where my office is," MacDonald said. "Here comes Bea's helper. I'll see if she can stay with the other dogs tonight. I expect by tomorrow I'll have found temporary homes for all of them." He looked at the quivering dog in my lap. "It appears I won't have to worry about Hooligan." He walked toward the kennel area.

Ian crossed the yard from where the coroner had parked his van.

"Blake said your hands need looking after. Give them here, lass."

He put his bag on the ground and bent over my outstretched palms. He focused on the one with the deepest scrape.

I clutched Hooligan to my chest with my other hand. "Has Bea regained consciousness?"

"No, Jax. She's gone," Ian said. "Annie and Maude will soon be here to take care of her house."

"Bea's dead? B-but she was fine this morning. So full of life. She enjoyed showing off her dogs. We shared a cup of coffee. She was so . . . nice."

"I heard she had one of her visions about you," Ian said.

"I got the impression she believed in them. Does anyone else?"

"Lass, you're in Scotland." He stood, his smile gentle and sad. "This is the land of kelpies, broomies, and fairies. Bea believed in her premonitions, and we were inclined to go along with them. Right, Blake?"

Blake stuck his hands in his jacket pockets. "I don't believe in the paranormal. There's a scientific explanation. Bea understood people and dogs. She was perceptive and intuitive."

"She mentioned her plans after she retired. Helping rescue dogs and entering her corgis in herding trials." I swiped a tear from my cheek. "How sad she won't be able to enjoy them. Was it a heart attack?"

A look passed between Ian and Blake.

"You're not telling me something."

The doctor didn't answer immediately. He put some antiseptic salve and gauze in a plastic bag and handed it to Blake.

"Have her wash her hands when she gets home. Make sure she gets all the dirt out. You can put the bandages on afterward." He turned to leave.

"Wait, Ian. What about Bea?"

Another of those looks shot between the two men. Ian said, "It wasn't Bea's heart that killed her, Jax. The coroner and I agree. She was murdered."

I held the corgi closer. "How can you be so sure?"

"She had a stab wound. In her back," Blake said. "The police think the fire was set to destroy the body and any evidence left behind."

I couldn't wrap my brain around the concept of murder. Not here in this quiet setting. Bea, that sweet lady, was dead. She had taken me under her wing and invited me into her home. I wanted more time with her.

It wouldn't happen. Some bastard had killed her.

I struggled to clear my throat of the tears hiding there. "Hooligan was special to her. I've never seen a dog so agitated when he insisted I follow him. He must have witnessed Bea's murder. The man I saw may have been the killer."

CHAPTER EIGHT

I HOBBLED TO BLAKE'S Land Rover while he put the bicycle in the back. I slid inside and motioned for him to put Hooligan in my lap. The bike was none the worse for wear, but my hand stung and my knee felt swollen. Blake strode to the kennel area and returned with a leash, water dish and blanket. On the drive back to town, he and the dog were quiet. I didn't feel like talking either. I struggled to come to grips with the first murder victim I'd seen in real life, not on TV. Worse, I knew and liked the person. We'd played cards and laughed together. We'd shared a cup of coffee less than three hours ago. And now, I'd never have the chance to know her better. Two people in this village were dead. I knew them both. Was there another connection ? Before I succumbed to emotional numbness, I mentioned my missed appointment with Elizabeth Coulter.

"I rang her from Bea's," Blake said. "She was shocked by the murder. Offered to reschedule."

I returned to my cocoon of silence. When we arrived back at Blake's building, Hooligan came out of his lethargy long enough to do his business on a patch of grass across from the parking lot. He attempted to follow us up the stairs. After the first step, he looked at me and whined. Blake stuck the baggie with the cream and gauze in a pocket and picked up the corgi.

"I should've asked. Is it okay to bring Hooligan here?"

"Hollister, I am not an ogre. I like animals."

"For an afternoon snack?"

He ignored my snipping. "While my aunt is in hospital, I'm keeping her canary. You may keep Hooligan in your flat."

There was that stuffy British accent again.

I managed the key in my least injured hand and opened the door. Blake brushed by, placed the towel on the sofa and set Hooligan on top.

"I'll bring up some dog food from the market. You wash your hands."

I used the sink in the bathroom. In the mirror, I noticed a smudge on my cheek. My hair was a total wreck. I washed my face and found no abrasion under the dirt. My right hand was another story. I soaked it in warm water for a few minutes before applying soap. I dabbed it dry and returned to the other room to find Blake seated on the sofa, stroking Hooligan's head. He jerked his hand back as if I'd caught him robbing a cookie jar.

He jumped to his feet and pointed to the bag on the table. "The salve Ian wanted you to apply is in there."

I held out my hand. "I'm right-handed. Will you put it on for me?"

"Shall I call your friend, Rosalind, to help?"

She was the last person I wanted to see. "There's no need to bother. You can put on the cream."

He looked everywhere except at the scrape. "Uh, um, I'll get the cream out of the bag for you, unscrew the lid. You can apply it yourself. I wouldn't want to, uh, hurt you. Here's the gauze, too. I'll get scissors to cut the tape."

When he handed me the tube, he ignored my scraped hand.

Aha! The big bad man couldn't stand the sight of blood, and Ian knew it. What a jokester.

I could've teased the heck out of Blake, but I found it surprisingly charming the way he tried to apply the adhesive without touching my injury.

He looked toward the door, the only escape from what was clearly an uncomfortable situation for him.

I held up my bandaged palm. "Well, thanks for the help."

"If you need . . ."

"I'll be fine."

"Right." He let himself out.

He hadn't been rude, but he left in a hurry. Was it because of my bloody, scraped hand, or my personality? Probably both. And he hadn't offered an explanation for his actions in front of my door last night.

Hooligan hadn't moved except to close his eyes. Do dogs feel grief? If they did, then sleep was the best thing for the little pooch.

The enormity of what I had taken on hit me. I had no experience with a pet, much less a deaf dog. How was I going to get him back to the States? What would I do with a dog while I worked and traveled? The problems of coping with Hooligan were huge, but I'd made my decision. I was keeping him. Bea would want this. Her dog chose me. He was not going to lose someone else.

Scarlet O'Hara had the right idea. The how-to of making it work could wait for another day. This afternoon, I needed to keep my mind off Bea's murder.

Thank goodness I could concentrate on my job. Since the fall hadn't damaged my fingers, I typed a report to headquarters. I explained the delay in my on-site observation of the manor house and told them of Bea's death.

The image of her lifeless hand flashed before my eyes. Someone had killed that sweet woman with a knife to the back. An attack from behind. The low-life coward.

CHAPTER NINE

MAUDE HAMPTON blew her nose before she turned the OPEN sign to CLOSED. She didn't need a note to explain why she'd closed Pins 'n Needles early. By now, the entire village knew of Bea's death. Maude backed her old car out of the alley and drove to the market. Annie's pale face and red-rimmed eyes echoed her own sadness. They didn't speak during the short ride to Bea's house.

Maude parked to one side of the police vehicles. Tape around the charred remains of the shed marked the scene of the on-going investigation. Annie's quiet sobs filled the car. Maude set the brake, her own eyes stinging.

"Here's a handkerchief, Annie. Pull yourself together. We'll have time for a good cry after we're done."

"Horrible, horrible," Annie said.

"Yes, it is. Who would murder our Bea?"

Annie looked out the windscreen of the car and shook her head. "Bea's death on top of everything else." Her shoulders slumped. "Whatever will I do?"

Maude stared at her life-long friend. "Everything else? What could be worse than Bea's murder?"

"Not worse, I dinna mean that. It's Bobby. My grandson has been stealing from the market cash drawer. Added to Bea's death . . . 'tis more than I can bear."

"Oh, Annie, I'm so sorry. How long has this been going on?"

"Too long. I've been making up the difference, but I canna continue. I'll have to tell Blake. He'll be so disappointed. Him trying so hard to be a friend to the boy. A good influence. He gave him a part-time job during the summer taking care of the rental bicycles and stocking shelves." Annie shredded her tissue. "I know it's because Bobby's fallen in with the wrong sort. Staying out late, not telling me where he'd be, and his grades have been slipping. I'm afraid he's using drugs again. I haven't seen him since New Year's day."

Annie blamed herself for Bobby's problems, a guilt she hadn't earned, in Maude's opinion. An unwed mother at seventeen, Annie had raised her daughter, Sara, alone. The father left Scotland before the baby was born. Sara repeated her mother's mistakes and had Bobby at sixteen, never marrying or identifying the father. A baby hadn't made her more responsible. Sara progressed from drug use and petty thievery to robbery and prison. Annie had taken in her rebellious grandson after Sara was incarcerated. Bobby had been a problem ever since.

"Make him pay it back, Annie. Blake won't have to know."

"I think Bobby took my extra set of keys. I'll have to tell Blake to change the locks and he'll ask why. What ever will I do?"

Maude patted her friend on the shoulder and jumped when someone rapped on the car door. It was Charlie Trask. Annie rolled down the window.

"Come inside, out of the cold," the constable said. "I need to ask you some questions."

Annie opened her door. "I wish we didn't have to do this."

"Sooner started, sooner finished," Maude said.

CHAPTER TEN

PROOFREAD MY email to headquarters with a copy to Mr. Atkins, anxious to find out if Bea's murder would change anything in our strategy or my bid. Because I didn't have a phone in my room and the market was closed for the day, Blake was the closest possibility for a dial-up connection. I tucked my tablet under my arm and walked in front of Hooligan. He was lethargic, but awake and watching me.

"Come on, little man. I don't want to leave you alone. Let's go down the hall."

He cocked his head.

I knew he was deaf, but it hadn't sunk in until that moment. "Now what? I can talk all I want, you still can't hear me. Bea trained you, but I'm the one who needs training. If I walk away, will you come with me?"

When I reached the door and looked down, there he was. He stared at it as if willing it to open. So far, so good.

He followed me and sat at my feet when I stopped in front of Blake's door. I knocked.

Ouch. I'd used my injured hand.

Blake opened his door. "Hollister." The surprise registered in his voice, if not on his stone face. "I was coming to bring you a message. Elizabeth Coulter rang, and wants me to bring you for our tour and luncheon at eleven tomorrow. Montoya will be there earlier for breakfast and his last look."

It seemed a bit crass to continue the tours until a respectful time had passed. Nonetheless, Miss Coulter owned the property and made the schedule. I prayed Raul would be gone when Blake and I arrived.

"Two tours at the same time?" I didn't like the idea of Blake looking over my shoulder while I worked. "Won't that make things . . . overcrowded?"

"Elizabeth wants this business done before Bea's funeral. We'll be in different parts of the manor at different times."

I couldn't argue with logic.

Blake leaned against the doorframe. "Why are you here?" His tone was not welcoming.

Would I react to his negativity? Not me. I'd be professional. "It's business. I need to send an email. The market is closed. May I use your internet connection?"

He contemplated my request as if I'd asked for a pint of blood. A slight dip of the head and he stepped aside. Every surface in the living area held a labeled plant. It looked to be more than a hobby.

Hoolie followed me inside, sniffed all the potted plants he could reach and settled in front of the electric fire. The high-speed modem was where I remembered it to be. Blake walked over to a roll-top desk, moved the modem on top and rolled the top closed. He might as well have put a NO PEEKING sign on his workspace.

I shifted a family photograph to one side to make room for my tablet. In the picture, a somber man and tight-lipped woman, both dressed in khaki shorts and pith helmets, stood in front of a tent. I guessed they were Blake's parents. Each rested a hand on the shoulders of a skinny young boy with dark brown hair. The photo of the child hinted at the man Blake would become. Serious. Unsmiling.

I sent my email and had another idea.

"As long as I'm on-line, may I look up information on training deaf dogs?"

I looked over my shoulder. Blake sat on the couch reading a magazine.

"If you must," he said without moving his attention from the page.

On-line, I found some training ideas. Hoolie already knew to focus on me for commands, and he followed me without hand signals. All I had to do was find out what other signs Bea had taught him and how she got his attention. Annie and Maude might remember something.

I swiveled the desk chair to face Blake. He'd set aside his reading to stroke Hoolie's head.

"Hoolie must heal fast. I didn't hear him cry when he jumped up on the sofa," I said.

"He didn't jump. I picked him up."

Hoolie gave his hand a lick and sprawled over his lap. Blake tried to hide a smile, unsuccessfully. I could tell he liked the attention. There *was* a feeling, caring human inside his rough exterior. If he dropped his surliness, we might get along. Maybe.

I brought up something that was bothering me. "How well did you know Bea?"

"As well as anyone."

"She was well-liked, wasn't she?"

"Yes."

"Then who would want to kill her? And why?"

"Why?"

"What was the motive?"

"Motive?"

I pointed to the birdcage in the corner. The yellow bird had been quiet. "When did that magical canary turn into a parrot? Why do I keep hearing my words repeated?"

Silence. At last, he said, "I can't think of anyone who would want to kill Bea."

"What about the man I saw behind Coulter manor?"

"It was your imagination."

"No, Blake, I did see someone. He ran when he knew I'd seen him. I'm not making it up."

"He may have had a logical reason for being there. Too bad you didn't get a better look at his face."

"Whoever it was didn't want to be seen." I stood and winced. My knee had stiffened. I tried to walk it off. "A friend of mine writes mysteries. When she begins a new book, she doesn't know who the killer is until she develops the victim and the motive. It's usually one of the deadly four: greed, love, jealousy, or revenge. Greed is the big one. How can we find out if Bea had any money?"

"We?"

"Back to one-word sentences, are *we*?"

A surprising twinkle made its way to Blake's eyes. It never made it to his lips. "The police will find the killer. Why are you interested? You barely knew her."

"Because." I sat on the other side of my dog. "I liked Bea. She was nice to me."

"And?"

"I feel I owe it to Hoolie."

"*And?*"

God, he was good at digging with one-word questions.

"And that cop, Trask, thinks I might've murdered her, doesn't he?"

"It's a natural assumption. You were first on the scene."

"Drop the lawyer act, Blake. Look at Hoolie. Would he be with me if I'd killed Bea?"

Blake remained silent, unwilling to apply my logic to the situation.

"Look, I don't like being Constable Trask's only suspect. Why didn't he believe me when I described the man I saw?"

"It was too detailed."

"I can't help it if I have a photographic memory. He asked me what I saw. I told him. I get the feeling Trask won't follow up. He thinks he's got a suspect. Me. What about that man who ran away? He could've killed Bea for her money."

"You're wrong. That can't be a motive."

The corgi turned on his back, tucked his short front legs to his chest and spread his back legs so I could rub his tummy. I used my good hand to scratch the white hairs on his belly.

"How can you be so sure? Aren't there endorsements and such when you have champion show dogs?"

"Not with travel, vet bills, feed. Bea did it for the love of the breed. She owned her place and had a tidy income from investments, but most years she barely made expenses for the dogs."

"And you know this because?"

"I drew up her will. I told Charlie Trask. He didn't think money was the motive, either."

Charlie? Blake was on a first name basis with the local police. Did good old Charlie believe Blake's account of my klutzy arrival at Bea's?

"In your experience as an attorney, isn't money at the root of most killings? Bea had property she could sell. It could be valuable if the buyers for the Coulter estate wanted to expand. Did she have any children?"

"No."

"Neither did Philip. Can you think of a motive for his killing?"

"No."

"Did you ask the constable for an update on Philip's case?"

"The police are still calling it an accident."

"You don't believe that any more than I do. Two murders so close together. Time and location. There has to be a connection."

Blake's face was one big question mark. "Bea's and Philip's deaths? What possible connection could there be?

"Uncle Philip was executor for the Coulter estate and was well-liked. Bea was the sweetest lady and well-liked. Her farm is next door to the Coulter land. Maybe someone wanted her property."

"That's a stretch, Jax. If it were true, it could point a finger at one of the bidders. One of us."

"The timing. I don't believe in coincidences. Was Uncle Philip worried the last few days? My father said he mentioned some problems that would be resolved shortly. Did he mention anything like that to you?

"No."

To extract more information from Blake required an energy I no longer had. It had been a long day. "I've overstayed my welcome." I struggled to stand and half-suppressed a groan. "Thanks again for the use of your internet access."

"I'll drive you out to the manor house tomorrow."

"Thanks, I can find the way."

"You're limping. You're in no condition to bicycle out there. I'll pick you up at ten forty-five."

I wanted to believe the offer meant his icy demeanor was thawing. One peek at his stony expression told me nothing had changed. With my first step, I knew Blake was right. Tomorrow I'd be black-and-blue and stiff as a robot.

I waited for him to help Hoolie off the couch. The dog preceded me through the open door. "Until tomorrow," I said. My landlord had already closed the door.

Blake might be polite, but warm, he wasn't.

CHAPTER ELEVEN

RICHARD HYDE heaved a sigh of disappointment and brushed the dirt from his knees. He'd been positive the notes in the old man's journal pointed to the ruined chapel for the location of the dagger. He'd been wrong again.

"It's got to be here," Richard said under his breath. He turned in a circle and studied the filled-in places he'd excavated.

The references to the Scottish hero's dirk couldn't be wrong. It was common knowledge that Elizabeth's ancestor purchased it on the black market and had it secretly authenticated. Word of its existence had leaked. Reginald Coulter fought with the Scottish historical societies and won a battle with Parliament to keep it out of museums and in his private collection. A final appeal decided ownership in his favor, but no one saw the knife again.

Richard had investigated every possible niche and corner of the manor house. He'd questioned Elizabeth but she hadn't a clue. Was it fact or a mere fanciful legend that said Reginald buried the dagger in a place so secret he'd been unable to find it again? Locals told the tale of his ghost walking the grounds at night, searching for the hiding place.

Ghosts? Rubbish. Richard didn't believe any of it. The old man was a selfish bastard. He carried the secret to his grave.

Unless, over the years, someone else discovered the dirk.

Impossible. A find such as that would have made the news. It hadn't surfaced because it remained hidden on the property. Was it possible another journal existed?

The old man had written his last entry two months before he died. Surely, he'd been too ill to start another volume. The inventory of his personal documents hadn't listed one. Richard had investigated all the boxes in the attic. Had he looked in the trunks tucked under the eaves? To make sure, he would have another go at the dusty alcoves.

Richard had resolved to find the blade before Elizabeth finalized the sale. The discovery would make him a fortune and secure his reputation. He could support Elizabeth in the style she deserved instead of living off her money. Offers to lecture or teach would flow his way. A prestigious museum directorship could be in his future. A book deal. Movie rights.

He examined his hands. Despite the gloves, he'd developed a blister. Elizabeth would fuss, make him forgo the search tonight. He cleaned off his trowel and pick, stored them in the gardening shed, and went inside to wash up for the evening meal.

CHAPTER TWELVE

BEA. MURDERED. Unbelievable. Maude Hampton punctuated each word by shoving a skein of yarn into its cubbyhole.

Oh, how she was going to miss her friend. Bea was such a gentle person. Never an unkind word toward anyone.

Maude could admit she'd been jealous of Bea's happiness with Ben Kestle. Heather Hill always had a shortage of eligible single men. Once Ben spied Bea at the church social, he'd paid court to no one else. Bea never remarried after his untimely death. She claimed Ben had spoiled her for any other man.

Maude envied her the memory of a happy marriage.

She should go to church to pray for Bea, but she needed to double-check the year-end inventory spreadsheet. She turned off the lights in the front of the store and moved to her office computer in the back room.

A headache provided an excuse to go home early, except Maude had another hour of work before returning to her cheerless house. She stopped off at the tiny sink, took two aspirin, and looked in the mirror. She didn't look as old as Annie—they were both fifty-three,

Bea had been the same age. Maude hadn't begun the change, and she didn't have Annie's problems, either. That Bobby would give wrinkles to a marble statue. She leaned closer to the mirror, checked for lines at the corner of her eyes.

Vanity, thy name is woman.

Humph! Wasn't that the truth.

Raul had used that sin, and the loneliness, to his advantage.

She was more alone than ever with Bea gone.

Who would kill her? And why?

Not Raul.

No, not possible.

He was a womanizer. He used women. He didn't kill them.

How could she be so sure?

They'd shared one kiss. If he had faked his passion, what other things was he capable of?

An inexplicable chill ran the length of her body.

If she hadn't seen Jax arguing with the hotel clerk, she would've gone to Raul's room. In hindsight, she was glad she hadn't. He never asked why she failed to keep their late-night rendezvous. It was as if they'd never kissed. The broken date had given her time to think. At the card game, the American woman's distaste for Raul was obvious. Either Jax was immune to his charm, or they had a past together.

In the harsh light of day, she knew Raul was underhanded enough to romance her for her vote. He probably thought she would sway the other members of the council.

Introspection wasn't one of her strong suits; a look in the mirror was all it took to see what Raul must have seen—a lonely woman past her prime, anxious to feel desirable one last time.

Fool me once, shame on you. Fool me twice, shame on me.

CHAPTER THIRTEEN

THE MEMORY OF Bea's murder destroyed my appetite and emotional exhaustion sent me to bed early. I feared the images of Bea's body in the burning shed would play in my head and make sleep impossible until Hoolie cuddled in the hollow of my back, and I slipped into sleep.

I woke to Hoolie's growl. He leaped off the bed and ran to the door. His sharp bark wasn't like the others I'd heard from him. This was vicious, an alarm. I heard footsteps clatter down the stairs followed by the slam of the outside door. Hoolie whimpered and scratched at the wood. I looked at the clock. It was after midnight. I crawled out of bed as fast as I could and stood beside him, too afraid to open the door. I wasn't taking any chances. Whoever had been outside might come back.

"Jax, what the hell set the dog off?"

I recognized Blake's voice and struggled into my parka before opening the door. "How long have you been standing there?"

Hoolie slipped outside before I could stop him. Nose to the floor, he dashed down the stairs and sat at the front door, scratching and growling.

"I think someone tried to break in," I said. "Hoolie heard—no, he must've smelled them. He wants to follow whoever it was."

"What's that on the floor?"

I picked up a note. Block letters in red ink on plain white paper.
GET OUT

With trembling fingers, I handed it to Blake. "This is different from the first one. Another one of your friends?"

"My friends wouldn't resort to such pranks."

"This one is hand-printed. It feels more . . . threatening."

"Did you lock up last night?"

"My apartment door. Did you lock the outside one?"

"Of course."

He sounded positive, but I saw the doubt in his eyes.

"If you locked the outside, how did he get up here?"

"Why do you think it was a man?" Blake was in lawyer mode again.

"I heard clomping footsteps going down the stairs. Heavy boots."

His penetrating gaze searched my face, then strayed to my chest.

It was true. Men *do* think of sex every five minutes, and we'd been talking that long. I looked down to see what he was looking at. Damn, he'd seen the effect of the cold air from the hallway on my breasts. I buttoned the coat up to my neck and pretended to study my toes. From my lowered eyes, I noticed he wore white boxer briefs and a T-shirt. That was all he slept in. The chill had no effect on his anatomy.

I shouldn't have looked.

Blake cleared his throat and handed me the note. "You need to give this to Trask."

"I don't think he likes me." I handed it back. "He might take it more seriously if you give it to him."

Hoolie climbed the stairs and returned to my side. "I'm sorry my dog woke you."

"Lucky you have him. Lock up. See you in the morning."

Restful sleep eluded my dog and me. Hoolie twitched and muttered in his sleep the rest of the night. I tossed and turned. Two threatening notes. Someone didn't want me in town. I hadn't run into anti-American sentiment in Scotland on my two previous trips. What was different this time? The Coulter property? The oyster lads?

The travel alarm went off at seven-thirty as usual. I dressed and took Hoolie outside, but the rain curtailed our morning duty walk. The corgi's droopy behavior and the confused, lonely look in his eyes wrung my heart. How could the dog understand Bea's absence and a new person in his life?

I offered Hoolie a bite of my cookie, but he ignored it.

On a television program, the police would have arrested a suspect by now. A village this size couldn't hide a killer for long. Blake would know if the local cops were closing in on the murderer.

The gusty patter of rain on the balcony sliding door drew me to the glass. The wind wailed out of the north and whipped white caps across the gray surface of the lake. No fishing boats braved the storm today.

What was Mr. Atkins thinking when he proposed a year-round golf resort in Heather Hill? Had anyone scouted the area in January? I doubted if the most rabid golfer would venture out in such a gale. Hiking? Not likely. Nearby skiing would offer a winter alternative. Not if it was this windy. I shuddered to think of children trapped inside during bad weather. In my opinion, the marketing department was going to have one helluva time filling rooms after the Christmas and New Year holidays.

At exactly ten-forty-four, I leaned casually, I hoped, against the stairway banister. I went over my parka for dog hair and lint and noticed the ornamental button on the sleeve was missing. Damn Raul! I hoped it wasn't noticeable. I needed to make a favorable impression on Elizabeth Coulter. I intended to snap up the property for Fairway Golf, collect my commission and promotion, and reclaim my condo.

My landlord's door opened promptly. I studied Blake's face for a clue to today's mood.

Ahhh, there it was—his perpetual scowl.

Gads, the man could out-glower a brooding Heathcliff.

"Good morning," I chirped, knowing a cheery greeting would throw him off balance and set his teeth on edge. "Isn't it a beautiful day?"

He raised one eyebrow. How did he do that?

"Have you looked outside? It's raining."

"Nice. So good for the trees." I carried my parka over my arm and worked my way down the first few steps. Walking wasn't so bad, but the stairs put a severe strain on my scraped knee.

"Where's Hooligan?" Blake said.

"I left him with Annie." I had this insane desire to make conversation. "Have you ever had a dog?"

"No."

So much for small talk. I concentrated on descending the stairs as normally as possible. I was slow and expected Blake to pass me on the stairs. He stayed two steps above me. I'd dressed for the weather in a tweed pantsuit and sweater. The slacks fit a bit snug. In the ensuing quiet, I swear I felt his eyes on my derriere. I tried to ignore the sensation.

On the last riser, he stepped in front of me and pulled an extra umbrella from the stand. I took it with my bandaged hand, winced and shifted it to left.

"Come on, then," he said. "The sooner we get to the manor, the sooner we'll be done."

Outside, I dropped my smile. Rosalind Sweet approached from the direction of the hotel. Her brassy red umbrella, matching raincoat and yellow boots were too bright even for my chirpy mood.

"Hi, Jax. I thought I'd go with you out to the manor house. I haven't seen it yet." Her false cheer put mine to shame. It gave way to a somber expression, equally false. "How awful you discovered that lady's body," she said. "You were playing cards together the other night, weren't you?"

I didn't want to open the subject with Rosalind. I didn't want her around at all. "You don't need to come with us. I wouldn't want you to catch cold in this damp weather. Why don't you go back to the hotel? I'll bring you up to date this afternoon."

"Oh, Jax, you are so kind to think of my health." She rested her hand on Blake's arm and smiled up at him. "Isn't she the nicest person, Blake? It is Blake, isn't it? I'm Rosalind. Rosalind Sweet, remember. You have room in your car for one more, don't you, Blake?"

Blake shifted from foot to foot and looked from Rosalind to me. He probably wanted to get rid of me so he could be alone with Rosalind. Tough. He offered me a ride first.

Blake must've had an upbringing as proper as mine. He was polite and put Rosalind in the back seat and opened the passenger door for me. I sat as far to my side of the Land Rover as I could. Rosalind kept up her incessant chatter. I made another try to draw Blake into a conversation.

"I noticed the bird in your apartment last night. How old is he?"

"What?"

"Your parrot-canary?"

He caught my grin before I could hide it.

"He's almost three."

Rosalind gave a gasp. Fake. "Jax, you were in Blake's apartment last night? Was that wise?" She gave Blake a playful tap on the shoulder. "Our employer, Mr. Atkins, demands discretion from his employees. He might not approve of Jax renting from you. Not that I think anything improper is going on, however, some might. Why don't you move into the hotel, Jax? The holidays are over, and there are plenty of rooms available."

I clenched my hands into fists so tight the nails cut my palms. Her hypocrisy had me seeing red. Blake or no Blake, I was ready to give her a piece of my temper. I had to bite my tongue during the time he parked the car.

We climbed the wide steps as a threesome. Blake used the stag head knocker on the carved wooden door. It looked like an antique.

A woman in housekeeper's attire opened the door and greeted us. "Good day. So nice to see you again, Mister Blake. You must be Miss Hollister. I'm Mrs. Casey. Come this way, if you please."

Blake introduced Rosalind to the housekeeper who led us into the formal parlor.

"Miss Elizabeth will be right with you," she said.

I declined to sit on the antique couch, fearing my knees would lock up as they had in the car. Rosalind removed her scarf and primped her hair and makeup.

I wandered the perimeter of the room, keeping in mind the structural engineers' report. The foundation was sound, no termites or problems with the mortar. If the designers expanded the parlor into the foyer, I calculated the area would be large enough to serve as a registration/reception desk. It would need a decorator's touch to remove the formality of the current sitting room. New possibilities crowded my imagination. I'd have to see if the rest of the manor could be adapted to my emerging idea. I kept my enthusiasm under wraps, away from Blake, the competition, and Rosalind, the credit-grabbing witch.

Elizabeth Coulter entered the room with practiced ease and held out her hands to welcome Blake. If she had been auditioning for the part of dowdy spinster of the manor, her clothes would have won her the part. Her unrelieved gray sweater and slacks matched the dismal sky and did nothing to brighten a muddy complexion. She was my height and, from experience, I knew she had to have her clothes altered. A big-boned woman, she weighed at least thirty pounds more than I did. Not to be unkind, she carried most of it below the waist. I guessed she was around Blake's age.

Elizabeth's expression became business-like when she turned to me and downright frosty when she saw Rosalind. My fellow employee's overt sensuality had that effect on many women.

"So nice to meet you, Miss Coulter. This is my associate, Rosalind Sweet." I extended my left hand, showing her the bandage on my right. "I'm sorry circumstances forced us to cancel yesterday. Were you and Bea close?"

Elizabeth made a pass at my left hand, barely touching it. "Bea was a wonderfully warm woman, a good neighbor," she said. Undistinguished brown eyes brimmed with tears. "I was appalled to hear of her death."

Blake put his arm around her shoulder. "There's no easy way to say this, Elizabeth. Someone stabbed Bea and set a shed on fire to hide the evidence and body."

"Richard told me the police were looking for suspects. I can't believe . . . stabbed. Right next door." Her hand went to her throat. She leaned on the desk for support. "Has there been any progress in the case?"

"No," Blake said. "The police aren't releasing any details."

"Then the murderer remains at large?"

Elizabeth's pallor concerned me. "Do you need a glass of water?"

She waved off my suggestion. "No, no, I'll be fine." She steadied herself on Blake's arm while he walked her to a chair. Elizabeth sat on the edge, ankles and knees together, shoes pointed straight ahead.

"Where are you from, Miss Hollister?"

"New York City." I ignored Rosalind and gave Elizabeth my attention. "I heard you were building a new home up the coast. How is the construction coming?"

"The weather has slowed things. One delay after another. I'll be happy when we can move in." She sighed, stood and motioned to the door. "But you're not here to listen to my complaints. Shall we complete our business? Cook promised a special luncheon when we finished. Blake, you remember the way to the north wing. I haven't used those rooms in years. I opened the doors to air them. Take Miss Sweet with you, if you please."

Oh, goodie. Let Rosalind put up with his bad mood.

Elizabeth led the way out the door. "I'll give Miss Hollister the tour. We'll start in the south wing, at the top."

"Call me Jax, please." I huffed up the stairs, mentally noting the need for the addition of an elevator. My knees complained with each step. On the second floor landing, I couldn't contain my curiosity.

"You and Blake have known each other a long time?"

"Since we were children." A quiet smile hinted at an inner beauty. "When I first came here with my father, I was the worst kind of outsider. A Sassenach, one of the hated English. Still am, to some. Surprising in this day and age, isn't it?" She tucked a loose strand of hair into her Eleanor Roosevelt style bun. "The Scots have such long memories. Blake had his own acceptance problems. So short and skinny, and half-English. His parents sent him to Heather Hill during school holidays to stay with his aunt Cora. Back then, to us she was old and didn't offer much to keep an active boy occupied. Happily, she loved him, and he knew it. It had to be wrenching for him to return to that English boarding school."

At the top of the third floor stairs, Elizabeth pointed down a long corridor. "These were servant's quarters until the beginning of WWII. There is a water closet at the end of the corridor. The rooms are small. I don't bother to heat them. When the original family took their holiday here, they used the other wing. Not quite like "Downton Abbey," but the same rigid segregation between servants and family existed. Nearly thirty years ago, dear Papa switched things up. He moved us into this wing and allowed the few servants he retained to use the larger rooms on the other side."

I looked into two or three empty rooms. Back in the day, they may have held a cot or a pallet. No closets. Hooks on the wall for hanging clothes. The rooms enjoyed great views of the lake. On the other side of the passageway, the rooms would overlook a putting green and golf course. I pulled a notebook from my purse, made a sketch, and scribbled a note to add bathrooms. Plumbing was a necessary expense. I had another idea. The design team could turn this floor into a dormitory for employees.

While we walked down one flight, I was determined to gather more information on my competition. "What did Blake do during his summers here?"

"It's no secret he was headed for trouble, until one year, Philip LeBeck took an interest in him. He involved Blake in his hobbies, hiking and gardening. Blake did a complete turnaround. I think that's why he tried to befriend that Bobby Duncan." Her frown echoed the disgust in her voice. "That hoodlum is beyond help. Cook says working with plants bores him, whereas Blake cherished the hours he spent tending to Philip's tomatoes."

Gardening. That explained the greenery in his apartment.

"Did you hear I'm adopting Bea's Hooligan? Yes, Blake agreed to let me keep the dog with me."

"Blake never had a pet. His parents were famous archeologists, always off on some dig during the summer, a full lecturing tour during the winter. I hold to the opinion that emotional neglect is abuse. I have no doubt the holidays Blake spent here in Heather Hill were some of his happiest times and the reason he made this his home. That and the partnership offer from Philip. I can tell poor Blake is devastated by that man's death."

On the second floor, she opened the door to a bedroom furnished with a Laura Ashley print spread and curtains. "This is my room."

Elizabeth showed me around the suite complete with sitting room and bath. She stood at a window and continued to reminisce.

"They were known as the Three Musketeers. Blake, Ian and Maggie. When I came on the scene, they made me D'Artangnan." Her voice took on a dreamy quality. "I suppose it was natural that I developed a crush on him."

"On Blake?"

Elizabeth eyes went tender at the memory. "I had a teenager's fantasy for him, but his affections belonged to Maggie. Always have. Unrequited love, on his part. Oh, he was engaged once. The woman said she didn't want to live in Scotland. I rather imagined she had seen how Blake looked at Maggie."

"Maggie who runs the pub?"

"Yes, she's always had a thing for Ian. A love triangle. Word is you and Blake might—"

"Impossible. No, it would be a conflict of interest." I was emphatic. "I want Fairway Golf to buy this wonderful estate fair and square. If there was any, uh, impropriety, it might cloud the issue. Besides, we are on opposite sides of the development debate."

"Whatever you say." Elizabeth dropped the subject and opened the door to her father's suite.

From what I could see, the room was the same size as Elizabeth's and had been preserved like a shrine. Before I could ask, she closed the door and said, "Next door is my fiancé, Richard's room. He doesn't like me to show it to strangers. It's the same layout as mine, with books and papers scattered everywhere. Men can be so disorganized, can't they?"

We crossed the landing to enter the north wing without passing Blake and Rosalind. Elizabeth explained they must have taken the other set of stairs from the kitchen.

"No sense straining your knees walking up to the third floor. The children's rooms up there duplicate the size of the servant's quarters you saw in the other wing. When the family's children were old enough, they moved down a floor."

We strolled through bedrooms occupied by her great-grandfather and his five brothers and one sister. Antique beds stripped to the frames were the size of current double beds. People were shorter in those days. Each room had a boarded-up fireplace dating back to the days before central heating. Dressing tables and armoires, covered by sheets, took up the rest of the bedroom space. There were no water stains on the ceilings. A good sign. Three of the rooms had connecting doors. With some remodeling, they could become suites. Add a bath or two, enlarge closets, update the beds, but keep the antique feel. I made another note.

Elizabeth led the way downstairs to where we began the tour. "I'm surprised we haven't bumped into my Richard. He must be on the grounds somewhere."

"In this rain?"

She chuckled. "If we waited until the weather cleared before going outdoors, we'd be shut-ins."

"Annie Duncan mentioned you were newly engaged. Congratulations"

"Thank you. Every day I thank God I found Richard. I hope each of the Musketeers can find the happiness I have."

We crossed the entrance foyer and stopped in front of a closed door. "This is the oldest room in the house," Elizabeth explained. "It has had several uses. My great-grandfather changed it into a study. The cornerstone is here and must be incorporated into your designs."

Rosalind and Blake joined us. Rosie the Devious wiped off a sly smile, stepped away from Blake's side and assumed a modest demeanor. Blake appeared grouchier than when he began his tour.

Elizabeth turned to him. "Remember the first time you visited, Blake? Dear Papa had added two walls of shelves for more books. You didn't think we'd ever fill them. However, we did. See?"

She turned the knob. "That's strange. It's locked." She called, "Mrs. Casey?"

The housekeeper appeared. "Yes, Miss Elizabeth?"

"Why is the study locked?"

"I-I don't know, Miss. I dusted it before breakfast. I'm positive it was unlocked when I left to help serve."

"It's never locked. The key, Mrs. Casey."

"Yes, Miss." She pulled a jangling bundle from a pocket on her uniform and inserted the correct one.

"Thank you. That will be all." Elizabeth pushed the door open and stood aside to allow Blake, Rosalind and me to enter. "This is the one room of the house I will miss the— what's the matter, Blake? Go on in."

"That's not a good idea, Elizabeth. You need to call the police."

Blake blocked the door, but not before I saw the body of a man in the middle of the floor. He was clutching his throat with one hand, the other lay limp on the carpet. Raul Montoya looked very dead.

CHAPTER FOURTEEN

I **HAD LOVED** Raul Montoya, once upon a time. After his betrayal, I loathed him. He was a womanizer with an ego the size of the Argentine pampas he called home. Handsome, amoral, now dead.

The police arrived, taped off the room, and called for their forensics team. We waited for the arrival of Constable Trask, who would do the official interviews. We weren't supposed to talk about what we had seen. Other topics of conversation seemed trivial.

During the delay, the reality of Raul's death wormed its way through my defenses. A shocked numbness spread and emptiness settled in my stomach. When an unexpected stab of pain hit, I wrapped my arms around my middle. Rosalind noticed. I saw the flicker of curiosity in her eyes before she reapplied her I've-seen-a-dead-body face. Had Raul revealed our past?

I straightened in the stiff chair, kept my head bowed and studied the pattern in the carpet. Two bodies in two days, and I turned up at both scenes.

The Constable would ask how well I knew the dead man. I couldn't lie, but how much should I reveal? My boss knew of my divorce. I didn't think he'd told the rest of the staff. I played with several possible responses until I decided to take my lead from the line of questioning.

Time dragged like it had when Raul was late for one of our dates. I always forgave him. His charming smile and laughing explanations made it difficult to stay angry. It wasn't until after we were married that evidence of the other woman became obvious. I could no longer believe his excuses or stay married to him.

An urge to scream and pound something threatened to break free. I needed to finish our last argument. Now, I'd never get the chance. I fought to keep the jumble of emotions off my face. In search of a distraction, I looked at the others in the room to gauge their reactions.

After the initial discovery of Raul's body, Rosalind had put on a great show. Her oh, my, God, I've seen a dead person act was over the top. A few tears would've been less dramatic. I overheard her tell the first cop on the scene that she knew Raul from the hotel. They'd met in the bar once or twice. True, I suppose, but she left out what happened after they left the lounge. When the young (and smitten) policeman finished questioning her, Rosalind assumed the pose of a person in shock.

Often, in the midst of business negotiations, I fell back on my friend Cindy's knowledge of poker. She'd taught me all about 'tells,' those mannerisms that give away what was in a player's hand. They were a handy people-reading tool, too.

Despite Rosalind's outward distress, her tapping index finger and occasional sighs signaled boredom. I knew that beneath her flashy exterior whirled a devious slyness. From the moment she arrived in Scotland, she'd been up to something. I wondered if anyone else could see how she was after my job. How far would she go to get it?

A sudden fear for my own safety edged out business concerns. Were the anti-American notes slipped under my door linked to Raul's death? I looked to Blake, wondering if he'd found time to turn them over to the police. He held Elizabeth's hands in a comforting way.

They talked in low murmurs. The housekeeper and cook sat in the corner without speaking. Their expressions of shock appeared natural.

With macabre fascination, we watched the coroner remove Raul's body from the parlor. The sound of the hearse driving away signaled a final end to what had been an important part of my life.

By mid-afternoon, the sun touched the watery horizon of Loch Linnhe and we waited. We fidgeted and looked everywhere except at each other. I suspected a police tactic—let the witnesses stew until they're ready to spill all the details. Periodically, I stood and wandered the room so my knee wouldn't stiffen.

When Trask arrived, he entered the study, inspected the floor where we had found Raul's body, then huddled with the crime scene man. He headed toward the kitchen at the back of the house and sent for Blake. One by one, the constable interviewed Elizabeth, then Rosalind. The cook and housekeeper were next. I was positive the constable was saving me for last, all the better to stretch my nerves to the breaking point.

It was nearing dark before a policeman showed me into the kitchen where Trask sat.

"Ms. Hollister." He motioned me to one of the chairs around the butcher-block table. "Two bodies in two days, and you're present both times." His smile was polite, at odds with his unfriendly eyes. "Do you believe in coincidences?"

His conversational tone didn't fool me. I'd seen enough cop shows to know that I was a stranger in Heather Hill and found at two death scenes. That would put me at the top of his suspect list. If the coroner ruled Raul's death a homicide and Trask discovered our acrimonious divorce, he'd order a hangman's noose for sure.

"Do I need a lawyer, Constable?"

He snapped his notebook open and glared at me.

Oops. I shouldn't have asked the first question.

"Now, now, Ms. Hollister, I need your official statement. It's standard procedure."

"You already have it. When your man first arrived, he asked what we'd seen. I told him we found the door locked. The housekeeper opened it. Blake went in first. He told us not to enter, but I could see Mr. Montoya's body on the floor. I have nothing more to add."

Trask didn't speak. He let the silence play out. I knew that ploy, too. It's an effective interview technique, a way to get a suspect to talk. This was not a television program.

It was time to take my brother's advice: the best defense is a good offense. Always attack. It worked for him on the tennis court.

"Have you found the man I saw behind the gazebo yesterday? What was he doing there? He could have been Bea's killer and came back to kill Mr. Montoya today."

"Ms. Hollister, there was no evidence anyone had been there. Are you certain you saw someone? Not an animal?"

Not good. He thinks I'm a liar, too. "It was a person. And last night, a man slipped a note under my door. I heard heavy boots going down the stairs after my dog barked. I gave the paper to Blake."

"And he turned it over to me. Blake thinks someone is stalking you. I don't see how that connects with Mr. Montoya's death. I understand you had a personal relationship with the deceased."

Damn Rosalind Sweet!

The constable's remark had a pointing-finger tone to it. The less I said the better. I met his gaze and stated, "We'd met."

"Is that all, Ms. Hollister? Concealing evidence is a crime in this country, as it is in the United States."

"I said I knew him. I also know the German and English representatives, Constable Trask. In my business, all of us know the other major players." Time to deflect the investigation away from me. "Uh, there are rumors." I hesitated and pretended to be embarrassed. "Mr. Montoya had a reputation for being a ladies' man. He wasn't always discreet. It might be wise to ask the desk clerk if he had any visitors."

For the briefest moment, I felt the teensiest bit of guilt. No, I had to make Trask look for other suspects. If it led him to Rosalind? Well, as the old saying goes, she made her bed and she certainly slept in it.

"Constable, I never visited Mr. Montoya at the hotel, and I didn't kill him." It was past time to make an exit. I gritted my teeth and prayed my knee wouldn't buckle when I stood. "Excuse me." Be polite, my mother told me, especially when you're angry enough to tear tin with your teeth. "I have nothing more to add." I did my best *Auntie Mame* impression and swept out the door without a limp.

Trask followed me. "One more thing."

I turned and almost stepped on his toes. He stood close, invading my space. I'd experienced his intimidation at Bea's. I hadn't paid much attention then, but I was more aware today. I recoiled from the stench of stale cigars clinging to his rumpled raincoat. His hair looked like it hadn't seen the teeth of a comb in a week. He was a taller version of the Seventies TV detective, Colombo, with a Scottish accent.

"Where were you this morning from nine until noon?"

"I worked in my room and sent some emails from the market. I left my dog with Annie Duncan at ten-thirty. She can verify the time. From ten-forty-five until noon, I was with Mr. Ramsey, Rosalind Sweet, or Miss Coulter."

He wrote on his pocket-sized spiral pad.

"How well did you know Raul Montoya?"

"You're repeating yourself, Constable, and I already told you. We were in the same business. Do you consider me a suspect?"

"More a person of interest, Ms. Hollister." He stood aside so I could enter the parlor. "I'll need your passport."

The first rule of travel, never lose your passport, loomed large in my mind. Trapped in a foreign country without it? Not good.

I held tight to my self-control. Please, God, let me get through the next few minutes. I joined Blake at the window. "I need some advice. The constable wants my passport. Can he do that?"

"Since global terrorism, he can do pretty much what he wants by invoking national security." Blake turned toward the constable. "Charlie, she's not a flight risk, she's here on business. I'll vouch for her."

"I need more proof that Ms. Hollister arrived after Bea Kestle was killed yesterday. Today, I have another body, and she's at this scene, too."

"You have my statement that I saw Jax arrive at Bea's. Are you doubting my word?"

"She doesn't have much of an alibi for this morning. Said she was working in her room before you picked her up."

"I believe her. She doesn't have a car. What she does have are bad knees from her fall yesterday. I doubt she could ride her bicycle out here and back. The timing is not right." Blake squared off with Trask. "I've been at both scenes, too. Do you want my passport?"

"No need to get huffy. Let's talk outside." Trask led the way to the foyer.

I couldn't hear the discussion, but Blake's posture was easy to read: arms crossed over his chest, upper body shoved forward, stubbornness in the set of his shoulders. Trask could gesture all he wanted. Blake wasn't giving an inch.

Raul would've used his charm, not English bulldog resolve.

Elizabeth's color had improved. She managed a weak smile and indicated the two men. "Blake can be positively obstinate when it suits him. You've found a champion."

Blake? Strange to think of him defending me.

I glanced at Rosalind for her reaction to my altercation with the policeman. She sat on the stiffest chair in the room, imitating Elizabeth's prim, lady-of-the-manor posture and watched the exchange between Blake and Trask with mild interest. When our gazes met, she tried to hide a smirk. She bit her lower lip, unable to keep her glee at my discomfort from reaching her eyes.

I knew for certain she had told Trask whatever she suspected or knew about Raul and me. Rosalind Sweet would do anything to get me out of the competition. Then she would take over my job. I'd worked too hard to let that happen.

Two minutes later, the constable turned toward the study, and Blake re-entered the parlor.

"Are you feeling better, Elizabeth?" Blake said. "Should I call Ian?"

"No, no. I'm fine. I rang Richard on his mobile. He should be here any moment. You needn't stay with me. You can take Jax and Miss Sweet back to town."

"Trask said we can leave?" I asked.

Blake helped me into my coat. "He's not happy, but you can keep your passport."

Rosalind held out her coat for Blake to do the honors. After sliding her arms into the sleeves, the minx leaned against his chest as if she were going to faint. Lousy actress.

Blake steadied her and led us to the door.

Outside, I relished the fresh air. The atmosphere in the house had closed in on me. I chalked it up to falling under the local cop's scrutiny. I couldn't ignore the constable's animosity and Rosalind's curiosity. I needed to clear something up. "Blake, when we first met, you didn't like me. The oyster lads aren't fans of mine, and Trask wants to make me a murderer. Are all Scottish men xenophobic?"

"Using multi-syllable words, are we—you?"

"Seems more mature than asking if all Scots hate strangers."

Blake did his death glower. "I am not xenophobic."

Rosalind tried to regain the spotlight. "The constable was rude. I felt as if he strip-searched me with his eyes. Did he do that to you, too, Jax?"

I looked at her chest and down at mine. There was no comparison. Before I could answer, a pristine, classic Austin Healy came to a screeching halt behind Blake's muddy Land Rover. Blake waited for the tall man with blond-going-gray hair until he scrambled out of the car and rushed toward us. He had a receding chin to match his disappearing hairline and was dressed in rustic hunting tweeds beneath his London Fog winter coat.

He gripped Blake's arm. "Elizabeth?"

"She's shaken, but bearing up. Richard Hyde, this is Jax Hollister and Rosalind Sweet."

"How do you do?" He gave my hand a cursory shake and lingered over Rosalind's for a second longer than necessary. Reluctantly, it seemed, he turned to leave. "If you'll excuse me, I must see to Elizabeth." He ran inside.

"So, that's Elizabeth's Richard," I said. "Annie and Maude worry he won't give Elizabeth the best financial advice how to invest the proceeds from the sale. What do you think?"

"Elizabeth has a man in London who advised her father. I suppose she asks Richard's opinion. She'll listen to all the suggestions and make her own decision. She's a smart woman." Blake started his car and flipped on the headlights to dispel the approaching darkness.

"Is there a restaurant nearby that has a decent salad bar?"

Rosalind's out-of-the-blue question was mind-boggling.

"All this fattening pub food," she continued. "Everything is fried. I've gained three pounds since I arrived."

Her self-centered babble was the last straw in a long day. "I would think that after discovering a body, food would be the last thing you'd want. There are more important things to consider." I shifted my attention to Blake. "Do you think we have to worry for our safety? What did Trask say when he saw the note? Will Montoya's death delay the sale? Does there have to be five bids? Why didn't Trask take my passport? What did you say to him? Where were you this morning before we drove out to the manor house?"

"Slow down, Jax. Take a breath."

He kept his attention on the road, but I swear the corner of his mouth twitched.

I was in trouble, and he thought it was funny?

"What note?" Rosalind said.

"Someone slipped a get-out-of-town note under my door last night. Did you get one?"

"Me? Why would someone threaten me? Am I in danger?"

I detected a hint of fear in her voice. It was tempting to say more and frighten her back to New York. Instead, I decided to let her imagination do the work.

Blake said, "You should be safe at the hotel."

She wouldn't have to leave her door open for Raul tonight . . . or ever again. I stared into the darkening gloom until I could speak without a tremor in my voice.

I asked Blake, "Did you ever meet him? Raul Montoya?"

"No, I was out of town when he arrived. I saw you talking to him in the pub the other night. You knew him, didn't you?"

"We bid on some of the same properties." I wasn't ready to say more. Rosalind kept her comments to herself, lucky for her.

Wait a minute. Blake had changed the subject. He never told me where he'd been this morning before he picked me up. Not that I seriously suspected him. Blake Ramsey struck me as an honest and ethical man, not a killer. But then again, once upon a time, I believed Raul was perfect and thought he loved me. When it came to men, my judgment was seriously lacking.

"Rosalind, had you met Raul?" I was curious if she'd reveal what she told the police.

"Briefly. We are-were staying at the same hotel."

I shifted in my seat so I could see her features. "What did you think of him?"

She didn't blink. "We barely spoke."

Too busy doing the horizontal tango? I didn't say it, but oh, how I wanted to.

Once more, my mind veered away from my feelings for Raul. I'd come to Scotland on a simple business trip and discovered my godfather was dead. Two more deaths had occurred in as many days. One in the manor house, one at the Kestle Kennels next door. The coincidental proximity of properties could be a link to a motive for all three deaths.

I remembered the previous day on the road when Raul and I argued. Where did he go after I pedaled away? He could have driven to Bea's farm. It would be logical for him to inquire if she was in the market to sell her land. Had Trask considered Raul a suspect in Bea's death? I didn't give voice to my opinions, not out of respect for the dead, but because it didn't matter. Raul was out of the picture. Permanently.

CHAPTER FIFTEEN

I **WAS HAPPY** when Blake dropped Rosalind off at the hotel and didn't prolong the parting. Within minutes, we were in front of Maude's two-story, white townhouse. Annie had called Blake to say she'd sent Hoolie home with her friend. Maude's house connected to several others with red roofs, similar to those pictured on postcards of Scottish coastal villages. The lights were on. I recognized Hoolie's bark before he bolted out the opening door. If Blake hadn't intercepted him, my dog would have bowled me over. When he handed over the wriggling fur ball, I received a face wash.

"I heard your car pull up," Maude said, "Hooligan couldn't have. I do believe he sensed you were here before Winnie did."

Maude was keeping Bea's newest champion until the estate was settled. Winnie sat politely at Maude's feet.

I tucked Hoolie under my arm and spoke to him. "Why can't you behave like Winnie? And darn, why do I keep talking to a deaf dog?" He licked my hand and quieted.

"Apparently, he understands you perfectly well." Maude turned to Blake. "Is there any news? What caused Ra—Mr. Montoya's death?"

"The coroner won't finish the autopsy report until tomorrow, toxicology sometime next week. I didn't see any signs of foul play."

I stared at him in disbelief. "You didn't? One of his hands clutched his throat. He could've been strangled or poisoned."

"You read too many mysteries, Jax."

His rebuke stung until I looked at Maude. Her expression of horror made me regret I'd been so insensitive.

"Another murder?" Her voice quavered.

"We won't know until the police get the results." Blake gave Maude a brief pat on the shoulder. "Lock up tight. If you need anything, give me a ring. Try not to worry."

"Easier said than done," she replied.

Blake parked in the lot by his building, and hesitated before opening the car door.

"Want a drink?" he asked.

I wasn't ready to be alone with my memories. "I'll keep you company." On the short walk to the pub, my knee acted up again. Hooligan slowed his pace to match mine.

The regulars were in their places, but the noise level in the *Heelster Gowdie* was subdued. I earned a few furtive looks and whispers. Maggie pointed us to a corner table and soon arrived with a shot glass and a bottle of Scotch for Blake.

"You'll be needing this, Blake. What will you have, Jax? You're looking pale."

I pinched my cheeks. "Better?"

"Not much." She returned with what looked like a cup of black tar. "Tea so strong a mouse could walk on it," she said. "Blake, add a wee dram for Jax." He poured, she talked. "We heard you found another body. 'Tis beyond belief. The entire village is in shock. Not another murder, surely?"

"The police won't know until all the reports are in," Blake said.

"Bad enough Philip and Bea's deaths have the village locking their doors." She looked down at my feet and the corgi spread across my shoes. "I'm glad Hooligan has found you. He'll do a grand job of protecting you."

"How much security can a deaf dog provide?" I asked.

Blake leaned down to scratch the corgi's head. "He used his other senses last night."

"Last night? What happened?" Maggie asked.

I told her I'd received a second threatening note.

"It must be someone having a joke on you."

"Regardless, Blake and I will make sure we're locked up tight tonight."

The door opened and the first footer from New Year's Eve rushed in. When he spotted me, his eyes widened. He spun on his heel, stumbled out the door, and slammed it behind him.

Maggie broke into giggles that progressed to hold-your-sides laughter. She fell into a chair.

"What's so funny?" Blake handed Maggie a napkin to blot her eyes. "Did Dickie do something?"

When she could speak again, she said, "He thinks Jax is a *selki*, one who came ashore to bewitch him into wedlock."

"He thinks I'm a seal that turns into a human?" I snorted a laugh. "Nonsense. It's a legend. B*roomies* and fairies aren't real, either. No one believes in them anymore."

A few of the patrons frowned and shook their heads.

"I didn't mean that the way it came out. They're lovely stories."

"Best quit while you're ahead," Blake said.

"Dickie keeps to the old ways, he does." Maggie pushed to her feet and gave the table an unnecessary wipe. "Can I get you anything to eat?"

"This is fine," I said.

After Maggie left, I spoke so only Blake could hear me. "That man was the one I saw by the river yesterday."

"Dickie? Are you positive?"

"Yes. N-no. I think so. I only had a glimpse of him."

"Why do you think it was Campbell?"

"His body size and shape. His clothes, and the way he moved."

"Not something the police can act on."

"I'm as sure as I can be. Does anyone have a guess why your town drunk was on the Coulter property the day Bea was killed?"

Maggie returned to refill my tea.

"Dickie is our local handyman," Blake said. "Maggie, didn't Bea hire him to do odd jobs?"

"Aye, he works for Elizabeth, too, when he's not on duty at the oyster farm."

"Why would he run off when he saw me yesterday at the manor? It can't be because he thinks I'm a *selki*."

Maggie didn't answer because Richard Hyde wandered in. "Be right with you, Richard."

"What's he doing here? I mean, doesn't Elizabeth have a cook?"

"Aye, she does. Richard phoned in the order for carry-out and told Sean that Mrs. Gordon has taken a few days off. I imagine she's feeling a bit unnerved after serving breakfast to that Montoya fellow, and then him up and dying in the study."

I caught Elizabeth's fiancé looking at me, a question on his face. I shifted my attention to my tea.

"Something wrong?" Blake asked.

"I wonder how well Richard knew Montoya."

Maggie said, "He introduced himself when Elizabeth and Richard were in last week with the English agent. I can't remember which day. Let me think on it. What can I get you from the kitchen?"

Blake ordered the fish and chips. "Bring Jax a bowl of soup."

I protested I wasn't hungry, but no one listened. Blake fell into one of his silent moods.

"Three deaths in less than a week," I said. "Don't you find that too much of a coincidence?"

"I do, but I can't connect them. The only thing they have in common is you."

"And the Coulter estate," I added.

Blake shook his head and returned to contemplating his Scotch. I twisted my teacup round and round, remembering another time and place when Raul and I sat in a cantina in Cancun. Candles and champagne. Soft ocean breezes. Raul smiled his brilliant smile for me alone. His gaze caressed my face.

My good memories shattered when Sean delivered our food. He was less than gentle setting my soup in front of me. He stormed back to the kitchen.

"I see your winning ways haven't won over all the locals," Blake said.

I ignored his mockery and played with my spoon. I'd had enough confrontation for one day.

Blake used the malt vinegar on his fish. "Where did you meet Montoya?"

His tone was what I imagined he used in court. I refused to look at him and took a spoonful of soup before answering. "We competed for the same property in Cancun a couple of years ago."

Maggie stopped by to refill my tea, again.

"What did you think of that Montoya chap?" Blake asked her.

"'Tis not what I thought of him that mattered," she said. "*He* thought highly of himself, he did. Fancied himself a lady's man. He flirted with all the women, Annie and Maude, too. Maude rather liked the attention."

I tried to hide my bitterness. "Yes, he was good at making a woman feel special." He was a charming man, courtly . . . and completely without a conscious. He used women as if they were paper napkins. I felt sorry for Maude if she had fallen under his spell.

After most of the pub's patrons called it a night, Maggie returned and took the chair next to Blake.

"Bea's funeral is tomorrow at one," she said. "I won't be opening the pub 'til five for dinner."

I pushed aside my half-empty soup bowl. "I knew Bea such a short time. Do you think it would be appropriate if I attended? She was so nice to me."

"She felt she'd met you before, she said, mayhaps in another life. Bea believed in things otherworldly. She'd be pleased if you attended." Maggie studied Hooligan. "I think she's happy that one is with you. He was a favorite of hers. The whole town likes him. How are things between you two?"

"He's a special dog." Hooligan stood and jumped into my lap. "See, he already knows how to do that."

Blake frowned. "I didn't see you make a hand signal. What did you do?"

"Nothing." Some people are so dense.

"Blake, Jax made a joke," Maggie said. "Hooligan jumped by his ownself."

"Oh."

I looked from Blake to Maggie. "I have an idea. I could take Hoolie to the funeral. I'm sure he was a witness to Bea's murder before he came and got me. He might be able to pick out the killer."

"Oh, the killer wouldna go to her funeral," Maggie said. "He's long gone. It has to be one of those senseless, random acts. Some hoodlums from Inverness or Glasgow."

"Bea lived outside town," I countered. "Wouldn't a burglar strike somewhere closer to the main road? Easy in, easy out."

Blake put his knife and fork on his empty plate. "If it was someone from around here, what was the motive? Annie said nothing had been disturbed in Bea's house."

"That rules out a robbery gone bad," I said. "Blake doesn't believe any of the deaths are related to the Coulter manor. But Bea's land is next door. It could be worth a lot of money."

"It wasn't for sale."

Ian entered the pub and took a seat next to Blake. "What's not for sale?"

"Bea's farm," Blake said. "Jax thinks it's a motive for murder. I haven't heard of any pending offers."

Maggie reached over and stroked the corgi's head. "Jax wants to take Hooligan to the funeral. He might pick out the killer."

"Not a good idea." Ian was emphatic. "What if he growls or reacts to the wrong person?"

"Does he usually bark or growl at people?" I asked.

Ian studied Hoolie. "Only when that Montoya fellow crowded you. I'd never heard one of Bea's dogs growl before."

"I agree with Ian," Blake said. "What if the murderer *is* there? And what if Hooligan makes a scene? The killer would notice. It would put you and the dog in danger. No, let the police do their job."

His argument made sense. I'd leave Hoolie in the apartment during the service. At that moment, my dog jumped to the floor, stretched and lay on his back. He looked at us upside down and closed his eyes. His short front legs relaxed on his chest, his back legs spread wide.

"He does that a lot," I said. "It makes me smile."

Ian used his thumb to make Maggie's sad lips tilt upward. "Every corgi Bea brought into the pub ended up on their backs, didn't they."

"A breed trait, Bea always said. 'Tis hard to believe she won't be coming in to play cards." Maggie swiped tears from her cheeks. "I best be getting back to the bar and send the rest of the oyster lads to their homes and bed. Sean'll have my skin if they're late for work tomorrow."

I dug in my purse to pay for my soup. "I need to go, too."

"Put it on my tab." Blake helped me with my coat and pointed to the cuff on my sleeve. "You're missing a button."

"I noticed it this morning."

No need to tell him Raul tore it off when we fought. For the last time.

It had been a long, emotional day. On the short walk to MacGloomy's building, I tried to make sense of recent events. I couldn't figure why Richard had been staring at me in the pub. Why had it made me feel so uneasy?

Raul and I were foreigners. The notes told me to leave town. Did Raul receive one? Could I become the next victim? It seemed unlikely, but I'd be smart to exercise some self-protective paranoia.

We approached Blake's building. Hoolie sniffed the bushes along the way. Blake hurried on ahead.

"Good night, and thanks for dinner," I called after his retreating backside. I hoped he'd slow down and wait for me. Instead, he hunched his shoulders as if I'd hit him with a stone. So much for using my oversized landlord for bodyguard duty.

Safely inside my apartment, I swallowed a couple of aspirin for my knee, clicked on the fireplace to take off the chill, made up the sofa bed, and crawled under the covers with my cell phone. My first call was to my parents. They were shocked and surprised to hear my news of Raul's death.

"Mom, should I call Raul's family?"

"No," was her immediate response. "Let the police make the official notification. Later, you can decide how to handle your condolences."

My father was on the extension. "You sound worried. What else is going on?"

I told them how I might be a suspect in Bea Kestle's murder and maybe Raul's death. My dad let fly with an expletive, or three.

"Dad, take it easy. You need to relax. You just had surgery. This is such a small town, the local cops will find Bea's killer soon. I'm sure Raul's death was accidental."

My parents were not easy to placate. Because I needed their fussing, I let them carry on. Mom finished by saying, "If you need, I can be on the next flight."

I promised to call or email with updates. I disconnected and the tight hold on my emotions shattered. A flash flood of Raul memories rushed in. Good ones, horrible ones, words said in anger, things left unsaid, sorrow and loss. Raul's death dealt me a final sense of closure, but not in a satisfactory way. On top of Philip's and Bea's deaths, the Grim Reaper seemed to be around every corner.

Hoolie surprised me when he licked wetness off my face. I didn't think I had any tears left after last year. He whined and rested his head on my heart, a solid reminder that I was responsible for another life. He needed me to take him outside and feed him on a regular basis. I had to do it. One step forward, one day at a time. I wouldn't let sorrow or fear get in my way. Still, I got up and rechecked my locks.

CHAPTER SIXTEEN

A T SEVEN THE next morning Hooligan needed to go outside. He was more reliable than an alarm clock. After I let him out and fed him, I resisted the urge to return to bed and pull the covers over my head. That action could lead me down the slippery slope to depression. Been there, done that. Work and Hooligan would be my salvation.

Before appearing in public, I used make-up to conceal the redness and puffiness under my eyes. My business mask firmly in place gave me courage to email the announcement of Raul's death, without speculating on how it might affect the sale of Coulter Manor. I'd leave that to the chief of my department. I forwarded more ideas for the manor house to the designers, and collected my correspondence, including one from accounting. They wanted me to stick to their bidding cap.

Damn bean counters. If I'd been in charge, I would've given me more room to maneuver. How the town council would vote was unknown. Worst case scenario? The entire process could turn into a popularity contest between SLFS's designs and Fairway Golf's. Blake and SLFS had the hometown advantage.

I'd never been good at the popularity game. At Stanford, I preferred the library to frat parties. I ignored the social aspects of college . . . or it ignored me. Fairway Golf recruited me at graduation and sent me to New York for training. Soon, I knew I had found my niche. Mike Lemon taught me the finer points of destination resort planning. It wasn't until I finished my apprenticeship and went solo on a job that I discovered my father and the owner of Fairway Golf were friends. Mr. Atkins swore he'd hired me based on my qualifications. It took a few years to realize I'd earned my way to the top.

And I'd dropped it all for Raul. Think of something else.

Hoolie moped around the apartment as if he knew today was Bea's funeral. When I looked at him, my mood fell in the dumpster again.

I needed some comfort food. Why not cook some chili? It would taste good on such a cold and somber day. A quick check of the refrigerator and cupboards sent me to the downstairs market for the rest of the ingredients. I opened cans of tomatoes and browned hamburger, minced meat in the UK. I'd never made a small batch before, always cooking my specialty for a crowd at the office. One pot expanded to fill two. I looked at the full pans of simmering chili and opened the freezer. There was room for the leftovers or I could give it away when it was time to go back to the States.

The idea of leaving Scotland brought mixed feelings—a sadness I attributed to the upcoming funeral and the memory of Raul's death. And I'd miss the new friends I'd made in Heather Glen.

I added the chili powder and cumin and was stirring the pot when Maude stopped by with a crate for Hoolie.

Maude had tears in her eyes when she said, "Bea crate-trained all her dogs. It made it easier when they traveled to shows." She set the neoprene approved-for-airplane-travel container against one wall, facing outward.

Hoolie explored the crate, did a quick turn around and settled on the cushion inside.

"He must think it's his den," I said.

"That's what Bea said. He feels safe. You can close the door when you leave so he doesn't get into trouble. Annie and I noticed he suffers from a bit of separation anxiety when you aren't nearby. Understandable after losing Bea . . ." She blotted her tears. "I'm going to miss her so."

I gave the older woman an awkward hug.

"The word is you're going to her funeral," Maude said. "I'll let you get dressed. The church is at the other end of the street. I'll see you there."

If the clouds are nae on the hills, t'will soon be rainin'. If the clouds are over the hills, it is rainin'. (Scottish saying)

SINCE THE CLOUDS were over the hills, I took an umbrella from the stand by the front door. Clouds and rain were appropriate on such a sad day. For me, sunshine and funerals don't mix.

The white, wooden church stood on the edge of town a short two blocks from Blake's market/apartment building. The dismal day surrounded me, muffling the footsteps coming from behind. I looked over my shoulder. No one was there. I quickened my pace and heard heavy shoes on the pavement. I wasn't imagining things. Someone was following me.

Omigod, I was next on the killer's list.

I ran up the steps and reached for the church door. A rough-clad man circled his arm around me.

"Let me get the door for you, miss," he said.

He ushered me inside. Once over the threshold, I waited. He went around me to sit with some of the men I recognized as the oyster lads. Their continuing animosity was apparent from their hostile looks.

I leaned against a pew to quiet my racing heartbeat. Memo to self—must manage overactive imagination. There may be a killer on the loose, but I didn't seriously think I'd be his next target. I had nothing in common with Bea Kestle except a card game and a cup of coffee, and Hooligan.

Uncle Philip? Raul? I had so much history with both men. Was there enough in common to put me on the killer's list? Tension re-tightened the knot between my shoulders.

Annie waved, motioning me to join Maude, Ian, Blake and Maggie. She made Blake scoot over until I settled next to the hard press of Blake's shoulder. Across the aisle, Elizabeth and Richard acknowledged me with polite smiles. The kindness offered by new friends offset the chilly gazes tossed my way by the oyster lads.

Soon, the peace and quiet of the interior worked its magic and allowed memories of murder and Raul to recede. The wooden surfaces in the church gleamed with fresh polish, reflecting the many candle flames. Evergreen boughs softened the austere alter and lent a piney aroma to the crowded sanctuary.

The minister rose to speak while I mulled over my new feeling of fitting in—something I seldom had experienced in my lifetime. My family moved often, until, at the beginning of sixth grade, we settled in Lake Tahoe. The social aspect of my education had been hell. The cliques had already formed and continued through high school. I was always the tallest, clumsiest kid in my class. Basketball should have been my forte. It wasn't. Not Jax the Klutzy Jinx. I was always the last picked.

New York and my job gave me a fresh start. I loved the benefits of world travel. The downside? I never stayed in any city long enough to sustain long-term relationships. Heather Hill felt different. I'd already made friends I'd miss.

The mourners took out their hymnals and sang their sorrow. I didn't recognize the songs. My parents didn't believe in organized religion, but the tunes were so simple I could hum along. Readings from the Bible offered comfort to some. Annie and Maude sniffled into their tissues. For the eulogy, several people spoke about Bea and what a good person she had been.

My musings came to an abrupt halt with the realization that Bea's killer might be in the church. I shifted on the wooden pew and squelched the urge to look around.

I bowed my head when the minister gave the final prayer. Bea was in a good place. I hoped Uncle Philip, and yes, Raul were, too. After the service, Blake stood and made an announcement.

"Bea wished me to read her will to as many of the town's inhabitants as possible, including those who adopted her dogs. I'll announce the time and place for the reading as soon as I can."

The mourners filed out the door. I followed them into the damp grayness and checked the crowd for a murderer. Dickie Campbell was nowhere to be seen. No one wore a sign saying I KILLED BEA/ PHILIP/RAUL.

The rain had stopped. Droplets dripped off the pine needles. The villagers broke into groups, some wandering among the tombstones in the adjacent cemetery. Others returned to their vehicles or walked to their homes. Bea's closest friends seemed reluctant to be alone.

"Come to my place," Blake said. "Bea would want us to raise a glass in her memory."

Annie and Maude declined, stating they were driving to Glasgow to search for Annie's grandson.

I followed Ian and Maggie into the foyer of Blake's building. I wasn't sure I'd been included in the invitation, so I traipsed up the steps on the right that led to my apartment.

Blake led the way up the left staircase to his flat. "What is that smell?"

Why did he make me feel so defensive? "It's chili." The *aroma* smelled wonderful.

Blake's eyes narrowed. "Real American chili? Not out of a tin?"

"It's been cooking all day. Do you like it?"

"I haven't had any since I spent a summer in America."

"There's plenty for everyone, but my apartment is too small to hold the four of us."

Maggie joined me on my side of the landing. "Blake, you and Ian make the table ready in your flat. Jax and I will bring over the chili. I'm anxious to try it. Blake comes close to waxing poetic when he speaks of it."

Minutes later, Maggie and I each carried a pot to Blake's. Hoolie followed us down the hall.

"These were the biggest pans that came with the apartment," I said. "They barely fit in that oven."

"Why not simmer it on the stove top?"

"It never sticks to the bottom of the pan when I cook it in the oven."

Ian opened the door for us. I heard Blake lock the market below and pound up the stairs.

He held a six-pack of brown bottles triumphantly in the air. "Imported beer! Texas long horns."

"Long necks," I corrected with a smile. It took me a second to realize that in Scotland, American beer qualified as imported.

"I stand corrected. Long necks it is. Let's eat."

It was a comfortable fit for the four of us around Blake's table. Maggie and Ian tentatively tasted my culinary efforts. Blake dug right in.

He rolled his eyes. "Perfect. Not too hot. Great flavor." He grinned at me.

A first. No wonder he didn't smile often. Scotland would have to declare they had a weapon of mass destruction.

I gave myself a mental slap. Blake was an interesting man and he might like my cooking, but this was a temporary truce, not a budding . . . anything. Innocuous conversation was the safest bet.

"Blake, you mentioned spending a summer in America?"

He swallowed. "Lake Tahoe. The Center for Environmental Studies at Incline Village."

"We were practically neighbors. My folks live up the hill from the center."

"Philip wanted me to call your father while I was there, but my schedule was jammed."

"What exotic place will you be heading to after Heather Hill?" Maggie asked.

"Wherever my boss decides to send me."

Ian said, "Doesn't the lack of stability bother you? I like knowing where I'll be one day to the next."

"The call to adventure is hard to resist," I said.

Spoons scrapping the bottom of bowls signaled refills. Maggie declined, saying she was full to the brim. Ian and Blake had seconds.

Blake picked up the questioning. "What would you do if your employer sent you to a place where you didn't think a golf resort was a good idea?"

"That has never happened. Mr. Atkins makes excellent choices. I don't expect him to change."

"You're convinced Heather Hill needs one of Fairway Golf's over-sized mega resorts?"

"Blake, I think once you see our plans you will agree they aren't oversized. Until then, let's agree to disagree."

Ian cleared his throat and said, "Great chili, Jax. If Maggie could make this, I'd marry her," he snapped his fingers, "like that."

"And who's to say I'd be accepting you, Dr. MacKenzie?"

Maggie's comeback and quick concentration on her bowl successfully hid her pain from the men. Not me. She was so in love with Ian, and he didn't have a clue. His expression was one of bemused curiosity when he looked at Maggie's bowed head. Maybe he wasn't as oblivious as I thought. Blake's phone rang, saving the moment.

All conversation stopped when Blake said "anaphylactic shock." A premonition set the hairs on my arms standing at attention.

He hung up and returned to the table. "That was Charlie Trask. He received the preliminary report from the coroner. Montoya had an allergic reaction to something in the breakfast at Elizabeth's. They won't know exactly what it was until they analyze his stomach contents. If we have any information, he wants us to call."

"Onions," Maggie said. "It had to be onions. When he came in for dinner last week, he questioned me. Right thorough, he was. Wanted to know if there were onions in the lamb stew. When I told him yes, he said he was allergic and ordered the fish. I dinna give it another thought."

"I've never heard of an onion allergy," Blake said.

"People can be allergic to the damnedest things." Ian uncapped another beer, offered it to me, then Maggie, before claiming it. "Food allergies can be sneaky and deadly."

"Someone could have overheard your conversation and put onions in something he ate at breakfast," I said. "Maggie, who was in the pub with Montoya that night?"

"We were busy, I remember. Sean's lamb stew is popular." Maggie frowned, concentrating on the memory. "Mr. Montoya had dinner with Richard and Elizabeth and the British real estate agent. Anyone could have overheard him. You were there, Ian. All my regulars. Maude and Annie, too. Why?"

Without thinking first, I said, "It could have been deliberate."

Ian set down his beer. "That would be murder."

It wasn't the right time to tell anyone I knew Raul had been allergic to onions.

"What possible motive could there be to killing him?" Ian asked.

Any jealous husband could have motive to kill the Argentine lothario.

Blake said, "Trask mentioned Montoya's reason for being here. The sale of the manor. There's a lot of money involved." He favored me with another frown. "The good constable reminded me I'd taken responsibility for you."

"He suspects Jax?" Ian and Maggie asked in unison.

Blake didn't come to my defense. That hurt.

"Not possible," Ian said.

"Bless you," I said.

"Mr. Montoya's death must've been an accident." Maggie stood and took bowls to the sink. "If he ate something bad at breakfast, you couldn't blame Elizabeth's cook. She wasna in the pub that night. She had no way of knowing he had an allergy."

Ian collected the beer bottles. "If Montoya was that allergic, I'm surprised he didn't question Mrs. Gordon regarding the ingredients."

"He might've thought Elizabeth would remember." Maggie leaned against the counter. "He'd also assume she told the cook."

"Perhaps she did," I said.

CHAPTER SEVENTEEN

BLAKE AND I CLEANED up the dishes after Maggie and Ian left. Rain pattered the window over the sink.

"Does it always rain this much in January?" I grumbled.

"Not this many days in a row."

"I wouldn't be surprised if I brought the bad weather with me. The New Year curse."

"I heard. I don't believe in curses," he said. "Bad luck follows you if you think it does."

Hah! He hadn't stumbled around all his life with a label of jinx over his head.

"I'll wash up," he said.

"Let me dry. It might go faster if we have some music." The quiet left too much room for thinking. I walked over to his entertainment center. "Do you have anything besides the three Bs? All I see are Bach, Beethoven, and Brahms."

"I have Bacharach, the Beetles and B. B. King, too."

"Why, Mr. Ramsey, I do believe you made a joke."

The corner of his mouth hiked a millimeter upward before he resumed his normal frown. "Not me. According to Ian, I never joke."

Blake had arranged his collection of CD's alphabetically by musician and category. I found the one I was looking for and popped it into the CD changer. I turned up the volume and filled the room with the musical score from *The Big Chill*.

"You're a fan of films?" he asked.

"And rock 'n roll." I did a boogie to *I Heard It Through the Grapevine*. Not the world's best dancer, I earned another lip twitch from Blake before I knocked into a side table that held a tray of seedlings.

Blake lunged. "Careful." He caught the baby plants before they hit the floor.

"What are they?"

"Tomatoes."

I tried to raise an eyebrow, but failed. Blake coughed on a chuckle.

"Why indoors?"

"Short growing season."

Succinct. Damn, he made lengthy conversations difficult. In the renewed silence, I returned to the problem of Raul.

"When Constable Trask called, did he say anything else about the case? Or Bea's murder? Does he think they are connected? I mean, *if* there is no connection between Bea, Philip and Raul, that might mean there's a serial killer on the loose. Someone who kills at random. From your expression, you don't think that's a likely scenario. Neither do I. Therefore, my dear Watson, it is logical these deaths must have something in common."

"Bea and Montoya never met. I'll double check with Annie and Maude. I think Montoya arrived the weekend of the Inverness dog show."

I stood looking out the kitchen window at the rain. "Wasn't that the same weekend Uncle Philip went hiking?"

"And was killed."

The fun feelings left-over from the evening with Ian and Maggie ran down the drain with the dishwater. When I thought of never seeing my godfather again, a void opened inside so huge I wrapped my arms around my stomach to hold in the pain. "Damn it, I miss him. Blake, I have to do something to find his killer. But what? I'm being unrealistic about finding evidence on the mountain, aren't I?"

"Yes."

"What else can I do? I'm not a detective. The police think it's an accident. They aren't looking for a killer."

"You're not giving up, are you?" There was a challenge in his voice.

"I will never do that. I won't stop pushing the police to keep the case open. It would help if you could lend your support."

"You still convinced Bea and Philip's deaths are connected?"

"Aren't you?"

"When the police find Bea's killer, will it lead them to Philip's?"

"I hope it will. Blake, we can do more than hope. We can be pro-active. We should question the locals. They might know someone who had a motive to kill Bea."

"No, Jax, if the killer heard you were asking questions, he could come after you. Let the police do their job."

"If we worked as a team, it wouldn't be so dangerous."

"Let Trask work the case." Blake looked at the calendar hanging on the wall. "What we can do together, if you're still in town, is go up Ben Nevis and spread Philip's ashes."

"Thank you, that's kind." To forestall an errant tear, I focused on one individual raindrop sliding down the window. "If you decide to postpone it, I could come back. Philip loved hiking in the spring, looking at the wildflowers."

"I suppose there's no hurry."

"My parents would like to be here. They mentioned some kind of donation to one of Philip's charities."

Blake's reflection in the window glass showed he, too, was concentrating on the rain. "That would be thoughtful." He gave my shoulder a brief touch like a comforting pat.

The phone jangled again. It was late for anyone to be calling.

I stopped stacking the dishes when I heard him say, "Annie, calm down."

He put his hand over the mouthpiece. "I've got to take this call, Jax. Thanks for the chili."

I stood in front of Hoolie and tapped the floor with my shoe. He woke and followed me to my apartment.

A few minutes later, there was a rap at my door.

Blake stood outside, a worried expression creasing his forehead.

"Annie found her grandson in the Glasgow jail. I told her I'd be there tomorrow morning to help."

"Thanks for letting me know."

"I'll leave my sealed bid with Bascome before I go, in case I don't get back by the five o'clock deadline."

Blake took a step toward me. "Thanks for dinner tonight."

Suddenly breathless, I stepped away.

Before I could close the door, he said, "I owe you a meal for the chili. Dinner tomorrow night?"

"No, you don't. It was nothing."

"Coward?"

"Yep. Smart coward. Conflict of interest."

"After we turn in our bids tomorrow, our business is over, for the time being. I'll pick you up at six."

He strode down the hall and turned at his apartment. "I'll leave word at the pub if this business with Bobby will make me late."

I locked my door and sank onto the couch. Hoolie jumped up and sat next to me. He licked my hand. Automatically, I scratched his chest.

Dinner with Blake? Simple as it sounded, nothing with Blake was simple. He would use it to throw me off balance. Yes, that was it. Just another move in his game plan to win the bidding.

I rubbed Hoolie's ears. "Okay, dog, no use making more out of Blake's offer than what it was. You agree, don't you?"

Deaf or not, I swear he bobbed his head before he curled into my side and fell asleep.

SCOTLAND IS SO FAR north that dawn comes late during the winter—it's dark at seven in the morning. I couldn't stay in bed. Today was a big day. I had to turn in Fairway's offer. I got up and took care of Hoolie's needs. Before I finished my first cup of coffee, my least favorite person knocked on the door.

Rosalind had a temper going on. "Let me in."

I wanted to block the entrance and send her on her way. Instead, being younger, and *much* more mature and polite, *and* curious, I stepped aside. Hoolie scurried to his crate and sat as far to the back as he could go.

"What did you tell that policeman about Raul and me?"

Ooooo, she was mad. I sat in the one chair and gestured to the couch. "Have a seat, Rosalind."

"That-that Constable Trask has been snooping around the hotel, asking questions."

"That's his job."

"You must've told him Raul was interested in me."

"Weren't you discreet? Oh, that's right. Discreet isn't in your vocabulary."

"How did you know we'd been together?" She remained standing, clenching and unclenching her hands. "Who told you?"

"Not everyone spreads rumors, Rosalind. No one told me any-thing. I smelled it. That night in the pub, he reeked of your perfume and you stank of sex."

Bright red spots stained her cheeks. Rosalind stuttered and stammered.

I'd had enough. I stood and walked to the door. "Get out. Go back to New York."

"After Mr. Atkins heard Raul was here, he sent me to make sure you didn't screw up this job."

"And look who did the screwing. Leave." I opened the door.

"We'll see what Mr. Atkins has to say." She glared at me. "I'm sure he'll be interested that you live down the hall from one of our competitors, had dinner with him last night, and left his apartment late."

"You can twist a story any way you want, *Rosie*. I trust Mr. Atkins to see the truth. Too bad he didn't review your credentials. You'd never have made it past the receptionist."

I shut the door in her face. My cell phone rang.

It was my boss wanting an update on Raul's death.

"The police say he died of anaphylactic shock. They won't know what he was allergic to until all the reports are back." It was best to tell my employer everything rather than have him find out from others. "Mr. Atkins, I knew Raul was allergic to onions. He may have eaten some by accident. He died in the study of the Coulter manor house."

A long pause. "What are the police saying?"

"That I'm a person of interest. Because I knew him."

"And this took place the day after you found Bea Kestle's body?"

"They were both dead before I saw them. You believe me, don't you?"

I heard a sigh.

"Of course. I don't think you had anything to do with either death, but this is an unexpected complication, and you're smack dab in the middle of it. Will Raul's death affect your ability to do your job?"

"It won't. I plan to file our bid on time today as planned."

"Who do you think is our toughest competition?"

"Blake Ramsey."

"Not the German or Mrs. Harris?"

"Helmut high-tailed it to Edinburgh after Raul died. I never considered he'd finish on top because he tries to low-ball his clients' offers. He'll probably have a courier deliver his bid, but I don't think his heart is in it anymore. Brenda Harris went back to London. She had breakfast with Raul that day and was one of the last people to see him alive. The police let her leave town. I'm betting his death took the luster off the deal for her."

"What makes this Ramsey guy such a threat?" Mr. Atkins asked.

"He lives three miles from the estate. He's convinced he knows what's best for the area, for the ecology. He's a rabid tree-hugger. And I think he holds the same beliefs as that actor who wants a free Scotland. Ramsey is against foreign investment in Scotland, too. His bid will be high."

"Go ahead and offer what you think is necessary. Remember, you don't have to beat everyone. You need to finish in the top two. We'll courier the plans to you if, I should say *when*, we make it to the show-and-tell phase."

We rang off. I wrote in the figure I believed would put my company's bid in first or second, said a prayer, and sealed the bid in a Fairway Golf Incorporated envelope I'd brought with me. I clipped on Hooligan's leash and went in search of the lawyer's office.

Gray clouds threatened to overpower the winter sun. I looked to Ben Nevis. Cloudy. More rain was on the way.

Mr. Bascombe's office abutted Maude's Pins 'n Needles. No one had changed the brass plaque next to the door. LeBeck and Bascombe, Solicitors. A separate sign beneath stated that Blake M. Ramsey, Solicitor, had his office in the same building. Inside, the receptionist bent over a cardboard box. She used strapping tape to seal it shut and jumped when I closed the door.

"I didn't mean to startle you."

"We're all on edge these days. The recent deaths have us looking over our shoulders." She extended her hand in greeting. "You must be Jax Hollister. Hello. I'm Jessica Brown, receptionist, secretary, and packing expert." She motioned to the boxes stacked along one wall.

"Nice to meet you." I waved the envelope. "I have the offer from Fairway Golf."

"Mr. Bascombe has been expecting you. I'll ring you in."

A half-minute later, the door on the left opened and Samuel Bascombe came forward to greet me. He was a good six inches shorter than my six feet, with a potbelly that strained the buttons of his old-fashioned vest. The lawyer looked more like an Irish elf than a professional man.

"Miss Hollister, a pleasure." He gestured toward the boxes. "Please excuse the cartons. I'm sure you've heard that my partner passed away recently. I can't bear to do more than box up his books."

"I'm sorry for your loss. I feel it, too. Philip was my godfather."

"Sorry I didn't make the connection right away. His death was so unexpected," he said. "I haven't had the heart to clean out his desk, but we are working on his files. Come inside, won't you? Bring Hooligan. Yes, I know the little devil. He earned his name as a rowdy puppy. He's grown up to be a right fine gentleman, he has. I'm so pleased he has picked an owner."

A cozy fire burned in the grate inside Bascombe's office. Law books lined two walls of the windowless room. Framed degrees and landscape paintings covered the remaining wall space. Very masculine and professional. Exactly what the locals would want from their solicitor.

Bascombe motioned me to take one of the client chairs across the desk from where he sat. Hooligan lay by my feet.

I handed the attorney the offer. "When will you announce the winners?"

"Elizabeth and I will open the bids tomorrow at nine. I'll call you with the results. I see you included your cell phone number on the back of the envelope?"

"Yes."

"If you are one of the two top bids, are you prepared for the next phase?"

"Yes. Because of the size of the presentation, Fairway Golf will send a courier with the sketches."

"We've set aside the church basement for the displays. After two days of public viewing, the town council will meet, take comments, and vote. Will Mr. Atkins attend?"

"I believe he has obligations elsewhere. I'm his authorized representative. Will Mr. Montoya's client be sending an offer?"

"I haven't received word. I'm afraid the death may have an unnerving effect on their desire to build in the neighborhood, but the bidding is open until five this afternoon. Mrs. Harris's company and the German firm sent notice to expect their offers by this afternoon's post. I see you didn't go scurrying off after Mr. Montoya's demise, Miss Hollister."

"I'm not easily frightened, Mr. Bascombe."

"One murder and two accidental deaths in the space of two weeks have shaken our quiet village."

"Two accidents?

"Mr. Montoya and Philip, of course."

No sense telling him I suspected the two deaths were murders until the police said so.

We did the polite chit-chat thing for a few more minutes until I was able to extract Hoolie and myself from the talkative lawyer's presence. Outside, the clouds had given way to a fog that shrouded the village. It was so thick a killer could be an arm's length away before I'd see him.

We met Maude and Winnie locking up for the noon hour. They were heading to the pub for lunch. I watched Hoolie and Winnie scamper to greet each other with the obligatory sniffing. Winnie yipped and smiled, Hooligan responded by bowing with a matching smile. Clearly, they had a bond.

I invited Maude to lunch and asked after Annie.

"She wasn't happy to spend the night in Glasgow," Maude said, "She insisted I come back to open my shop." She snorted in disgust. "That grandson of hers. Driving the car for his thieving hoodlum friends. Poor Annie."

I pushed open the door into the crowded pub. The smell of fresh coffee and fried foods was familiar. Neighbors gossiped over the day's events like small town coffee shops wherever I traveled. Raul's death was the main topic of interest for the somber crowd.

"Constable Trask called Blake last night," I told Maude. "Mr. Montoya died from anaphylactic shock."

Maude eyes widened in apparent shock. Maggie came from behind the bar with a cup of coffee for me, tea for Maude.

"Have you heard anything more about Raul's death?" I asked her.

"No, but I dinna think we would. We're not directly involved like those who were there." She called to Richard Hyde, who sat at the far end of the bar. "Richard, did the constable say he'd be letting you know the test results on Mr. Montoya?"

"Not me. I expect he'll be speaking to Elizabeth and Mrs. Gordon once he gets the analysis of Montoya's stomach contents."

Maude shifted in her chair. "If Rau-Mr. Montoya died from something in his food . . . well, it would have to be an accident, wouldn't it?"

Hmm. Three times Maude had stopped before using Raul's first name. "How well did you know him, Maude?"

"Oh, not well at all." She stared at her tea. "He was a handsome man and knew it. Not to speak ill of the dead, but he was so conceited. Maggie, you noticed. He was positive he knew what a woman wanted. I don't think anyone would kill a man for that. It must have been an accident."

How could Trask prove otherwise? "Philip's death, Bea's murder, and now Raul Montoya. Doesn't it feel like too much of a coincidence, Maggie?"

She cleared dishes from a nearby table. "Malicious mischief is the extent of our past crime wave in Heather Hill. If Mr. Montoya was killed . . ."

"I cannot believe he was murdered," Maude said.

Methinks she doth protest too much. Did she have some kind of personal relationship with Raul? If he had led her on, then dumped her, she'd have a motive. But how would she have the opportunity and the method? Before I could play sleuth and dig deeper, Richard brushed past, knocking my coat and purse from the back of my chair.

"I do apologize, Miss Hollister. I'll hang them on the rack behind you."

"Thanks. Give my regards to your Elizabeth for me."

He exited the pub, shaking hands with Ian who was on his way in.

"Ach, here's a sight to behold." Ian used his exaggerated highland brogue. "Three lovely lasses to brighten a gloomy day."

Maude gave Ian a wan smile. Maggie set a cup of tea in front of him. She imitated his over-the-top burr.

"Have ye been to Ireland today, Doctor? Kissed the Blarney Stone, did ye?"

In that moment, my Machiavellian brain cells found a solution to a problem. After I ordered my sandwich, I looked at my new friends. "Blake invited me to dinner tonight," I said. "I'm having second thoughts. It could give the wrong appearance. The Coulter Manor? If our offers are the top two, it might look as if we were in collusion. Let's make it a party. That way, no one would think twice. Maude? Maggie and Ian? Won't you join us?"

"Thanks for including me," Maude said, "but Annie will need some comfort when Blake brings her back from Glasgow."

"What say you, Maggie?" Ian's eyes held a devilish glint. "You're due for a night out. Shall we chaperone Blake and Jax?"

From his tone of voice, Ian believed Blake had made romantic dinner plans. He was so wrong. Blake's offer of a meal was repayment for my chili and nothing more.

CHAPTER EIGHTEEN

AFTER LUNCH, I was too restless to stay indoors and needed exercise to work off my luncheon calories. My knees felt almost healed and the joints barely twinged. Maude kept Hooligan while I took my rental bike for a reconnaissance trip around Heather Hill. The fog had lifted and with it my somber thoughts of death and dying. Fingers of clouds clutched the hills. The sun did its best to dry things and raise the chilly temperature. Despite the damp chill, there was no wind. It wasn't a half-bad day. New growth evergreens planted as part of Scotland's reforestation program sparkled with leftover moisture. Even in winter, Scotland was green. The cold weather had its upside— no dreaded "midges." It was rumored the miserable "no seeum" insects considered the summer busloads of tourists their meals on wheels.

The road forked at the town limits. I turned away from the A82, the main road to Fort William, and headed in the opposite direction on a side street. I pedaled along with no particular destination in mind. It felt good to get my pulse rate out of couch-potato range. Another hill beckoned—the same hill Coulter Manor sat atop. I pushed aside the recent images of Bea and Raul and concentrated on business.

The Fairway Golf site selection committee reported the properties on either side of the estate weren't for sale. The name of the owner on the far side hadn't been included in the reports. Mike Lemon mentioned that Mr. Atkins would be pleased if someone could get an option on it. I relished the challenge of an unwilling seller.

Before I tracked down the owner, I wanted to see the land for myself. I had to ride beyond Bea's place to get there. I couldn't bear to see the charred ruins of the shed. Head down, I pedaled hard to gain momentum for the uphill climb toward Coulter Manor.

A quarter mile beyond the manor's driveway, I rode past plowed fields waiting for their spring planting. A one-story farmhouse sat at the end of a gravel lane. Double gates denied entry. A keep-out sign warned off trespassers.

DO NOT DISTURB! NOT SELLING!

The signs were a silent challenge. They cemented my desire to meet the person who didn't want to sell. I'd ask Maude or Maggie the name of the owner. Since I was here, I decided to see as much of the property as possible from the vantage point of the Coulter estate. I changed direction and rode to the manor house.

Elizabeth was out hiking, Mrs. Carson said. The housekeeper didn't think Elizabeth would mind if I had another look around the grounds. I walked my bike along the fence line between the two properties. Beyond a thick, six-foot high privet hedge there were glimpses of tilled ground and a neat farmhouse in the middle of empty fields. When I reached the river, the adjacent acreage continued beyond the water until an outcropping of weathered rocks hid it from view.

I stared across the river at the spot where I'd seen Dickie Campbell three days before. What had he been doing there?

This day, not a breeze stirred the trees. Not a bird chirped. The afternoon sun was fast giving way to clouds and the early evening gloom. Damn, I'd run out of daylight and time to play detective. My reconnaissance of the farm would have to wait. I retraced my steps and bicycled out of the Coulter's driveway. I coasted down the hill, gained speed, and remembered how I'd gone ass-over-teakettle to land face first in Bea's yard. I applied the brakes. The bike didn't slow. I looked down to locate the problem and saw a pothole the size of Texas. My front wheel dipped and bounced. The handlebars wobbled loose in my hands.

Oh, shit! Not again.

I skidded one foot along the pavement in an attempt to slow my momentum. No such luck. I swung my other leg over the center bar to get off before I crashed. Difficult to do under the best of circumstances. Impossible while speeding downhill.

My left ankle collapsed.

I went down hard on my butt and immediately grabbed my foot.

The pain was so excruciating I couldn't manage more than pitiful gasps. I heard the bicycle crashing across the road.

It took five minutes for the agony to subside. Between gulps of air, I repeated every cuss word I'd ever learned.

The late afternoon sun hid behind a cloud and a deep grayness spread over the hills. I hoisted myself upright, unable to put weight on my foot. The bike lay across the pavement in two parts. The frame was twisted; the handlebars a few feet to one side.

I dug in my back pocket for my cell phone. When I snapped it open, the lid came apart in my hand. No light came on. I shook it. The rattle of parts inside confirmed my worst diagnosis. Angry at the whole world in general and my klutziness in particular, I flung the worthless phone at the useless bike.

I looked up the slope toward Coulter Manor. A half-mile uphill to a phone or the same distance downhill to the next intersection. The thought of hiking the steep incline on a bad ankle decided matters. I could flag a ride up ahead.

A light mist added to my misery. I looked at my still-working watch. Where had the time gone? At this rate, I wouldn't make it back to Heather Hill for dinner. Three limping steps later, the first raindrop plopped on my nose.

CHAPTER NINETEEN

A FEW MINUTES after six, Blake clattered down the stairs in time to catch Annie locking up the market for the night.

"That temporary girl did right good when I was in Glasgow," she said, holding out the bank deposit bag. "You should think of hiring her for the summer."

"Blast it, Annie, where is she?"

"The part-time help?"

"Jax. We were supposed to have dinner, but she's not answering her door."

"I haven't seen her since we returned from Glasgow."

Maude rapped on the glass. She had Winnie and Hooligan in tow. "Hello, Blake, Annie. I brought Hooligan back. I'll run him up to Jax."

"She isn't here," Blake said.

"That's strange. She usually parks her bicycle over there." Maude pointed to the corner. "She said she'd be gone for an hour or two, at the most."

Annie looked worried. "She's out riding? In this rain?"

"Something must be wrong," Maude said.

Ian drove up to the door, Maggie in the passenger seat.

Blake flung open the outside door. "We'll go look for her."

Maude kept Hooligan from following. "I'll keep Hooligan until you find her. Call us when you do."

"Right." Blake dashed for Ian's car and climbed inside.

"Ready to buy us dinner?" Ian's laughter stopped when he saw Blake's expression.

"Jax is missing." Blake reined in his rising panic. "She didn't come back from a bike ride this afternoon. Any idea where she could be?"

"She must be lost," Maggie said. "I don't think she'd ride all the way to Fort William. Turn left here."

Blake wavered between worry and anger. "That woman doesn't have an ounce of sense."

Maggie and Ian looked at each other.

"What? You think this is funny?" Blake realized he was taking his anxiety out on his friends. "Doesn't Jax realize the police haven't caught the killer? She could be lying in a ditch, unconscious. Or worse."

That concept brought him up cold. Jax injured or worse? When had she managed to get under his skin? From competitor to . . ?

Ian sped through the rain and scanned the side streets and driveways. Maggie and Blake did the same on the other side. The windshield wipers beat a furious rhythm, struggling to keep up with the downpour.

"There she is." Ian aimed the car straight ahead. The headlights picked out a limping figure in driving rain.

"Damn blasted woman." Before the car came to a stop, Blake threw open the door and ran to Jax's side.

"Bloody Hell, woman. What are you doing walking in the rain?"

The headlights captured Jax's smile of greeting when it froze. Her expression of gratitude morphed into one of steely-eyed anger.

"What the hell do you think I'm doing? I'm getting *wet*, you idiot." She limped toward the car. "Typical man. Someone gets hurt and your first reaction is to rant and rave."

"You're limping."

Jax stopped in her tracks and shot him a look of incredulity. "What a genius! Of course I am. I twisted my ankle and it hurts!" She turned toward the car and yelped with pain.

Ian helped her into the backseat. "Get in, Blake. Let's get the lass home before she catches a chill."

Jax protested. "The bike—"

"We'll come for it tomorrow," Maggie said. "You're soaking wet. You need to get warm. Blake, call Annie and Maude and tell them we found Jax."

I COULDN'T CONTROL my chattering teeth. I handed Maggie the keys. She ran ahead to unlock my door while Blake carried me up the stairs. I'm not a light load, but he made me feel petite and vulnerable. I held myself away from his chest, resisting the impulse to snuggle and capture his body heat. Blake set me on the sofa. Maggie started water running in the bathtub. Ian pulled up a chair and sat in front of me. He gently peeled off my boot. The relief from the throbbing pain was instantaneous and brief.

He tsked.

I fought to keep from whimpering. "Why do doctors tsk that way?"

Ian winked. "I suppose so we don't shout, 'Bloody Hell, woman what did you do?'"

Blake appeared embarrassed. He found the teakettle and turned on the water.

Ian poked, prodded and pronounced a sprained ankle. "Not broken. You won't be riding a bicycle for a time."

"Not ever again," I said.

"You know the cure, Jax. Rest, ice, elevate. Here are some anti-inflammatory pills. They'll help with the swelling and pain. Add a compression bandage before bed. Not too much walking for a few days."

Maggie reentered the main room, followed by a fragrant cloud of steam. She scolded Ian and Blake. "Where are your senses? Can't you see she's shivering? She needs to get into a hot tub." She shooed the men out the door.

Before it closed I said, "I want my dog."

"Blake, go get Hooligan," Maggie ordered. "Ian, call your service and tell them you're back in town, then leave us alone. Come, Jax, let's get you out of those wet clothes."

Maggie helped lower my icy body into the bubble-filled water. Delicious warmth seeped through layers of skin. She brought me a cup of tea to remove the last of the chill from the inside.

"You'd make a fantastic drill sergeant the way you took command of Blake and Ian. Better yet, a nurse or doctor. What about taking classes?"

"I thought about it when Ian went off to medical school. Then Pops had a stroke, and Mum quit the pub. They retired to the family farm. I took over running the pub, 'twas expected of me, you see. There's always been a woman publican in our family." Her voice sang with pride.

"Would you give it up? After you marry Ian?"

"Marry? Ian and me? I think not. He doesn't look at me in that way."

"In that dress?" I drew an hourglass shape in the air. "He would have noticed you tonight, if he hadn't had to fix my ankle."

Maggie suffered from the redhead curse. Her cheeks flamed crimson. "I bought it special for him."

"The neckline frames your pearl necklace. I don't think I've ever seen one that color of pink. Fresh water, isn't it?"

"From the River Tay. Yes, Scotland has pearls. My great-grandfather gave it to his wife. 'Tis passed from mother to daughter. I treasure it, but don't often dress fancy enough to wear it."

"Let's reschedule dinner for tomorrow night. You wouldn't want that dress to go to waste."

"You're a horrible matchmaker, Jax Hollister. After all this time, I think Ian is a lost cause." She tested the cooling water. "Time's up. You're starting to wizen like a prune."

She helped me out of the tub, gave me a towel to dry off, and handed me my pajamas. "Oh, my. You'll be havin' a nasty bruise back there."

The full-length mirror reflected a red area on my left bum in the shape of my cell phone.

"It'll turn all the shades of the rainbow. It should match my knees and ankle. It's a blessing it's in an area no one can see. I wish I weren't so clumsy. The harder I try, the worse I get. I blame my brother the tennis player. He got all the athletic genes. I got the accident-prone ones."

I balanced on Maggie's shoulder and struggled into my long johns. "Thanks for the help. I'm sorry I messed up the plans for tonight. That dress is a knockout."

There was a rap at the front door. I pulled an afghan from the back of the couch and wrapped it around my shoulders. Maggie let Blake in. Hooligan launched himself into my arms. I tumbled onto the sofa, hugged the wriggling, licking bundle of fur to my chest, and buried my face in his neck to hide my tears from Blake. The stress-filled week, Philip and Bea's murder, Raul's death, and two falls caught up with me. Through my sobs, I heard the door close.

When I was done with my crying jag, I found a tissue, sniffled, and blotted my eyes. Maggie was gone. Blake stood over the stove, stirring something in a pot.

I love a man who cooks.

Oops. I will *not* go down that road again.

"Is that tomato soup I smell?" I said.

"And a grilled cheese sandwich." Blake turned from the stove and waved a spoon in the air. "Not exactly the dinner I had planned. If you feel up to it, we'll go to Fort William tomorrow night. Wait, I'll be right back."

He returned with an extra chair, an opened bottle of red wine and two glasses. Blake helped me to the table, propped my foot on the second chair and wrapped an ice pack around my ankle.

He poured the wine.

"I didn't know red wine went with grilled cheese."

"It goes with spaghetti, which is made with tomatoes." He indicated the soup. "Therefore, it is the perfect choice."

"Lawyer logic? Or are you, God forbid, teasing me?"

"Teasing? Me? I never tease. Ask Ian. Eat. You've had a long day."

A seldom-seen smile softened his command. I picked up half a sandwich.

"Not to bring up a touchy subject," he said, "but how did you manage to wreck your bicycle?"

"I hit a pot-hole, then the handlebars wobbled. They came off in my hands."

His eyebrow rose in an unspoken question.

I ignored the steaming soup. "Handlebars aren't supposed to do that, are they?"

"I'll take a look when I pick it up in the morning."

While we ate, Blake reverted to his usual silent mode. Just as well. I was so tired I could barely hold my head up, much less my end of a conversation. The rain had lessened to an occasional tap dance on the glass door of the balcony. Soothing.

Blake cleared the table. "You look done in. I'll unfold the sofa."

Never had a bed, iron support bar and all, looked so welcome, but Hooligan stood at the door, wanting to go out. Blake noticed.

"I'll take him. You shouldn't do the stairs tonight."

I folded the afghan into a thick pad to keep my ankle elevated and crawled beneath the covers.

The door reopened. Hooligan jumped on the bed.

"I wiped his paws downstairs," Blake said.

"Thanks." I balanced on the edge of sleep and tucked Hoolie against my side.

"Lucky dog."

CHAPTER TWENTY

IT TOOK A LOT of moaning and groaning to get out of bed the next morning. My butt was sore, muscles ached in places I never knew I had muscles, and my ankle and foot were so swollen the only shoe that fit was an unlaced sneaker. What a fashion statement.

Blake appeared at my door, took Hoolie out, and brought him back to me. I thanked him.

"It's what a neighbor would do." He had reverted to his stuffy Brit routine.

I couldn't handle an entire night of that. I was ready to call off our dinner when he came back with a newspaper and a replacement cell phone. Hoity-toity one minute, considerate the next.

Blake put the paper on the kitchen counter and handed me the phone. "I activated it for you and called in the new number to Bascombe's office."

"Thank you." I'd forgotten the lawyer was supposed to call with the results of the bidding. I offered my limited hospitality. "Would you like to wait here for the call? I could make some instant coffee?"

Already at the door, he said, "No, I have paperwork to do."

"So do—"

He left before I completed my sentence.

Nine o'clock came and went. I couldn't concentrate on the newspaper. The minutes dragged toward nine-thirty when my new phone beeped.

"Samuel Bascombe, here, Ms. Hollister. I'm pleased to report your offer was one of the two highest bids. I'll send a registered letter of confirmation to your home office."

"Thank you, Mr. Bascombe. May I ask who the other finalist is?"

"Scottish Lands for Scots. I look forward to seeing the two displays."

The proverbial lead weight hit the bottom of my stomach. Blake and I remained competitors. After Bascombe disconnected, I jumped to my feet—foot—and did a limping version of a happy dance. Hoolie raced around the apartment barking up a storm, and came to a stop in front of me. Anyone would think he was panting; I knew he was grinning. I grinned back.

A knock at the door sent me maneuvering around the energized fur-ball. I expected Blake had come to share his news.

Constable Trask, attitude and all, waited on the other side of the door.

Hooligan slipped around the cop and ran to Blake's apartment. He scratched and barked until Blake opened the door.

"Hooligan, what the hell . . ."

Hoolie raced back to my side. Blake followed.

"Charlie?"

"Morning, Blake. I'm here to speak to Ms. Hollister. No need for you to stay."

"He can hear anything you have to say, Constable." I motioned them inside. "Did you find out what caused Mr. Montoya's death?"

"There was onion seasoning in the haggis he ate for breakfast. He was allergic to onions. I think you already knew that."

I had a premonition where Trask was going with this. I didn't offer him a seat.

Blake made me sit on the sofa and put my foot up. "Why are you here, Charlie?"

Trask pulled his notepad out of his pocket and flicked it open. "I have new information that you had a hostile relationship with the victim. Isn't that correct?"

I stalled for time to think. "I'm not sure what you mean."

Trask wet his finger and turned another page. "You were seen arguing with Mr. Montoya on the road outside Coulter Manor."

I couldn't deny it, so I kept quiet.

"Most curious of all," Trask said, "we found a button in Montoya's jacket pocket. It matches a coat you were seen wearing, Ms. Hollister. That one." He pointed to where it hung on a wall peg.

The way the constable stressed the 'Ms.' when he said my name grated on my nerves.

Trask snapped the pad shut. "All totaled, it goes to motive. I'm here to take your passport."

I stood and moved a foot closer to Trask than necessary. Two could play the intimidation game. He could threaten all he wanted, but I wasn't going to act guilty. I had done nothing wrong.

"I didn't put onions in his haggis, Constable. How could I?" I crossed my arms over my chest. "Do I need an alibi? Are you charging me with Mr. Montoya's murder?"

I didn't yell or shout. I kept my tone polite. Icy polite. Blake stifled a chuckle when Trask took half a step back from me.

"I have it on good authority you hated Raul Montoya," the constable said. "You fought. Motive, Ms. Hollister. Your passport, please."

If Trask had been more certain of the evidence, would he have said 'please'?

"I'm here on business, *Constable*, and it's not finished. I am not going anywhere. I am not a flight risk. Blake?" I turned to him for support.

"Might as well turn it over, Jax," he said. "When Charlie solves the case, he'll give it back."

"How can he do that when he's wasting time and energy looking for ways to connect me to Raul's death? In the meantime, the real killer is out there." I limped closer to Trask, getting in his space again. "You haven't caught Bea Kestle's murderer either, have you. Any leads in *that* killing, *Constable?*"

Trask glared at me and held out his hand. "Your passport. Now."

I hobbled to the closet, found the document, and slapped it in his hand.

Without another word, Trask stomped out of the apartment.

My anger vanished. "I'm in trouble, aren't I?"

"It doesn't look good." Blake put his arm around my shoulder and gave me a quick sympathy hug. "Trask's superiors must be pushing him for results. He needs a suspect for at least one of the murders. It didn't help your case when he found your button on Montoya's body."

"Raul and I had a fight on the road the day before he died. A car drove by at the same time he ripped my coat." I sank into the couch. Hooligan jumped into my lap. "Why did he have to keep a lousy button?"

"One good thing, Charlie didn't connect you to Bea's murder. That case has the locals upset. Montoya's death has international implications. There's bound to be pressure from above to solve that one. He had to do something."

"The fact that Raul and I argued doesn't mean I killed him." I propped my foot on the chair Blake provided. "The constable may think I had a motive, but opportunity? I was here that morning. I knew Raul was allergic to onions. But how could I put onions in the haggis, or know that Elizabeth Coulter's cook would serve it for breakfast? Hell, I've never tasted the vile stuff."

"Never?"

"It's cooked in a sheep's stomach. Yech."

"Don't turn your nose up at something you haven't tried," Blake said. "Walter MacTavish is proud of his haggis. It's the best in the area. His shop is always busy, and he delivers to most local restaurants."

"Does Maggie buy from him?"

"She serves a brunch on Saturdays and sometimes has it on the menu for lunch. I wager Sean keeps it in stock."

"I can't sit here doing nothing. It's up to me to find some evidence that will steer Trask's investigation in a direction away from me. I better taste the murder weapon. Let's go see if Maggie has some haggis."

"CONGRATULATIONS, Jax, Blake." Maggie greeted us from behind the bar. It was early, and we were her first customers. "The whole town is talking. I canna wait to see your plans for the manor."

I'd been so preoccupied with Trask's accusation I'd forgotten Mr. Bascombe's good news. When I got back to my apartment, I'd report my success to headquarters, but I'd have to tell Mr. Atkins that I'd been forced to give up my passport.

"Charlie Trask stopped by this morning." Blake pulled out two chairs, one for me and one for my sprained ankle. "The toxicology report came back. Montoya's allergic reaction came from onions, as we suspected. After talking to Elizabeth's cook, Charlie said it had to be in the haggis. Jax has never tasted our national dish. Does Sean have any left?"

"I'll see. Anything else, Jax?"

"No, I don't usually eat breakfast."

I regretted the words as soon as they left my lips. I'd told Blake to deduct breakfast off my rent. He didn't say a word, but his wooly caterpillar eyebrows inched toward his hairline.

Maggie returned with a plate. I stared at the grayish square. I knew haggis originated during hard times when no food was wasted. A mixture of kidneys, lungs and various other innards of sheep, mixed with oats, was a thrifty way to use the entire animal. The crofters boiled the mixture in a bag made from the sheep's stomach.

Double Yech.

It didn't smell bad. In fact, it had a delicate, undefinable aroma.

"It's not cooked in the old way," Maggie said. "Today, our butchers use artificial casings, like sausages."

The haggis appeared to have been sautéed. I stabbed it with my fork. A piece broke off the slab. I put it in my mouth. The flavor of butter hit my tongue first, then dissolved and allowed the haggis to saturate my taste buds.

Not bad.

I chewed, swallowed, and took another bite. "It's good," I said with my mouth full.

Someone huffed. "Of course it's good. I know how to cook Walter's haggis."

I looked up to find Maggie's brother, Sean, hovering nearby.

Was this a test?

I crumbled the slab, shredding it. "I don't see any onions." If I hadn't known what killed Montoya, and I hadn't known he was allergic, I wouldn't have been able to guess what killed him.

I took another bite. "Are onions traditionally used in haggis?"

"It depends on which school of haggis the butcher belongs to," Sean said. "Some think onions are traditional, some think not. Walter's claim to fame is his secret blend of spices. I already guessed he'd used a wee bit of sage. Now I can add onion flavoring to the list."

When Raul and I dined out, he always quizzed the chef. Walter the butcher's recipe was a secret. Elizabeth's cook couldn't have told Raul about the onion seasoning.

Blake pointed to the dish. "If you didn't suspect onions, would you be able to taste it?"

"You mean if Raul hadn't expected it, would he have known he was eating onions? I don't know."

Ian wandered in and made his way to our table. "How's the ankle, Jax?"

I lifted my foot off the chair. "Still where it belongs. Can you taste the onion in this haggis?"

Sean handed him a fork. Ian took a bite. "I can't, but I'm no gourmet."

"I suppose Raul's death could've been an accident," I said. "Someone should explain that to Constable Trask. He thinks Montoya was murdered, and I'm his main suspect."

"Oh, Jax, no," Maggie said. "Why would he think that?"

I calculated the speed of gossip in a village this size and concluded that with Rosalind in town, trying to keep any secret was useless.

"Raul Montoya and I had, um, a history. We argued the day before he died. There was a witness. Trask thinks I had a motive. He took my passport this morning."

"I don't understand," Maggie said. "How could you know that Mrs. Gordon would serve haggis?"

Ian reached for another bite. "Or that it had onions in it."

"Trask can't link me to the method and opportunity. That's not to say he'll stop trying." I'd lost what little appetite I'd had and pushed the plate over to Ian.

Richard Hyde entered the pub.

"Congratulations, Blake. You, too, Jax. The offering amounts were higher than Elizabeth expected. Money can't buy happiness, I'm told, but it will make parting with her home a bit easier. When can we expect to see your designs?"

"SLFS will send our chief designer day after next," Blake said.

I checked the time. "I have to notify my office when it opens. Fairway's courier should arrive in two days. Because of the time difference, it may be late in the day."

Ian swallowed the last of the haggis. "After the viewing, the villagers will give the town council their input. You'll hear comments from all of us, I'm sure."

"SLFS could have the home field advantage. I hope Blake living here won't influence their decision."

"I think they can be fair," Maggie said.

Richard took his sack of take-out food from Sean. "To be honest, Jax, much depends on the plans. Elizabeth wants to follow her father's example and do what is best for the area. Remember, she has the tie-breaking vote."

The second phase of the sale process was irregular but legal. The town council having the vote usually happened in the zoning phase.

Hadn't Richard been one of the last people to see Raul alive? In light of Trask's accusations, I wanted his take on the situation. "Mr. Montoya's death won't delay the sale, will it?"

I would've missed the brief flicker of reaction if I hadn't been looking for it. I didn't understand what it meant, but I would give it more thought.

"No. Elizabeth is anxious to move ahead as quickly as possible," he said. "She's already looking at paint samples for the new house."

There was something in his voice, a note of displeasure? Was the engaged couple arguing about paint or were they having financial troubles?

Ian interrupted my thinking. "To change the subject to something more pleasant, are we going to reschedule our double date, Jax? I'm not on call tonight. Do you think your ankle will be up to it?"

"If you don't make me walk to Fort William. You should ask Blake. He's the one picking up the bill."

Ian tried to keep a straight face, but his eyes twinkled. I'd backed Blake into a corner, one he couldn't get out of without appearing to be cheap. Ian waylaid Maggie's brother before he went back to the kitchen. "Sean, can you cover for Maggie again tonight? Give her another night out? You know last night's dinner never came to pass."

Sean's harsh manner softened when he looked at his sister. He agreed to our plan. I had the impression he believed his sister and Ian made a nice couple, too.

"Since I'll be buying dinner," Blake gave a fake sigh of resignation, "Ian can drive and pay for the petrol. Pick us up at half-past six."

CHAPTER TWENTY-ONE

SPENT THE afternoon catching up on emails to my family and headquarters. The announcement that Fairway Golf and SLFS had been
the top two bids was purposely placed before I notified my boss that
the police were holding my passport. I explained it was all a misunderstanding and hoped my employer would take my word for it. Because
of the time difference, I had to wait for a reply.

Evening arrived and I spent an inordinate amount of time getting
ready for a simple, courtesy payback dinner that was not a date.

Blake arrived at my door at six-thirty on the dot. His white turtleneck
sweater set off his dark hair. Navy slacks and trench coat completed his
dinner attire. My attempts to dress fancy with my limited travel wardrobe evidently didn't pass muster. He gave me a cursory once over and
focused on my tennis shoes. I limped to remind him I couldn't get
my foot in anything else. I'd hoped for an obligatory you-look-nice
compliment. Instead, he scowled and handed me a fancy carved walking
stick.

"Some tourist left it in the market last summer. For balance. Are
you ready?"

I put Hoolie in his crate and fed him a dog snack to let him know I was coming back.

Ian and Maggie were waiting in the car. On the short ride to Fort William, we three had to carry the conversation. Blake was at his taciturn worst. I'd given up trying to figure out the reason for his moods.

His choice of restaurants met with our approval. White lights surrounded the windows of Pietro's Italian Restaurante. The mouthwatering aroma of tomato sauce, Italian spices, and garlic greeted us when we entered. The red-checked tablecloths, red cloth napkins, and dripping candles in straw-covered Chianti bottles were a cliché, but the décor was similar to my favorite Italian restaurant in New York.

Ian's smile broadened when he helped Maggie take off her coat. If she intended to make him notice her as a woman, not a childhood friend, she succeeded. He stared at her green wool dress where it clung to her petite curves. The color went well with her auburn hair. Maggie's pink pearl necklace nestled a half-inch below her collarbone. She had the same pink glow when she looked at Ian.

If I hadn't invited them to come along tonight, Ian might never have seen Maggie out of her normal surroundings. Her usual bartender attire was utilitarian, not sexy at all. Smugness isn't a nice attribute, but damn, I *was* a good matchmaker.

The food was as tasty as any I had eaten in Italy, and I told the chef/owner when he visited our table. He accepted our compliments and suggested a dessert special. Then sadness replaced his smile.

"Mr. Blake, I am sad. I know Mr. LeBeck, he was your friend. When he did not keep the reservation the week past, I worried. So did his lady friend."

Blake and Ian stared at each other. "A lady friend?" Blake said.

"Yes. When he called, he told me he would have a guest. When he didn't arrive . . . if I telephone the *policia* . . .?"

Ian set his glass aside. "The police said his death was instantaneous. Nothing you could do, Pietro. Tell us more about the lady."

"She wait for him, but after one hour go past, she write him a note and she leave."

"Was she young? Old? Did you recognize her?" Blake said.

"She was of the age with Mr. LeBeck, I think, but she no been in here before."

"Did you keep the note?"

Pietro hung his head. "No, Mr. Blake. I already told police. When I heard he died, I was upset. I throw the paper away. Was it important?"

"It could be." Blake pulled out a business card. "If the lady comes in again, will you have her call?"

"Yes, of course."

I didn't understand the puzzled expressions on everyone's faces. "Why do you act so surprised?"

"Philip had a lunch date with a woman on his birthday," Blake said.

"Yes, so?"

"Philip was gay."

"He told me. It doesn't mean anything," I said. "Why schedule it for his birthday? It must have been an important business appointment."

Blake refilled our glasses. "What was so important he would schedule it for that day? And who was the lady?"

"Hmmm. He didn't keep the meeting because he was already dead." I turned to Blake. "Maybe his appointment book had the name of the woman he was meeting?"

"I'll have Sam Bascombe look into it."

Ian scraped up the last of his spumoni ice cream. "Jax, you're holding on to the idea Philip was murdered?"

"Maude mentioned you gave Uncle Philip a clean bill of health a month before he died. He was an experienced climber. We know Bea was murdered. Let's assume Montoya was, too. What connects the three deaths?"

"I don't see any connection," Maggie said. "Bea and Montoya never met, to my knowledge. Or Philip and Montoya. What possible motive could there be?"

I folded my napkin and placed it on the table. "Coulter Manor is a connection. Montoya was bidding on it, Bea's place is next door, and Uncle Philip was the executor for the estate."

Blake snorted. "Bea was killed because her property adjoins the Coulter estate? Ridiculous."

"'Tis a bit of a stretch," Maggie said.

"Why? Property equals money. People kill for less. You knew Bea better than I did. Can you think why someone would kill her?"

We tossed around ideas on the return trip to Heather Hill. Bea had no enemies, according to the others. I remained convinced the manor house was the common thread. An idea niggled at a corner of my brain. It had something to do with Raul's death, but I couldn't bring it forward.

Ian pulled his car in front of Blake's building and let us out. "I'll drive Maggie home," he said.

"You don't have to, Ian," Maggie protested. "I can walk. The pub isn't far."

"You shouldn't be walking by yourself with a murderer on the loose." He set the brake. "I'll see you to your door." He draped a protective arm over her shoulder.

I slid a glance at Blake. If he *was* in love with Maggie like Elizabeth said he was, would he be jealous of Ian's romantic interest? It could explain his sour mood.

I hobbled up the stairs at top speed.

Blake said, "In a hurry? Trying to avoid a good-night kiss?"

"I'm not trying to avoid anything. The swelling in my ankle has spread to my foot. I need to get out of these shoes. And this was not a date." I used the walking stick for support and struggled to kick off my tennis shoe.

Blake extended his hand for my key and inserted it. "Didn't you lock up before leaving?"

"I always lock my doors."

"You didn't this time." He held up a hand. "Wait." He eased the door open.

"Gas," he said, and pushed me toward the stairs. "Get out!"

"Hooligan." I tried to move past him.

Blake blocked the doorway. "I'll get your dog, you get Ian. Have him ring the fire department."

I picked up my shoe, raced downstairs and outside as fast as my bare foot and ankle would allow. Ian and Maggie hadn't reached the pub. They spun around when I screamed Ian's name. "Gas," I shouted, motioning them to hurry. "Blake says to call—"

"On it." Ian punched in numbers on his cell phone and rushed back, Maggie right behind.

Blake hurried outside, cradling my limp corgi in his arms.

"Hoolie." I died inside until the little guy gave my hand a lick.

"He needs air," Ian said. "Set him down, let him get his bearings."

I sank to my knees, ready to catch Hoolie if he lost his balance. His short legs quivered. He sank back on his haunches, head bowed, wheezing for breath. A dry, hacking cough wracked his body.

"Ian, isn't there something we can do?"

"His instinct tells him what's best. See, he's trying to stand again, but I can call MacDonald if you like."

I sat on the ground, heedless of the wet pavement. Hooligan quit coughing and wobbled into my lap. "I think he's better." I hugged him close, relief making me weak.

"Blake, what happened?" Ian asked.

"I smelled gas when I opened Jax's door. The stove's pilot light was out. The burners were on."

I put Hoolie over my shoulder as I would a baby, ready for burping. He breathed easier in that position.

"An accident?" Ian directed his question to Blake.

Before he could answer, I said, "It was no accident. I didn't turn off the pilot. I did not leave a burner on. And I always lock my door.

Someone tried to kill Hooligan while he was in his crate. Who would do such a thing?"

"You could've been killed, too," Blake said. "Any explosion would have been catastrophic."

Maggie gasped. "Both of you could have been killed."

I'd never feared for my safety before. My stomach clenched with dread. "Remember the warning notes, Blake. The gas was meant for me. Someone was trying to kill me. You would've been in the wrong place at the wrong time."

The local fire department arrived, suspending further speculation. Blake explained how he'd turned off the gas. He asked the fireman to relight the pilot in my apartment and make certain his was clear of fumes. He handed over our keys.

"Anyone hurt?" A fire fighter squatted by my side.

"My dog, but he seems better."

"He probably survived because his crate was on the floor." The fireman stood. "Good thing you didn't turn on the lights. A spark in ten or fifteen percent gas-to-oxygen, and you can have an explosion. There was no sign of forced entry. I take it none of you thinks this was an accident?"

"Absolutely not," I said.

Who hated me enough to kill me? Why?

One of the oyster lads doubled as a firefighter. He returned with his report. "Five minutes longer and I don't think the dog would have made it. Blake, your apartment is clear. No gas there." He took off his helmet. "Did you see anyone near the building?"

"No," Blake said.

The fireman gave me a hand up. "It will take a few hours to clear the remaining fumes. You both should stay somewhere else tonight. As a precaution."

Blake took Hoolie from me for a moment, so I could put on my shoe. The wet pavement had soaked through the seat of my slacks.

Maggie tugged on Ian's sleeve. "I have an extra bed for Jax. Sean is down the hall. She'll be safe with us."

The fire crew climbed aboard their vehicle and left. I tried to sling my purse over my shoulder. It fell from my shaking fingers and up-ended on the grass.

Ian knelt to pick up my scattered belongings. "What are you allergic to, Jax?" He held an EpiPen.

"That's not mine."

But I knew someone who'd always carried one.

CHAPTER TWENTY-TWO

MAGGIE AND HER brother lived above the pub. She tossed my damp clothes in a dryer after Sean loaned me some sweatpants and a shirt. He'd closed the bar early and sent the few stragglers home. I expected to fall asleep as soon as my head hit the pillow, but I couldn't shut my brain off. I went downstairs for a glass of milk. Loud voices met me halfway down the steps. I peeked into the pub's main room.

"Ian, that damn thing may be evidence. Jax has to turn it in."

Blake and the others were in front of the fireplace. Blake stood next to a table that held the EpiPen. Sean and Maggie's expressions changed from concern to neutral when they saw me enter. Blake noticed their shift of attention. He remained standing with arms crossed across his chest.

"I'm glad you're here, Jax," Ian said. "Tell us what you make of this thing."

I took an empty chair. "You're the town doctor. You treat most of the people in Heather Hill. Have you prescribed an EpiPen for any of your patients?"

"No."

"I knew Raul was severely allergic," I said. "He always carried one. If the police didn't find it on his body," I pointed, "that one might be his."

Blake sat next to Ian. "How did it get in your purse?"

"I didn't see anyone put it there. It seems obvious someone wants to frame me, make it look like I killed Raul. Whoever planted the EpiPen had to take it from him. The question is was Raul alive, or dead when it was removed?"

During the silence that followed my assumption, Hoolie jumped in my lap. I settled him and turned to Ian, Sean and Maggie. "I hope you all believe me."

Blake leaned against the mantle. "They barely know you, Jax."

His refusal to jump to my defense stung. Resignation was the only emotion I hadn't used that day. It took a moment to dredge up my resolve. When I felt I could talk without falling apart, I said, "I'm sure you've heard Raul and I had a past. We didn't part friends, but I didn't dislike him enough to kill him."

I searched their faces to see if I'd convinced anyone. "The police won't find my fingerprints on that EpiPen."

"Mine are," Ian said. "Blake, did you touch it when you held the bag open."

"No. If Jax didn't touch it, the police should find your fingerprints and the person who put it in her purse."

"The other night at the pub," I said, "Dickie Campell looked guilty of something. Why else would he run away from me? He did the same thing at the manor house? He must be involved somehow."

Ian frowned. "Where did you see Dickie?"

"Across the river behind the Coulter's gazebo."

"When was that?" Sean asked.

"A few minutes before noon the day Bea was killed. I reported it to the police, and I mentioned it to Blake the other night when Dickie wouldn't come into the pub."

"He couldn't have been at the manor." Certainty flared in Sean's green eyes. "He patrols the oyster beds during the day, a good mile from the house. He takes his lunch with the other lads. Dickie couldna be in two places at the same time."

I tried to placate Maggie's brother. "I might have seen someone who resembled him. Does Dickie ever wear a brown cap?"

"Aye, but I canna believe he'd leave his post."

Maggie patted Sean's arm. "He did the odd job now and then for Bea and Elizabeth, remember?"

"The policeman didn't believe me. I doubt they investigated his whereabouts. They need to ask him if he was anywhere near the estate the morning Raul died."

"Do you think Dickie put the EpiPen in your purse?" Ian said.

"I don't see how. He never came near me."

"We're back at the beginning." Ian drained his beer. "Who put the EpiPen in Jax's purse?"

"Could it be the same person who turned off the gas and tried to kill me?"

They sat there trying to make sense of the facts the way I presented them. No doubt, it sounded like I was trying to blame someone else. Hell, I was. I wasn't guilty.

"You have to turn the pen over to the police," Blake said.

"I know that." I reached for it in vain. Blake put it in his pocket.

"It's evidence in a possible murder. I'll keep it until you meet with the police."

"I can imagine the expression on Trask's face. He'll slap me in jail and throw away the key."

Maggie stood and picked up the glasses with practiced ease. "I don't think Jax killed Mr. Montoya. I *do* believe someone wants her to look guilty. If we think of a reason, we may find the murderer, but I'm tired and canna think straight. We need our sleep. A trip to the police station can wait for morning." She led the way to the staircase. "Blake, will you take Jax to Fort William tomorrow?"

"I can't. We're competing for the Coulter property. It wouldn't look proper."

It had been a trying day. My temper snapped. "For *who?*" I stalked to where he stood by the door. "Things can't look much worse for me. It's you who's afraid for your precious reputation."

Ian stepped between us. "I'll drive you."

"What if Trask throws me in jail? Can you convince Blake it won't sully his pristine standing in the community if he recommends a lawyer for me?"

Blake maintained his stone-face. "I'll take you to Fort William."

"Don't do me any favors, Mr. Ramsey. However, I would be oh so *eternally* grateful if you would make one itty-bitty phone call to a lawyer. Then you can stay in Heather Hill. God forbid you should be seen with a suspected killer." I limped up the stairs, certain I left a trail of steam behind.

Minutes later, all my bluster vanished with the realization that I might have different accommodations tomorrow night. I shuddered at the idea of going to jail. I hadn't done anything wrong, but that wasn't what people would remember. No matter if I was proven innocent immediately, the fact that I had been arrested was all people would remember. My career would be over. My reputation, destroyed. Mr. Atkins would fire me. I'd lose everything I'd worked for. It was the look of disappointment in my parents' eyes that was the hardest thing to consider.

I went to the dormer window and looked down on the deserted street. Someone out there was trying to frame me for murder. The same person who rigged the gas? What was the motive? Who would benefit from my death? Was it related to Uncle Philip's death? Bea's? Raul's? I closed the curtains and scurried back to the bed with icy fingers and feet. I'd never felt so alone.

If I went to jail, I'd have to give up Hooligan. Maybe for good. I'd fallen in love with the corgi. For the first time, because of him, I could understand the maternal instinct. I'd do anything to protect him. He had become my child.

Maggie entered the room with an extra blanket.

"Trying to kill me is one thing, but making Hoolie a victim is low." I crawled beneath the covers. "If I ever find out who did it, I'll make mincemeat of them."

"He can sleep on the bed, if you wish."

"Thanks." I patted the covers. Hoolie joined me, gave my cheek a dry kiss, lay with his head in my lap, closed his eyes, and snored. I stroked his head, the action soothing away the last of my stress. An uncertain future threatened a sleepless night, what was left of it.

I plumped the pillows against the headboard, leaned back, and watched Maggie hang her dress in the closet. "Be honest, Maggie, do you think I could have had something to do with Raul's death?"

"My female intuition is all I have to go on, Jax, and it says you're a nice person. Ian and Blake may not say so, but they don't believe you could have killed him, either."

"I wish Blake had been more encouraging. It was nice of Ian to offer to drive me."

Maggie glowed at the mention of Ian's name.

Her happiness pushed away my black worries. "I think I understand why the Mona Lisa smiled."

She perched on the side of the bed. "What do you mean?"

"She was thinking of a man. You and she have the same smile. Boy, did you catch Ian's attention tonight. I can't imagine he'll be thinking of you as a childhood buddy again. I bet he was going to kiss you before the gas leak. I'm sorry I interrupted your date. Again."

"No need to apologize, it wasn't your fault. Don't worry, he will kiss me."

"It'll be more than a kiss, if the way you two were looking at each other over dinner means anything."

She giggled, very un-Maggie-like, then pointed at me. " 'Tis a case of the pot and the kettle, I think. You and Blake?"

"No, no. There's nothing between us. We weren't out on a date tonight. Dinner was pay back for the chili I fixed. Besides, he knows I'll be leaving soon."

"I think you are wrong about Blake. Over the years, I've seen how he acts with other women. He's different around you. Ian agrees. He told me Blake is worried about the attempt on your life. He won't be letting you out of his sight anytime soon. And you should be keeping a close eye on that woman, Rosalind, from your office. She has been asking about him. She's no friend of yours, Jax."

"Thanks for the warning. I know what she is."

"Aren't you jealous?"

"Of her?" I tried to laugh, but it came out wrong. I had to ask. "He hasn't shown an interest in her, has he?"

"Believe me, Blake is interested in you. And a blind person can see the attraction is mutual."

"Not after tonight. How could he be so self-serving? His reputation?" My anger made a resurgence. "I'm being framed and could go to jail."

"He dinna mean—"

"In case you didn't notice, Maggie, we don't get along. There's no way we could. We're bidding for the same property." I pulled the blankets up to my chin. "I do wish I hadn't told him to stay here. I think I'm going to need a lawyer."

"He knew you were angry." She walked to the door and switched off the light. "Get some sleep. If I know our Blake, he will be here at cock's crow."

CHAPTER TWENTY-THREE

BLAKE OPENED ONE of the Fifties-style metal cabinets in Ian's kitchen. He knew where his friend kept a bottle. Blake removed a glass from the drain board, poured a shot, tossed it back, and refilled his glass. Jax's remark about his concern for his reputation had cut too close.

"Pour me one, too," Ian said, "while I lock up."

Ian strode to the front door and locked it. He checked the examining rooms opening right and left off the hall, then turned off lights on his way back to the kitchen. His office and waiting room were at the front of the old house. The sleeping quarters were on the second floor.

To avoid the subject of the argument with Jax, Blake said, "This kitchen is old. Maggie will want a new one after you're married."

Ian sipped his drink and ignored the misdirection. "You'll stay with Jax in Fort William tomorrow until your friend arrives? I heard the call you made on the way over here. I hope you picked a good one. The EpiPen is a damning piece of evidence. It will make Jax look guilty as hell. She's going to need solid legal advice. Despite what she said, she's frightened."

"Never thought I'd see the day."

"Only natural. She believes someone wants to hurt or kill her." Ian recapped the bottle of Scotch. "Frame her for murder? I believe that, too. How to convince the police?"

"Accidents can explain all the incidents, even the gas tonight. It could have been a leak."

"You don't believe that. Drop the pretense, my friend, you're worried for her. Good thing you were alert after opening Jax's door. Could she have left her door unlocked?"

"They lock their doors in New York, and she wouldn't leave her dog without locking up. I'm having the locksmith in tomorrow."

"It could be anti-foreigner sentiment. The German and English agents left after Montoya's body was found. Could be someone is trying to scare Jax into leaving town?"

"That's a better reason than the alternative."

"That we have a serial killer on the loose in Heather Hill?"

"Exactly." Blake couldn't conceive of it. The same killer for Bea and Montoya? Philip? Jax was in danger. None of it was possible. He knew everyone in town. Had since he was a child.

"Montoya was from Argentina, Jax is a Yank," Ian said. "There's your foreign connection to one element of dissent in town."

"Can you think of anyone who would hate Montoya or Jax enough to kill?"

"Not because they represent foreign companies. There might be another reason. By the by, I went online and looked up the Fairway Golf's resort on the Solway Firth. Took the virtual tour. Nice. It fit into the surroundings."

"Don't tell me you're switching sides? Going with the developer way of thinking?"

Ian sipped the last of his Scotch. "No, I'm not convinced the silt won't get into the oyster farm."

"One of the oyster lads could feel his livelihood is in jeopardy, which brings us back to tonight. Was tonight's attempt on Jax's life meant to scare her or kill her?"

Ian drained his glass. "I wouldn't want to guess wrong on that one."

"This might not be the first attack. I picked up her bike this morning. The mechanic at the repair shop said it could've been tampered with."

"Could've or had been?"

"He wasn't sure. It was a new bike. Worn brake pads? A loose cinch bolt? The handlebars shouldn't have come off. I turned it over to the police."

Ian stood and put the bottle away. "Do you believe her about the EpiPen?"

"I have to. She couldn't have biked to the manor early, stood over Montoya while he had his allergic reaction, stole that damn pen, then made it back to her flat before I picked her up."

"Well, someone took it from Montoya or from his body. Planting it in Jax's purse? The police will find that hard to believe."

"How could the person know when Jax would find it? That she wouldn't throw it away?"

Ian leaned against the counter. "If she had known it was there, she could have."

"She didn't."

"That's why I believe her story."

Blake stood and stretched. "I've never known one woman could attract so much trouble. Jail might be the safest place for her until the police find out who is behind this."

"Sounds like you care for the woman. Haven't fallen for another Yank, have you? Didn't learn your lesson with Caroline? She wouldn't stay in Scotland. What makes you think Jax will?"

"Jax and me?" If pressed, Blake might admit to a physical attraction, nothing more. Her gray eyes, red hair and her lips . . . . No, he had to stay away. "It's strictly business. She's staying in my spare flat. If there'd been an explosion tonight, she could've sued."

"Oh, is that all it is?"

"Of course. And you shouldn't be pointing fingers. I saw how you looked at Maggie over dessert. Good thing you've finally come to your senses. She's been in love with you since we were children. Treat her right, or I'll have to hurt you."

CHAPTER TWENTY-FOUR

GNAWED ON the problem of who wanted me dead until dawn. There had to be a connection between all the murders and the gas near-explosion. I couldn't believe someone would use such an extreme measure to force me out of town. Unless the killer believed I knew something else and was trying to silence me.

What did I know? I played with various theories and came to a conclusion. All the deaths had a connection to Coulter Manor. And I'd given myself a headache.

Thick fog shrouded the walk from Maggie's pub to Blake's building. I looked over my shoulder at the slightest sound. Paranoia isn't paranoia when you've suffered an attempt on your life. Back in my apartment, I took a couple of aspirin, fed Hooligan, took a shower, and dressed in my most professional suit. First impressions, and all that, but I had the feeling that turning over the EpiPen to the police was handing over my freedom, no matter what I wore. I was on my last sip of coffee when Ian knocked on my door.

It wasn't Ian. Blake walked in. "The fireman's report concluded you forgot to lock up."

I stared at him. The jerk was going to pretend we hadn't argued. I was ready to square off, then stopped. Some men can't apologize. Pride, manliness, and all that. Best tuck my hurt feelings inside for the time being. I needed all the friends I could muster. "Did you and Ian come up with any new ideas?"

"I've a few things to investigate."

I looked around the one room apartment. "It's scary knowing a stranger was in here. At least the firemen didn't make a mess."

"They checked the oven and the fireplace." Blake handed me a piece of paper. He'd written:

CAREFUL WHAT YOU SAY. POSSIBLITY YOUR FLAT IS BUGGED.

I pointed to the paper, shook my head in disbelief, but kept quiet. Blake's note did nothing to alleviate my anxiety.

Blake said, "I'm going to Glasgow to file papers and look in on Bobby Duncan. You're not due in Fort William until later. Want to ride along?"

What a nice way to remind me of my impending doom. But a car trip was better than bouncing off these four walls as I imagined a stay in the Fort William jail.

"Can we go through Glencoe?" I pulled on my coat. "I'm tired of work. I want to be a tourist before I'm incarcerated for life."

"Gather up Hooligan's things. I'll bring the car around."

The corgi joined us in the front seat. He sat with his front legs propped on my knees and peered out the window.

Blake kept one hand on the wheel, dug in a pocket and handed me my passport.

"I saw Charlie this morning," he said. "After the bike mishap and the near miss at your apartment last night, he's seeing you as a possible victim, not so much a suspect. I didn't mention the EpiPen. It'll sound better coming from you. He agreed to meet with us this afternoon."

Never had the sight of one document given me more relief. I was free to leave Scotland, if Trask didn't throw me in jail by the end of the day. Blake's reticence to discuss the subject worried me. "You think I'll end up staying there, don't you."

"The Fiscal, he's like your DA or coroner, he'll examine the evidence." Blake cleared his throat. "Uh, the maximum he can keep you is one-hundred-five days."

"Don't I *love* the Scottish justice system." I couldn't keep the sarcasm and bitterness out of my voice. "When my time is up, when I'm proven innocent, I'll be out of a job, a home and, and, Hoolie will have forgotten me."

"Giving up, Hollister?"

I disliked his goading tone. "Not in this lifetime. I'll think of something."

Blake had nothing to add. For once, his lack of conversation was welcome. The Land Rover entered the road that sliced through the treeless mountains hulking over the valley of Glencoe. Hoolie whined and tucked his head under my elbow.

I stroked his back. "Is it too far-fetched to think he senses what happened here so long ago?"

Blake rubbed Hoolie's neck. His hand touched mine, gave it a brief squeeze, and re-gripped the wheel.

A comforting gesture. It wasn't personal. Not to him. I couldn't ignore the hormonal rush. In the time it took for my heartbeat to return to normal, I examined my feelings for Blake. I hadn't felt anything for another man since Raul. I studied the strong line of Blake's jaw, the lock of dark hair persistently flopped over his forehead. I had to admit, there could be a physical attraction if I could get over my trust issues. We didn't agree on much, but I recognized he was a good man.

Blake interrupted my thinking and returned to Hoolie's woo-woo paranormal response to gloomy Glencoe. "Hoolie sensed when you arrived at Maude's the other night. It's possible he could have extra sensitivity to feelings, past and present?"

I studied the sodden clouds that crept down the peaks. I could imagine they were herding the ghosts of the MacDonald clan to the valley floor. Raindrops splattered the windshield. Boulders and sheep dotted the steep hillsides. No trees or buildings. No people.

"Even if I didn't know there had been a massacre here, I think I would feel a lingering sorrow. There is definitely something sad about this valley."

"Some Scots carry a grudge. To this day, there are pubs that won't serve a Campbell. Never have forgiven them for helping the British troops betray the MacDonalds." Blake switched on the windshield wipers and kicked the heater up a notch.

We didn't stop at the visitor's center. I wasn't up to a vivid recreation of the bloody splotch in Scottish history. No use thinking on the past. Or the future. It was time to tackle present-day problems.

"I guess you checked your car for a listening device?"

"Couldn't find anything."

"Did you find one in my apartment?"

"It could have been removed last night during the time I was sleeping at Ian's."

I stroked Hoolie's ears. "Why do you think someone put a bug in my apartment?"

"There had to be one. How else would someone know our plans and that your flat would be empty?"

"I think you've read too many spy novels. Anyone in the pub could have overheard us planning our night out. Richard Hyde was there."

"You can't think he had something to do with the gas leak or your bike mishap?

"He was one of the last people to see Raul alive. And he was in the pub yesterday when we made our plans. Wait, what do you mean, my 'bike mishap'?"

"I picked it up and took it to a repair shop. It had worn brake pads. The cinch bolt came loose. It was a new bike. I turned it over to the police. That's where I collected your passport."

"My bike was tampered with? Who could have done it?"

"You parked it downstairs, inside the front door. Easy access during business hours."

"Too risky. Annie would've seen someone messing with it." I shifted in my seat to watch him think. "Someone could have come in after the market closed."

"They'd need a key. I've accounted for yours, mine and Annie's."

"There's another one," I said. "The first night I was here, in the pub, Annie said Ian knew where the extra key was. Anyone could have heard that, too."

"No matter. I'm having the locks changed today."

"Annie's grandson took care of the bikes, didn't he? Could he have tampered with mine?"

"Timing isn't right. He was in Glasgow before you rented the bicycle. Last night, he was in the detention center. No way to fake that. He's innocent of anything recent. He confessed to breaking the furnace shunt and turning off the breaker in the fuse box the first night you stayed in the flat, but he didn't mention the bike. And he wrote the first note you found under your door. When I see him today, I'll ask if he gave a key to one of his gang."

"Why would he vandalize your building?"

"Annie thinks it's a case of misplaced loyalty. When Bobby first came to live with her, I spent a lot of time mentoring him."

"I don't understand."

"Bobby believed he'd be doing me a favor. Chase you out of town. One less bidder for the property, a better chance for SLFS. You didn't leave. Then he heard how angry I was about the broken furnace shunt. He knew I'd suspect him, so he ran off to Glasgow."

I tried connecting the dots. "Bobby's escapades involved you. You are bidding on Coulter Manor. Bea's death was next door. Raul died in the study. My bike mishap happened on the road outside the manor. I'm bidding on the estate. The gas leak last night has to connect, too. That property has to be the common denominator."

"Possible."

"I don't understand the who and why of it."

"We could hire a detective."

"If I'm arrested, I may have to."

After that, Blake fell back into his normal, non-communicative mode. The situation seemed so hopeless I stopped over-analyzing it. I was glad when we left Glencoe. The dismal valley had done nothing positive for my mood, and the unremarkable countryside did little to cheer me. Few buildings and fewer trees sprouted along the roadway. In the distance, an occasional cow or sheep grazed in the poor grass.

A few miles later, we left the harsh land for a complete change of scenery. Blake drove south along the bonnie, bonnie banks of Loch Lomond. When the sun broke through, the lake sparkled and, like magic, my spirits lifted. With wooded hillsides and small islands, I could imagine Rob Roy hiding here after his cattle rustling raids.

When we drove through the more populated areas of Alexandria, Renton and Dumbarton, I closed my mental tour book. The depressing suburbs of Glasgow shared a sameness I'd seen in industrial cities around the globe. Hoolie woke and looked out the window.

Blake broke his silence. "It won't take me long to file my papers."

"Find a bookstore nearby and you can leave me there. I need to stock up on reading material to carry me through another week. You did hear I won the bid." I couldn't resist the dig.

"I had the winning offer."

"I did." I hooked Hoolie's leash to his collar and peeked at Blake. His perpetual scowl had lessened. "Ramsey, you are teasing me again. Bascombe never said who had the top offer, did he?"

Blake parked two doors from a combination bookstore-tea shop, opened my door, and helped me out. "There's an internet café inside. If my future was as uncertain as yours is, I'd email my employer. You won't have internet access in jail."

I bit my tongue before I said something he'd regret.

He asked the clerk if I could bring in my dog. Once inside, he said, "I'll see you in an hour. Don't get into trouble."

"Right. Like I go looking for it," I said under my breath.

I found a vacant computer and composed a note to Mike Lemon with a copy to Mr. Atkins. It would be better if he heard it from me than from the police or the press. I could see the headlines. ARGENTINE PLAYBOY CHOKES TO DEATH ON HAGGIS. AMERICAN QUESTIONED. Please, God, keep Montoya's death out of the papers.

What to say? I'm in trouble, future unknown, HELP. Not professional. Whiney.

The police are questioning me this afternoon regarding Raul Montoya's death. More details to come.

I proofread my message. It was a triumph of understatement. I clicked send, logged off, and went in search of a book.

I should've been as happy as a cat in a sardine factory as I hobbled up and down aisles of well-stocked bookshelves, but I couldn't lose the feeling of doom hanging over my head. I wandered until the latest Ian Rankin mystery jumped off a shelf at me. An entire section of Robert Louis Stevenson, Robert Burns and Sir Walter Scott caught my attention. When my arms were full, I juggled my walking stick, Hoolie's leash, and paid for my purchases. Blake walked in the door in time to take my packages and help us into the car. He was fastening his seatbelt when his cell phone rang.

"Yes, I understand," he said. "I'll be right there." He snapped it shut. "Cora is demanding my presence."

"Cora?"

"My aunt. She's in a rehabilitation hospital on the outskirts of Fort William." Blake kept to the speed limit. Barely.

"Why does she want to see you?"

"The nurse didn't say."

We arrived at the rehab center set in a quiet neighborhood of Fort William. I offered to stay in the car.

"Oh, no you don't," Blake said. "She specifically asked to see you and Hooligan."

"How did she know we were together?"

"She has legions of spies." He favored me with a quirky grin.

We entered, walked down a hall, and approached an open doorway. A commanding voice carved the air.

"You tell me to do things by myself, and then you hover over me as if I'm an invalid. Leave me be, girl."

The "girl" who left the room was over forty and wore a stethoscope and white lab coat over a conservative brown sweater dress. Blake introduced me to Dr. Irene Peters, who was in charge of his aunt's therapy.

"How is she today?" he said.

"If you gauge her recovery by the level of impatience, then I'd say she should be out of here in a few days. She is," Dr. Peters smiled, "unique."

"It can't be easy having a former teacher as a patient," Blake said.

"So true. I'm behind schedule. Ring me if you want an update. If you want to know how she is, ask her. She's anxious to see you."

We entered a room where the attempt to make it feel more homey had not quite succeeded. The paintings and furniture had the same institutional look I'd seen in most hospitals and extended care facilities in the states.

I expected Cora Ramsey to be a large-boned hefty woman, someone capable of doing farm work and wrestling milk cows. Petite as her canary, Blake's aunt appeared engulfed by an overstuffed chair. White hair waved away from her face. Sharp blue eyes sparkled in a porcelain face etched with fine wrinkles. Her expression softened when she saw Blake; I quailed when she turned to me.

"Come closer, Jax Hollister, and allow me to look at you. With that red hair and those fey gray eyes, I'll wager you have the blood of the Celts running in your veins. Where do your people come from?"

"Other than paternal Scottish grandparents, I have no idea, Mrs. Ramsey. No one has done the research."

"Every person should know their family tree. You make that your top priority, young lady. Right after my Blake, of course."

"Now Cora, darlin'." Blake patted her on the shoulder.

"Don't 'Cora darling' me, Blake Ramsey. What are you doing to find Philip and Bea's murderer?" She shook her finger at him. "You will have to find their killer. Charlie Trask won't," she grumped in obvious exasperation. "He couldn't find his arm at the end of his elbow. Sit, Hooligan."

He did. I didn't think he could read lips and Cora hadn't used a hand signal or tapped the floor. She'd merely aimed those commanding eyes at him.

Blake pulled up two chairs. "Why do you think Philip was murdered, Aunt Cora? And who told you about Bea?"

"Maude and Annie visited. I'm not in my dotage, young man. I continue to read the papers and watch the telly. I've heard of Jax's accidents, too, if they were accidents. A gas leak doesn't happen by accident."

"The police ruled Philip's death accidental," he said.

"I don't give a horse's hiccup what the police called it." Cora straightened a lap robe over her knees. "I believe the term they used was 'inconclusive.'"

"You mentioned one killer, Mrs. Ramsey," I said. "Why do you think Bea and Mr. LeBeck were killed by the same person?"

"Deductive reasoning, my dear. Bea had an appointment with Philip the day he died."

Blake and I looked at each other.

"How do you know——" Blake said.

"Because she visited me that morning before meeting Philip for lunch. She was on her way to the dog show and brought Winnie and Hooligan in to say hello. I assume Philip was unable to keep the appointment?"

"The owner of the restaurant said a woman waited an hour, then left." Blake sat back in his chair. "So, it was Bea."

"Did she mention why they were meeting?" I said.

Cora's brow creased the same as Blake's. "Bea hadn't a clue. Philip asked her to bring her birth certificate. Blake, do you know why he would want that document?"

"Until this moment, I didn't know Bea had a meeting with Philip."

"Bea couldn't find a copy." Cora studied her clasped hands. "What did Philip expect to find? He already knew her mother's name. It's possible he was hoping her father's name would be on it. I doubt it would be." Cora leaned toward me in a conspiratorial pose. "In addition to having an alcoholic mother, Bea had to bear the burden of illegitimacy. Fifty years ago, having a child out of wedlock simply was not done. Her mother moved here when Bea was a baby. To escape the shame, I would think. In spite of it all, Bea turned out to be a fine person. She was a good student, loved her husband and her dogs. Her happiness was easy to see."

She shrugged her shoulders, as if to shake off her sorrow. "That birth certificate may be important. Philip wouldn't have asked her to bring it otherwise."

"I'll need Bea's maiden name to get a copy."

"Clooney, like the actor. Bea was born in that big hospital in Edinburgh, I believe. I can't recall its name. Find that certificate, my boy."

"Yes, ma'am."

"You take good care of Hooligan, Jax Hollister. And my Blake."

"Yes, ma'am."

With that, we were dismissed.

I staggered into the hall and leaned on my walking stick. "I feel as if I've been sent to the principal's office."

Blake chuckled. "Her students called her the Little General. You can see how she earned the nickname."

He took Hoolie's leash and walked to the Land Rover. "She loved all of them, especially Maude, Annie and Bea, then later, Ian and Maggie," he said. "Looked after them, but in the end, she had to let them make their mistakes and live their lives. Setting them free to make their way she called it."

I looked at Blake out of the corner of my eye. He was smiling. That gruff exterior held a soft spot for Cora Ramsey. Bless her for loving him.

On the drive to the police station, I mulled over the problem of Bea's birth certificate. "You were Bea's lawyer, don't you have a copy?"

"Bea never gave me one. I'll call the Registration Office in Edinburgh and have it sent."

All too soon, Blake turned into the parking lot next to a gray building scarcely more than a storefront wide.

"Hoolie will fare better in the car." Blake cracked the windows.

I fought tears. "Goodbye, Hoolie." I feared this would be the last time I would see him. I held his foxy head between my hands and stared into his questioning eyes. "I'll be back." I fed him a treat, hugged him, and hoped I was right.

I felt Blake's hand on my shoulder. "I'll keep him until this is resolved. Come away." He locked the doors and guided me toward my fate.

I looked over my shoulder. "Hoolie didn't howl, Blake. He knows I'll see him again."

CHAPTER TWENTY-FIVE

RICHARD HYDE rushed into the study. "I found it, Elizabeth, I found it!"

"Look at you. You're covered in dust and cobwebs. Where have you been?"

"In the attic looking for your great-grandfather's last journal. I thought I had already found it, but the one I was using ended six weeks before he died. On a hunch, I looked for a box of Reggie's personal belongings. You know, those things he might have had on his bedside table during his last illness. And there it was; a package on top of another, shoved behind a rack of clothes. Inside were his reading glasses, pen and inkwell, and this book." Richard held up a small, leather-bound journal. "The maids or your great-grandmother must have packed it away. I knew Wallace's dirk was too important. He had to mention it one more time."

He coughed and pounded his chest. "Damn dust."

Elizabeth poured him a glass of water from the decanter on the sideboard. "Here, sweetheart."

"Thanks, Lizzie. Exactly what I need. After you help me decode Reggie's last entry, we'll uncover the hiding place of the dagger and celebrate with champagne."

They settled in their chairs. He jiggled his foot while Elizabeth perched reading glasses on her nose. "The clue is there." Richard drummed his fingers on the arm of the chair. "On the next to last page."

She read the passage out-loud. " *'After I am gone, my Son will Search for that which is my Passion. He knows the History.'* That's all? It's hardly a clue. What does it mean?"

"Obviously, my dear, he is referring to the dagger. That was his passion. The reference to history must mean one of these books." He gestured, pointing to the shelves. "A history book on William Wallace."

"My dear, I do believe you're correct."

"All we have to do is find the right book. The location might be underlined. Perchance. he used a slip of paper to mark the page."

"Must we read all the books on Wallace? There are so many." With a frown, she opened her day calendar. "I best reschedule my appointment with the contractor until next week. I suppose the dirk is more important than our new house."

Richard heard the edge of annoyance that slipped into her words. "Finding it could pay for a round-the-world honeymoon cruise." Her frown gave way to a smile. He knew he'd struck the right chord. "It's a huge task, luv, but we can narrow the search. Your great-grandfather couldn't have hidden anything in books published after he died. Our first job is to look at the copyright dates. Then we can go through the oldest ones, the ones he would've read."

"How brilliant, Richard. After we sort out the newer books, we can crate them up for the move, something I meant to do this week. Killing two birds with one stone, as it were."

He pointed to the book-lined walls. "I hope this is the only room with books."

"There are two trunks along the far wall of the attic. I think they're full of the oldest ones. We'd best start there. We'll begin tonight, dear, after we eat. We haven't much time to complete such a large job."

Richard stood and turned in a slow circle, studying the ceiling-to-floor shelves. "So many books."

CHAPTER TWENTY-SIX

THE FOUR STEPS to the double doors of the police station felt like forty. I stopped to retie a shoelace, pull up a sock, then leaned heavily on my walking stick. I inhaled what I feared would be my last breath of freedom, and dragged one foot at a time until we reached the top stair.

Please let the doors be locked, the office closed for the day, I prayed.

Blake opened the left glass panel, took my arm, and guided me through.

"Keith, good to see you." He shook hands with his business look-alike. Tall, dark, rugged. Same black overcoat, same dark suit, different tie. Lawyer attire. Dressed to convey competence, inspire confidence.

I wanted hope.

"Jax Hollister, this is Keith Kirkley." Blake released my elbow. "He's handling Bobby Duncan's case and has agreed to act as your solicitor. He's experienced in criminal law. Will you have him represent you?"

Would I reach for a life preserver if I were going down for the third time?

I thanked Blake for calling in the cavalry. I'd almost overlooked that he'd called Kirkley a *criminal* attorney. My spirits sank another notch. I gazed into the attorney's brown eyes and imagined I saw a glimmer of compassion.

"I'm not guilty, Mr. Kirkley. Someone is framing me."

"It's Keith. May I call you Jax?"

"Certainly. All my problems began when—"

At the sounds of footsteps, I looked to my left and swallowed my words.

Raul's younger brother, Marcos Montoya, followed Constable Trask into the waiting area.

Blake stood behind me, blocking my escape from the impending train wreck. I straightened my spine and prepared for the inevitable.

The Montoya resemblance ran strong in the men of the family. Marcos was as handsome and as slender as Raul had been. He had a body-builder's sculpted physique and hair jelled into a modern spiky style. A scar that slashed through his left cheek detracted from his perfection, not his masculinity. It created a dangerous appeal.

Trask said, "Blake, Keith, I don't believe it takes two of you to help Ms. Hollister take care of the paper work for Montoya's body. You made the trip for nothing. His brother, Marcos, is here to claim it."

Raul's brother inserted himself between the constable and me. The scar flared scarlet against skin washed white from obvious rage. He leaned his face into mine.

"My family, we did not know you were here. We hear nothing from you."

"I'm sorry for your loss, Marcos."

"Sorry? You are a hypocrite. I would not be here if you did your duty. You should bring his body home to Argentina, not me. You are Raul's widow."

Oh, God, why did my marriage have to be made public now? In the police station in front of the constable, my lawyer. And Blake. I couldn't look anywhere but at the floor until Marcos stabbed me with a finger.

"Raul never changed his will." Specks of saliva flecked the corner of his mouth. "You are glad he is dead."

So great was his anger, I was afraid he'd strike me. "Marcos, I didn't marry him for his money. I never wanted it."

"My mother said—"

"Your mother did not want us to divorce."

"We are of the Catholic faith," Marcos said. "You married in the Catholic Church. You knew divorce could never be an option."

It was the same argument I had with Raul and his mother before I left Argentina. The Montoyas never understood my side. When I told them the Catholic Church didn't approve of adultery, they brushed off my objection as if I should've ignored Raul's infidelity.

I did my best to be civil. "The Catholic Church didn't tell me your brother had a mistress. No one told me. I didn't find out until after he saw the sonogram. Once he knew he sired a son, he left our bed for hers. It was your sister who confirmed it."

Marcos said, "It is a custom in my country—"

I'd heard that before. I couldn't let it pass. Not this time. I lost it. "Don't give me that cultural differences crap. I can play that game, too. Raul married an American woman. In *my* state, adultery is grounds for divorce. In *my* country, my divorce is final. Why does your mother continue to deny it? I am sad he is dead, but I am no longer Raul's wife. It was more appropriate that your family take care of the arrangements."

His jaw clenched with restrained fury. "You are his widow. A very rich widow. A motive for murder, no?"

"I didn't take anything for the divorce. All I wanted was out." I was speaking too loudly and needed to calm down. I regained some control over my resentment. "When I returned to the United States, I took back my maiden name."

Trask said, "She is correct, Mr. Montoya. We couldn't find a legal connection. Your brother's papers listed your family in Argentina to contact in an emergency."

My ex-brother-in-law's shoulders slumped, his expression one of remorse mixed with loathing. He brushed by and headed for the door. At the last moment, he whirled to face me.

"If you try to get money from us," he said through gritted teeth, "I will fight you with all my family's power and might."

"That's not going to happen."

He slammed the door so hard the glass rattled.

His hatred staggered me.

Up to this point, my failed marriage had been a private matter. It couldn't have come out at a worse time.

Blake said, "Find us some privacy, Charlie."

Trask led the way. He turned left into a room with a metal table, four chairs, and a reflective mirror. I wondered if anyone was behind the glass watching us.

"Ms. Hollister, I take it you're here for reasons other than claiming Raul Montoya's body. I'm busy, let's get to it."

My reaction to the confrontation with Marcos would have to wait. Suck it up, Jax. "I've come across some evidence that may pertain to Raul Montoya's death. The police should have it."

"Something that will require the presence of a solicitor, I assume." The constable looked from Blake to Keith. "Which of you will represent Ms. Hollister?"

Keith helped me off with my coat and draped it over the back of the chair. "I'll represent her," he said, "if it comes to that."

"She doesn't need two. You can step out, Blake."

"I'm a witness to the reason Jax came in today," he explained. "I can verify what she says."

I was surprised he wanted to be in the same room with me after what he'd heard from my ex-brother-in-law.

Blake withdrew the baggie from his coat pocket.

I took it and placed the wrapped EpiPen in front of Trask. "I want to turn this in. I think it belonged to Raul Montoya."

Trask stared at the bag. "Where did you find it?"

"In my purse. It fell out last night after the firemen left. Did they report the gas leak to you?"

"Of course. Why do you think it belonged to Mr. Montoya?"

"Dr. MacKenzie was with us when it was found. I asked if he'd prescribed an EpiPen for any of his patients. He hadn't. Raul Montoya always carried one."

"You know this because?"

"As you heard, I was married to him."

Trask flipped the page in his ever-present notebook. "When I first interviewed you, you said you were acquainted with Mr. Montoya. Why did you lie?"

"I didn't lie."

"You weren't complete in your answer."

"What does it matter now? He's dead." I noticed he wasn't recording this. Maybe our conversation wasn't official.

And maybe I was Mother Fricken Goose.

"It matters because you knew he was allergic to onions."

I looked at Keith. He gestured that I could respond. "I knew he always carried an EpiPen."

"Where did you find this one?"

"As I said, in my purse."

"Ms. Hollister, where was the pen before you found it in your purse?"

"I don't know."

"How did it get there?"

"I don't know."

Trask threw his notes on the table. Blood raced to his face.

I hadn't meant to set him off. Honest.

"That thing appeared in your purse by magic?"

"No need to badger my client," Keith said. "She's here voluntarily."

"Constable, someone put it in my purse." To demonstrate, I hung my bag over the back of the chair. "See how the side pocket hangs open. Anyone could have dropped it inside. I think the killer did it to make me look guilty."

Keith tapped me on the shoulder and whispered in my ear. "Keep your answers brief."

Trask leaned over me so I had to look up at him. "When did this occur?"

I refused to back down. "I don't know."

"Let me see if I have this correct." He scanned the items on his notepad. "The day Bea Kestle was murdered, you and Mr. Montoya argued on the road. There were witnesses. He tore a button off your coat." He pointed to where it hung over the chair. "Our lab will prove it matches. You say you saw Dickie Campbell on the river behind the gazebo around the time of Mrs. Kestle's death. No one else saw him. The next day, you and your associate, Miss Sweet, Blake and Miss Coulter discovered your husband's body. You have no alibi for the three hours before you came upon the body."

Each item was a nail in the coffin of his case against me.

"Correction, my *ex*-husband's body."

"Twenty-four hours later, you had a so-called accident on your bicycle. The repair shop said the handlebars and brakes *might* have been tampered with. And you claim someone broke into your flat. No sign of forced entry. That same someone rigged the gas to explode when you turned on the light. No proof of that, either. That's when you found the EpiPen. You don't know how it got in your purse or when."

"Your list is complete." I crossed my arms over my chest, determined not to show weakness. "I'm not a stupid person, Constable. I know the circumstantial evidence looks bad. You must realize I didn't know Raul would be eating breakfast at the manor. I never met the cook until after Raul was dead."

"How did you find the EpiPen last night?"

"I didn't *find* the pen. It fell out of my purse. Dr. MacKenzie picked it up."

"Are your fingerprints on it, Ms. Hollister?"

"I didn't see her touch it," Blake said. "Ian put it in the plastic envelope a short time later. His prints will be on it. It's conceivable the killer's fingerprints are there, also."

The policeman glared at Blake. "You should have turned it in last night."

"It was two in the morning. Since I am an officer of the court, I kept the evidence with me until this moment. Jax would've come sooner, but Keith couldn't meet us until now."

I picked at a hangnail. Blake and Trask engaged in a stare down.

When the cop blinked, I said, "Did you ask Dickie Campbell where he was at the time Bea Kestle was murdered? Or the morning Mr. Montoya died?"

Trask gaze swung to me. His face reddened, again. "Dickie denied being anywhere near the manor either time. It's well known he patrols the oyster beds all day."

"Could I have seen one of the other oyster lads? They dislike me because I represent a company that will develop the estate. Any one of them would be happy to see me in jail."

"You think the oyster workers or Dickie Campbell placed the EpiPen in your bag? One of them is trying to frame you for your husband's death?"

"*Ex*-husband."

I'd watched enough cop shows on television to know I fit the embittered spouse profile. Raul had a mistress. I knew of the affair. Motive enough for an American jury to convict me in a New York minute. I could expect the same in Scotland, unless the police had another suspect. "Did you investigate to see if Mr. Montoya entertained any visitors at the hotel?"

"Yes."

"And you found out he invited a woman to his room." I needed to throw suspicion elsewhere. "You know I don't match the description. I can imagine he might've had a rendezvous that went bad. I'd look deeper into it, if I were you."

Trask went rigid. His face turned from red to purple. His jaw muscles clenched.

Oops. No one likes being told how to do their job.

"You're correct, Ms. Hollister. While I gather more evidence for the Fiscal, I have a vacant cell with your name on it. You'll be safe there from that infamous *someone* who is trying to do you harm. Be my guest while I investigate the death of YOUR HUSBAND."

"*Ex*-husband."

Me and my big mouth.

CHAPTER TWENTY-SEVEN

BLAKE WALKED HOOLIE and Keith to the nearest pub. Blake needed a drink.

Bloody Hell. He hadn't suspected she'd been married to Montoya. How long had she been divorced? And the son she mentioned? What other secrets was she hiding? And why was it important to him?

He had more investigating to do. When he researched Montoya and had all the facts, he'd figure it out.

"Jax should be glad you called me, Blake," Keith said. "Her temper makes her an interesting woman, but it didn't help her case with the constable. She'll keep you on your toes that one will."

"Not me, she's your client." Blake ignored Keith's implication of a personal relationship. He couldn't afford to get involved. After the altercation at the police station with Montoya's brother, he wasn't sure how much he could trust her. Why had she kept her marriage a secret? No, best keep things as they were. He ordered a pint. Hoolie plopped on the floor, head between his paws.

"Not much I could do to keep her out of jail," Keith said, "not after that argument with her ex-brother-in-law. I had to admire the way she held up during his attack. I got the impression she didn't know he'd be there. Too bad the constable thinks her marriage to Montoya adds to motive." Keith chuckled. "It's funny in a serious way how she stood up to Trask, too. I half-expected fisticuffs. As it was, her attitude earned her a stay in a jail cell."

"Jax and Trask have mixed it up before."

"Obviously." Keith took a sip of his lager. "I don't think he has enough evidence to keep her long. Is there another suspect?"

"The good constable isn't looking at anyone else."

Hoolie whined. Blake picked him up, and the corgi huddled against his chest.

"Is this the dog Jax says can identify Bea Kestle's killer?" Keith stretched out his hand for Hoolie to sniff.

"Jax thinks he was there."

"The constable doesn't credit the idea much. No connection between the Montoya and Kestle murders?"

Blake finished his beer and declined another. "Jax is convinced the estate is the common factor. Until the EpiPen showed up last night, we thought Montoya died alone. An accidental death." He stroked the corgi's fur. "Now, I have no doubt someone removed the EpiPen from Montoya and planted it in Jax's purse. If that someone kept Montoya from getting to it, that makes it murder. Depraved indifference at the least."

"You believe the lass's story, then?"

"She can be pugnacious and headstrong and may have lied by omission, but she's not a bad person. Certainly not a killer." Blake sobered at the vision of Jax in a cell. "She doesn't belong in jail, Keith. Get her out tonight."

"It's too late today. I'll ring up the Fiscal handling the case first thing in the morning. I have a copy of the police report. There are two pieces of solid evidence that I can see. The button and the EpiPen. It helps that Jax turned in the pen and readily gave up her coat." He flipped open a file folder. "The coroner narrowed time of death to a three-hour time span. Seven to ten. We need to confirm Jax's alibi for the morning before you drove her to the manor. I'll suggest she provide Trask with her computer password so he can go through her emails. Time stamps will verify she sent them when she says she did. And her remark regarding Montoya's visitor? Is there anything behind that?"

"It's likely Jax was throwing suspicion elsewhere. She suspects Rosalind Sweet, her associate from New York, of having been intimate with Montoya. She wouldn't mention the woman by name. I believe her loyalty is misplaced. Miss Sweet strikes me as someone who uses her sexuality for personal gain. If you met her, you'd see what I mean. Think sexual predator. She was with us when we discovered Montoya's body."

"How did she react?"

"Shocked. I don't know if it was an act or not. She might not be the killer, but can you use her to create reasonable doubt?"

"You need to find out if the Sweet woman has an alibi for that morning. If she and Montoya were lovers, they could have had a fight over Jax. And get an affidavit from the woman Jax left the dog with that morning."

"Can't help you on this, Keith. Jax and I are competing for the same property where Montoya died. If I interfere, people could construe it as a conflict of interest and it might worsen her case. That's one reason I called you. You can hire an investigator to do those things, if it comes to that."

"You should call her employer. We may need his money for bail."

"You'll have to do that, too. Drew Atkins has a reputation for having an over-zealous sense of propriety. He doesn't condone intimacy between competitors, perceived or otherwise. The best way I can help Jax is to keep it professional and stay out of it as much as possible. Atkins should know what is happening to one of his employees. You call him."

CHAPTER TWENTY-EIGHT

J AIL COTS ARE NOT conducive to sleep. First, it's where you are. Second, the question of how long you'll be stuck there is enough to keep Rip Van Winkle awake. The real or imagined bedbugs, lice, and spiders in my one blanket kept me tossing, turning, and itching all night. I assumed I was in a holding cell since it lacked a toilet and washbasin. In the morning, my tongue felt like a tribe of baboons slept on it. A female police officer appeared and gave me a comb, soap, toothbrush and paste. She walked me down the hall to the water closet. (The UK's term for restroom is so much more accurate. How many people actually rest in a restroom?)

The comb barely made a dent in the rats nesting in my hair. The toothpaste helped. The mirror confirmed that I looked like crap. No purse (they'd taken it along with my cane), no makeup. The same female officer escorted me back to my cell. She refused to answer my questions. My abode lacked a window giving me no clue what time of day it was until the matron brought me breakfast. I wasn't hungry.

Where the hell was Blake? My lawyer, Keith? Time stretched until I knew no one was coming. I felt abandoned.

Jax the Jinx strikes again. I shouldn't have pushed Trask into a corner. Damn it, I was innocent. I wanted to kick something, but the cinder blocks would hurt my toes.

I eyed the opposite wall of my cell, then paced off the steps. Six limping paces wide.

The Scottish system of justice couldn't be that different from the U.S. Innocent until proven guilty. Right? Or was it the other way around?

My ankle had stiffened overnight. I hobbled the length of the rectangle.

Eight paces. Six by eight.

I hugged Blake's overcoat tight against the chill of the cell. He insisted I take it after I gave up my parka for evidence. Trask should have cut me some slack for turning in my coat and the EpiPen.

Hah! I always was an unrealistic dreamer. How could I believe Raul would love a klutz like me? His spiteful sister confirmed it. The family considered me "good breeding stock."

I couldn't afford the energy to get angry again. I had to think of something else.

Let's see, if I remembered my high school geometry, the imaginary line from one corner of the cell to the one kitty-corner from it formed the hypotenuse of a right-angle triangle. If I used my photographic memory to dredge up the page that had the formula for computing the diagonal, I wouldn't have to think about my current problems.

I needed to believe prison was not in my future. From television, I knew that once released, I'd be out of a job. Family friend or not, Mr. Atkins couldn't risk the reputation of his company. He'd done so much already, holding my job open, giving me time to heal, and I'd blown it. Word traveled fast in my elite community of real estate acquisition experts. *My* reputation would be shot. I'd lose everything. I'd have to start over. Doing what, I had no idea.

I'd been thinking I should go home for a vacation. That plan went in the dumpster. I could not return a failure. My parents would be so disappointed.

Tears threatened. If I allowed one to break loose, I'd never stop crying.

I'd slept in my clothes and they looked it. The jail weekend shift didn't have access to prison garb. Good thing. Prison orange would have clashed with my red hair. What if they made it out of plaid?

Hell, I hadn't been in jail twenty-four hours and already I was going crazy. A plaid jumpsuit. I shoved down the insane giggle bubbling inside. I remembered an old black and white movie where a prisoner went crazy. He shook the bars of his cell door and screamed. And screamed.

I refused to look at the bars.

I plopped on the cot, wrapped my arms around my legs and rested my head on my knees. I was subterranean deep in self-pity.

It was the not knowing that wore on my nerves. They couldn't keep me forever. I'd get out. I had to believe it, but when? I wished someone had told me what to expect. Given me some hope.

If there was any.

I slumped to my side and curled into a fetal position. I wanted my mommy.

"Have you ever seen such a sad sight, Blake?"

Oh. My. GAWD!

What was left of my world shattered. Mr. Atkins was in Scotland. Here. Outside my cell.

Where to hide? Dignity be damned, I would've crawled under the cot if there'd been room. Instead, I forced a smile and jumped to my feet.

A guard unlocked the door. I rushed to embrace my boss. He patted my back. I wanted to hug Blake. This was not the time or place.

"Your cryptic email concerned me," my boss said. "I was already in the air when Keith Kirkley called me. He arranged for Blake to pick me up at the airport."

Reality overcame my elation. Mr. Atkins was here to salvage the sale.

"Am I free to go?"

"Drew paid your bail," Blake said.

Omigod, number two. Bad enough Mr. Atkins knew I'd been in jail. He'd paid to get me out. I wanted to die.

OMG3. Blake and my boss were on a first-name basis. My life couldn't get any worse.

Mr. Atkins escorted me to the front desk. "I'm acquainted with the judge who knows your Fiscal. I told him I didn't think you were guilty of anything more than being in the wrong place at the wrong time. I did assure him you would stay here until the situation was resolved."

"Keith is taking care of the paper work," Blake said. "Your personal belongings are on the way."

Mr. Atkins prepared to leave. "I've got business in Inverness and called for the company limo. Blake, will you drive Jax back to Heather Hill?"

"Mr. Atkins, how can I ever thank you?"

"Convince the village to choose our plan. And stay out of trouble." My boss headed for the exit. "Chad is bringing Fairway's display. He'll be here tomorrow. He has my itinerary."

Blake and Keith walked me through the release procedure. I found my voice on the way to the car. "I can't believe I still have my job."

I knew Mr. Atkins wasn't happy with the situation. Under normal circumstances, my boss was the epitome of politeness. His abrupt departure spoke volumes.

I had my orders. I'd do as he instructed. I'd win the bid and repay my bail. In my mind, there was only one way to regain his trust. I had to erase my "record" by finding Raul's killer.

Outside, in the free air, I thanked Keith and promised to call him if I had to talk to the police again.

I tried to return Blake's coat, but he wouldn't take it, insisting instead that we stop and buy me a new parka. In the men's department of a sporting goods store, I found one with long enough sleeves. Back in the car, a strained silence rode with us to Heather Hill. I had so many questions.

How much was my bail? When did I have to go to court? How would my new friends treat me after my time in jail? Would it affect the chances for an unbiased vote from the town council? I wasn't ready to hear the answers, but one question couldn't wait.

"Has Marcos Montoya left the country with Raul's body?"

"This morning. You weren't expecting him to come for the body. What—"

"I-I can't go into it. Not now, Blake."

He didn't push, but I knew the subject was far from closed.

I collected an ecstatic Hoolie from Annie and escaped upstairs. We had a brief romp and tug-of-war. I had missed him and it was mutual. After I scrubbed off the prison grunge, I dressed in comfortable jeans and a cozy top. All I wanted was a quiet evening with my dog and a good book.

Blake knocked on my door.

"Sean is serving the first sampling of oysters. There's a celebration at the pub. Join us."

"Thanks but no thanks, Blake. I, uh, planned to go to bed early. And besides, I don't like oysters."

He took a step back and gave me the once over. "Coward."

"I-I—"

Blake silenced me with a stop-sign hand signal. "Don't play dumb, Hollister. I never thought I'd see you tuck your tail between your legs and run away."

Double damn. He was beginning to know me too well. In another time I'd flutter my fan and simper, "Why, whatever do you mean, Mr. Ramsey?" in true Scarlett O'Hara style, including a southern accent. That wouldn't work. Not on Blake.

"You'll face the entire village, and you'll do it this minute," he said. "No excuses."

"But—"

"If you're innocent, you have nothing to be ashamed of." He shoved me into my coat, took Hoolie's leash, and pushed me out the door.

"What do you mean 'if'? Of course I'm innocent."

"Then act like it."

My embarrassment stayed with me during the short walk to the pub. Blake let go of my arm long enough to open the door. I wanted to bolt back to my apartment.

Hoolie pulled me inside. Traitor.

Heads turned. A momentary silence reminiscent of New Year's Eve struck. I longed for the nearest hole.

"Jax!" Maggie rushed to my side. "I'm so glad you're here. 'Tis a big day for Sean and Ian. Have a seat."

Blake steered me toward Annie. Hoolie headed for Winnie and Maude. After we settled in at "our" table, the normal level of noise returned. No one mentioned jail. No one pointed. There were a few looks from the oyster lads, but they didn't like me before I'd done time in the slammer. Ian sat at their table, said something I couldn't hear, and the young men stopped staring.

Sean entered with two huge trays of oysters on the half shell. He placed one in the center of the table occupied by Ian and the oyster workers and passed the other tray to Maggie.

"To our investors and those who've worked so hard to make it happen," Sean said. "You've earned the right to taste the first Loch Linnhe Oysters." He reached in, took one and waited while the others did the same. He held it high. "*Lang may yer lum reek!*"

"Translated it means long may your chimney smoke," Blake said. "Same thing as have a long life."

My stomach rebelled when the honored few upended the gray slimy things into their mouths. The crowd held their breath until Ian slapped the table.

"Excellent! Succulent. Imagine how bonny the autumn harvest will taste. Time to talk expansion, Sean. More investors, more beds, more men and more money."

The oyster lads whooped and shouted and the villagers beamed. Maggie passed the tray and everyone took one. When it came my turn, I pretended to drop something. I bent over and felt Blake reach past me. By the time I sat upright, Maggie and the tray were at the next table.

"They're more delicate than the oysters from Loch Fyne," Maude said. "Don't you think so, Jax?"

Before I could stammer an answer, Blake said, "Sean was wise to wait until the fourth year. The three-year-olds were too small. These are the perfect size, nice and fat." He winked at me, stood, and clanged a spoon against his beer mug. "Here's to Loch Linnhe Oysters."

The crowd cheered. So many people had a stake in the venture. I promised myself I'd contact New York first thing in the morning and make certain our environmental impact studies ensured the safety of the oysters.

"Where's Dickie?" Sean asked. "He's guarded the beds from the beginning. He should be here to celebrate with us."

Heads turned. Dickie was not in the pub or the adjoining kitchen. Sean sent one of the oyster boys to find him, but before he could leave, Constable Trask entered. When his gaze swept the crowd, a chill ran down my spine. He frowned at me before he spoke to Sean and Ian. Those nearby overheard. Whispers flew from person to person.

"Dickie's dead? No, it canna be," Annie said. Her shocked expression mirrored others in the silent room.

Trask came to our table. "Is this the man you saw across the river from Coulter Manor?" He placed a photo in front of me. Annie gasped.

I didn't want to look. The policeman tapped the picture, forcing me to focus. I reached under the table for Blake's hand and squeezed until I ground his knuckles together.

The picture was a head shot of Dickie Campbell. Eyes wide, unseeing, and dead.

I looked at Trask. Nothing but accusation in his expression. Sean, Ian and the oyster lads crowded around our table.

"How? Where?" I asked.

He slid a second photo onto the table. In it, Dickie lay on his back, legs splayed, his sightless eyes turned toward the sky. Blood stains spread on the front of his sweater. Was that a pitchfork stuck in his chest?

"Part of an oyster rake," Sean said.

"Not an accident, was it," Blake said. "Where was he found?"

"A few meters beyond the footbridge behind the gazebo." Trask stared at me. "Where you said you saw him the day Bea Kestle was killed. Where were you this morning, Ms. Hollister?"

I couldn't allow him to accuse me. Not in public. I dropped Blake's hand and pushed to my feet. I must have looked fierce because Trask and the others stepped back.

"If you'd been in *your* office, you'd know I was in *your* jail in Fort William."

"And at noon?"

I wanted to scream in frustration.

Blake stood by my side. "She was being released at noon. The Fiscal didn't have enough evidence to hold her." He spoke to the constable, loud enough for the patrons of the pub to hear. "Then I drove her back to Heather Hill."

The constable's expression changed from accusatory to momentary confusion. He shifted his attention to Sean and the oyster lads. "Anyone know why Dickie would be near the manor this morning?"

"He helped us fish the oysters early on, right after first light." Sean couldn't take his eyes off the photos. "Dickie said his Wellies leaked. He went to change shoes and socks before going on patrol."

Dickie's boots showed in the photo. Were his feet wet or dry?

CHAPTER TWENTY-NINE

WHEN I CRACKED an eyelid the next morning, the dial of my travel clock showed five twenty-five. By six-thirty, I decided searching for snooze land was a lost cause. I'd never had this much trouble resting in a foreign place. My sleep deprivation didn't bother Hoolie. No matter what time I woke, he wanted out. I tested my ankle. It felt better. I left my cane propped by the door. My new coat kept out the morning cold, and the wool cap kept body heat from escaping. Hoolie acted invigorated by the chill air and romped on the end of his leash. I crossed the A82 highway and found a path leading down to Loch Linnhe.

The rising sun brightened the sky. North toward Fort William, clouds cloaked the summit of Ben Nevis. I couldn't remember seeing the top of the mountain after I arrived. Someday I hoped to hike to the top in memory of Uncle Philip.

A few fishing boats cut white vees across the water, disturbing the mirror image of the surrounding hills. No other early walkers dodged the wavelets breaking on the sand. I let Hoolie off his lead and watched him herd the shore birds. Up ahead, a yellow machine worked the shallows, its engine growling. The sound of a hammer striking wood played the backbeat to the squawk of the ubiquitous seagulls.

All memories of dead bodies drifted away in the normality of the morning. Hoolie brought me a piece of driftwood, and we played fetch until he decided it was a stupid game. I kicked a discarded plastic water bottle up the slope beyond the reach of the incoming tide. The next time we walked here, I'd bring a trash bag.

"You're trespassing." A male voice boomed from behind.

I yelped in surprise and tried to whirl toward the threat, one leg half-raised for a self-defense kick.

Wrong leg. Ankle pain. I hopped to the other foot and lifted my fists to chest level.

Six feet away stood one of the oyster lads. He was the biggest one from the pub. I didn't remember his name. His heavy work coat and wool pants strained over bulging muscles. Huge waders encased legs the size of telephone poles. The behemoth's face had never known sunscreen lotion. Folds and wrinkles covered a weathered skin and made it difficult to tell his age or intentions. I looked into his eyes for a clue to his mood. Nothing there. However, the shotgun over his shoulder was a dead giveaway.

Should I take a step forward and call his bluff, or run like hell?

The closest human was far down the beach.

I lowered my leg, but stood ready to move into flight mode. "I didn't see a No Trespassing sign. I was walking my dog."

"We don't allow strangers 'round the oyster farm."

"I'll leave. I apologize, Mr. . .?"

Silence.

"Mr. . . . ?"

"Gordon. Niles."

I ignored his surliness. "Isn't your mother the cook at the Coulter Manor?"

"Aye. 'Til it's sold, and she loses her job." He swung the gun into the crook of his elbow.

I edged backward. "That depends on who buys it, doesn't it?"

He shrugged his eyebrows.

"A golf resort will need to feed its guests," I said.

"Think ye'll win? Ye haven't got the town council's vote yet. I'll be speaking agin ye. The oysters come first."

Think fast, Jax. "I'm glad I met you, Mr. Gordon. Would you show me the farm? You can point out where there might be problems. I'll make sure the engineers at Fairway Golf have included plans to protect the oysters. You have my word."

A shadow of disbelief flickered in his eyes. "Doc Ian spoke to your people months ago."

"Ian doesn't work the beds, does he? He's got book smarts, but he doesn't know the water, the tides. Not like you do. Were any workers interviewed?"

When he didn't answer, I said, "Help me correct that oversight. Talk to me."

Hoolie came to sit at my feet. Niles regarded him, then me.

Before his wall of animosity could rebuild, I said, "If we work together, the village could benefit."

He gave a noncommittal "um."

A tough sell.

"Fairway Golf has an interest in keeping the beds safe, too. Our menu could feature your oysters. Another marketing possibility, for both of us. A win-win."

I could see him thinking it through.

"What have you got to lose, Niles? Give me a tour."

Hoolie whined, placed his paws on Niles's knee and turned pleading eyes upward.

"Come along, then. Put him on his lead so he stays clear of the machines."

My dog, the closer.

In the next ninety minutes, I learned how much the village of Heather Hill had staked its financial future on an ugly bivalve. Niles pointed out the oblong-shaped floats that marked the boundaries of the oyster farm. In the past, humans had fished the native wild oyster to near extinction, he explained. Currently, the government regulated and controlled the wild oyster harvest. Farmed oysters sought to answer an increasing demand. Loch Linnhe was a salt-water lake, perfect for farming. Sean and the other investors imported the Pacific (yes, as in Pacific Ocean) oyster spats—baby oysters. The oyster lads placed them in mesh bags and attached them to wooden trestles. I watched a few of the men hammering new frames. When completed, they would secure the frames to the lake bottom.

I pointed to several men wading in the shallows. A man pulled something out of the mud and put it in a bag hanging from his waist. "What are they doing?"

"Year-round we have to search the beds for invaders like starfish. Disease be another problem. Those lads also monitor the size of the oysters."

Niles confirmed that oysters mature in three to four years. It seemed a long time to wait for a return on an investment. And each year, the investors had to purchase new spats to replace what disease or a harvest took. It was a labor intensive and expensive undertaking. So many things could go wrong.

"Oysters breathe the same as the fish, ye ken."

"I didn't."

"They have gills. The saltwater brings them oxygen."

"Ah. If the water is polluted . . ."

". . . or the silt increases, the oysters die."

We walked back to the place on the beach where we'd met. "You're worried about the runoff into the Muckle River during construction, aren't you?"

"Aye. When it starts high in the hills, the river is pure and clean. As fresh as it can be. It curves past the farms, 'rounds Coulter Manor and drops behind Mrs. Kestle's place. Goes underground at the village and empties into the loch a kilometer south of here. The fresh river water gets diluted by the salt loch."

"The oysters are well north of where the river flows into the lake." I reasoned it through. "Normally, the tides should disperse the silt in the water. If there was too much silt . . ."

"Aye."

"Niles, I'll make sure Fairway Golf plans include filters and other safeguards. There's someone in New York who solved a runoff problem in Ireland. Don't get your back up, he's not Irish. The drainage situation there was similar. I'll have him double-check everything."

A grin split his face. "Ye must truly love oysters, miss."

"They are, uh, unique." I controlled my gag reflex. "And they're important to Heather Hill."

The sun warmed the air. I watched a lone bicyclist on the road upslope from us. His cap was like the one Dickie wore. "You worked with Dickie Campbell, didn't you?" I drew a sand doodle with the toe of my sneaker. "Any idea who killed him?"

He studied my drawing. When he met my gaze, sorrow replaced the brief smile in his eyes. "Me and the lads, we talked. Came up with nuthin'." He shoved his hands into his pockets and hunched his shoulders. "Dickie had his trouble with the bottle, he did. Still, the man wasn't a mean drunk. A good sort, always lookin' for a way to make money. It all went to drink."

"What was he doing on the estate yesterday?"

"Had to change into dry socks. A short cut?"

We looked across the road, up the slope to the back of the pub and the village.

"Where did he live?" I asked.

"A cousin gave him a room behind the church." Niles pointed to the spire on the north end of town.

Coulter Manor sat hidden behind a rise in the land. I knew it was well south of Heather Hill. Dickie had gone out of his way to die.

CHAPTER THIRTY

STOPPED IN the parking lot to make sure the beach sand was out of Hoolie's paws. A quick ruffle through his fur and he was good to go. The market was open, and the smell of fresh-baked scones tempted me. I bought one and told Annie how easy it was to keep my dog clean.

"You wouldna be wanting an animal who'd spent the day with sheep and cattle bringing the barnyard inside with him. Breed a proper coat, Bea said, bless her soul."

We looked down in time to catch Hoolie begging for the last bite of my pastry. I resisted his pleading eyes, mindful of his weight. I'd researched corgis and discovered the breed, with their long backs, was subject to arthritis—a problem made worse by extra pounds.

"Oh, I've a note for you from that Rosalind woman." Annie wrinkled her nose as if a bad smell lingered. "She stopped in but you were out." She handed me a piece of butcher paper, obviously borrowed. I unfolded the square and read:

Shopping in Inverness. Rosalind

She'd added a heart-shaped, smiley face. Ack.

Rosalind on the prowl made me uneasy. When would she be back? As if I cared. I did wonder who gave her a ride. Blake's car wasn't in the lot. I bit back the impulse to ask Annie where he was.

Wait a minute. Rosie was shopping in Inverness? Mr. Atkins would be in Inverness. Rosalind and my boss in the same city? Was she after my job or my boss? Maybe both. I suspected she would use my recent brush with the law to her advantage. Best adhere to the old adage: keep your friends close, your enemies, closer.

My cell phone rang. Chad Stillwell, the western-dressed Texan and talented designer for Fairway Golf, called from the second company jet. He needed to know where to bring the plans when he arrived in Heather Hill. I gave him directions to the church basement and told him I'd meet him there. What to do for the rest of the morning and afternoon until he arrived?

I called Elizabeth and asked if I could hike the back part of the estate. I wanted to see if the slope and grade for the proposed turn-around holes was too steep. She warned me that Dickie Campbell's body had been found by the river. I told a little white lie and promised to stay away, but I wanted to see where the murder had taken place. Not inclined to morbid curiosity, I was looking for a clue that would clear me of Raul's murder. What did my ex-husband's death have to do with Bea, Raul and Dickie? And Uncle Philip's? Was the estate the only connection?

Despite my plan to never ride a bike again, I needed a way to the manor. Annie found me a new bike. I promised her I'd be careful. I had no intention of falling off again. I left Hoolie with Maude and Winnie and followed her directions to a path that entered the Coulter's land from uphill. I left my bike by the side of the lane and walked down a gently worn corridor through the thick stand of pines. A game trail? Through a gap in the trees, I glimpsed a herd of local red deer. They raised their delicate heads and gazed at me with soulful eyes, untroubled and unafraid.

The sun, where it filtered through the greenery, felt good on my shoulders. The lack of wind was a welcome respite. All in all, a good day for a hike. The sight of an occasional footprint visible in patches of soft dirt gave me pause. I assumed the police had been all over the trail for signs of the killer. Caution slowed my headlong push through the undergrowth. A rustle in a bush ahead frightened me to a standstill. I bit back a scream when a rabbit dashed in front of me. So much for a relaxing stroll.

The sound of rushing water led me to the river. The Muckle, swelled by the recent rain, roared through the deep channel. The dirty brown flow was colored by runoff filtered through the peat. A local distillery claimed the "peat tea" gave the national drink a distinctive flavor. No wonder I didn't like Scotch—a blasphemy I avoided divulging by drinking the local beer instead.

The path ended some thirty feet north of the footbridge. Disturbed grass and footprints covered the site where the police had found Dickie Campbell's body. Evidence of the Scottish equivalent of CSI littered the area. There were grid markings and too many boot prints to pick out any one pair. I wondered who discovered the body.

I backed away and moved twenty paces to the right where, eight days earlier, I'd seen Dickie Campbell's face in profile before he disappeared through the trees. From where I was standing on a low sandy place near the steep bank, I could see the Coulter's white gazebo, not the main house. I avoided tracks in the muddy earth. They led in the direction I'd come from. Uh, oh. The prints appeared to be recent. I hadn't passed anyone on the path. I looked around for the person who made them and listened. Nothing. When I was positive I was alone, I placed my boot next to one of the prints. Dickie was five foot five, at most. The print I was looking at was close to the same size as mine. Could be someone near six foot or so. The sole had a heavy tread. It could be a hiking shoe or a work boot. Plenty of those in Heather Hill.

Near the edge of the water, I noticed an odd-shaped stone sticking out of the mud. I bent over, grasped and wriggled it out. I removed my sunglasses to inspect the object.

A split second later, I was in the middle of the river.

I couldn't touch bottom. I fought to keep my head from going under. Failed. Panic increased when my parka filled with icy water. My brain refused to work. The blood in my veins flowed like molasses. The memory of my father's voice broke through my terror.

"Wet clothes can drown you."

I'd hated the childhood swimming lessons, but they were necessary because we lived at Lake Tahoe. In the middle of a Scottish river, I thanked my parents for their foresight.

Underwater, I held my breath and struggled with the zipper tab. The job was impossible with gloves on. I worked them off, kicked to the surface, and inhaled a gulp of air. My head dipped below the surface again. I unzipped the coat, clawed and tugged my arm free from one sleeve, then the other. My lungs burned with the need for oxygen. I shook my shoulders, let the sodden coat fall to the bottom, and stroked toward the light. Seven feet of murky water felt like seven thousand.

I broke the surface, gasped for air, swallowed water and gagged. A hard cough cleared my chest.

Where was I? I swiped gritty water out of my eyes. The current had carried me beyond the shallow area of the riverbank where I'd gone in. The steep sides offered no handholds, no way to climb out. I twisted to my right and saw the footbridge. I quit fighting the swift water, let it carry me to the central supports, and clung to the wood.

My survival instinct kicked adrenaline into my chilled veins. It wouldn't last. I had to get out of the water before hypothermia set in.

Two flailing strokes against the fast moving water brought me closer to the next piling and the shore.

My boot touched bottom. Hope surged.

I lunged for the next upright. The water no longer covered my face.

I threw myself at the next vertical support. Progress.

I was chest-deep in the icy flow. The last pole was near the end of the bridge, five feet away.

It might as well have been a mile. I hugged the wood, afraid to let go, afraid my strength had run out. A hard shiver shook my body.

Don't shut down, my inner voice screamed. I looked to heaven for help and saw the underside of the bridge.

I uncurled my fingers and pried one hand from the wooden pole. I reached up and gripped the under edge of the walkway. Forced my other hand to do the same. Splinters dug into fingers. Legs were blocks of ice.

In another minute, I'd lose my grip and the current would take me.

I rested my head against my left arm and slid my left foot along the rocky bottom. What upper-body strength remained I focused into lifting my left hand and advancing it a few inches along the edge. Forced my right to follow.

Inch by inch I moved numb hands and shifted heavy boots, one by one up the incline. Two feet to go.

"Jax! My God. Let me help you."

A hand came into my field of vision. I grasped it and followed the tug for the final few steps out of the water.

"Take my coat. Steady. No, don't talk. Back to the house. We have to get you warm."

CHAPTER THIRTY-ONE

I HAVE NO IDEA how I traveled the distance from the river to the manor house. Once inside, my mind worked in fits and starts. I have a vague memory of needing help to climb a set of stairs. Voices were an unintelligible babble, a mixture of male and female. I recognized Elizabeth and Mrs. Casey. They tried to take off my wet clothes, but the heavy wool clung to me like the skin to a tomato. Hands plucked at me from all directions. They peeled me in sections. I should have felt the difference between wet clothes and the warmer air of the upstairs bathroom. All I felt was cold, freezer-burn cold. Modesty was useless. I shook so hard I couldn't cross my arms over my breasts or any other place.

Elizabeth tested the water in the tub. "More cold, less hot. We have to warm her gradually."

Mrs. Casey adjusted the tap. "I'll get her other sock." She stripped the icy wool off my foot.

"Jax. Jax! Open your eyes. No sleeping." Elizabeth slapped my face, not too hard, just enough to bring me back from wherever I'd gone. "Can you stand? Help us move you into the tub."

They hoisted me to my feet, but my legs wouldn't cooperate. Before a foot could slide out from under me, Elizabeth picked it up and lifted it into the water.

"Ow, ow, ow." Red-hot pinpricks stabbed my foot. Tears streamed down my cheeks. I rested on Elizabeth's shoulder while Mrs. Casey shifted my other leg over the rim of the tub.

"Too hot, too hot." I tried to jump out of the water. The message from my head short-circuited somewhere around my neck.

"It's cool water, child. It only feels hot. Lower your body," Mrs. Casey said. "We'll support your arms."

My butt hit the water first. The stinging there wasn't as bad as my feet. More padding. I would have giggled at my lame joke, but it took too much effort. Inch by inch I sank into the water until my keester hit the bottom of the tub. I pulled my knees to my chest and wrapped my arms around them. I held tight until the violent shaking lessened. Mrs. Casey added more hot water. I released the tension in my legs and let the water cover them. The shaking decreased to shivers. The housekeeper turned on the hot tap again. Gradually I slid under the water until I was up to my chin. Pinpricks of heat gave way to delicious warmth. Elizabeth went to get me a cup of tea.

Before I slipped into semi-consciousness, I heard Elizabeth and Richard outside the door.

"How the hell did she fall in the river?" Richard's angry voice carried through the wood. "Didn't you tell her about finding the body yesterday?"

"I warned her," Elizabeth said. "Whatever was she thinking? She doesn't strike me as one to visit a crime scene out of morbid curiosity. It was a good thing you heard the flood warning and went to check the river. Otherwise, we might have had another body to report. What do you think . . ."

Their voices trailed off, and I closed my eyes. I could have stayed there forever.

"Ian said half an hour should warm her, Mrs. Casey." Elizabeth patted my shoulder. "Jax, wake up. We need to get you out of the tub."

"Noooo. Warm. Wanna sleep."

"Doctor's orders, miss. Stand up."

I had no strength in the cooked noodles that substituted for my legs. I wobbled onto the bath mat where Elizabeth and the housekeeper used towels to scrub my skin until it turned pink. Fingers and toes continued to prickle where warm blood replaced the cold. They dressed me in a pair of Elizabeth's wool slacks and a sweater. I wasn't much help. My synapses weren't snapping, not in unison. Heavenly fuzzy socks warmed my feet. The two of them helped me downstairs to the kitchen where I sat in front of the stove, toes toasting on the open oven door, a mug of tea in my hands.

"That will warm your insides," the cook, Mrs. Gordon, said.

I wrapped my hands around the heavy crockery and sniffed. "No brandy?"

"Doctor Ian says that's an old wives' tale. It does the opposite it should to the blood vessels. Myself, I would've add some, but Miss Elizabeth—"

"Ian said regular hot tea." Elizabeth sat at the table sipping at her own cup, a pale rose pattern on porcelain so delicate it was almost transparent. "He wants you in his surgery later this afternoon," she said.

"Surgery?"

"Surgery, office, same meaning. No need to worry, he's being cautious." Elizabeth directed Mrs. Casey to place my boots on electric warmers. "I hope you'll be careful the next time you walk along the river."

"I will." Whatever I had left of my wits whispered I shouldn't reveal the whole truth. "My foot hit a muddy patch, and clumsy me, in I went." They were satisfied with my explanation.

More frost melted from around my memory cells. I remembered a shove to my back before I landed in the river. I wasn't hallucinating, I had felt two hands.

Who pushed me?

"Was it Richard who helped me out of the water?"

"We were worried the river would overflow its banks. If he'd gone out earlier or later, you might not be sitting here," Elizabeth said.

Where had she been when I took the plunge? The housekeeper? The other help? In light of their current hospitality, it would be impolite to interrogate them. I needed to use an indirect approach.

"How awful to have Dickie Campbell killed on your land. Who discovered the body?"

"Terrible, simply terrible." Elizabeth closed her eyes and shuddered. "I couldn't bring myself to walk out this morning."

"What do you think Dickie was doing over there, Elizabeth?"

"I have no idea. These days, some private landowners post no trespassing signs. My father never denied access to the locals. They weren't a nuisance." Elizabeth drained the last of her tea. Mrs. Gordon refilled her cup and mine. "Dickie and some of the others fish the Muckle when they tire of the saltwater fish from the lake. It's not unreasonable to assume he was on his way to a favorite spot."

My dad never fished in fast running water. What kind of fish would see bait in that brown muck? "Dickie did some odd jobs for you and Bea Kestle, didn't he?"

Elizabeth gave a rueful smile. "When the poor man remembered."

"Miss Elizabeth is too kind to say it straight." Mrs. Gordon patted her employer's shoulder with obvious affection. "Dickie would come to work when he pulled himself out of the whisky bottle. He was a special project of Mrs. Kestle's, too. She got him his job at the oyster farm. Sometimes she made extra work for him, I think. You did, too, Miss Elizabeth. Right kind it was of you both."

I hadn't received an answer that satisfied me, but when I looked at the kitchen clock, I set my tea aside. "Where has the time gone?" Much as I wanted to know who pushed me in the river, it would have to wait. "I have work to do before our drawings and plans arrive. I've intruded on your hospitality much too long."

A familiar knocking came at the back door. I'd recognize Blake's pounding anywhere.

The housekeeper went to retrieve my clothes from the washing machine. The cook answered the door. "Mr. Blake. Come in, come in."

Elizabeth and Blake exchanged friendly hugs. "Not that you aren't welcome, Blake, but what brings you to the back door?"

My, my, my. I stared in amazement. Blake's face was flushed red, and I didn't think it came from the cold outside. Why was he embarrassed?

"I, uh, no, uh, Annie, yes, Annie and Maude were worried about Jax. There's been so many accidents. And bodies, Maude said. She knew where Jax had gone hiking. I followed the trail. When I didn't see her, I came here."

"You're just in time," I said. "You can drive me back to my bike."

"And make sure she sees Ian." Elizabeth stepped aside when the housekeeper handed Blake a bag with my damp clothes inside. "Jax took a nasty spill in the river."

Blake's left eyebrow climbed to a record high. To avoid further explanations, I felt my boots. "Nearly dry. Thank you, Elizabeth. I'll return your clothes and jacket. Be sure to thank that man of yours. If he hadn't come when he did, I'd still be hanging from the bridge."

In the car, Blake said, "You didn't fall in, did you."

"I told Elizabeth I did."

"Bollocks. That's not what happened."

"Damn it, Blake, this has been the worst week of my life. Someone tried to blow me up, the police have accused me of murder, I spent the night in jail, and today someone tried to drown me. Who hates me that much?"

"If you're through feeling sorry for yourself, tell me what happened."

He didn't sound the least bit sympathetic.

So much for my pity party. "It's easier to show you."

"We'll do it tomorrow. We're going to Ian's first."

"I'm fine. I may never be warm again, but I'm fine. Turn here."

Blake drove to the spot where I'd left my bike. We followed the path until we arrived at the crime scene.

"What the Bloody Hell were you doing here? You shouldn't have crossed the police tape."

"It was already down. I was careful not to disturb anything. I wanted to see where Dickie was killed, to see if it was close to where I'd seen him the day Bea died. It was." I pointed to the low, sandy spot on the riverbank. "That's where he was, and this is where he was killed. Less than twenty paces apart."

Blake walked around the police tape.

"Wait." I grasped his arm and motioned toward the spot where I'd gone in the river. "Did you walk down there?"

"When you weren't here, I took the bridge."

"Where are your footprints?"

"I don't see any."

"Because there are none. Not here and not where I was walking. My sunglasses fell off before I was pushed in. You should be able to follow my footprints to the edge. The person who shoved me should've left prints. They're gone. All of them. Someone came back after you left for the manor." I crouched and examined the sand. "Look close. Here and here. See the brush marks."

I stood and found a downed pine branch. I used my boot to smooth out the prints we'd made and brushed over the plot with the branch.

"Compare this area to that. See? Effective as a broom. Less obvious, too."

Blake knelt by my side. "Not a single footprint. You're positive this is where you were standing?"

I walked to the exact spot. "Right here. There are my glasses." I bent over to pick them up and it triggered a memory. "I leaned over to examine something, and the next thing I knew, I was in the middle of the river. The bank's not muddy. I didn't slip, trip or fall. I felt hands in the middle of my back."

"Who?"

"The same person who killed Dickie?"

"I suppose that makes sense. Why? Before you were pushed, you were leaning forward. What were you looking at?"

"It happened so fast." I scanned the area to see if I had dropped the object. Nothing. For all I knew, I carried it into the water with me. It had stuck out of the sand. I scraped my boot across a patch, dug below the soft, top layer and rubbed against something. I knelt to pry out part of a shell.

"It doesn't look like an oyster shell." I held it out to Blake.

"Different shape. Smoother." He looked at the river. "A fresh water mussel. I didn't know the Muckle had any."

I continued to dig with my boot and found one more half shell. I worked my way to the edge of the clearing and brushed away dead leaves and pine needles. Blake did the same, but we failed to uncover more.

Why would someone push me in the river over a stupid shell? We returned to the car where Blake put my bike in the trunk.

"You're limping again. What happened to your ankle?"

"I must've hit it on something in the river. Damn, I've been limping the entire time I've been in Scotland."

On the short trip back to town, I transferred the shells from one hand to the other. It helped me think.

"Was Dickie poor? Poor enough to need the mussels for food?"

"No one in Heather Hill goes hungry."

Blake sounded offended I'd suggest such a thing.

"I didn't mean—"

"We're a small village, Jax, we take care of our own."

Jeesh! Who put a burr under his saddle?

"No one would have let Dickie go without food," he said. "Dickie fished the lake. He caught game. He had a job."

Another subject we couldn't discuss.

Back at my apartment, I changed into my own clothes and set aside Elizabeth's. I'd take them to a drycleaner on the way to buy another coat. My poor credit card. I tied my unruly hair into a ponytail, tucked my tablet under my arm, and hobbled down the hall, Hoolie close behind. Blake was getting better at reading my mind. The door was open. He pointed me toward his dial-up modem, brought me a cup of coffee, and looked over my shoulder.

I searched under fresh-water mussels. "The shells we found resemble the ones from the River Tay." I scrolled down. "The article doesn't say they are inedible. The mussels produce rare pink pearls. Oh, my God. Dickie wasn't eating the mussels, he wanted the pearls. Blake, Maggie has a pink pearl. She wore it the other night."

"I noticed."

I drank coffee to hide my frown. So what if Blake continued to have feelings for Maggie? All the more reason not to get too involved with him. I scanned the rest of the article. "Since the wild mussels are near extinction, it's illegal to take them. Dickie was poaching."

"Appears so. Print out the information. Poaching deserves a fine, not murder. And it doesn't explain why someone pushed you in the river." He reached under the desk and pulled the sheet of paper from the printer. "We should take this pearl business to Trask."

"What do you mean 'we'? I'm staying as far away from the police as I can."

"Good point. I'll call and find out where he is."

Before I could caution him to be careful what he said, he was on the phone.

"Charlie, we found something that may be important. Did you find any pink pearls in Dickie's belongings? Uh, huh. I'll explain when we get there."

I wanted to bang my head against the wall. "Again with the 'we'? You had to bring me into it?"

"He asked if you were with me."

"And it never entered your thick cranium to sidestep the question? What kind of lawyer are you?" The fickle finger of fate was definitely pointing at me. "I'm not going."

"It's too dangerous to leave you alone."

"I have Hoolie to protect me."

"He's not much of a deterrent. If someone wants to kill you, they'll kill him, too."

His logic won me over. "The constable won't be happy to see me."

"On the contrary, you're his suspect. He'll want to know where you've been."

"That's what I'm afraid of. He won't believe me when I tell him someone pushed me in the river."

"Best to get it on the record. Elizabeth can verify it."

"All she can say is that I was in the river and got wet." I sighed. "Where are we supposed to meet the good constable?"

"At Dickie's place." He looked at my ankle. "Get your cane. We can walk. It's not far."

"I'm bringing Hoolie."

"Of course. I assume your coat is at the bottom of the river. Take this jacket. I'm not using it."

I knew someone wanted me afraid and/or gone. I didn't say it out loud because I didn't want to test the "third time's the charm" theory. Putting the words out in the universe might make them come true.

CHAPTER THIRTY-TWO

B LAKE MOTIONED for Jax to catch up. She ignored him and took Hoolie for a walk around the church. Stubborn woman. And too damn curious for her own good. Why go to Dickie's crime scene? What did she expect to find that the police hadn't? Blake had panicked when she wasn't where Maude said she'd be. Sheer instinct sent him racing to the manor. Bloody good thing no one from the house could see the footbridge because he'd made a spectacle of himself racing over the span. Almost fell to his knees with relief when he saw Jax in Elizabeth's kitchen. She had looked bedraggled and . . . beautiful.

Too bad Annie and Maude hadn't missed her sooner. He could've stopped the bastard who tried to drown her. His anger resurfaced and warred with the need to protect. Damned if he'd let her out of his sight again.

Charlie Trask and one of his men stood in the doorway of Dickie's shack. He approached Blake, but kept an eye on Jax wandering near the caretaker shed. "What do you have for me, Blake?"

"Mussel shells." He handed them over and added the printout. "We found the shells near where Dickie's body was found."

"Shells? You and that woman? What were you doing at the crime scene?"

"Someone pushed Jax into the river this morning. She took me to the spot where it happened."

"I'd wager she fell in. That woman is an accident waiting to happen. There were no footprints, were there?"

"Mine should have been there. I'd gone looking for her, stood where she had, in the same spot, and mine were gone, too. Someone removed them. Brushed them out with a pine branch. I'm sure you found Dickie's killer did the same to the footprints around his body."

"Very clever thinking, Blake."

"I didn't figure it out, Jax did."

The amazed look on the constable's face was laughable, but Blake was serious.

"Someone is trying to kill her, Charlie."

"Impossible. No one has a motive." He turned toward the tool shed. "Why is that damn dog howling?"

Jax waved her arm. "Blake, Constable. I think you better come here."

When they arrived, they saw Hoolie pawing at a loose slat.

"He won't leave it alone." Jax struggled to pull the dog away.

Blake and Trask knelt to inspect the area.

The constable pulled on some gloves. "I'll do it." He tugged at the board until, with a screech of nails against wood, it gave way.

Hoolie continued to whine. Charlie used his flashlight and peered inside. He reached into the dark space.

"What have we here?" He removed a plastic bag and stood. "Well, well, well." He held up several bundles of bills wrapped in more plastic, a paper envelope, and a swatch of cloth. The constable handed the money and envelope to his sergeant and who unwrapped the material.

"Bloody Hell, it's a knife," Blake said.

"Bloody is right." Trask inspected the design of corgis. "With all these dogs in the pattern, it must be Bea Kestle's scarf. It's logical to guess it's her blood. Dickie's fingerprints could be on the knife, too, if he didn't wipe them off. How much money, Sergeant?"

"I reckon five thousand pounds."

The constable shook his head, his bloodhound sad eyes more pronounced than ever. "Dickie murdered Bea for her money."

"I don't think so," Jax said. "Bea befriended Dickie. Why would he kill her?"

"I know Bea never kept that much cash at hand," Blake argued.

"What if someone wanted it to look like Dickie killed her?" Jax pointed to the money, knife and bloody scarf. "Those could've been planted to frame him."

Trask snorted. "Another frame-up? Why would anyone frame Dickie? More likely, he knew she'd come back from a dog show. He might've read she was going to retire. He figured Bea sold some dogs or her kennel and received a down payment. He hid the money with the knife and scarf."

"What's in the envelope?" Blake asked.

The constable retrieved the packet from the other policeman. He shook the contents into his gloved palm. Seven large pink pearls.

"Fresh water mussel pearls. Those are huge." Jax's eyes were wide with wonder. "They're larger than the pink pearl Maggie has. If Dickie found someone who bought illegal pearls, it would explain the money. He was on the bank of the Muckle looking for more." She pointed to the pearls in the policeman's hand. "Dickie must not have had time to sell those."

"It's possible." Trask didn't sound convinced. "I'll send someone to see if Dickie did business with any of our known less than reputable jewelers." He aimed a stare at Hooligan then Jax. "How did you know to look in the shed?"

"I didn't. I was trying to stay out of your way. I mean, away from the investigation. Hoolie led me here." She knelt and hugged the whimpering dog. "He sniffed around until he came to this board. He smelled Bea's scarf with her blood on it."

"Humph! How can I write that into my report? I'll be laughed at from here to Glasgow."

"You could always claim it was 'an anonymous tip,' " Jax said. "Hoolie won't mind sharing the credit."

Her cell phone interrupted further questions.

Blake recognized the tinny tune. "*Scotland the Brave.*" Politically correct. Jax knew how to play all the angles.

"Yes, Chad," she said. "What do you mean, 'over your dead body'? No, don't do or say anything until I get there. I'm behind the church right now. Give me three minutes."

The moment Jax finished her conversation, Blake's cell chirped. He answered and said, "Calm down, Tilly. Not another word. I'm on my way."

"Trouble at the church?" Jax said.

"Why am I not surprised?"

Inside the church basement, Blake strode toward diminutive Tilly Markham, chief designer for SLFS. Tilly the Terrible, as people who'd incurred her wrath, called the blue-eyed blonde behind her back, glared at a man who stood talking to Rosalind Sweet. Jax and Hoolie crossed Tilly's line of fire toward the object of her anger. Blake assumed the red-faced, thirty-something in the Stetson hat shouting into a cell phone was Jax's associate from New York, Chad.

Shorter than Jax by two or three inches, the cowboy quieted when Jax tugged his elbow and turned him toward a corner. Blake couldn't see their expressions. The question of how well-acquainted they were concerned him for a moment. He assessed the man's physical attributes. Skinny. Cocky posture. Not Jax's type. The Texan was a business friend, he decided. Nothing else.

When Chad pointed at Tilly, Jax whispered something in his ear. She ignored Rosalind Sweet, who smiled at Blake.

Tilly tugged on his jacket. Blake gave her his full attention and walked her into a neutral corner. "Explain from the beginning."

The tiny blonde's cheeks reddened. "That-that *cowboy* insists Fairway Golf should set up their display at the entrance. Blake, it's the best location. *Our* plans should be the first thing people see when they walk in the door. Let the Americans have the rest of the room."

Blake was curious how Jax would handle the situation. She limped confidently toward them, Chad stomping behind her, Rosalind bringing up the rear. Hoolie sniffed Tilly's shoes, sat and looked up at her. She leaned over and stroked his head before he returned to sit by Jax.

After introductions were made, Jax said, "Chad tells me we have a stalemate over whose display will go where. Why don't we flip a coin for first choice?"

Blake admired how she took control. He pulled out a coin and followed her gracious lead. "You call it, Chad."

The coin tumbled in the air. Chad called heads, Jax snatched it before it hit the floor, and slapped it on the back of her arm. She showed it to Blake.

"It's heads," he said. Tilly's shoulders slumped.

"We'll take the far corner," Jax said.

"B-but," Tilly pointed at Chad, "he said you wanted the entrance."

"I changed our mind." She waved her walking stick at the equipment stacked inside the door. "Chad, let's move this gear closer to the kitchen counter."

Blake applauded her strategy. She was being gracious in victory and let Tilly have her way. At the same time, Fairway's display would be near where the tea and biscuits would be set out. Shrewd.

Jax said, "Here's your coin." She looked at the other side, handed it to him and winked before moving to the far corner.

Willpower alone kept him from laughing. She had looked to see if it was a two-headed coin.

It was late afternoon and dark when Blake and Tilly covered their display at the same time Jax and Chad covered theirs. Jax had given Rosalind the job of opening boxes. When she broke a nail, she complained loud enough for all to hear. She left to fix it, but not before simpering over to invite Blake for a drink later, which he declined. Jax and Chad's conversation was more interesting. He'd overheard the redhead exclaim that the artists had captured her ideas to perfection. Gamesmanship prohibited him asking for a preview showing. He'd wait for the unveiling in the morning.

Everyone gathered their coats and prepared to leave. Chad and Tilly seemed to have struck an uneasy truce. With a devilish gleam in her gray eyes, Jax said, "I'm hungry. Let's go to the pub for some dinner. Fairway Golf's treat. Chad, you've already met Hoolie and Blake, I want you to meet my other new friends."

Blake was absurdly pleased Jax thought of him as a friend, except she'd lumped him in with her dog. And he detected a plan behind her words. What crazy ideas were scrambling around in that unpredictable brain of hers?

CHAPTER THIRTY-THREE

BLAKE WALKED ME home from the pub, muttered that he'd had a long day, and left me at the stairway. He'd been in a bad mood all night. I took small comfort that I wasn't the only one he ignored. I'd had a full day and was too tired to analyze the cause of my landlord's sour mood. I fell into an exhausted sleep.

A pounding on the door penetrated my dreamless slumber.

"Wake up, Jax."

"Didn't anyone teach you how to knock on doors, instead of breaking them down?"

"I've been knocking for five minutes. You sleep like the dead." His gaze never strayed below my messy bed hair. "Get dressed. Charlie called. There's been a break-in at the church."

I jumped into some clothes and met Blake and Hoolie downstairs. We walked as fast as my ankle would allow and entered the brightly lit basement. Constable Trask met us at the door, cautioning us not to touch anything. I gagged on the smell of rotting garbage, gripped Blake's elbow for support, and surveyed the damage.

Someone had demolished the Fairway Golf display. Metal easels lay dismembered in the middle of the floor. They would never hold another show card or drawing. The noxious odor came from a slimy mess strewn over the papers that had once been artist drawings and blueprints.

"Of all the childish, stupid . . . all that work, gone." My immediate reaction of disbelief turned into anger.

Blake moved to inspect SLFS's display. "Nothing damaged here," he said.

Rosalind's perfume announced her arrival. Chad bumped into my back and peered over my shoulder. He exploded with a list of cuss words, some so inventive I believed he made them up. He stalked over to Blake.

"This is your fault." He poked Blake in the chest.

I was afraid my hot-tempered associate would take a swing at him. Blake held up his hands in surrender.

Brave Tilly stepped between them. "SLFS had nothing to do with this-this outrage."

"The proof is on the wall." Chad pointed to the fluorescent red spray-painted graffiti on the whitewashed bricks.

FAIRWAY GOLF, GO HOME and SLFS FOREVER stood out in glaring red paint."

"SLFS doesn't resort to tactics like these," Blake said.

I pulled Hoolie away from the garbage heap he was sniffing and studied the writing.

"Blake's right. It's supposed to look as if SLFS destroyed our chances, but it's too perfect. Too staged. SFLS is being framed. There's a lot of that going around."

Trask observed our reactions. "I read the scene the same as Miss Hollister," he said to Blake. "That color paint should be easy to trace if it was bought locally." He turned to the crime scene crew. "Photograph everything, fingerprint the doors, and then, wrap things up."

"Why would the killer want to frame SLFS?" I said.

"You think the murderer did this?" The constable shook his head. "No, it has to be some kids. Vandalism, nothing more." His cell rang. "Shots fired?" Then, "Right. On my way." He rang off and pocketed the phone. "A shooting in Fort William," he said to Blake. "Full moon. Busy times." He hurried away.

"What do you mean the killer did this?" Chad asked. "What killer?"

Blake and I explained the events of the last few days.

Tilly motioned to the stinking pile of debris in the middle of the room. "What do the murders have to do with this mayhem?"

"I'm convinced it all ties to the sale of Coulter Manor," I said. "Trask disagrees. The common denominator in the vandalism and the killings is the estate. We need to look at this," I swept an arm in the direction of the heap, "from another angle. Who gains by the destruction of Fairway Golf's plans? What's the end result?"

"SLFS wins the sale." Chad glowered at Tilly. "We can't compete in the final phase without a display."

"I don't think it was meant to knock us out of the competition. Whoever did this must've known we'd send for back-up plans."

Rosalind held a lace handkerchief to her nose. "I'll call Mr. Atkins."

"It's too early. No sense waking him," I said. "I'll call later. Go back to the hotel and get some sleep. You, too, Chad."

"I'll stay." He found a chair for me. Blake set one up for Tilly.

Bone weary and dispirited, I sagged into the seat and waited for the crime scene unit to finish. I sorted through other motives for the vandalism. "Who benefits from a delay in the sale? Elizabeth?"

Blake shook his head. "She told me they have a construction loan due next month on their new house. They need the sale to proceed. Elizabeth isn't unreasonable. She'll grant you a few days."

"Who else would want to slow things down?" Chad asked.

"Good question. Someone with a secret agenda?" I remembered my conversation with Niles Gordon. "Someone who doesn't want to lose their job at the manor house before they find another? Blake, you know the staff, don't you?"

"Most of them. It's worth looking into. I'll talk to Elizabeth."

I stared at the shredded papers. "Chad, tomorrow, when the stores open, you'll have to locate some easels in Fort William or Oban. And it might be a good idea if *you* left Mr. Atkins a voice mail message. He's heard enough bad news from me."

The rumpled Texan, minus his customary Stetson, patted down his pockets. "Damn. Left my cell in the hotel."

I handed him mine. Blake was already talking on his. Tilly pulled hers from a pocket and punched in some numbers. They finished their conversations at the same time.

Tilly looked from Chad to me. "I called my brother in Oban. He's in construction. He'll send a crew over to repaint the walls."

Blake said. "My janitor service is on the way to clean up."

I thanked them for their quick thinking and generosity. Moments later, the CSI guys left and half the town poured through the doors.

Maggie rushed to my side. "We heard the sirens and saw the police." She tried for the innocent-maiden look, but her flushed face, swollen lips, and rumpled clothes gave her away. When Ian arrived moments later, smoothing his hair and adjusting his coat collar, his expression left no doubt that Maggie had received her good night kiss. Neither could take their eyes off the other.

I was glad someone was having a nice time.

The crowd gathered around the remnants of Fairway Golf's exhibit. I searched each face for some sign of glee at my company's misfortune. Instead, I saw expressions of shock and dismay.

Maude opened the back door. "A cross-draft will help clear the smell. It's a cruel prank."

Annie motioned me away from the crowd. "Speaking of pranks, this might not be the best time, but I've had a note from my grandson, Bobby. He apologizes to you for the furnace and electricity. 'Twas as I guessed. He wanted Blake's approval and his friends pushed him into it. I'm right sorry."

"No need to apologize, Annie. You didn't do anything."

"He was living under my roof. He was in my care. He'll repay Blake for the damages."

"His apology might be a good sign. I hope it means he's turning over a new leaf."

Annie's plump body straightened. "You think so?"

"Yes, I do." I gave her a reassuring hug. Maggie's actions caught my attention. She bent over the pile of garbage and used two fingers to pull out a fragment of paper.

"We might be able to save some of these drawings." She shook coffee grounds off one corner. "This looks like a crazy golf course."

"Your plans include one of those garish American miniature golf parks?" Blake sounded appalled.

I took the paper from Maggie, flicked off some green thing I didn't want to identify and held it in front of Blake's face. "I don't do garish."

He pointed. "What's that? A pirate ship?"

"It's supposed to be the 'Hispaniola,' in miniature of course. It's anchored in a little lagoon. And this is the stockade."

"Ben Gunn's cave?" Blake's eyebrows were doing their reaching-for-the-sky act again. "Skeleton Island?"

"It's a *Treasure Island* theme, isn't it?" Maggie grinned. "What fun."

"So much for keeping that a surprise," I said. "There should be enough room for it on the front lawn, if we incorporate some of the trees along the road. I suggested Fairway Golf open it to the public during the summer time."

The townspeople, as a unit, swung their gazes toward Blake to watch his reaction. I was more interested in the local response. To judge by the pleased expressions on nearly every face, my special part of the project met their approval.

"It's an interesting concept," Blake said, no emotion in his voice.

Faint praise. Could he be trying to hide a wee smile? Very wee.

The paper, upon closer inspection, was worthless. Smeared ink and goop hid many of the details. I dropped it on the pile and dug a tissue from my pocket to wipe my fingers. "Nothing can be salvaged, Maggie, thanks for trying."

With a clatter of buckets and mops, Blake's clean-up crew swept into the room. The crowd filtered out the door, back to their beds for a few more winks until it was time to start the day.

"Come to the pub," Maggie said. "Sean will fix breakfast."

"Thanks for the offer, but I'm not hungry. I need sleep more than food."

"I'll walk you back," Blake said.

Outside, the moon had retreated, leaving the pre-dawn stars to light our way. I filled my lungs with the crisp fresh air, but was too emotionally wrung-out to be invigorated. I burrowed into Blake's jacket and longed for my bed. As usual, Blake had nothing to say. I was used to his silence, but not the nearness. His hand on my shoulder burned through the layers of cloth. Some claim chemistry is what sparks the attraction between male and female. For me, it's thermal.

Halfway back to Blake's building we waited while Hoolie prepared to do what male dogs do. Instead of lifting his leg, he lifted his head, stared at the shrubs and growled. A figure stepped out of the shadows.

"Richard," Blake said, "what are you doing here?"

"I must insist you and Miss Hollister accompany me to the manor."

Ambient starlight glinted off the revolver aimed at Blake's chest.

CHAPTER THIRTY-FOUR

"LEAVE THE DOG," Richard commanded.

"Never," I said.

"Stop worrying. Someone will find him."

"Won't that look suspicious?" I asked. "Everyone knows Hoolie and I are inseparable." Why was I trying to reason with someone who had a gun pointed at us?

Richard glanced over his shoulder. "Keep your voice down. Bring your damn dog. Any funny moves, I'll kill him."

Fear for the three of us threatened to give me the screaming jee-bees. I shoved down the futile instinct to run. I had to stay alert for a chance, any chance to shift the balance of power, to neutralize his gun so we could escape.

"Start walking." Richard directed us up the hill.

"Let Jax go," Blake said. "We can't all fit in your Austin Healy."

But when we turned the corner, Richard pointed toward a sedan.

"Elizabeth took my car into Edinburgh yesterday. She's staying with a girlfriend for a day or two. Stupid wedding plans. Blake, before you open the door, take out your cell phone."

Blake reached in his pocket.

"Use two fingers. That's right. Drop it and step on it."

Richard kicked the pieces into the gutter.

"Give me yours, Miss Hollister."

"I gave mine to my associate."

"So you did. Blake, you drive. Miss Hollister and I will sit in back."

Hoolie refused to jump in the car. He'd never done that before. He enjoyed riding in Blake's car. The fur on his back stood on end and he growled.

"Get him in the car or leave him," Richard said.

I tossed my cane into the backseat and picked up Hoolie. We sat as far to one side as possible. A familiar trace of perfume hung in the air. Rosalind had been in the car. If I got out of this alive, I had a lot of questions for her.

"No sudden stops or swerves, Blake. I'd hate to shoot Miss Hollister. Blood is so difficult to remove from upholstery."

My dog shivered. He must've sensed the man with the gun had evil intentions. I hugged him and he quieted.

"Why kidnap us?" Blake said

"None of your business."

"Your gun makes it my business."

I prayed Blake wouldn't antagonize Richard further. To switch attention to me I said, "So far, you've done nothing wrong. Let us go, now, and we won't press charges."

"It's too late for that, Miss Hollister. I have plans for you."

"We'll be missed by Blake's friends, my boss. The police will search for us."

"I'm not worried about Trask and his minions. Such an incompetent. It'll be a few days before he misses you." Richard's teeth gleamed in a malevolent smile. "As for your friends, a rumor dropped in the pub and anyone who notices will think you two are off on a lovers' holiday until New York sends your replacement drawings."

Blake looked in the rearview mirror. "You were listening—"

". . . at the back door of the church." Richard turned the gun in Blake's direction. "I had to know the results of my handiwork. Clever, Miss Hollister, to see through my attempt to turn suspicion on SLFS. I would have planned better, if I'd had more time. When my ruse failed, I had to improvise an alternative way to slow the sale process. With the top two bidders out of the way, I'll have the time I need. Speed up, Blake. Don't spare the petrol."

Another stuffy Brit! If we weren't up to our knees in alligators, I would've laughed at his pomposity. At the moment, anxiety threatened to freeze my funny bone. Whatever Richard's motive for kidnapping us, I realized he'd confessed too much to let us live.

"Turn off the headlamps when you pull into the drive. Don't want to alert the help, you know. Park at the side entrance so Mrs. Casey can't see us from her cottage."

Richard backed out of the car, careful to shift his aim from Blake to me.

"Open your door, Blake. Careful, Miss Hollister, slide over the seat and follow me. Keep that damn dog quiet."

We did as instructed and entered the mansion through a side door. Richard directed us down a dimly lit hallway until we came to the study. Hoolie refused to enter the room. I gave Blake my cane and tugged on his leash.

Richard cursed. "You should've left him behind."

He aimed a kick at Hoolie's head. Blake stepped between Richard's foot and my dog. Richard's shoe plowed into Blake's shin. He hobbled back, and despite the pain etched on his face, took a swing at Richard with my walking stick. He stopped when Richard turned the gun on me.

"Get inside and keep quiet."

We walked into the study. Once inside, Hoolie tugged his leash out of my hand. He ignored Richard, sniffed, and growled at chairs and bookcases until he crouched in front of the fireplace. My dog's eyes continued to search the room.

A lamp glowed on an end table. With the drapes closed, no one could see inside. Richard locked the door behind us and flicked on the overhead light.

Blake returned my cane with a meaningful look. I nodded, silently agreeing to use it when I had the chance. At present, the urge to bash Richard's smirk off his face was overwhelming. Instead, I leaned heavily on the stick and pretended to be more crippled than I was.

Think. Stall for time until we can find a way to escape. "Why did you push me in the river?"

Richard's jaw dropped with surprise. "A gentleman would never do such a thing."

"I suppose it's okay for a gentleman to kidnap us? I bet you had something to do with all the recent murders."

"Wait a minute, young lady. I didn't kill anyone. Not Bea Kestle. So common. And certainly not that drunk, Campbell."

I believed Richard hadn't killed Bea. Hooligan would've torn him to pieces. "You didn't mention Raul? You were at breakfast with him that morning."

"That fool. What a glutton. He had seconds on the haggis. When he excused himself from the table, I followed him into the study. He was staggering and reaching for his EpiPen."

"And you must have kept Montoya from using his antidote," Blake said. "At the very least it's depraved indifference. You might as well have shot him.

"Blake, Blake, Blake." Richard wagged his head and chided Blake as if he were a child. "I hear he had an allergic reaction to the haggis. Why would the police suspect me?"

"The EpiPen," I said. "The police have it."

"I hear Ian found it in your bag and the police think you took it from Montoya's body, not me."

Parts of the puzzle snapped into place.

"In the pub, when you knocked my purse off the chair, that's when you put it in there. You planned to set me up."

"It would've worked, but you got out of jail too soon." A frown replaced his self-satisfied smile. "If the police had kept you longer, the sale would have been delayed until your employer could send someone else. How unfortunate for me you had a rich boss who was willing to post your bail. This time with you *both* out of the way, I'll have plenty of time."

"Time for what?" I asked.

His exasperated expression told me I was trying his patience. He gestured at the bookshelves. "It's time-consuming looking through these books."

Blake picked one off the table, checked the title, and chuckled. "Don't tell me you're looking for William Wallace's dirk? The gardener told me you've been digging up the estate. It's a legend, *old man.*"

"What legend?" I said.

Richard's temper flared. "It is not a legend. The dagger exists. I found evidence." For a moment, pride overshadowed the cold calculation in his eyes. "The location is recorded in one of these books."

"I can't believe you'd go to such lengths to find a stupid dagger," I said.

Blake shook his head. "It won't matter if you find it or not. You'll never be able to sell it."

"Yes, I will. I planned ahead, you see. I've already found a potential buyer for the dirk on the Internet. I'll have enough money to purchase a new identity and live abroad for the rest of my life."

"Third world non-extradition countries aren't known for their luxuries." Blake shifted his weight to the balls of his feet.

"Wrong, old boy. Only you and Miss Hollister can tie me to Montoya's death. The police won't be searching for me."

In all the movies and books, when the killer confesses, he doesn't leave anyone to retell the tale. Richard's plans for us were clear.

"All hell will break loose when the police find my body," I said. "The U.S. doesn't take kindly to one of their citizens turning up dead."

"Not to worry, Miss Hollister. I'll call from the airport before I leave the country and tell the police where you are. You'll be dehydrated, that's all."

I didn't believe him.

"Does Elizabeth know what you're doing?"

"She's been helping me go through the books. I'm closer to finding the dirk than her father ever was."

"What makes you think she'll agree to leave the country with you?"

"She'll want to come, of course. She loves me."

Blake and I exchanged another pay-attention glance. I pointed to the partially-filled boxes on the floor. "If you're going to leave the country, why pack up the books?"

Richard looked at them, as I hoped he would. Blake stepped forward and launched a punch.

Richard dodged. Blake's fist grazed the shorter man's jaw.

Quicker than a blink, Richard backhanded Blake. The gun connected to skin and bone, with a sickening sound. Blake fell to his knees.

I hefted the stick like a baseball bat.

"Don't do it, Miss Hollister. I'll kill him."

"A gunshot would wake the household. You don't want to do that." Logic seldom works with someone who has a screw loose.

"Do you want to take that chance, Miss Hollister?"

I lowered my cane. At that moment, the thought of Richard killing Blake crystalized my emotions.

I had "feelings" for Blake Ramsey.

Of all the times to figure that out.

Blake staggered to his feet, and I helped him to a chair. His jaw muscles bunched. I hoped he was gritting his teeth at the situation, not because he was in pain.

"I thought we had him."

"Me, too." I tossed my staff on the couch and found another tissue in my pocket. I wiped up the blood oozing from the nasty welt on Blake's cheekbone.

"As an expert on bruises, I'd say this one will be a beaut by morning." I smiled to show Blake I wasn't giving up. I shifted my attention to Richard and played for more time. "Why did you kill Philip LeBeck?"

"Never said I did. He had a hiking accident. I don't climb mountains for entertainment. Stop stalling." He sidestepped to the cartons, picked up a roll of strapping tape, and tossed it to me. "Blake, hands behind your back. You, tie him up."

I did as I was told.

"Tighter," Richard snapped. "Tear off the roll and hand it here." He lay the gun on a table within reach. "You next, Miss Hollister. Turn around."

I tried to keep my hands apart for some give, but he used several turns of the tape to secure them.

"Over by the fireplace." Richard pointed the gun at us, walked to the opposite side of the mantel, and felt around on the second shelf. He removed a book and took out a remote control. He pushed a button. At this point in a movie, an entire section of wall would swivel to reveal a dark hole.

Life imitated art. The bookcase rolled outward.

Hoolie investigated the opening before I could stop him.

"Follow your dog, Miss Hollister. You too, Blake."

A memory clicked into place. "The morning Raul died, the study door was locked from the inside. You were in here with Montoya."

Blake's expression changed when he reached the same conclusion I had. "How did you get out?"

Richard gestured toward the other side of the fireplace. "Through the wood box. It loads from outside. I went into the cave and took the remote with me. I waited until the help had gone about their business, re-opened the wall, crawled through the wood box to the outside, and drove into town. No one saw me leave. The locked door should have confused the police. You can imagine how unhappy I was when Trask missed that detail."

A knock sounded at the door. "Mr. Richard? Are you in there?"

He pointed his gun at Blake's temple and motioned us to keep quiet. "Yes, Mrs. Casey. I couldn't sleep. I'm crating books. It'll save Elizabeth some work. I'll be ready for breakfast in an hour."

"Yes, sir."

Richard waited until the sound of the housekeeper's footsteps faded in the distance. He appeared visibly shaken by the interruption, then his expression tightened with resolve. "Get in there." He waved the gun toward the dark hole.

I hobbled toward the opening, pretending more pain in my ankle than I actually felt. "My cane?" I wasn't sure what I'd do with it, but I wanted it.

"Of course." Richard shoved the remote in his pocket, picked up my walking stick, and lobbed it into the darkness. "Don't want to leave any evidence around."

Damn, I hadn't considered that.

Hoolie whined from inside the dark cavern. He knew something was wrong or felt my panic. I dreaded being locked in a cave that looked too much like a crypt.

"Move," Richard said.

I limped past the entrance, into the gloom, and turned to face the light.

Blake resisted. Richard shoved him inside. The wall slid into place.

CHAPTER THIRTY-FIVE

WHEN THE LIGHT completely disappeared, I leaned against Blake. "This is my fault. If you hadn't been with me . . ."

"You didn't get us into this fix. Richard's obsession with that damn dagger put us here."

Claustrophobic darkness pressed down on every part of my body except where my back touched Blake. I held my terror at bay and told him to turn around. "Back to back. I left a corner flap of tape turned under."

Blake's hands found mine. I fumbled to find the tab, but Blake's arms were shaking.

"Hold still."

He burst out laughing.

I stopped groping. "What's so damn funny?"

"You are," he said. "Not funny. Clever. To think of a way to get our hands free. Jax Hollister, you are a marvel."

A marvel? A declaration of undying love would have been nicer. I liked the undying part.

Love? Where had that crazy idea come from? Blake and I? Never happen. He was handsome. I liked him, but not in that way. Did I? No, we were business acquaintances and competitors, nothing more.

I concentrated on finding the turned-under corner. "Here it is." I pulled the tab to the side. "Hold your hands away from your body." I had to bend my knees, work my hands under Blake's hands, and twist the tape toward the top again. "Awkward. Not as easy to unwind as I imagined it would be. Backwards, upside down . . . ah! Got it."

He sighed. "Feels good to get the circulation going again."

"Now do mine." I felt Blake move in front of me. "No, no. My hands are behind my back."

"I know."

He fumbled for my face, traced my lips with a finger, and tilted my chin. His mouth sought mine.

A lava flow of heat stretched from head to toe. Good God, what a kiss!

I pulled away, my lips tingling. "This is not a good idea, Blake."

"We aren't going anywhere. I've been wanting to do that for some time. One more."

"This is not ration—" I couldn't finish. My tongue became otherwise engaged. Blake wrapped his arms around me, pulled me close against his hard chest. A groan rumbled deep within his body. He feathered light kisses along my jaw. When he nipped my earlobe, I exploded. That wonderful heat shot to a thousand different locations. My knees turned to jelly.

"Blake." I moaned, the sound echoing off the stones.

"Bloody Hell, we've got to get out of here and find a bed."

"Unless you're into bondage, undo my hands. I can help find a way out of here."

"Did you see this place? It's solid rock. There is no way out."

"Undo my hands anyway."

With considerable fumbling, Blake found the end of the tape. When my hands were free, I rubbed my wrists to get the blood flowing again. "Where's Hoolie?"

"I can't see him. I can't see a damn thing."

"If I lean down and tap the floor, he'll feel the vibration. He'll come to me. He likes to give me kisses."

"He's not the only one."

"I heard that. Oh, there you are, Hoolie. Such a nice boy." I stroked his head and looped his leash around my wrist.

Blake reached for me, and we held each other, a solid unit against the oppressive dark. Eons of cold poured from the rocks I couldn't see. Ice seeped into my bones. I shivered, more from the image of boulders crushing me than the chill of the enclosed space. Buried alive.

"Cold?"

A lump of horror made it difficult to swallow. Words were impossible. All I could manage was a nod, which was nonsensical. Blake couldn't see me. He hugged me close, but his warmth did nothing to assuage my fear. I widened my eyes to help them adjust to the dark. It was useless. There was nothing to focus on. When I closed my eyes, the dizziness eased.

An idea nibbled through my numbing fright. "Richard locked us in here thinking we couldn't escape. Let's hope he was wrong. If this is part of the original structure built back in the fifteenth century, there might be a way out."

"I don't follow."

I recited page two-hundred-fifty-seven of my college English History text. "'To escape from English soldiers, tunnels were hidden behind false walls, often extending for miles underground.'"

Blake's silence demanded an explanation. "Photographic memory, remember?" I said. "If I understood the data, tests were easy. Anyway, as old as this part of the house is, this hidey hole might be a priest's hole that will lead to an escape tunnel. Let's look for another exit."

"Richard wouldn't lock us in here if we could get out."

"He's into archeology, not history. Maybe he didn't know."

"Elizabeth would've said something."

"Not if she didn't know the tunnel was here."

"That's a lot of maybes and ifs," Blake said. "Which way is the exit?"

"Seems logical it would be the rear wall, wherever that is. Damn, I'm turned around. We need to find the way we came in and walk in the opposite direction." I walked forward a few steps, stumbled over something and pitched forward to my knees, hitting my head on wood.

"Jax, what happened?"

"Klutzy me, I tripped over my cane and hit the back of the book-case. A clumsy way to find the way we came in."

"You're not clumsy. Anyone would have taken a spill in this dark. At least we know which direction not to go."

I stood and stuck out the stick in the direction of his voice. "Take my cane and hold it in front of you until it hits the back wall. I'll hang onto your waistband and Hoolie."

Four short steps and the stick knocked against rock. "I found it. Not much space to hide," Blake grumped.

Memories of reading Edgar Allen Poe surfaced. Walled in alive scared me to death as a teenager. Fifteen years hadn't lessened the fear. "If there is a secret exit to an escape tunnel, I think the builders would hide it by carving it out of the surrounding stone. You take your side of the end wall, I'll do the other. Feel for a seam or a rock that moves."

Long, silent minutes passed. Nervous sweat dripped from my fore-head in spite of the cold. There had to be a way out. I poked and pried along a corner where the end wall met the side. From top to bottom. Nothing.

Before I could start on the next line of rocks, Blake said, "I'll be damned. I found it. Stand back."

A grumble and scraping of rock against rock broke the unnatural quiet. The entire wall slowly swiveled inward. Blake found my hand and moved forward.

"Ow. Bollocks!"

"What happened? Why did you stop?"

"Because I hit my head on the top ledge of the opening."

"Remember, men were shorter in those days. Hold the cane over your head to gauge how high the ceiling is. Please tell me this is a beginning of a tunnel."

Blake led me around the edge of the stone door and stepped forward. Wood rapped on stone. "The ceiling is a few inches taller than I am. The sides are little more than an arm-span wide."

"You described a tunnel. Now what are you doing?"

"I'm going to find the closing mechanism. It was a small rock that sprung the release. Aha." The stones grated against each other when the wall closed. "In case Richard looks for us. We'll be gone, but he won't know how we got out. He won't be able to follow us. Get behind me and hold on. I'll take Hoolie and let him lead the way."

My eyes strained for focus. "It's black as pitch."

I'd hope for, yes, you guessed it, a light at the end of the tunnel.

Unsure of our footing, we shuffled forward.

"Careful," Blake said. "The ground slopes down."

"We're going underground?" We could be walking to a dead end. Fear got another stranglehold. No way out. Sealed in, tons of dirt and stone overhead, waiting to crush us. In my imagination, Edgar Allen Poe rubbed his hands and chortled with glee.

"This has to lead somewhere. We're going to get out." Blake's confidence was reassuring.

"Right. Think positive." Like a mantra, I mentally repeated my wish for escape. The sound of our footsteps, my breathing, and the clicking of Hoolie's nails on the stone floor was supernaturally loud.

"Shit!" Blake said.

"What's the matter?"

"Cobwebs. Ugh."

I giggled.

"It's not funny, Hollister. I walked right into them."

"Cobwebs spook men. That's why they use them in horror movies. Women think it's a sign of sloppy housekeeping."

"That gives me *so* much comfort. Keep talking."

I could take a hint. A moment of silence passed.

Blake cleared his throat. "No, I'm serious, keep talking."

I should've wanted to talk about our shared kiss, but I needed time to sort through my emotions. Instead, I asked, "Did you believe Richard when he said he didn't kill Bea? Or Dickie?"

I felt Blake shrug. "Can we believe anything Richard said?"

"Good point. My instinct says he didn't kill Bea. Hoolie didn't attack him. Bea's murderer is still out there."

"At least we discovered how the pen got in your purse. When we get out of here, Trask will arrest Richard and have to drop the charges against you."

"And Mr. Atkins will get his money back." We continued our shuffling walk in silence for a moment or two. "What's Hoolie doing?"

"Tugging on his leash, leading the way. He acts like he knows where he's going. Do you suppose he smells fresh air?"

"I hope so. This place stinks of damp and—" I yelped and bumped into Blake's back.

He stopped. "What's the matter?"

I buried my face between Blake's solid shoulders and dug my fingernails into his belt.

"Where's Hoolie?"

"In front of me. Why?"

"Something furry brushed against my ankle."

"Probably a rat."

Hoolie growled. A high-pitched screech sounded from in front of Blake.

"He got it. You okay?"

"Great." I shuddered and pushed at Blake's back to keep moving. "How did it get in here?"

"Good question. At least we won't starve."

"Ick."

"And we shouldn't run out of air."

"We could die of thirst." Immediately, my mouth felt like the Sahara. We must've walked a mile when Blake cussed again.

"What?"

"The wall turned," he said. "I missed it and barked my shin on something."

"No barking allowed. Hoolie has that covered."

"Not funny. There's a wooden barricade in front of a gap in the wall."

"Is it a side tunnel? Should we try it?"

"Your dog wants to go straight."

We eased forward, afraid of stumbling and falling. We couldn't afford an injury if we were going to get out of here. No, not if, when.

A pull in the back of my calves caught my attention. Were we going uphill? Wishful thinking? No, the ground definitely sloped upward.

My nose plowed into Blake's back. "Why did you stop?"

"Hoolie stopped. I can feel rocks in front of me. Loose rubble."

My worst fears had come true. It was a dead end. I sucked air, ready to vent my frustration with a scream when I noticed . . . "What's that sound?"

"Hoolie's digging at the stones. He must smell fresh air. Stand by my side and help me clear these rocks."

We stood shoulder to shoulder, removed stones, and tossed them behind us.

"No mortar between the rocks," he said. "A landslide?"

"Or someone walled up the exit?" We tugged at the rocks. A pin-prick of daylight appeared in front of me, illuminating a wall of boulders blocking a narrow opening.

"Take out the ones up high so they don't fall on us," Blake instructed.

One by one, my fingernails broke, but I continued to drag away the smaller stones. Fresh air and light poured through the opening. Hot damn! We'd found an exit. One large boulder blocked our escape. Blake braced his feet against the wall and put his shoulder to it.

He grunted. "I can't get an angle. I need leverage."

"My stick."

"I tossed it aside. There, to your left."

I picked it up and handed it to him.

Wood scraped against the edge of stone. "Get Hoolie out of the way. Stand behind me."

Blake leaned into the wooden staff, gently at first. When it didn't break, he applied more pressure.

The gap of light widened. "It's moving, it's moving." I whispered, afraid to speak louder for fear I would jinx it. "Come on, rock, pop out of there."

It didn't exactly pop, but out it came. I shouted with relief, jumped up and down, and pounded Blake on the back. "You did it, you did it."

"We're not out of here yet. The opening is too narrow for either of us to climb through."

"The rocks at the top are smaller. We can move those and work our way down."

We cleared a hole big enough to crawl through. Gray sky and damp air never looked or felt so good.

Hoolie scrambled over the rocks, looked outside and whined.

"Why doesn't he go on through?" I asked.

"Take his leash. I'll look."

Blake found a finger-hold, used his upper body strength to pull himself up and halfway through. An eternity passed before I heard another sound.

"I know this place." Blake's words drifted over his shoulder. "Come on up."

"The opening isn't big enough for all three of us. You go on through and take Hoolie with you."

Blake eased around until he was facing me. I handed him Hoolie. They squirmed backward through the opening, hesitated, then dropped out of sight.

His voice filtered back. "Come on. Be prepared for a bit of a drop."

"How much is a 'bit'?" I scrambled up and over the jumble of rocks and looked through the opening. Four or five feet to the ground looked like fifty. Immobilized, I searched for another way. No such luck. Hoolie barked his encouragement.

"I don't want to land head first."

"Turn around. Twist your legs until they point outside like I did. Hang on to the rocks until you're all the way through, then let go."

It wasn't an easy maneuver, but if a man of Blake's height and broad shoulders could do it, so could I. Rocks scraped my knees through my jeans. After I turned around and faced the way I had come, I inched backward until my legs and behind dangled into nothingness. Cold rain found the gap between my jeans and sweater and pounded the small of my back. I hung from the edge of the opening by raw fingertips, feet searching for a toehold to take some of my weight.

What the hell. After everything I'd been through, what was a little fall?

I turned my face skyward and said a prayer.

"Let go," Blake shouted. "Bend your knees when you hit the ground. It's not that far."

Ha! To someone afraid of heights, there is no such thing as 'not far.' Hoolie barked again. The scene from *Butch Cassidy and the Sundance Kid* flashed before my eyes. The one where Redford says he can't swim and Newman replies not to worry, the fall will most likely kill them. Yes, that one.

Since I didn't want Hoolie to think I was a coward, I let go.

In similar situations, people say their whole life flashes in front of their eyes. They're wrong.

No matter how young you are, there's not enough time.

Miraculously, I survived.

I tested my arms and legs. No pain. I'd taken the fall like a pro. What an adrenalin rush. "Where are we?"

"That shed over there is my Uncle Roland's workshop and where he stored his tools. After we repaired fences or some other chore, we'd go there and clean up. We're on the back of Aunt Cora's property."

"You never found this cave or the tunnel?"

"Judging by the amount of brush hiding it, I'd say the mouth of the tunnel was filled in decades ago."

"Or centuries." I turned in a circle, trying to orient myself. "Where's the Coulter house?"

"On a diagonal line, through those trees. Come on, we'll ring up the police from my aunt's house."

"I left the walking stick behind."

"You're not limping. You don't need it."

Moments later, I stood under the eaves of the farmhouse. Blake removed a key from a fake rock by the back porch step.

"Isn't it a conflict of interest, your aunt owning the property next to the property you're bidding on?"

"I don't see it that way." He opened the door. "In a village this size, it's difficult to avoid a conflict of interest. Besides, it doesn't matter to Aunt Cora who buys it. There are over five acres between her place and the estate with a line of trees for a buffer. She won't sell her land to SLFS or anyone else."

"Won't you inherit this someday?"

"She's said she'd will it to me if I married and passed it on to my children. Better get towels before Hoolie muddies her kitchen."

CHAPTER THIRTY-SIX

WHEN THE COPS arrived, they allowed us to change clothes before the trip to Fort William where we'd make our statements. I'd asked Annie to keep Hooligan and located Chad to retrieve my cell phone. He'd been busy rounding up items for the replacement display and hadn't noticed I was missing.

"My God, Jax. Heather Hill is supposed to be a quiet village, not a hotbed of kidnappers and killers."

"The police arrested Richard Hyde, Elizabeth Coulter's fiancé, for the kidnapping and the murders. I'm convinced he's guilty of killing Raul Montoya. The other murders? I think there's another killer out there. Be careful."

"I will, and I'll call headquarters to report what happened. Oh, the duplicate set of drawings should arrive in a couple of hours."

After I spoke to Chad, the police escorted Blake and me to the same police station where I had spent a night at their expense. Constable Trask's attitude toward me had changed. During the interview, he was not quite apologetic, but he was polite. And he fairly radiated pleasure. All the murders were solved. I hated to burst his bubble of happiness.

"Constable, I don't think Richard killed Bea. Is there any evidence to prove he did? Are his fingerprints on the knife you found?"

"Wiped clean."

His two and two didn't equal my four. "What possible motive could Richard have for killing Bea? And how did the murder weapon get in Dickie Campbell's shed?"

"Miss Hollister, I don't expect you to understand police work. The evidence is circumstantial. Hyde's motive for killing Mrs. Kestle is the same motive for kidnapping you and Blake. Delay the sale until he could find Wallace's dagger."

"But Hooligan didn't attack Richard. If that man killed Bea, I'm positive he would have."

Trask drummed the table with square, blunt fingers. "He's a dog, Miss Hollister. How he reacts or doesn't can't be considered evidence. It's early days. After a few nights in the nick, Hyde will confess. I'm sending the investigative unit to Mrs. Kestle's again this afternoon. We'll find enough evidence to convict him for her murder, Campbell's, too. Thanks to you two, we have him for Mr. Montoya's death. He claims the man was dead when he removed the pen. He had no answer for why he took it. It's murder, plain and simple. Blake, I have your statements. You and Miss Hollister are free to leave."

In the foyer, the interior lights switched on and brightened the afternoon gloom. We walked out of the station to find the streetlights glowing. It wasn't that late, according to my watch, but this far north, the dark came early.

"Blake, not to belabor the point, but Richard didn't kill Bea. Her death wouldn't have delayed the sale."

"Agreed."

"What about Dickie Campbell?"

"I can't see a reason there, either."

"Uncle Philip? Richard is an archaeologist. They have to do some climbing. He could have been on Ben Nevis."

The arrival of a distraught Elizabeth ended our conversation.

"This is unbelievable, Blake, Jax. I'm so thankful you're not hurt. Mrs. Casey had my cell number and found me in Edinburgh. When she told me Richard had been arrested, I left immediately." Elizabeth sobbed and turned toward the entryway. "I have to see him. It's a terrible mistake. My Richard couldn't kill anyone. He's so gentle, kind." She covered her face.

Blake put his arms around her shoulders. "He kidnapped us, Elizabeth. He confessed to watching Montoya die. Claimed it was an accident."

"Yes, that must be it. An accident. It's all a misunderstanding. I'll talk to him. We'll straighten things out. You'll see." She dug in her purse for a tissue. "We're getting married in six weeks. The police must drop the charges. Richard couldn't have done those horrible things."

Elizabeth was close to hysteria. I caught Blake's attention. "She needs a friend. You stay with her and help her get through this."

"How will you get home?" he asked.

"I'll call Chad to pick me up."

"Thanks for understanding." He helped Elizabeth through the double doors into the police station.

Chad answered his phone. "How are you feeling? How'd the inquisition go?"

"I'm okay. Elizabeth Coulter just arrived. Blake is with her. I need a ride."

He put me on hold then came back on the line.

"Mr. Atkins and the company limo should be coming down that street as we speak," he said. "The boss didn't want to take any chances. He's bringing the drawings from the airport to Heather Hill. I'll see you when you get back to the church."

I walked outside. A stretch limo so long it should have had a stabilizing set of wheels in the middle turned the corner and stopped in front of me. The chauffeur doffed his cap and opened the back door. I slid inside, surprised to see Rosalind sitting next to my boss. A sinking feeling washed up old insecurities and fresh worries. No doubt she had used her time with Mr. Atkins to further her own future. What lies and gossip had she been spreading?

"Good news, Mr. Atkins. I'm not a suspect for Raul's death. You'll get the bail money back, and I can concentrate on successfully finishing my job."

"What an awful experience for you, Jax," Rosalind said. "I can't believe you and Blake were kidnapped."

I couldn't see her expression in the dark of the car. She sounded sincere but was a tad heavy on the gush factor.

Mr. Atkins took my wrists and turned my hands over. The bandages on my fingers appeared white in the passing streetlights. "You're hurt. What happened?"

"We had to move some rocks to clear the tunnel exit. Scrapes and bruises, that's all."

Rosalind leaned across Mr. Atkins for a closer look. "Oh, your poor nails. We simply must find you a manicurist."

"Thanks for your concern, Rosalind." I kept my sarcasm and scorn under control. "I'll settle for a bath and a nap. First, I'll check with Chad and see what I can do to help set up."

"Rosalind and I will take care of it." Mr. Atkins patted my shoulder. "Will the arrest of Miss Coulter's fiancé delay matters?"

"I'll call Mr. Bascombe."

"Give Rosalind the number. Fairway Golf needs you at your best. You rest, and I'll see you for dinner. The hotel has a remarkable dining room. Meet us there around seven."

Mr. Atkins's kindness didn't alter the fact that I needed to finish this job and win the contract. What would Rosalind do to sabotage my efforts and, at the same time, take a step up the corporate ladder? In her short time in Heather Hill, she'd been everywhere. At the pub. The church. Richard's car.

Did she know he had plans to kidnap us?

The limo dropped me at Blake's building. I went inside the market and retrieved a joyous Hooligan. Annie demanded all the details of our abduction. It wasn't until I leaned against the counter that she noticed my exhaustion and sent me upstairs.

Once inside my apartment, I bathed, turned on the fire, and snuggled into the afghan on the couch. Hoolie fit into the comma of my body. Before I dozed off, I reconsidered THE KISS. Already it was taking on capital letter significance. I had enjoyed it. Was I foolish to hope it signified there could be more? The physical attraction between us was undeniable. Unfortunately, I knew my emotions were unreliable. I was on the rebound from Raul, and his death had reopened old wounds. Could I trust Blake? The Coulter estate had personal significance for him. Could THE KISS have been part of a plan, a game he was playing? With the answers to those questions eluding me, I drifted into a deep sleep.

BLAKE REFILLED the water and seed bins in the birdcage. The tiny canary peered up at him. "You agree Jax Hollister is all wrong for me, don't you?" The bird gave a non-committal chirp. "I admit I'd like to bed her, but anything more than that? Not bloody likely. She's just another American who'll leave Scotland when her job here is done."

The bird blinked his beady black eyes. "Yes, she could be playing me. That kiss might be nothing more than part of a grand scheme, a tactic to distract me from acquiring the estate for SFLS." The canary ruffled his feathers. "I agree it doesn't seem in character. It's more like something her devious associate, Rosalind, would do."

The yellow ball of feathers gave him a wink. Blake used his lightest touch to stroke the bird's back. "Jax was surprised by our kiss. She liked it. I felt her response. No faking that."

Blake draped the cage with the black-out cloth to keep out drafts. His aunt said canaries were susceptible to them. "Go to sleep, little guy, while I consider the future. Can I trust Jax? And why do I care?"

The canary didn't answer.

∾

A LIGHT TAPPING on the door woke me. I felt as if I'd dropped off the face of the earth for a few minutes; my wristwatch told me it was a quarter to seven. I opened the door to find Blake standing there, dressed in the same clothes he wore when we went to dinner with Maggie and Ian. If he were mine, I'd never let him wear anything except that white turtleneck sweater.

If he were mine? Where had that idea come from? Not from Blake Ramsey. He hadn't mentioned our kiss. He hadn't said much at all. We'd been busy with the police, then with Elizabeth, and then my boss. And yet I expected . . . what?

"Your employer invited me to dinner at the hotel and suggested I walk you over."

"Have a seat. I need a minute." I took my one dress from a hanger and went into the bathroom to change. I refreshed my make-up, pulled my hair into a low short ponytail, and secured it with a barrette. To change up the look of the dress, I draped a colorful scarf over the shoulders. Blake held my coat (his extra jacket) and I dove into it on the fly. He opened the door, motioning for Hoolie to precede us.

"That set a speed record for changing clothes." He added a quirky grin that had my heart doing gymnastics.

"Does the dining room allow dogs?"

"I know the manager."

On the short walk to the hotel, my misgivings kicked up a notch. I'd had dinner with Mr. Atkins before, usually to celebrate a successful acquisition. This time we were in the middle of the sales process. It set my nerves on edge that he'd invited the competition to join us.

Halfway to the hotel, Blake stopped and pulled me into a quick embrace and kiss.

I pulled away. "What was that for?"

"You look lovely tonight." He ran a finger down the side of my face. "And because I can't deny it any longer. You have bewitched me. I want time to find out who you are."

"Bewitched?" I took another step away. "I'm not one of your Scottish other-worldly beings. I'm simply a business woman who will be off on another job after the town council makes their decision."

"I'm not interested in your business plans."

I longed to return to the comfort of his arms, but cleared my mind and throat. "We need to talk."

"Okay."

"When I married Raul, I gave up my career. We moved to Argentina and lived on his family's horse farm. After I recovered from my miscarriage—"

"Miscarriage? You didn't mention that before. Did it contribute to the divorce?"

Blake's tone was compassionate and non-judgmental. Unbidden tears threatened. "Raul blamed me for going riding without an escort. When the horse stepped in a hole and threw me, that's when it happened. He couldn't . . . wouldn't forgive me. When his mother suggested we try again, I felt like one his family's brood mares. I was a mess of sadness, guilt, and anger. And I knew Raul wouldn't give up his mistress."

I couldn't look at Blake and continued to stare at the ground. "I wonder if he ever loved me."

Blake pulled me into a loose embrace. "You loved him?"

"I did, but after I lost the baby, we couldn't make it work. Too many bad memories." I emerged from Blake's warmth, determined to finish what I had to say. "The Coulter job is a chance to prove to Mr. Atkins that he made the right choice holding my job for me during my reovery. I told you he has his rules."

"No mixing business with pleasure."

"No impropriety."

Blake leaned into me and lowered his lips to mine. "None of this?" He kissed me softly.

"No."

"And none of this?" He kissed me again, harder.

When he finished, I put my hands on his shoulders to support my rubbery legs. "None of that."

"And certainly none of this." His head dipped and his tongue stroked mine.

How could I not react? There was definitely something between us—a strong physical attraction and who knew what else. I'd been divorced less than a year and Raul had been dead less than a week. Was Blake the right man at the wrong time?

I pulled away. "Why did I have to find you now?"

"I've been wondering the same." His thumb brushed my cheekbone. "We'll figure it out. I'll mind my manners around Atkins."

We completed the short walk to the hotel. The freshening wind cooled my cheeks. By the time we entered the Smuggler's Roost, I had my emotions under control. Mr. Atkins, Chad and Tilly were in the bar. They acknowledged us then returned their attention to the television. The weather report was featured, the sound turned up.

"There's a big *blaw* coming," the bartender said over the noise.

Chad leaned near my ear. "Hurricane-force winds possible with rain turning to snow. The west coast is in the path of the storm."

The television camera switched from the map of Scotland to an anchorwoman who told the audience to stay tuned for updates.

Rosalind arrived and Mr. Atkins took her elbow. "Let's go into dinner, shall we. We can watch the news when we finish."

The restaurant was what you would expect to find in a Scottish fourteen-room hotel. Quaint and rustic, filled with antiques, plaid upholstered booths and subdued lighting. After not quite two weeks in Scotland, you'd think I would be fed up with plaid, or "played" as the Scots pronounced it. Instead, I wanted to take some home.

Other than an elderly couple seated in the corner, we had the room to ourselves. The menu reflected the local specialties: venison ragout, fresh langoustines from Loch Linnhe, tatties and neeps, which were a mash of potatoes and turnips.

Blake sat next to Tilly. I was between Chad and Rosalind, and Mr. Atkins presided at the head of the table. Throughout dinner, Rosalind did her best to capture a share of the attention. Blake and Chad ignored her overtures. A brief pout played over her perpetually plump lips before she hid it behind her I'm-all-business mask. My boss charmed Blake and the chief designer for SFLS. Without visible effort, Mr. Atkins steered the conversation away from controversy until it appeared he and Blake viewed stewardship of the land in the same light. When they reached a truce of sorts, he changed the subject.

"I heard your aunt broke her hip, Blake. I called to see how she was getting on with her rehabilitation. Ready to come home, she said."

I couldn't hide my surprise. "You know Cora?"

"Certainly. I had the pleasure when I first surveyed this location. She introduced me to Mrs. Kestle. Such a nice lady. I was upset to hear of her death. The police think they've caught her killer?"

Blake recapped the case against Richard Hyde while I tried to figure out why Mr. Atkins hadn't told me he was acquainted with Cora and Bea. A small detail. What else hadn't he told me?

Mr. Atkins turned in my direction. "You don't believe Mrs. Kestle's killer has been apprehended because your dog didn't react to him?"

I looked down at the corgi, sleeping at my feet, flat on his back, short front legs relaxed against his chest. "Hoolie led me to Bea's body. He had to be there when it happened. I'm positive he can identify the killer. He didn't react to our kidnapper. My intuition agrees with my dog. It wasn't Richard Hyde."

Mr. Atkins looked at Hoolie and smiled. "I can see why you've become so attached. A dog as a detective? Only happens in the movies. Best leave it to the police."

"I don't think the police have all the details." I turned toward Rosalind. "When were you in Elizabeth's car, Rosie?" I used her hated nickname on purpose.

"Uh, yesterday afternoon, I believe." She fidgeted in her chair. "Yes, I was walking, and she gave me a lift. Why?"

Blake stared at her. "Elizabeth couldn't have done so. She took Richard's sport car and drove into Edinburgh day before last."

Rosalind twisted the napkin in front of her. "I must have my days mixed up. I lose track when I travel, don't you, Mr. Atkins?"

"Richard drove Elizabeth's sedan when he kidnapped us. We smelled your perfume in the car," Blake said. "You were with Hyde in that car. When? Were you aware of his plans to vandalize the displays? To kidnap us?"

I was glad Blake was in lawyer mode. I'd be pulling her hair to get the answers.

Rosalind's face flushed beet-red. She pushed to her feet. "I don't appreciate your questions, Blake Ramsey. Jax put you up to this, didn't she?"

Mr. Atkins set his fork on the plate. "Why don't you answer the questions, Rosalind? What did you know and when did you know it?"

She stood there, her mouth opening and closing like a fish out of water, gasping for air. "I didn't know what he planned to do, Mr. Atkins. Honestly, I met him once for a drink in Fort William."

I couldn't resist. "Is that all you did with him?"

She turned on me with fury in her eyes. "Look who's talking. You're the one who's bedding down with the competition."

"That's enough." Mr. Atkins stood. "I heard rumors in New York, Rosalind, but I wanted to give you a chance. When I arrived, your clandestine visits to Montoya's room came to my attention. And you have been with Miss Coulter's fiancé. Your sexual misadventures have caught up with you."

"No one has proof. I've done nothing wrong. I won't stay and listen to this-this slander." She faked a sobby gasp. "This is so unfair." Always the consummate actress, her shoulders shook when she left the room.

For a brief moment, I enjoyed my enemy's defeat. I was tempted to gloat, but my parents raised me better than that. I *did* believe in the old adage that if you gave someone enough rope, they'd hang themselves. Thanks to Blake's astute questioning, my boss had seen Rosalind's true colors. My job was safe from her.

Maude entered the dining room and hurried to our table. "Blake, Jax, I'm so glad Richard didn't hurt you."

"Maude Hampton, this is my employer, Mr. Drew Atkins," I said, "and my associate, Chad Stillwell. I think you've met Blake's associate, Tilly Markham?"

"Yes. Please sit, gentlemen. I've been in a meeting with the town council. You may have heard we're in for a storm. It could strike as soon as tomorrow night. We need to postpone the unveiling of your designs until the weather is more agreeable. Blake, that includes the reading of Bea's will tomorrow morning. The village needs to prepare for the worst."

"What can we do to help?" I said.

Maude appeared surprised by my offer. "That's nice of you, Jax, but we don't expect visitors to shoulder our burdens."

"We hope to be neighbors, Ms. Hampton," Mr. Atkins said. "Tell us where we can be of the most use. We'll do our part."

Blake offered Maude a chair.

She declined. "I have to get back to the emergency center. We get a bad storm every winter and know the places that have flooded in the past. However, this could turn into the storm of the century. We'll take a pounding if the disturbance brewing in the North Sea makes landfall at the same time as the one coming from the west. We'll need more sandbags than usual at the church. Mr. Atkins, Blake, I'd advise you to remove your displays from the basement and store them here at the hotel. We've never had any problems with this building holding against the water or wind."

"Yesterday, I saw the river had nearly reached the banks," I said. 'What if it floods? And what about the oyster farm?"

Maude buttoned her coat. "Town first, river second. The oyster lads have done this before. They'll be fine. See you in the morning."

The bill arrived, and Mr. Atkins signed for it. "It's late and we have a full day ahead. Chad, if you or Miss Tilly would care for an after-dinner drink in the bar, put it on my tab." He shooed them off with a wave of his hand. "Jax, I'll get my coat and walk you and Blake back to his building. After that fine dinner, I need the exercise. Blake, you run an excellent establishment."

After Mr. Atkins went upstairs for his overcoat, I turned on Blake. "You own the hotel?"

"Yes."

"Why didn't you mention it?"

"Is it important?"

"I guess not."

Blake looked at me as if to say if it wasn't important, why should he mention it.

My confidence plummeted. I assumed I knew all there was to know regarding the competition. I believed I'd done my homework on SLFS. I hadn't. A background check on Blake should have been at the top of my list. His aunt's ownership of the land next to the estate would have been in the report. Blake's controlling interest in the hotel would have surfaced. Dumb, dumb, dumb.

On the short walk to Blake's building (how many more properties did he own?), Mr. Atkins and I arranged to meet at the church in the morning to move our plans and drawings to the hotel. I said goodnight and walked up the stairs to my apartment, relieved the night was over. Before unlocking the door, I peeked over the banister. Mr. Atkins had detained Blake, and they appeared to be in a serious discussion. My insecurity resurfaced. Would my boss bring up the subject of my safety? Or how my living down the hall from a competitor was inappropriate? My previous excuse of keeping an eye on my rival sounded contrived.

After all the bad things that had happened, a normal person would be scurrying for the safety of the hotel.

CHAPTER THIRTY-SEVEN

THE HAMMERING BEGAN as soon as night changed to dawn. It came from outside the building. I opened the sliding door on my patio and peeked out. Blake stood on his balcony and pounded a nail into a piece of plywood covering his kitchen window. He saw my head sticking out the door.

"Ah, good. You're up."

"How could I sleep, oh ye mighty pounder of nails?"

Did Blake smile at my quip? If so, by the time I rubbed the sleep from my eyes it was gone.

"Your windows are next." He hit another nail. "Get dressed."

I hurried into clothes and mixed a cup of instant coffee. After the first sip, I opened the door to find Blake struggling with the unwieldy plywood to cover my windows. I guided him onto the narrow patio and held the sheets of wood in place while he wielded the hammer. The job looked easy when I'd seen people preparing for a hurricane on television. It wasn't.

When we were finished, he said, "Annie opened early. Get what food you'll need for a couple of days. Water, too."

We rushed down the stairs. Blake pulled boards from behind the alcove and moved on to the market windows. I went inside where several people were stocking up before the storm.

Annie motioned me forward. "I've set aside a bag of food for Hooligan and two gallons of water. What else do you need?"

I wouldn't be able to cook if the electricity went out. I reached for some of my favorite shortbread cookies. "These, some candles and matches."

Annie had the necessities under the counter. "I'll bill you for them. Kent MacDonald has set up a doggie day care at his office. Workers can leave their pets. I'll be closing early to help at the children's nursery. If you need anything else, ring me there."

I took my supplies, stepped aside to allow the next customer access to the cash register, and ran upstairs. I'd been through power outages at Lake Tahoe and New York and knew what to expect. I placed candles and matches at strategic places in the apartment. Hoolie picked up my anxiety and retreated to his crate. I gave him a treat, promised I'd be back soon, and went to help Blake.

Outside, I found two teenage boys manhandling an unwieldy piece of plywood over one of the market windows. I added my hands to the task. Blake pulled up in his car as we finished the last window.

"Go get Hoolie. We'll take him to MacDonald's."

My dog and I were back in a flash.

"Is it my imagination, or is it warmer than yesterday?"

"Nearly twenty degrees."

I took off the jacket he'd loaned me. "In Tahoe, we called it the warm before the storm. What's the latest weather report?"

"The winds are strengthening in the Atlantic and heading for the Hebrides. The islands will take the first hit after sundown. It may weaken over land."

"And the storm in the North Sea?"

"Same time table, the location of landfall is uncertain."

It had all the makings of a perfect storm. I shuddered at the memory of what happened to the fishing boat in the movie of the same name. George Clooney and the crew didn't have a chance. I sent up a prayer for all the ships, villages and towns in the path of this monster storm.

We arrived at MacDonald's office. A quick word with the reception-ist, and I was back in the car, sans dog. "He'll have lots of company. Winnie and several other corgis were already there. On to the church."

It was a hectic beginning to the busiest day of my life. We moved the displays down the street to the hotel. Chad kept our set in his room. Tilly shoved SLFS's plans against the inside wall of her closet.

Sandbagging was next on the schedule. On TV, it looked like back-breaking work. It was. Blake handed me a shovel to fill the bags. He took over the heavy lifting and loading the cart that would carry the bags around the foundation. Before the sun climbed over the hills, I was laboring for oxygen.

The pub and hotel provided sandwiches and drinks for lunch. I opted for a swig of beer, drank gallons of water and wolfed down a toad-in-the-hole (a deep-fat-fried sausage, covering a hard-boiled egg) and a banger on a bun—a Scottish hotdog. Fuel is fuel. Maggie sat down beside me in the grass where I had collapsed.

"Sean and I decided the town needs a *ceilidh* after all this work. You'll come, won't you?"

I shielded my eyes from the sunshine growing weaker by the hour. A thin overcast spread inland ahead of the storm. "What's a 'kaylee'?"

"A gathering. Some people will bring their fiddles and whistles. A wee bit of music and laughter to help make the time pass. Sean's fixing fish 'n chips for a crowd."

I pushed myself to my elbows. The muscles in my shoulders pro-tested. "I have a feeling that by tonight the spirit may be willing, but the body might not make it."

"I doubt Blake will be letting you stay alone. Not with a killer roaming the hills."

"You don't believe Richard killed Bea, either, do you. Why?"

"What you said. Him not having a motive and Hooligan not attacking."

"Could Dickie Campbell have killed her?"

"Sean and I donna think Dickie would. When he was a lad, Bea protected him from some bullies. He loved her. I suppose 'tis a possibility Richard killed them both. Do you think he fits the serial killer type?" Maggie's expression was a mixture of sadness and disbelief. "Word is he's not talking."

"No matter what the police say, Richard didn't kill Bea. Hoolie knows who did. And all that cash found at Dickie's shack? Blake doesn't think it was Bea's."

Maggie gazed westward, concern wrinkling her brow "You should ask Annie or Maude about the money. They knew her best. You'll see them tonight."

"Will your family be at the pub?"

"They'll stay near their animals."

"Blake and I could take some men out to help."

"Our farm is inland. Flooding has never been a problem. I'm more worried for the oysters. Mr. Atkins called from the emergency center and said he'd send help if the lads needed it."

"My boss is working with Maude?"

"Aye, she says his organizing skills are a big help. Logistics, he calls it."

We helped each other to stand. I searched the crowd of resting workers and saw Chad and Tilly lunching together. "I don't see Rosalind. Is she working with Mr. Atkins?"

"From what I hear, she was on the first bus out before breakfast, bags 'n all." Maggie's eyes twinkled. "I'm thinking the news won't bring a tear to your eye."

"What gave you that idea?"

"Oh, mayhaps the grin splitting your face from ear to ear."

"I'll admit it's the first good news I've had in some time. I hope she keeps on going, all the way to New York." I shivered. "The temperature is dropping. What's the newest storm update?"

"There're some mandatory evacuations in the Outer Hebrides. Never a good sign. I best be getting back to the pub. See you tonight." She waved and walked down the hill.

Blake appeared from around the corner of the church. "That's finished. There's a lorry full of bags and workers on the way to the river. We'll take Chad and Tilly and as many as can fit in my car and follow."

Tilly drove so Blake could eat on the way. He finished the last crumb at the same moment we pulled into Bea's place.

"This is the lowest of the three farms along this part of the river. We'll start here, then check the manor and then Cora's."

I avoided the area where I'd discovered Bea's body and concentrated on the placement of the buildings.

"The trees are far enough from the house that if the wind knocks down some limbs, they shouldn't do much harm. I think the situation is the same at the manor. How is it at your aunt's place?"

"Uncle Roland planted trees on the sides and back of the property, away from the house. Not much to worry there. It's the river that's the potential problem."

And something I'd have to write into our plans for the resort and golf course. I'd left out contingencies for storm disasters. After the damage Hurricane Katrina caused and all the recurring floods in the Midwest, I didn't have much faith in levees. Sandbags? I'd have a chance to see how effective they were at holding back the Muckle River.

By the time we finished building up the banks and surrounding the foundations of the three houses, little light remained in the sky. The wind from the west carried the scent of rain, and the temperature continued to plummet, a clear sign it would be below freezing before morning. We stopped and picked up Hoolie on the way to the hotel where we dropped off Chad and Tilly. They agreed to meet us at the pub for dinner.

Mr. Atkins rushed out the hotel entrance with a picnic basket on his arm. He'd changed his everyday golf knickers for a dark plaid pair, with a white shirt under a dark sweater and camelhair coat. Very dressy. He hurried to Blake's car before we drove away.

"Blake, just the man I want to see. I called the rehab facility. Fort William has done all that can be done for the safety of the residents. I'm taking Cora her dinner, a change of pace I think she'll enjoy. Perhaps I'll stay there until the storm passes. With your permission, of course."

Blake's expression of concern changed to one of bewildered amazement. "Of course. Tell her the farm is as secure as we can make it."

"She'll be glad to hear it. I'll leave Jax in your care. See you in the morning." He climbed in the limo and pulled away.

Blake parked the car in the semi-shelter of the east side of his building, out of the wind. "Now's the time I wish I had a garage. This will have to do."

I couldn't hold my laughter any longer.

"What's so damn funny?"

"The look on your face when Mr. Atkins asked permission to stay with your aunt tonight."

"I don't care if she thinks she is ready to come home. It hasn't been that long since she had hip replacement surgery."

"That's not what's bothering you." I bit back a giggle. "It's the thought of what they might do after dinner."

"At their age?" He unlocked the outer door. "I never—"

"Kind of like imagining your parents having sex, isn't it?"

"Oh, God. Enough. Go. I'll see you in a couple hours."

I couldn't wipe the smile off my face. Blake was so much fun to tease. We had worked well together. Not a cross word between us.

I'd seen, up close, how much he cared for his adopted home. It was a feeling I was beginning to share. I filled the tub and settled in for a long soak. I'd stretched my muscles to their limit and was tired. It was a satisfying, good kind of tired.

TWO ASPIRIN and a nap and I still ached in places that had never hurt before. I stretched to work out the kinks and groaned. My ankle was acting up again. Lordy, I was tired of being a cripple. Whining was so not my style.

A single tap on the door. Blake was ready for dinner. He took Hoolie's leash, and we stepped outside into a gust of wind that blew me off balance. Blake pulled me into his side. We ran from the cover of one building to the next. His overcoat shielded me from the worst of the rain. Hoolie's low undercarriage was soaked. He gave a mighty shake before we entered the pub.

Cries of "Blake" and "Jax" greeted us. Winnie barked, and Hoolie scrambled to meet her. Maude motioned for us to take our seats at a table already occupied by Annie, Tilly and Chad.

The crowd was in high spirits despite the day's hard work. They laughed and toasted all for a job well done. I soon forgot my pain and joined in the merriment. The noise stopped for a moment when Ian arrived. He had to hold the door to keep it from blowing off its hinges. The air that blew in with him was frigid. He looked exhausted, went to the bar for a kiss from Maggie before he joined our table. Blake crowded next to me on the bench to make room.

"Two smashed fingers, MacCafferty stepped on a nail, and Ed Mitchell sprained his ankle in a fall off a ladder," Ian said. "All that before noon. I'm praying everyone stays inside tonight so I won't have to leave my warm bed."

Maggie came to see if we needed refills. "According to the telly, good news. No deaths so far. Jax, have you asked Annie or Maude about Bea? The money?"

Maude set her teacup aside. "I heard. The five thousand pounds the police, excuse me, Hooligan found at Dickie's. I don't think it was Bea's. She wouldn't keep that much cash at hand. She believed in banks. Dickie didn't steal it from her, and I don't believe he killed her.

I searched for another explanation. "If she sold the kennel when at the dog show, she might not have had time to deposit the down payment."

"She didn't sell." Maude looked to Annie for confirmation. "Quite the opposite, I'm certain. She retired from showing, not breeding. She was ready to stay closer to home."

I looked at my friends gathered around the table. "Dickie had Bea's scarf with a bloody knife. If it wasn't her money, where did Dickie get it?"

Ian pulled Maggie into his lap. "Five thousand is a nice round sum."

Two plus two equaled four. "Blackmail money."

Shocked silence met my comment. "Dickie would never blackmail Bea," Annie said.

"Not possible," Ian agreed. "But what if Dickie saw who killed her?"

I leaned forward. "And saw the murderer get rid of the scarf and knife. He could've taken it, hidden it away, and blackmailed whoever murdered Bea."

Blake set down his pint. "The killer might've paid the blackmail. That would explain the five thousand pounds."

"What if Dickie asked for more?"

Blake filled in the blanks. "The murderer decided it was cheaper to get rid of him."

"He should've followed Dickie back to his hiding place to retrieve the knife," Ian said.

"You're assuming the killer is a man?" I asked.

"I did say 'he', didn't I?" Ian paused. "A natural assumption because of the way Dickie died. The oyster rake went into his chest, not his back, so he knew his killer. He didn't run. The coroner said the angle of entry was downward. Forceful. Whoever did it was tall and strong, therefore a man."

I remembered the shove into the river. Yes, someone strong. One of the oyster lads?

Maude said, "Jax, you better call Constable Trask and tell him the blackmail theory."

"Not me. I'm not the one to point out something he might have missed. Blake, you do it."

Maggie shuddered. "Enough talk of crime. 'Tis too nasty a night for such things. We need music and laughter."

Most had finished their meals. A few families took advantage of a lull in the storm to hurry home. Sean came from the kitchen, reached into a cupboard and brought out a concertina. One of the oyster lads produced a fiddle, and Blake prodded a blushing Tilly to join them with her penny whistle. They struck up a merry tune.

My toes were tapping to the music. "Why isn't anyone dancing?"

"Too crowded," Blake said. "That's why the Scots dance with their arms at their sides."

I thought he might be teasing until I remembered it was something he didn't do. Foot stomping and clapping was. There was not a dour Scotsman or woman to be found that night in the *Heelster Gowdie*. Chad tilted his cowboy hat back on his head. His unobstructed gaze never left Tilly's face. I admired a man who wore his heart on his sleeve. I tipped my chin at him and looked toward Annie and Maude. They smiled in unspoken agreement that the poor guy had it bad. I hoped their romance could survive a cross-Atlantic commute.

The impromptu musical trio took a break. The wind whistled around the eaves and there was a clap of thunder. From the next table, Rob, a truck driver I'd stacked sandbags next to said, "Ach, the *kelpie* is wandering tonight."

I poked Blake in the side. "Is that similar to a *selki*?"

"Ian, explain the difference."

"Both are shape shifters, but the *selki's* romance with humans always ends sadly. They eventually give in to their seal nature and return to the sea."

"The *kelpie* is a nasty beastie," Annie said. "There be nothing romantic concerning its contact with people. It traps mortals and drags them into deep water, drowning them."

Ian settled back in his chair. "Sometimes it takes the form of a horse, white or dark, with a dripping mane. When its tail slaps the water, we hear thunder. Sometimes it appears as a man. He disappears with the flash of lightening. That's why we associate a *kelpie* with storms. The bigger the storm, the bigger the *kelpie*. Must be a huge one roaming tonight."

Sean set mugs of beer in front of all. "Give us a tale, Ian."

"I will if my girl will hold my hand. I'm thinking of a fearsome and frightful story."

Hoots and whistles encouraged Maggie to sit next to the doctor. When she threaded her fingers through his, he began.

"We all know the *kelpie* is most active during storms, and it can be devious. Sometime it hunts when the sun shines bright." He turned to Blake. "Isn't this a perfect story for the unbelievers like Jax here?"

I played along. "True, I don't believe in faeries, either."

Boos and whistles bounced around the room, as I knew they would.

"Beware, Jax Hollister." Ian winked at me. "We've not seen lightening yet, and ye must walk home tonight."

"Blake will protect her," Annie said. "Get on with your story, Ian."

"Patience, lass. I need to wet my vocal chords." He took a sip.

"There once was an old crofter" he began, "called Donald MacGregor, whose summer holding lay near a large and deep loch. Friends told him to move his cattle, for they grazed on the wrong side of the burn, the side the *kelpie* claimed as his own."

"Jax, a burn is a stream or river," Maggie said.

"Donald MacGregor didn't believe in the monster. 'Until I see it with me own eyes, I'll not be movin.' My herd deserves the best grazin' and it be on this side of the burn.' "

The crowd grew silent. The fire hissed, the wind howled, and Ian's brogue thickened.

"Now Donald MacGregor had a bonny daughter. Morag be her name, and she spent the summers at her father's holding. In the sunlight of the morning, she sat in the doorway of the wee white cabin, spinning at her wheel. When purple shadows fell, she skipped across the heather until she came to the side of the loch and called in her father's cattle. She knew the many dark tales of the shape-shiftin' water devil, and each night she had her misgivins as she approached the deep water. But her father told her she had nothing to fear. There were no such beasties as *kelpies*. And so, every sundown Morag raced o're the heather and round the hillocks to gather the cattle and made it back safe to her father's wee white cabin.

"One morning as Morag spun her wool, a dark shadow fell o're her wheel. Startled, she looked up. A handsome lad blocked the sun. 'I dinna mean to startle ye.' His mellow voice charmed her, yet his hair and clothes dripped with water.

" 'How came you to be so wet?' she asked. 'Tis nary a cloud in the sky.'

" 'My foot slipped out from under and I fell in the water. Ye should-na worry, the sun will make quick work of the damp.'

"Morag felt uneasy, tho' there be no threat in his words. When the stranger turned his beguiling face to the sun and brushed his dripping hair from his face, Morag's heart became his.

" 'Rest your head in my lap,' she said, 'and I'll comb your hair. It will dry much faster.'

"This he did and many a quiet moment passed until Morag notice the teeth of her comb were choked with wisps of green and mud, the very same as were in her father's net when he fished the great loch. She leaned close to inspect the young man's hair. Closer. Closer."

On cue, Maggie screamed.

I jumped. Annie muffled a cry. Next to me, Blake gave a start.

Ian winked at Maggie and resumed his tale. "The handsome lad's hair was full of green water plants and silt. Morag realized this was not a mortal man. It be none other than the monster *kelpie* come to spirit her away to a watery death. Up she jumped, feet flashing o're hillock and heather. Behind her, she felt a dark presence, huge and terrifying. On she ran, until she came to the burn. She cleared it in a mighty leap. When she turned, not a shadow or the lad lingered in the meadow. Morag was safe, for as you know, *kelpies* cannot cross running water.

"Shaken by his daughter's encounter, Donald MacGregor recanted his words against the *kelpie's* existence and abandoned his summer holding for safer ground. The ruins of his wee white cabin can still be seen on the hill across the loch. As for Morag, she learned to guard her feelings around a handsome lad, for men are not always what they seem."

Ian shifted in his chair until he faced me. "Be verrra careful on your way home, Jax Hollister. We've not seen lightening. The storm *kelpie* is out there, waiting for YOU."

On Ian's last word, Blake tickled me. I'd been so caught up in the spell of the tale that I shrieked. Good-natured laughter erupted from the pub's patrons.

The mood of the story broken, Maggie called chug-a-lug last call. We gathered our things and made a dash through the wild wind and sleet.

CHAPTER THIRTY-EIGHT

"**C**OME TO MY flat for a nightcap," Blake said. "We'll warm up quicker in front of my fireplace. It's larger."

I hesitated, unsure if he remembered our agreement to abide by Mr. Atkins' rules. "Let me change out of these damp things."

The storm bore down on Heather Hill with renewed intensity. The roar of the wind bothered me most. I waited for a window to implode or part of the roof to blow off. The gale blew with huge gusts, one after another, like the cartoon of the big bad wolf trying to blow down the brick house of the third little pig.

I wasn't the only one on edge. Hoolie paced the room. He followed me as I changed into my thermal underwear, the least sexy thing I owned. I added two pair of socks and used the afghan for a shawl. Seductive? Glamorous? Not hardly.

I was exhausted from the day of hard labor, but wired and wide-awake. I remembered I'd sent a request for information on silt prevention to the New York office. If I used Blake's internet and printer tonight, I'd have the report to show Sean, the oyster lads and the town council when business as usual resumed. If I was in work mode, it might send

Blake a no-funny-stuff message, in case he had an ulterior motive behind his offer of a drink.

"Men are not always what they seem." Ian's story had ended with those cautionary words. A nightcap might mean something else. With my past history, I questioned my new-found feelings for Blake. I might be suffering from nothing more than a bad case of loneliness or homesickness. I didn't trust myself to find out if I was wrong. Whatever our relationship turned out to be, it couldn't amount to anything permanent. I'd be back in New York in a week.

With my tablet under my elbow and a firm grip on my resolve, I scurried down the cold hallway, Hoolie at my heels. Blake brought me into the living room where the fire blazed and the television news anchors were updating the storm. The on-site reports from the Hebrides were scarce. Communications from the outer islands were failing. The storm had lost none of its strength as it made landfall. Currently it was wreaking havoc on the western edges of the mainland. Power outages darkened towns up and down the coast. Injuries, so far, were few.

Before Heather Hill lost its power, I rushed to use Blake's equipment. I accessed my email and printed out the material I'd requested.

"That must be important," Blake said.

"You can read it. After I give a copy to Sean, Niles Gordon and the town council, it won't be a secret." I traded him the printout for a mug of tea. "The last page has the summary, if you don't want to wade through the engineers' report."

He read the final sheet and flipped to the cover letter. "This is good news. Your independent engineering firm confirms that precautions are planned so the golf course construction won't send silt into the river. The oyster farm will be safe." Blake looked up from the papers. "Why the frown?"

"I thought you'd be angry. The report erases one of the biggest objections the villagers have to the Fairway Golf resort. SLFS will lose the deal."

"Not so fast. *Our* plans will win over the town council. Drink your tea before it gets cold."

"There's booze in it."

"Drambuie. A Scottish liqueur. Sit by the fire."

I sat in the corner of the couch, tucked my feet under a pillow, and rearranged the afghan. Not an inch of skin showed. Blake joined me on the other end and rested his head against the back of the couch. The distance between us equaled a dog's length. I patted the seat cushion. Hoolie filled up the space and fell asleep. I relaxed.

"How's your ankle?"

"Better. If I weren't so clumsy, this would've healed last week. Usually, I bounce back faster."

"Were you accident-prone as a child?"

"By the time I was twelve, I'd seen the doctor so many times, he gave my parents a discount card. It included five visits get one free. I got my growth spurt when I turned thirteen, and, by the next year, my clumsiness was legendary. I was always picked last for any team sport." I nestled into the cushions and turned sideways so I could watch Blake's expression. "With my height, I planned to be a physical education major in college. When I developed water on the knee, in time for my sixteenth birthday, that ended plan one. At seventeen, my mother resigned herself that I was too awkward to be a model or make it in the beauty pageant world. 'Use your brain, find something you're good at, and stick to it,' was her advice. So I did."

"Did your parents take you to a specialist?"

"For being a klutz?"

"Ian said you should be looked at for a balance problem. He mentioned something to do with your inner ear."

I didn't remember having my ears tested. "You talked to Ian about me?" I wasn't sure how that made me feel. I wanted to believe it meant Blake cared for me. Or it might be exactly what it was; two friends discussing a clumsy American.

Blake got up to refill my drink. "Bad balance could explain some of your mishaps." He lit a candle and placed it on the kitchen counter alongside a flashlight. "In case we lose electricity." He returned to the couch and sank into silence.

I jerked as something hit the plywood covering his patio door. It clattered along the wall and continued on its wind-driven path to the other side of Scotland.

"A tree branch." Blake reached for the control, turned off the TV, took up another remote and turned on the music. I recognized one of the Strauss waltzes and concentrated on the lilting tune, not the sounds of the storm. The more I relaxed, the more I had an urge to move Hooligan and cuddle against Blake. I squashed the idea. How could I think I had feelings for a man I'd known less than two weeks?

"What was your childhood like?" I asked.

"You want more storytelling, do you?"

"Aye, Mr. Ramsey, I do."

"Hard to imagine I was small for my age. Half-English, and last picked, too. Back then, Heather Hill had a pack of louts who bullied the smaller lads. One day, Ian and I stood up to them."

"Good. Strength in numbers won the day."

"Not so good. They beat us to a pulp." Despite his words, Blake smiled. "Maggie played nurse and wiped off the blood. From that time on, we were three."

Blake's expression was the same one he used when he spoke of his aunt. Happy.

"One day, we were swimming in the lake, and the bullies stole our clothes. We went after them. Cornered them, too, but we were out-numbered. Spunky Maggie stood in front of us. The tallest taunted us that we were hiding behind her skirt. We knew they wouldn't hit a girl."

He chuckled, enjoying the memory. "Maggie walked up to him until she stood less than two feet away. Her head barely reached his shoulder. She reared back and punched him in the stomach. He never expected it. The last we saw of him, he was on the ground, doubled up. We grabbed our clothes and ran like hell."

"And you've loved her ever since." My eyes drifted closed.

"She always loved Ian. I'm glad he finally saw it at dinner that night. He's taken her for granted much too long." Blake's voice faded into the music and the wind.

When I opened my eyes again, the lights were off and the fire was out.

"Power's gone," Blake said.

"It's freezing in here. I better get to my apartment." I struggled to my feet. "Oh, ouch, ouch."

Blake put his arm around my shoulder. "Where does it hurt?"

"Everywhere." I leaned on him. My ankle buckled before we reached the door. He lifted me in his arms, walked to his bedroom, and deposited me on his bed.

"I can't be here."

"You can. You stay dressed, I'll stay dressed. Crawl under the blankets. We'll conserve body heat."

Before I could protest, he matched action to words. I tried to escape to the far side of the bed. He followed and pulled me against his body.

"Go to sleep. I'll be a proper English gentleman."

"You're half-English. It's your Scottish half that worries me."

Hoolie jumped up on the bed and scratched at nest by my feet.

Blake rubbed the ache in my tense shoulders. "Shhh. Go to sleep."

The warmth and the soothing action of his hands on my sore muscles eased me into dreamland.

Some hours later, the lack of noise awakened me. The wind had stopped, but the power hadn't come on. The exact time wasn't important. I was cozy and warm. I snuggled back against Blake.

Blake! Omigod! Paralyzed with shock and wide-awake, I assessed the situation. Blake's hand rested under my shirt and cupped my breast.

We radiated so much heat, I felt inflamed, as in, uh, romantically-inclined inflamed. Wrong thinking. My urge to flee increased when I heard and felt heavy breathing in my ear. I moved a leg toward the edge of the bed. Blake shifted, and his hand fell away. The breath in my ear became a snore.

I relaxed and stifled a chuckle. Come morning, this could be awkward.

MY ARMS WRAPPED around the dark horse's neck as it dove into the water. Deeper it swam. It was taking me to the bottom of Lake Tahoe. Let go or drown. I flung my arms wide, pushed off, and kicked toward the surface. Seaweed wrapped tentacles around my legs. There's no seaweed in Lake Tahoe! The black horse changed into a monster shadow and aimed its gaping maw at me. My lungs burned with the need for air. I fought clear of the ensnaring kelp and surged upward. Heavy arms. One more stroke. The sun shone through the surface of the water, beckoning . . .

Brilliant sunlight blinded me. Outside, Blake's silhouette removed the plywood from the windows. The bedclothes were in a tangle around my legs. Part of the sheet covered my head and wrapped around my arms. My nightmare-induced sweaty clothes stuck to my breasts.

The memory of Blake's hand touching the same breast nudged aside the last remnants of the bad dream. A quick survey of my clothing revealed Blake had been true to his word. No button was undone. Nothing had happened. I felt disappointed? Embarrassed?

Time for another Scarlett O'Hara moment. Tomorrow would be soon enough to think how I felt about Blake not succumbing to temptation.

My wristwatch confirmed it was after eight. I'd overslept. I swung my legs over the side of the mattress with surprising ease, stretched both arms over my head, and didn't feel a single strained muscle. A slight twinge when I put my weight on my ankle. That was all. Spooning with Blake had generated warmth comparable to a full, body-length heating pad. I scurried to my apartment, unable to erase that image out of my mind.

Blake exited my apartment carrying the wood that had covered my windows. Hoolie ran to greet me.

"Dress warm and come outside. It snowed last night."

I made quick work of my morning routine, bundled up and raced outside.

"You call this snow? If you'd been in Tahoe during the winter, you'd know this wouldn't qualify even as a dusting. Why, there's hardly enough for a snowball."

It was a nice mixture of wet and dry snow. Perfect to pack into a sphere. Blake pried a board loose from the market window before I hit him in the back of his head, exactly where his coat met his neck. I couldn't do that again in a million tries.

He yelped. I rushed to hold up a side of the board before it hit him in the forehead. We propped it against the wall.

"Damage assessment?" I said.

"Snow dripping down my back."

Laughter would exacerbate the situation, but I couldn't help it.

Blake leaned down, made his own snowball and advanced. I backed away.

"No, no. I meant damage to the village."

He threw a bullet. I dodged, slipped on the ice under the snow, and landed on my butt. Blake took his turn laughing.

"I never figured you for a slapstick fan, Blake Ramsey. Remind me to get you the complete collection of Laurel and Hardy movies."

He hauled me to my feet.

I looked around. "Where's Hoolie?"

"Over there." Blake pointed to the far side of the parking lot where my corgi romped from one snowdrift to another.

"He's like a kid," I said. "Finds a fresh patch of snow and messes it up."

Down the street leading to the pub, shop owners were opening shutters and removing the boards from their windows. In the direction of the church, a few people stepped from their homes and inspected for damage. The villagers gravitated up the hill to their house of worship. Greetings came in subdued voices. Most people wore dazed expressions, as if shocked to find they had escaped the storm in one piece.

I left Hoolie with Annie before we walked to the church. "Have you heard from your aunt?"

Blake shook his head. "Has Atkins called?"

"The power could be out."

"If they don't call by noon, we can drive up."

The windblown snow had piled over the sandbagged foundation, creating a quilt of puffs and pillows. Behind the main building, Dickie's shack hadn't escaped the wind. A heap of boards lay where his home had been.

The crowd parted to allow members of the town council to move to the front. They surveyed the rubble and then turned to face the increasing number of people.

"What a miracle," Maude said. "This is the worst of the damage. The main force of the storm veered to the south. Let's take a moment to give thanks."

We bowed our heads. Moments later, the vet said, "We're lucky. Power crews are already here. We should have electricity in an hour. The southern coast areas sustained massive damage. Our emergency center can tell you what help is needed there."

"Blake and Jax?" Maude searched for us in the crowd. We stepped forward.

"Could you have your displays ready to go by, say, five-thirty tonight? I see no need to delay the viewing."

"Good idea," Blake answered. "Any problem for you?"

"We'll be ready," I said.

"Pass the word to the corgi owners to be there at five," Blake said. "I'll read Bea's will when everyone is present."

We spent fifteen minutes removing sandbags from the basement entrance of the church. The emergency radio reported weather for the rest of the week. It was not good. More storms could batter the coast. The council issued a statement to leave the remainder of the sandbags in place until the danger passed.

Blake, Tilly, Chad and I set up our drawings. By the time we finished, the power had been restored, and we stopped in the pub for lunch. Sean and Maggie were busy serving cock-a-leekie soup, similar to our chicken soup, with the same physical and psychological benefits. Maggie's brother was jubilant. Only two bags of oyster spats broke loose and washed up on shore.

Halfway through our soup, Blake's cell phone chirped. "Hi, Aunt Cora. How are you? Any damage to the center? No? Good. Yes, it was nice of Drew to visit." He listened then handed the phone to me. "Your employer wants a moment."

Mr. Atkins said he would return to Heather Hill as soon as possible.

"Take your time," I said. "The viewing is tonight after five-thirty. No, Chad and I can handle it. You stay as long as necessary. Make sure Mrs. Ramsey is secure."

I gave the phone back to Blake. "Mr. Atkins wanted me to assure you your aunt is doing well."

"She said they'd had a delightful evening. Delightful." Blake had that bemused expression again.

We finished our meal then it was off to check the river. The sandbags had done their job. A few shingles from the manor roof were missing, that was all. A future golf course should survive the worst Mother Nature threw at it. Trees that acted as a windbreak had lost a few branches, but they had fallen well clear of any of the proposed outbuilding sites. Bea Kestle's place had fared well. The farmyard was a muddy bog, but the sandbags held the rushing river at bay. The

Muckle was already a foot below its banks and would continue to recede if fresh rain didn't renew the flow.

The afternoon passed quickly. I returned to the market and made copies of the engineers' report for distribution at the meeting. Hoolie slept while I dressed in my most professional outfit, the same one I wore to spend the night in jail. I hoped a different scarf and pin would change my karma.

Blake waited in the foyer.

"Am I that predictable?"

"You're never late."

It was five in the afternoon, and stars sparkled overhead. Our feet crunched in the snow and the cold nipped my nose. It reminded me of winter nights at home in Lake Tahoe.

Hmmm. Lake Tahoe was home, not New York? When had the city become nothing more than a place where I worked? I searched my feelings and found I had no emotional attachment to the Big Apple. Fairway Golf had its headquarters in New York, but I could live and work out of a suitcase. How sobering to realize I'd been all over the world and had no place to call home. Except my parents' house in Tahoe.

Heather Hill, above the banks of Loch Linnhe, tugged at an inner need for permanence. The people touched a place in my heart and filled an emptiness I hadn't known existed. Or was it the man who dominated my thinking . . . and my dreams? I knew Blake wanted me in his bed. In his life? If he loved me . . . no, that would make things more complicated. If he loved me, I'd have to make a decision. Leave or stay? Risk loving again?

I stopped and rubbed at my tightening neck muscles.

"What's the matter, Jax?"

I'd been thinking so hard I'd forgotten where I was and who I was with. I continued to massage my neck. "My neck hurts. I must've slept on it wrong."

In the light from the street lamp, Blake's teeth flashed a wicked grin.

When would I learn to think before speaking? "Don't you say a word, Blake Ramsey. Do not mention last night."

Inside the church basement, Blake found the lights. I beelined to the back of the basement where cloths draped our drawings. Chad and Tilly entered moments later. They'd brought the refreshments. A yip of excitement came from the doorway. Winnie tugged Maude into the room. Kent MacDonald followed with another corgi. Soon, seven dogs were sniffing their hellos, happy to see one another and oblivious to the growing throng of villagers.

Blake cleared his throat and the crowd fell silent.

"Bea would be cheered to see her dogs so well taken care of. Are the seven of you going to keep your dogs?"

"Yes," I said, and six other affirmatives followed.

Blake continued. "The delay in reading Bea's will meets her instructions to make sure the adoptions were permanent. She didn't want anyone to be influenced by the fact that she left each new owner a stipend of thirty pounds a month for the rest of your dog's natural life."

Thirty pounds was plenty of money for food and anything else the animals would need. The owners who were on limited incomes would welcome it. Murmurs of surprise and appreciation circled the room.

Blake cleared his throat. "The money will come from Bea's savings account until the sale of her property. When the sale is final, ten percent of the proceeds will establish a trust account for the continued support of the dogs. Ten percent will go to a distant cousin of her late husband. Ten percent will go to the Corgi Rescue Foundation. She left the remaining monies to Heather Hill for the purchase of any land that will benefit the town. The Council must have approval of two-thirds of the villagers before any purchase is possible."

A stunned silence followed the announcement.

Maude asked, "Can Heather Hill use it to purchase Coulter Manor?"

"You could, but you don't have time," Blake said. "The legal process for the town to acquire any private land is a lengthy one. Michael Coulter's will mandated the speedy sale of the property and made no provision for a delay. Remember, it took several years for the crofters' union to buy their land. And the John Muir Trust took two years to negotiate for Straithaid. Heather Hill may form a foundation and would have to follow the time-consuming government legalities. Elizabeth isn't willing to wait for that to happen."

I sighed with relief that there would be no delay of this sale. From their expressions, Tilly and Chad had been thinking along the same lines.

"Before leaving tonight," Blake said over the excited chatter, "I suggest you look at the two sets of plans. The council needs your input before they vote."

Chad and I hurried to uncover our display. Tilly and Blake did the same. The crowd strolled between them. Some people stopped before the drawing of the miniature golf course. One pointed at the restaurant design. Smiles passed between neighbors. Excited murmurs came from across the room. I was dying to see SLFS's drawings.

Chad tapped me on the shoulder. "What do you think?

I whispered, "Let's go see what the competition has done."

CHAPTER THIRTY-NINE

BLAKE WATCHED a nervous Tilly. She fidgeted with the four easels, repositioning each drawing so they were perfectly square.

"Let's switch the conference center design," she said. "Put it before the tea room drawing."

"Good idea." Blake moved the placards.

Tilly looked over her shoulder. "Uh, oh, here comes the enemy."

"Yes, I noticed." He'd caught the movement in his peripheral vision. Tried to ignore the quickening beat of his pulse. Ever since Jax removed her jacket, he'd been unable to put her out of his mind. Her dress was the same she wore to the Italian restaurant. The scarf was different. He noticed how the greens went well with her flaming hair. The dress fabric flowed over the body he remembered so well from the night before. He'd had a devil of a time going to sleep when she snuggled her bottom against him.

Jax exuded confidence with every stride. Not a hint of a limp or clumsiness. She was in her element.

"Hi, Tilly." She shook the designer's hand. "I enjoyed your contribution to the music last night." Jax wore her poker face while she studied the display. Blake couldn't read her expression until she gave Tilly a genuine smile.

"I like how you made the study into a tea room." Jax indicated the drawing. "Who made the artist's rendering?"

"I did," Tilly said.

"You are so talented. If I were here on vacation, I'd want to stop in for a cup. The lacy fabric you used in the curtains and the plaid chair cushions make the room homey. You kept the fireplace, which lends warmth and coziness."

"The Conference Center is another good idea," Chad said. "Nice use of the second floor bedrooms for meeting rooms."

Tilly acknowledged their compliments with a blush. "Because SLFS is a non-profit, we'd need several ways to pay the bills. The small third-floor rooms can be used for break-out sessions. Blake, can you stay here while I look at Fairway's plans?"

"Of course."

Chad took her by the elbow. "Right this way."

Jax brushed by to follow, and Blake inhaled her distinctive scent. Apples.

A voice interrupted his distracted thinking.

"Blake, someone here wants to see you." Drew Atkins wheeled Cora Ramsey through the doors.

"Aunt Cora. Why didn't you tell me you were being released?"

"I told you he'd be surprised, Drew. Go see if your associates need any help. I want a moment with my nephew."

Blake squatted beside the chair.

"Thank you, Blake. Peering up at you would give me a crick in my neck."

"You look wonderful, Cora. I haven't seen the peaches in your cheeks for a long time."

He followed her gaze as it searched for Jax's employer.

"It's been ages since a handsome gentleman has been so attentive." She beamed. "When I told Drew I couldn't stay another day in that place, he charmed the doctor into releasing me. He arranged for a caretaker until I'm back on my feet. We stopped by the farm and turned up the heat. It'll be so good to sleep in my own bed and eat my own cooking when I want to, not on someone else's schedule." She patted his arm. "Have the police found who killed Philip and Bea?"

"They think Richard killed everyone. Jax believes Hooligan can identify Bea's killer, and he didn't react to Richard. She thinks Bea's murder and Philip's death, all the deaths in fact, are connected somehow to Coulter Manor. I agree."

"She makes a persuasive argument. I'm not surprised that dolt Trask wants to tie up the case so fast. I have a feeling it will unravel soon enough. Now, show me what you and Tilly have been working on."

Blake explained what SLFS wanted to do with her neighbor's house.

"What do you think of Fairway Golf's plans?" she said.

"I haven't had time to see them. Shall I wheel you over?"

"The doctor said no unnecessary walking, yet. Drive on, dear boy, no speeding."

Jax met them in the middle of the room. "Mrs. Ramsey, it's so nice to see you."

"You, too, my dear. Will you give me a tour? Drew raved over your ideas."

Blake made to follow them, but Atkins asked him to stay a moment. "My boy," he said, "contrary to your denials, I believe you have feelings for Jax. Your aunt confirmed it. She told me you were smitten. Yes, that's the word she used. I've seen it myself."

Blake tore his gaze away from Jax. "I admit SFLS would steal her away from you in a snap. However, she has made it plain she'll return to New York after the winner is announced." He hoped he'd deflected the issue of his personal feelings. Whatever the Bloody Hell they were.

Maggie breezed in the door. She radiated happiness. "Blake, I left Sean to handle things at the pub. I had to see your plans for the manor."

"Maggie," Blake said, "Meet Drew Atkins, Jax's employer."

"She speaks highly of you, sir. And Maude Hampton said you were such a help organizing people and supplies for the storm."

"You must be the publican at the *Heelster Gowdie*," Atkins said. "Jax said your game pie could win awards. I hope I have a chance to sample it before I leave." He looked toward the door. "More people. Please excuse me. I must join Chad and Jax. It was nice meeting you, Maggie."

"Quite the gentleman, isn't he?" Maggie indicated the retreating entrepreneur. "Blake, show me the drawings, then I'll go speak to Jax."

Moments later, Tilly joined them. "Hi, Maggie. You and Blake must see Fairway Golf's display. Their presentation is much more sophisticated than ours. Much as I hate to admit it, they have some good ideas."

Curious, Blake followed Maggie to the back of the room. They studied the first exhibit.

"The Treasure Island crazy golf is more elaborate than I'd imagined. The model ship is perfect on the pond." Maggie went from easel to easel. "What are these buildings scattered 'round the main golf course? Be they crofters' huts?"

"A bow to Scottish history," Jax said. "Replicas of traditional huts, designed for golfing families. I suggested the decorations inside simulate the homes of famous Scottish people. The one in the trees is the John Muir cottage. The Sir Robert Scott cottage will overlook the first fairway."

Blake gestured to a sketch. "And the restaurant?"

"With floral arrangements and other decorations, we can change the theme with the seasons," Jax said. "And in the summer, if the midges behave, we would open the doors onto the patio for casual dining and special events, such as concerts and plays. The restaurant will be open to the public. In the winter, as shown here, it's dining with a medieval theme from *Ivanhoe*. We'd move the suits of armor around in the summer time."

Maggie pointed to another drawing. Jax squealed and grasped her hand.

"You're engaged!" Jax hugged her. "When did this happen?"

Maggie showed off her ring. "Ian proposed to me last night after I closed the pub." She showed the diamond to Cora.

"It's about time," Cora said. "I was going to give him a good talking to if he waited much longer."

"I'm happy for you," Blake said, surprised how much he meant it.

"I believe the dinner Jax arranged for us in Fort William must've cleared the fog from Ian's thick head." Maggie hooked an arm through Jax's. "And after your kidnapping, Ian said life was too uncertain to waste time. We'll be married next week." She clasped Blake's hand. "Ian wants you to be his best man. He'll be asking you later tonight. We'd want you to be there, too, Jax."

Atkins stood nearby. "You have vacation time coming, Jax."

Her expression changed from joy to regret. "Thanks for the invitation, Maggie, I wish I could stay. I find I'm suffering a bout of homesickness. I'm going to visit my family."

Blake's heart stuttered. His hopes for more time with Jax died.

Why shouldn't she leave? She'd warned him she would return to the States after the job was over. He hadn't believed her. But he hadn't said or done anything to convince her to stay. What were a few kisses? They'd meant nothing to her.

He had to get out of this room.

He gulped air, spun on his heels and hurried into the frosty night.

I TRIED TO IGNORE how Blake's abrupt leave-taking hurt my feelings, but my heart sank to the bottom of my stomach like the Titanic. His actions told me a permanent relationship was not what he wanted. I should've been more prepared. It could never work. We came from two different worlds. We wanted different things.

I missed him already.

Maggie and Cora exchanged curious looks, which I disregarded. I smiled and gave a skeptical Oyster Lad a copy of the engineers' report. I explained the filtration devices and used the time it took to get my emotions under control.

In two days, the town council would make its selection. The day after, I'd leave Heather Hill forever. Blake knew that. Maybe he decided a clean break was the best solution. No long, drawn out farewells. No last kiss to remember.

I needed to concentrate on work, to focus on the crowd. Mr. Atkins sat in a neutral corner with Blake's aunt. Hoolie lay in her lap and watched the progress of people in and out the door. Chad answered questions. I continued to monitor the villagers' reactions.

"You've been in town the longest, Jax. How are we doing?" Chad said.

"From what I've overheard, most everyone has found something to admire in each presentation."

"Too bad we both can't win."

Mr. Atkins strode our way. "SLFS has done a good job." A wry grin accompanied his observation. "The conference center is an idea Fairway may incorporate into our revised plans. Chad told me about Mrs. Kestle's bequest. I'm glad it didn't come at an earlier time. Communities that buy back their land is an idea that's spreading fast in Scotland. The town council could have given us a run for our money. No telling what they would have bid."

During a lull, I suggested that Chad approach Tilly and get her take on the public reaction to SLFS's plans.

Mr. Atkins observed the couple on the opposite side of the room. "First your friend, Maggie, and now our Chad. The poor boy is twitterpated."

I giggled, a complete lapse in professionalism. "I haven't heard that word since the last time I watched *Bambi*. If I may be so bold, Mr. Atkins, you're acting a wee bit twitterpated yourself. I better warn Mrs. Ramsey."

"Tease me all you want, Jax, but there's magic in the Scottish air. I saw how you looked at Cora's nephew."

I felt the blood rush to my cheeks. "Nothing has happened. I swear."

"I know. Blake assured me that you would not allow anything to jeopardize the firm's reputation. No conflict of interest or collusion. I believe him."

I made a mental note to thank Blake for protecting my reputation.

Chad returned. "Jax, your idea for the Treasure Island miniature golf is a hit."

Mr. Atkins gave me a literal pat on the back. It was nice to be appreciated.

"Shouldn't Elizabeth Coulter be here?" I said.

"Excellent idea. Blake said she's become a recluse. She hasn't been out of the house since her fiancé was arrested." He used his smart phone. "I'll call the limo. If you show up at her door, she won't be able to refuse you. She needs to see both presentations."

Within minutes, the chauffeur picked up Hoolie and me and whisked us to the front entrance of Coulter Manor.

"I won't be long," I told the driver.

"I'll keep the heater going and stay in the car, miss. It's brisk tonight."

"Freezing, you mean."

Hoolie and I climbed the stairs and lifted the heavy brass knocker. Once. Twice. The housekeeper opened the door and fussed over me as she led the way into the study.

"It's sorry I am to leave you in this room again after knowing what Mr. Richard planned." Mrs. Casey blushed. "Miss Elizabeth keeps the heat turned off in the other public rooms when she's not expecting visitors."

Hoolie refused to enter the study. Again. He growled, the fur on his back rose, and he planted all four paws on the carpet. I tugged on his leash to no avail. I picked him up and carried him inside.

"Richard's scent must be in here." I held him against my chest.

"Aye, he must remember. May I bring you some tea?"

"No, thank you. I do need to speak to Miss Coulter. I want to take her to see the plans for the manor on display at the church."

"Oh, excellent idea, miss. The poor woman needs to get out of this dreary house. She has spent enough time in her room crying. I'll tell her you have a car waiting. I won't let her say no."

After she left, I set Hoolie down. He approached one chair, then another, growling the entire time. He returned to my side and stayed close to my feet while I wandered. If there was such a thing as bad energy, I imagined it remained in the study.

Richard's plan had almost succeeded. Although I knew there was a secret door, I searched and couldn't see the seam along the fireplace mantle. Richard had reached behind one of the books for the remote control that triggered the mechanism. I shivered. Blake and I had been lucky to find another exit.

The shelves in the study were emptier than when Richard brought us here. More cartons lined the wall. Elizabeth was keeping busy. I understood the need to work when your life turns upside down.

An open box caught my eye. I squatted to inspect the contents. A gently read copy of short stories by Robert Louis Stevenson lay on top. Underneath, Scottish history books predominated, several on the subject of Robert the Bruce. I set them aside and picked up one featuring William Wallace, another of Scotland's heroes and the subject of the movie *Braveheart*. I planned to visit the battleground and monument in Sterling before I returned to America. Richard had been searching for Wallace's dagger.

The aged book required delicate handling. The pages were yellow and brittle. When I opened the cover, a musty smell reached my nose. I was curious how old it was and turned to the copyright page. Published in eighteen-hundred-eighty-three. A black and white drawing of Wallace wielding his huge sword followed the title page. When I turned it, a corner of paper sticking out of the binding snagged my attention.

My calf muscles twinged from my awkward position. I stood, carefully eased the piece free, and took it to the desk. The folds were grubby from handling and age. The paper itself wasn't as yellowed as the pages of the book. How had it slipped into the binding? I spread the paper open, careful not to tear it. It was a bill of sale dated March 4, 1906, for a nine-inch dagger.

Three things happened in the next second. Elizabeth Coulter entered the study, Hoolie snarled and hurled himself at her leg, and I discovered who killed Bea Kestle.

The corgi sank his teeth into Elizabeth's calf and held on. She screamed and batted at his body.

I stood frozen in place, immobilized by disbelief. "You killed Bea?"

Elizabeth swung a fist at Hoolie's muzzle. "Get him off me!" She pounded his head. Before she could hit him again, I charged forward and grabbed her fist.

Elizabeth used her other hand and slashed at Hoolie's eyes with her nails. He yelped and let go. She jerked her clenched hand out of my grasp and struck me across my ear. Then her shoe grazed my shin. I did some fancy footwork to avoid another kick. She smashed a fist into my face. Shards of pain exploded inward. I feel to my knees, cupping my cheek in my palm.

Damn, if she'd fractured a bone, I'd . . .

Hoolie renewed the attack on her leg. Elizabeth staggered to the fireplace, dragging a firmly attached dog with her. She seized the iron poker from its stand. The awkward, downward position didn't stop her from bludgeoning him.

Before I could regain my footing, Elizabeth struck again. Hoolie collapsed on the floor.

Elizabeth drew back her foot to kick him.

"Nooooo!" I jumped between them.

Her kick landed on my other shin. I yelped and hobbled backward. She swung the poker at me. I ducked, but not fast enough. A numbing blow to my left shoulder forced me to change tactics.

Close-in fighting would render her weapon useless.

I muscled my body against Elizabeth's, pinning her against a bookcase. I wrenched the iron bar from her with my other hand.

Feeling returned to my injured arm. I stepped back and slashed at her with her own weapon of choice.

Elizabeth came in low under my swing. I used the poker like a club, the way she had. It was a bad angle. I was able to hit her once before she wrapped a leg around mine and jerked my feet out from under me.

We landed on the floor, Elizabeth on top. The poker rolled under a table. She straddled me, her extra thirty pounds crushing the breath out of my lungs.

Her hands found my throat and squeezed. I tried to wedge my fingers under hers to relieve the pressure and failed. The face above me, twisted with hate, grew dim. A move from my self-defense class wavered at the edge of consciousness. I pried one of her fingers loose, bent it back, and had the satisfaction of hearing it snap. She shrieked and loosened her hold. I gasped for air, pumped my hips toward the ceiling, and bucked her off.

Elizabeth clutched her broken finger and used her elbows to crawl toward the poker.

I caught her foot. She kicked to dislodge my grasp. I hung on and stopped her forward progress.

Hand over hand, I pulled myself up her leg. When I came to the tear in her trousers, it was slick with blood. I dug my fingers into the site of Hoolie's first bite.

She screamed, reached down, snatched my hair with her uninjured hand, and yanked.

My turn to yell. I released her leg and went for another finger. Before I could break it, she gave up her grip on my hair and raked her claws down my cheek.

We shoved to our knees at the same time and faced each other.

Our sides were turned to the open door. My peripheral vision caught sight of the housekeeper and cook standing on the threshold, wide-eyed, immobile.

"Call the police," I yelled.

Elizabeth took advantage of the distraction and lunged. I feinted to one side. She wrapped me in a bear hug, the better to bind my arms to my sides. She was strong. I wrestled free, but I was tiring.

I had to end it. Fast.

Elizabeth fought like a girl, pulling hair and using her nails.

I didn't.

I curled my fingers into a fist. The first rule of my self-protection boxing lessons: don't telegraph your blow. Keep it short and sweet.

I concentrated my power from the elbow to my hand. My knuckles connected under her chin.

The sound of lower teeth driving into upper ones was immensely gratifying.

Elizabeth's eyeballs rolled, and she fell sideways on the carpet.

I looked for Hoolie. He hadn't moved. "Please, God, let him be all right." I crawled over to him, pulled him into my lap, and buried my face in his thick fur.

CHAPTER FORTY

A COMMOTION SOUNDED at the front door. Constable Trask, Blake and the chauffeur burst through the entrance to the study. Blake rushed to my side.

"You're hurt." He used a handkerchief to dab the blood from the scratches on my cheek.

Meanwhile, the constable helped a dazed and wobbly Elizabeth to the couch. Between sobs, she pointed to her legs and Hoolie. Trask called in another cop with a first-aid kit who fashioned bandages for the bites.

Blake concentrated on me. He brushed a tear off my chin. "How do you feel?"

"I'm okay, but Hoolie . . . he hasn't moved. I'm afraid . . ." I couldn't finish. I cradled his limp body to my chest.

"Jax, I saw his foot twitch."

I wasn't sure I'd heard correctly.

"Yes, there it is again." Blake hugged us.

I held my hand in front of Hoolie's nose. "H-Hoolie."

I bent down to see if I could feel his breath against my cheek.

A dry tongue licked my wet face.

"Oh, Hoolie, you're alive. Blake, he's alive." I wiped away my tears and pointed at Elizabeth. "She killed Bea. Hoolie knew it and attacked her. She hit him with the poker."

My dog panted weakly and closed his eyes.

Blake took out his phone. "I'm calling MacDonald."

A moment later, he said, "He's on his way." Blake gave my shoulder a reassuring squeeze. Wrong shoulder. I winced.

"She hit me, too."

Blake glared at Elizabeth.

Careful to avoid the bump on Hoolie's head, I continued to stroke his ears. "The cops couldn't have received and responded to the housekeeper's call for help so fast. You must've already been on the way. How did you know to bring the police?"

"After I left the basement, I went to my office. Bea's birth certificate was in my mail. The space for the father's name was blank as expected. Samuel came in and asked for help going through Philip's desk. We found a handwritten letter to Philip from Michael Coulter, written shortly before his death. He didn't want it attached to his will, but expected Philip to execute his wishes. In it, Michael explained he was Bea's father."

"No one knew Mr. Coulter had an illegitimate daughter?"

"Michael wanted it to remain a secret, unless Elizabeth sold the estate. At that time, Philip was to tell her of Bea's existence. Michael wanted her to share the proceeds with Bea."

It took a moment for the new information to sink in. "Bea was Elizabeth's older half-sister. Did Philip have time to tell her before his death?"

"There were two significant dates in Philip's appointment book. Two months ago, he met with Elizabeth. The secretary heard shouting from his office and saw how angry Elizabeth was when she left. We think that's when she found out about Bea. And on Philip's birthday, there was a notation on his calendar confirming a luncheon with Bea in Fort William. We can assume he didn't trust Elizabeth to tell Bea, so he was going to do it. He died first."

I glared at her. "You killed Uncle Philip so he couldn't tell Bea, but you couldn't take a chance that Bea would find out some other way, so you killed her, too. Hooligan's attack proved that. Plain and simple, you didn't want to share."

Constable Trask had been listening to our conversation. He took a seat by the fireplace. "It would be difficult to prove she was on Ben Nevis with Mr. LeBeck. Damn near impossible after all the rain and snow."

"Blake, you can't believe any of this." Elizabeth whimpered and brushed away a tear. "I'd never kill anyone."

Blake patted her arm. "You're a good person, Elizabeth. A good friend." He stood over her, his face a mask of concern, his clenched fists the single clue to his real emotions. "You loved your father." Blake's voice was deceptively calm. "You tried to protect his reputation, his good name. I'd do the same. Anyone would. You met Philip on the mountain because he might leak the information about Bea. That would drag your father's name through the mud. You couldn't let him do that, could you?" Blake rested his hand on her shoulder.

Elizabeth leaned her head against his arm. "Philip wouldn't listen to reason. I begged him not to tell Bea. Once the news got out, it would ruin the Coulter na—"

She stopped and clamped her mouth shut.

Oh, Blake was good! He'd tricked a confession out of her. He didn't appear pleased. Instead, he looked as if he wanted to choke her. Gone was the friendly tone.

"You couldn't chance that he'd already told Bea, so you killed her. Dickie saw you coming from her place and demanded money to keep quiet. The next time he asked, you killed him."

Elizabeth broke into fresh crocodile tears. "How can you think that? We've known each other for ever. I'm not a murderer."

"I think you are." He took a step away from her, as if distance would help him keep his self-control. "Three times over."

"You have no proof I was on the mountain. The constable said so."

"You killed Bea, not to protect the family name," I said, "but for greed. You didn't want to share the money from the sale."

"Please, Blake, stop her from saying those terrible things." She broke into wrenching sobs.

She deserved an Oscar, but Blake saw through her act.

"I believe the dog, Elizabeth. He knows you killed Bea."

Her face, splotchy red from the fake tears, hardened with anger. "No jury will consider evidence based on a dog's actions. They'll return a verdict of not proven."

"Not proven? Can they do that?" I asked.

"Scottish law is different from yours," Blake said. "It provides for three possible verdicts. Guilty, not guilty and not proven. She has a two-out-of-three chance to get off."

Trask searched the pages of his notebook. "It'll be harder to get off if the murder weapon came from your kitchen, Ms. Coulter. After Mr. Montoya's death, I interviewed the staff." He motioned to the pad of pages. "Yes, here it is. The cook, Mrs. Gordon, was searching for a knife that had gone missing from her carving set. We'll compare the knife we found at Dickie's place to the ones in your kitchen. Our lab found a partial print on the bloody handle. I believe there is enough for a match."

Elizabeth wobbled off the sofa. Blake pushed her, none too gently, back into the cushions.

"I have an alibi for the morning Bea was killed." She wrung her hands, the picture of the wrongly accused. "I never left the study. Mrs. Casey said so."

"Not exactly true, Miss Coulter," Trask said. "Your housekeeper said she saw you enter the study. She couldn't say exactly when you left."

"Blake and I can tell you how she got out without being seen." I gestured to the vicinity of the fireplace. "She used the tunnel. Blake, remember the side branch that was barricaded? I bet it comes out on Bea's property."

Blake pulled books off the half-empty shelves at random. When he removed the second book on the third shelf closest to the mantle, he found the remote. He punched the button, and the wall swiveled inward.

"That's where Richard locked us in. He didn't know there was an exit in the end wall. Elizabeth knew, didn't you? She kept the secret to herself." He stared at Bea's killer. "You used the tunnel to go to Bea's, stab her, set fire to the shed, and get back here without being seen."

"Except Dickie Campbell saw you hide the scarf and knife," I said. "He dug them up and blackmailed you. When he went back for more money, you killed him. That's where you made a mistake." I turned to the Constable. "She killed him before he told her where the knife and Bea's scarf were hidden, the things Hoolie sniffed out at his shack. After Dickie was killed, I went to the river to see where his body had been found, looking for clues. It had to be you, Elizabeth, who pushed me in. Were you afraid I'd found something incriminating?"

Elizabeth crossed her arms over her chest. "Your American play-mate is delusional. Dickie Campbell wasn't blackmailing me because he didn't see me coming back from Bea's. I wasn't there. The rest of your wild story doesn't follow."

My anger toward Elizabeth never wavered. I was on a crusade to see her in jail and offered Trask a suggestion. "I think Richard will tell you where Elizabeth was the morning Bea was killed. He knew how to get out of the study without being seen."

"He'll never testify against me," Elizabeth said. "He loves me."

"He might not feel that way after the police inform him you knew Wallace's dirk had been sold years ago." I pointed under the table where the bill of sale had fallen. "You let Richard believe it hadn't been found. Let him spend all that time searching. You strung him along. Were you afraid he'd leave you if he knew his treasure hunt was useless?"

Elizabeth's lips peeled back in a feral smile. "You can't prove I knew there was a bill of sale stuck in the spine of a book."

"I didn't say it was a receipt or where I found it. You knew it was in the binding because you hid it there. The police will find your finger-prints and mine, not Richard's, on the book. You packed it away before he could see it, didn't you? You were afraid you wouldn't have a new husband in your new house."

One of Trask's men put on gloves and carefully placed the paper in an evidence bag. The book went in another.

Blake stood over his childhood friend. "The scene at the police station, after Richard was arrested, was all an act, wasn't it? You make a fine pair of killers."

She kept her mouth shut.

The vet arrived and got an update on what had happened while he ex-amined Hoolie. He gingerly probed the edges of the bump. MacDonald pulled a penlight from his pocket and looked at my dog's eyes.

"Has he tried to move?"

Oh, no, he's worried about paralysis. Please, God, no. "He twitched his paw and licked my cheek."

"Walk to the door and see if he follows," MacDonald said.

I moved carefully from under Hoolie. He lay on the rug, eyes closed. I held my hand under his nose and tapped my foot on the floor before walking to the door.

Slowly, ever so slowly, the corgi stood. He hung his head for a moment, as if gathering his strength.

I tapped the floor again. He looked at me. I motioned with my hand for him to come.

He hesitated, then put one foot in front of the other. When he staggered near Elizabeth, he bared his teeth. A growl came from deep within his chest.

Elizabeth cringed deeper into the sofa. "Keep him away from me. He's vicious. I'm going to need rabies shots."

Gone was the mild-mannered vet. "This dog's vaccinations are current."

"Hoolie is the one who'll need a shot after biting *you*," I said.

The constable stood between Elizabeth and my dog. Hoolie sat, lifted his head, and gave the constable his panting smile.

"I wouldn't have believed it if I hadn't seen it for myself," Trask said. "There's no doubting the dog has a strong dislike for Miss Coulter."

I tapped the floor again. With a final stare at Elizabeth, Hoolie came to sit in front of me.

I knelt and scratched his chest. "He's going to be okay, isn't he?"

"He might have a concussion, but he appears to be recovering. I'll need X-rays to be sure. Bring him to my office when you're through here."

Trask motioned to the door. "You can go now, Miss Hollister. I'll send someone from the Procurator Fiscal office to take your statement later. I assume you'll want to press assault charges"

"Will that keep her in jail long enough for you to make your case?"

"Until we match her fingerprints to the partial on the knife."

"I'll be thrilled to put her in jail," I said, "and you can throw away the key."

"Sergeant, call for a search warrant. There must be clothes from the stabbing with Mrs. Kestle's blood on them. We might find Dickie Campbell's blood, too."

"Oh, miss, how could you?" Everyone in the study turned in time to catch the housekeeper's stricken expression. "When I saw you with that bundle of clothes, you said they were muddy and needed to go to the cleaners. I offered to take them meself. You said you had errands to run. Not to bother."

"Have the clothes come back?" Trask said.

"Yes, sir. They're in their bag hanging in her closet."

"Would you go get them for us, Mrs. Casey? Sergeant, go with her." The policeman looked at Elizabeth, his gaze sharp with appraisal. "A new high tech lab in Glasgow has a special test. It can determine if blood is in the fibers of the garment, even after it's been cleaned."

Blake carefully picked up Hoolie. "You're going to prison for Bea's death, Elizabeth. You might as well tell me what you did to Philip."

No remorse or apology showed on Elizabeth's face. "I'll get a solicitor and be out before morning."

"I'll speak to the Fiscal myself," Blake said. "I'll see to it he keeps you locked up."

"If you do, I'll counter sue your Yankee girlfriend for assault and for keeping a vicious dog."

I turned to the vet. "Are any of Bea's dogs biters?"

"No. She was well known for breeding well-mannered, people-friendly dogs."

"He savaged me." Elizabeth held up both bloody pant legs as evidence.

"And we know why," I snapped back. "Because you killed Bea, and Hoolie was there when you did it. If you bring legal action against me or Hoolie, I'll go to the press. I'll make a stink so huge the animal rights groups world-wide will throw their lawyers against you. That and my assault charges should hold you while Constable Trask builds an airtight case. You deserve to rot in jail."

Satisfied with having the last word, I slammed the study door on my way out.

CHAPTER FORTY-ONE

B LAKE AND I were alone in the vet's office waiting for Hoolie. Dr.
MacDonald had to administer a light anesthetic to take X-rays
of the corgi's head. He'd taken my dog into a side room.

Blake ended a lengthy call on his smart phone. "Good news. Elizabeth
will have to stay in jail. Charlie told the Fiscal she was a flight risk."

"What if she cuts a deal? She can testify that Richard followed Raul
into the study."

"She can't plea down the murder of Bea. One bit of bad news. The
prosecutor is going to hold up the sale of the manor house until after
Elizabeth's trial."

I twisted Hoolie's leash into a knot. "Four victims. Over a legend
and a piece of property. Does Scotland have a speedy trial system?"

"No faster than America. The sale could be tied up in the courts
for a long time."

"And speculators will snap up Bea's house because of its proximity
to proposed development. And Heather Hill's town council will have
time to find the funds to purchase the manor house. There goes all
my hard work."

And I knew my boss. He wouldn't wait for the red tape to unravel. He'd cut his losses, pack up and go to the next project. Hoolie and I would go with him. I had no ties, no excuse to stay in Heather Hill. Unless Blake . . .

We barely knew each other. It had been less than two weeks since we met. Two intense weeks, to be sure. We'd crammed a lifetime of experiences into those few days.

It hadn't taken me long to see and admire Blake's honesty and passion to his cause. His loyalty to his friends and his country. My bad timing, again. I was leaving Scotland the next day, and I'd discovered I'd fallen in love with Blake Ramsey. I couldn't tell him. Strange how I'd trusted Blake with my life when we were in danger, but I didn't trust him enough to declare my love. I wasn't strong enough to risk his rejection.

The idea of leaving Heather Hill and my new friends burned an ache in my heart. The thought of not seeing Blake again felt like a herd of elephants stomping on my chest.

My love for Blake was impossible. How could I be sad to lose something I never had? It was time to accept a crappy situation and move on. God, it hurt.

I pretended to study a poster of a dog's skeleton on the white walls. The silence stretched to the breaking point. I spoke first. "Thanks for showing up at Elizabeth's when you did."

"You had the situation well in hand." He kept his gaze glued to the floor.

"Yeah, it felt good slugging her after what she did to Uncle Philip, Bea and Hoolie." I rubbed my abraded knuckles.

"I had no doubt after reading Michael's letter. Bea's mother had kept the birth a secret from him until the week before she died. When he learned of his other daughter, Michael decided to keep it quiet. He saw no point in bringing scandal to Elizabeth or Bea. After he sickened, he wrote the letter to Philip instructing him to tell Bea who her father was. If she needed money, she could claim half of the proceeds from the manor sale. When I read that Elizabeth had a half-sister, I knew it gave her a motive."

"The same motive she had for killing Philip. Too bad we can't prove it. I need that closure."

Blake propped his elbows on his knees and rested his face in his hands. "I can't believe I misjudged her. We grew up together. She was our friend, Ian's, Maggie's and mine."

"Elizabeth told me about your summer friendships."

"All those memories. Mucked up." He slumped back in his chair.

"Keep your memories, Blake. The Elizabeth who killed Bea isn't the same person you grew up with."

"I understand that, but what made her change?"

"You may never find out. Some questions have no answers."

Blake shifted so he faced me. "When did you become so wise?"

I melted under the spell of his navy blue eyes until a disoriented Hoolie weaved into the waiting room on wobbly legs.

"His x-rays are negative," MacDonald said. "No fracture. Don't let him drink too much water when you get him home, and keep him quiet for a few more hours." He handed me an envelope. "Here are all his health records, vaccinations and my personal letter verifying he is rabies free. These should help get him through customs when you arrive in America."

I accepted the package of papers, and with it, the reality of my imminent departure.

I picked up Hoolie and cradled him in my arms. When we reached the car, Blake helped settle us in the front seat. Without a word, we drove through Heather Hill.

"Let's stop at the pub," I said. "Ian and Maggie will want to hear the news. It's best if it comes from you."

"Right."

Back to one-word sentences.

A subdued crowd gathered around the bar. All the talk was of Elizabeth. A tearful Maggie ran to Blake. He held her tight. Ian joined the pair and they shared a group hug.

" 'Tis a bit much to take in." Maggie dabbed at her tears.

Blake put a consoling arm around her shoulder and led her to the table where I set Hoolie on the bench next to me.

Our regular table.

Maggie sat next to my dog and absentmindedly stroked his back. "I can't believe Elizabeth is a killer."

Ian agreed. "Bea was her neighbor. They were supposed to be friends." He noticed my face. "Good God, did Elizabeth do that to you? Sean, fetch the burn cream you keep in the kitchen. It'll work on these scratch marks."

"I'll get some ice for her cheek," Maggie said.

I'd been so preoccupied with Hoolie's injury and adjusting to the idea that I'd soon be leaving Heather Hill, that I'd forgotten my appearance. In a flash, the memory of my struggle with Elizabeth returned and with it, a throbbing cheekbone. Ian used gentle fingers to probe my injury and declared a possible fracture. When he applied the cream to the open scrapes, it stung.

The pub door opened and Mr. Atkins rushed in, followed by Chad and Tilly.

"We heard the news." My boss pushed his way through the crowd. "It was on TV." He looked at my damaged face. "Is she all right, Doctor?"

"It looks worse than it feels." I tried to sound brave but was embarrassed by all the attention.

Chad indicated Hoolie. "The reporter said your dog identified the killer. Elizabeth Coulter?"

Happy to have the attention shift to Hoolie, I explained how he had attacked Bea's killer.

Maude approached our table. "He deserves a steak dinner."

"And one for breakfast, too." Annie stood next to her friend. "You were right, Jax. Hooligan was there when our Bea was killed." She gave Blake a brief hug and patted Ian's shoulder.

Maude included the previous Musketeers in a compassionate gaze. "You must feel so betrayed. It's a tragedy your childhood friend turned out to be the killer. Will she stay in jail until her trial? What will happen to the sale?"

"If they allow bail," Blake said, "Elizabeth won't have money to travel. There will be a trial unless she confesses. The sale of the manor house will be tied up until it's over."

"It may be difficult to see it tonight, but some good might come of this," Maude said. She and Annie took their seats. "The delay gives the council time to look for some matching grant funds. I'll contact the John Muir Trust. They might help purchase the estate. With the money from the sale of Bea's land, we could have enough to do it."

Mr. Atkins sat at the head of the table and directed his comments to me. "I'll call our attorneys in New York. It could take at least a year to free up the Coulter estate, or longer, especially if Elizabeth is found guilty. I understand she is the sole heir. I'll reassess our plan to buy after the legal dust has settled. We might have to let this one go." He directed a piercing look at me. "Some things are worth staying and fighting for." His eyes shifted to Blake and back to me. "Are you sure you don't want to take your vacation time here in Scotland?"

"I'll miss my new friends, and all the people of Heather Hill." I stared at the table and waited for Blake to make some comment. And waited.

Ask me to stay. Give me an excuse so I don't have to leave. Please.

I risked a peek at him. He stared into his empty beer mug.

Maggie brought Blake another and nudged Ian. He looked from Blake to me and shrugged as if to say, what can I do?

"You must stay for dinner, Mr. Atkins." Maggie's voice was a bit too loud. "Game pie is the special tonight." She winked at him.

"Wonderful idea, Maggie. It will take time to round up our pilot and fuel the plane. And we have to eat. Game pie sounds tasty. Let's all enjoy a last meal together."

Maggie went back to the kitchen while Chad held a chair for Tilly. She leaned over and whispered in my ear. "Chad invited me to come to New York as soon as I can take some time from SLFS. I'm due for holiday leave. Is there a possibility you can take an afternoon to go shopping?"

"I'd like that. I'm glad you two hit it off."

Her I'm-in-love-with-a-wonderful-guy smile chipped away at the dam holding back my tears. Maggie's returned and sat next to Ian. Their obvious happiness increased my misery.

I tried mental telepathy one more time. *Blake, look at me.*

He didn't.

I love you so much. I know it's too soon. You don't have to say it back to me. Ask me to stay.

He continued to concentrate on his beer.

Remember our time in the tunnel. Our kiss.

He took a drink and set the glass back on the table. Somehow, he managed to do it all without glancing in my direction. Damn stubborn Scot.

No, I was the stubborn one. It was time to face facts. I was a pawn in his game. He'd used me, and now I wasn't necessary. Our time together didn't mean a thing to him.

A huge feeling of emptiness washed over me. I had to get out of there before I made a fool of myself. I snapped on Hoolie's leash and made my excuses. "I'm not hungry. I'll go pack."

"Pick you up at eight," Chad said.

CHAPTER FORTY-TWO

BLAKE WATCHED JAX hug Ian, Maggie, Annie and Maude before she rushed out the door. She didn't look at him. She didn't say goodbye.

The first forkful of pie stuck in his throat. He ordered another pint of lager. He separated the meat from the vegetables and rearranged them on his plate. By the time Atkins and Chad left for the hotel to pack and arrange transport to the airport, Blake's food remained on his plate. He ordered a whisky.

Ian slapped his hand on the table. "No, Maggie, whisky is not what Blake needs. What the idiot needs is a brain transplant. I always thought you were an intelligent man. I'll have to revise my opinion if you let that woman go."

Blake sat rooted to his chair, stunned.

"Aye," Maggie said. "Jax belongs in Heather Hill. With you."

Everyone at the table agreed.

"She doesn't . . . uh, love me."

"Sweet Jesus," Maggie said. "He's blind, too."

"Cora told me she was hoping you and Jax would come to an understanding," Annie added.

Maude indicated his cell phone on the table. "Call her and convince her to stay."

Blake hit the speed dial. "There's no answer. She must have turned it off."

"I'll try Chad." Tilly punched in a number. "The reception is bad, but we can text. He says they ran into fog up the coast. Blake, you might catch her."

"Go bring the lass home," Ian said.

Minutes later, Blake gripped the steering wheel in desperation. He must have lost all sense and reason. He was breaking the land speed record to chase after a hot-headed American. They had nothing in common. She worked for a developer. She'd never leave her job. She was loyal to Atkins. And she was good at what she did. Capable. Dedicated. Trustworthy, too. Bloody Hell, she was a perfect Girl Guide.

No, not perfect. Not with that temper when her back was up. Theirs would not be an easy relationship. They'd fight. She was passionate when she believed she was right. Yes, they'd argue. But the making-up promised to be passionate, too.

Blake made a right turn onto the airport road.

He'd never known a woman so brave. Foolishly fearless, like her dog. She been willing to take on Richard with only a walking stick. And she was resourceful. How did she think to turn an edge of tape under? And she knocked out Elizabeth. Put her flat. God, he'd been proud.

He'd never have to guess what she was thinking, once they were married. She'd let him know exactly how she felt. She had a sentimental streak, especially for family and Hooligan. When she laughed, she didn't hold back. And she'd made *him* laugh more in the last two weeks than he had in the last two years.

He followed the signs to the terminal for charter and private plane departures.

Interfering matchmaker. Not content with bringing Ian and Maggie together, she had worked her magic on Chad and Tilly. Now there was an unlikely pair.

Long distance romances didn't work.

Could Tilly and Chad make a go of it? He didn't want to risk Jax putting an ocean between them. Could he convince her to stay?

He remembered the kiss they'd shared in the cave.

Soft lips.

The night of the storm. In his bed.

Her curves fitting him in all the right places.

The Land Rover jumped the curb when he swerved into the parking lot. He barely eased off the accelerator. Tires squealed into a parking space. He stomped on the brake.

Inside the private terminal, he endured the short line at the security station. He ran through the concourse for the departure gate. His stomach dropped. The waiting room was empty except for an airport employee at the counter.

The young lady answered his query and explained. "You just missed it. Fairway Golf is preparing to lift off." She indicated the green jet hunched at the end of the runway, visible through the windows.

Blake rushed to the glass and shielded his face from the reflection. He could make out the distinctive logo on the side of the plane in the glow from its running lights. The jet sped down the tarmac, lifted its nose and cut through the glare of airport lights until it reached the black sky, and disappeared.

Too late.

He leaned his forehead against the cold window.

"Arf!"

What the hell?

He searched the reflection in the glass. There she was, seated on her luggage behind a pillar. Hoolie strained at the end of his leash.

Blake turned, afraid he was hallucinating, that the image he'd seen would disappear.

Jax stood. Her welcoming smile broke the gloom of the empty room. Hoolie tore free and scampered toward him, four paws churning for traction on the linoleum floor.

Blake took a step toward the woman he loved in time to catch her when she tripped over Hoolie's leash and into his arms.

I CURSED MY eternal clumsiness before Blake's kiss knocked every self-deprecating notion out of my mind. We broke apart to the sound of applause. We'd gathered an audience of passengers waiting for the next flight to depart.

"This is such a cliché." My cheeks heated with embarrassment. "The whole airport scene."

One of Blake's eyebrows arched a question.

"In the movies," I said, "the handsome hero races to stop the heroine from leaving.

"I was rushing to stop Hoolie from getting on the plane." Blake's amusement sparkled in his eyes.

"You didn't have to." I played along with his teasing tone. "My dog didn't want to leave."

"And here I was afraid I might have to bribe you to let him stay." He reached inside his coat and handed me a bronze-colored jeweler's box. Inside, nestled in white satin, were a pair of pink pearl earrings in a marquisette setting.

"I found them in an antique store. They reminded me of you. I was going to ask you to stay tonight, but you left without saying goodbye."

"I'm not a mind reader, Blake. I didn't think you wanted me to stay. You didn't say anything."

"I'll say it now. Don't leave."

I clutched the jewelry box to my breasts. "If I accept your bribe, I can't leave. It wouldn't be ethical."

"No, it wouldn't. Besides, in some cultures, accepting a bribe is the same as accepting an offer of marriage."

"I've never heard that one before." Had Blake proposed to me, or had I misunderstood.

"You're going to refuse my bribe?"

Bribe? What happened to marriage? I was so confused. "I didn't say I'd give you back the earrings. I think I'll need time to, um, research that cultural thing."

If he could be obtuse, so could I.

He kissed me again. "Take all the time you want. I'm not going anyplace."

I bent to pick up my dog's leash and found it wrapped around our legs. Hoolie grinned at us.

Blake stepped out of the snare. "We can tell our children it was the dog's fault."

"Are you complaining?"

"Would it do me any good?"

"Nope."

His smile reached those deep blue eyes. "Excellent, because I'm under orders to bring you back to Heather Hill."

"Do you always follow orders?"

He pulled me into his arms. "I do when they concern a certain red head and her dog."

About the Author

After living in the Reno/Sparks area for over forty years, J. Lee Taylor considers herself a native Nevadan. At the University of Nevada, Reno, she discovered her love for writing fiction. Mysteries became her genre of choice the day she killed off a villain and enjoyed it. She enjoys the change of seasons living in the Sierra Nevada foothills, and shares her home with an in-corgi-able Corgi where she is busy writing her next novel.